# FOUR DOMINIONS

Eric Van Lustbader is the author of twenty-five international bestsellers, including the most recent Jason Bourne novels. His books have been translated into over twenty languages.

# BY ERIC VAN LUSTBADER

# ERIC VAN LUSTBADER

# FOUR DOMINIONS

HEAD
of ZEUS

First published in the UK by Head of Zeus in 2018

9 7 5 3 1 2 4 6 8

A catalogue record for this book is available from the British Library.

ISBN (HB): 9781788540186
ISBN (TPB): 9781788540193
ISBN (E): 9781788541084

Printed and bound by CPI Group (UK) Ltd, Croydon, CR0 4YY

Head of Zeus Ltd
First Floor East
5–8 Hardwick Street
London EC1R 4RG
WWW.HEADOFZEUS.COM

*For Linda & Dan,*
*who help keep me sane in an increasingly insane world*

# SHAW FAMILY TREE

## LAST FIVE GENERATIONS

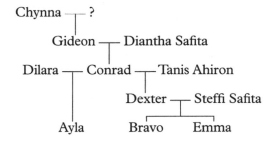

Chynna — ?
      |
   Gideon — Diantha Safita
         |
Dilara — Conrad — Tanis Ahiron
      |          |
              Dexter — Steffi Safita
                    |
   Ayla      Bravo    Emma

# THE HISTORY
# BEHIND THE FICTION

The Franciscan Observatines, here known as the Gnostic Observatines, are recorded in history, as are the Knights of St. John of Jerusalem, who inspired the story's Knights of St. Clement of the Holy Land. In those early days, the pope was the most powerful monarch in Europe. Like all monarchs, he was obliged to maintain his power in the face of rivals and enemies. Thus were the Knights created, as a form of papal army, who fought in the pope's name both at home and in the Levant.

From as far back as the early 1300s, there was a deep division within the Franciscans regarding the strict vow of poverty demanded by Saint Francis upon the founding of the Order in the beginning of the thirteenth century. The Observatines believed in it; the Conventuals did not. The dispute came to a head in 1322 when Pope John XXII sided with the Conventuals and their allies, the more established Dominican Order.

The papal bull *Cum inter nonmullos,* which stated, among other things, that the rule of poverty was "erroneous and heretical," was likely a subterfuge. It seems far more plausible that the pope wanted to stamp out a faction of the Franciscans bent on roaming the world, spreading their gospel and, in the process, their power and influence, rather than staying put *intramuros,* within the walls of their monasteries, as the Conventuals were bound to do.

However, the papal bull was hardly the end of the Observatines. Quite the opposite, in fact. In the latter part of the fifteenth century and the first two decades of the sixteenth century, a good number of Observatines who had accepted the pope's ruling were settled in the Middle East, especially the area in and around Trebizond and Istanbul, serving as emissaries of Christ, proselytizers of Catholicism. It is here that I have imagined my Gnostic Observatines discovering many of their secrets, including the Quintessence, which is recorded in history as the so-called fifth element, sought after by every alchemist on earth, but perhaps created by the cadre of alchemists employed by King Solomon.

Gnosticism is, in and of itself, anathema to the Vatican and its staunchly traditionalist orders. The name derives from the Greek word for knowledge. Gnostics, to put it simply, believe that the physical world is corrupt, evil, and that the true path to salvation lies in adhering to spiritual truth and goodness. Some Gnostics pursue study in the so-called esoteric mysteries, which lie beyond normal human comprehension. The Church, in its infinite wisdom, has, sight unseen, always judged these mysteries to be magic and, so, heretical.

The Knights, champions of both Christ and the pope, would naturally be predisposed to despise and fear the Order as much as the Holy See. It's entirely logical that the Knights would be only too happy to do the pope's bidding in dismantling the Order's power.

# PROLOGUE

ONE YEAR AGO

BRAVO SHAW SAID, "AFTER SEEING YOUR VISION RESTORED, after Fra Leoni told me what had happened to you, I—"

"Bravo, Bravo, my brother." Emma Shaw, in his embrace, pulled her head back so their eyes locked. "I told you. I'm fine." A hand gentling his cheek. "Please believe me."

"I do, Sis. It's just that . . . I missed you more than words can explain."

She beamed. "We're always in each other's hearts. What more is there to say?"

Bravo and Emma Shaw, along with the newly orphaned Ayla Tusik, were aboard one of the Observatines' private planes, twenty thousand feet above the Mediterranean, starting the first leg of their journey back to New York City. Bravo, as he'd promised his sister, had no more use for Istanbul. They'd been away for two years, since the explosion in the Greenwich Village town house that had killed their father and blinded Emma. They both missed home far too much to stay away any longer.

Ayla was sitting back in her seat, an ice pack on her throat. She was completely recovered from the fire and the thing that had crawled out of it; no mark remained on her forearm. It was as if the shadow-serpent's coiling had never happened. She had tried to talk as Bravo and Emma were taking her out of the library, but all that had come out was a dry croak and an awful clicking sound painful enough to cause her to stop trying.

"You're good," Emma had said to her, over and over in the private ambulance. "You're not going to die."

Ayla had looked up at her and smiled, but it was Bravo's hand she clutched tightly all the way to the airfield, while a doctor who worked with Bravo's Order of Gnostic Observatines tended to her neck, injected her with a mild sedative, before checking Emma's head bruise, cleaning and dressing Bravo's wound. When the ambulance arrived at the airfield it had been met by the three-person flight crew. They didn't blink an eye at the physical state of the trio. It seemed they were getting used to helping their passengers board.

The moment Bravo and Emma had seen to Ayla, made sure she was resting comfortably, they had fallen into each other's arms. The return of Emma's sight was a miracle. For Bravo, it was as if the clock had been reset to a time before the explosion. There would be a right moment for exploring the reasons and mechanisms behind the miracle, but now was not it. They were spent physically and emotionally. Now all they wanted to do was hug each other, drink the lemonade made with fresh Egyptian lemons that Lida brought them, and slide into a well-earned sleep.

Bravo went out like a light, as had Ayla. As for Emma, her sleep was fitful, shallow, stalked by creatures that were no more than shadows. She awoke with a start, her hair and brow slick with sweat. Her armpits felt swampy. She rose, went to the lav, and, after voiding, threw cold water on her face. Though it had only been three years in real time, the face in the mirror staring back at her seemed so strange. She had aged since last she had seen herself. She had to remind herself that everything had shifted while she had been sightless, the world had moved on, rolling from day to day without her. Looking back upon those years, she realized that she had felt marooned in a land of perpetual night, darker even than the dark side of the moon. And yet here she was now on the other side of it— fantastic luck or something else altogether, she couldn't say. A surge of gratitude flushed her cheeks and neck, but soon enough the strangeness of it all began again to overwhelm her. She didn't look the same—this was to be expected, she supposed—but not to feel the same was a mystery that, deep down, frightened her. Who was she now? Exhausted, she felt inadequate to the monumental task of finding out.

When she returned down the aisle Lida was refilling her glass. Bravo's mouth was partly open, his features at rest. She felt such love for him. Everything they had been through in the last days had been worth it for this . . . for them to feel closer to each other than ever.

He had fallen asleep while looking at the *Nihilus Inusitatus*. On the seat beside him was the rolled manuscript that was supposed to have been the Book of Deathly Things, The Testament of the First One to Fall, Brother of Michael, the Seraph Lucifer, King of Kings. But Aither, the curator of the library at Alexandria in Egypt, had claimed that it was blank. In a way, she was glad that it was blank, that the real Testament remained hidden. The manuscript was terribly dangerous. It was even dangerous for the reader, for, as Fra Leoni had told them, anything to do with Lucifer, with that ultimate evil, was seductive. It could drag you into the abyss before you knew what was happening.

Even if the manuscript was blank, it did appear very old, but who knew if it was. She had read about numerous archeological finds purported to stand ancient history or the foundations of religion on their head, only to be revealed as fakes, ingeniously doctored by clever scam artists wanting to make a quick buck or be spotlit by their fifteen days of fame.

Idly, she reached over, took it up, settled back in her seat. Before she'd been blinded, and following her brother's lead, she'd become an expert in the identification of artifacts. Within thirty minutes or so, she'd be able to tell whether its apparent age was real or fake.

The manuscript was covered in what seemed to be calfskin, or something like it, the sickly yellowish hue of an onion's skin. A strip of some unidentifiable black cloth wrapped it tight, held it in a roll. That was enough to set off alarms inside her head. No cloth she knew of would have survived the centuries intact.

Unrolling the manuscript, she studied the first page. The paper was undeniably ancient—just how old she couldn't tell without a laboratory. A conundrum, then. She leafed through page after page. Aither hadn't been lying; not a single letter, character, or rune was to be seen; the pages were blank. She sighed. Now the whole thing seemed worthless. Who cared how old it was?

Her gaze drifted to the window. She watched the clouds, fascinated by their changing shapes, their seeming contradiction, so solid in their weightlessness. She was like a child again, remembering how it had been the first time her parents had taken her and Bravo on a plane. How her face had been plastered to the window, nose mashed nearly to the cartilage, her breath fogging up the Perspex. She could not get enough of the clouds and what wonders lay spread out beneath her, shifting with every breath she took.

The drone of the plane's engines lulled her back to sleep, into a dream where a creature of immense size—not man, not lion, but a combination of both—was speaking to her with its tawny, final gaze. The light was dense, filthy, as if shining underwater or in a deep cave, its source some other place Emma could not imagine.

The beast crouched on a vast plinth made up of naked humans bent over double—thousands of them, tens of thousands, hundreds of thousands, all bowed down in obeisance. It stirred its heavy thighs, half-rising, launching itself toward her.

At that moment, the plane hit an air pocket, and she awoke with a cry lodged in her throat like a bone. As the turbulence accelerated, everything around her trembled and resonated, as if in a wind tunnel. Her ears popped as the plane was momentarily sucked downward. Her shivering glass began to tip over. She reached out, caught it, but some of the lemonade slopped over onto the manuscript.

She cursed wildly, unsure what to do. Bravo would kill her. But then everything changed. The moment seemed to go on forever as secret writing slowly appeared on the ancient paper, invisible until sprayed with lemon juice. Something in the acid reacted with the kind of ink used to hide the text. It was an ancient method of keeping secrets—no one really knew how old. But the fact was before her: a text that had not been visible moments before.

Slowly, with infinite care, she spread more lemon juice on the pages until all of the text had been revealed. She knew she should stop, put this thing aside, wake Bravo, and tell him what she had discovered. But there was something pulling on her, a pinprick of envy, dark and heavy, that had caught her, a fishhook dragging her down to another place.

Why was it Bravo who found everything first? Why was it Bravo who got the special training? Why was it Bravo who received all the credit, all the accolades from the Order? Who had been elected *Magister Regens*? All because of their father, when she had been the one taking care of Dexter ever since their mother had died? She was as smart, she was as clever, but it was never her. Never her. Where was the fairness in that? And now, now, when they were becoming even closer, there was Ayla, insinuating herself into their lives. She saw how Ayla had hung on to Bravo all through the hectic, dreamlike drive to the airfield, clutched his hand like the two of them were bonded somehow, like she, Emma, was the outsider.

No, no, no. The fishhook was tugging, tugging, tugging at her. Not this time. This time was different. This time there would be an alternate ending.

Without a second thought, she flipped to the first page, where the first words had by fateful accident come alive, and started to read the mixture of High Latin and Old Greek, two languages in which she was fluent:

HEREIN THE TESTAMENT OF THE FIRST ONE TO FALL,
BROTHER OF MICHAEL,
THE SERAPH LUCIFER, KING OF KINGS

# PART ⊙ ONE

## THE APPLE

# 1

UNDER A PORCELAIN-BLUE SKY, STRIPED WITH WHIPPED-cream clouds, Lilith Swan strode along the rue du Faubourg Saint-Honoré. She was tall, lissome, athletic. Dressed in a flowing ankle-length oyster-gray coat over a charcoal pencil skirt and a lacy blouse buttoned to her throat, she cut a stylish figure even among the chic Parisian, Japanese, and Arabic women entering and exiting the ateliers of the Faubourg's high-end couturiers. The only curious note was the pink ballet flats on her feet, which were certainly not made for walking the sidewalks of any city. Her thick hair, the color of midnight, reflected both light and shadow. A raven's wing dipped down from her sharp widow's peak partially obscuring one eye. Her gait was both provocative and artless, as can be typical with athletes of a certain type. It obscured an inner tension, which was, perhaps, simply nerves.

She turned into a narrow storefront between Bottega Veneta and Prada, its only sign a discreet brass plaque that unknowing tourists passed by without even noticing. Inside all was cool, dim, perfumed. One wall held three shelves of meticulously handmade shoes, below which was a large mirror. On the opposite wall, above two leather chairs, hung a chart of the thirty-five steps taken by the shop's master craftsman in assembling his made-to-measure footwear.

The master himself emerged from his workshop in the rear to greet Mlle. Swan. In one hand he held a pair of black suede shoes with five-inch heels.

"Finished," he said with a huge smile, after they had exchanged familiar greetings. He held the shoes aloft. "Every detail precisely to your specifications." He gestured. "Sit, sit. Please."

Lilith lowered herself into one of the chairs, slipped off her ballet shoes, offered the shoemaker her right foot. The shoe fit like a glove, felt exquisitely cushioned, and yet when she tried both on, rising and walking toward the mirror, they felt sturdy, not even a hint of a balancing wobble from the stiletto heels.

"Magnificent, Albrecht," she said, for the shoemaker had been born in the north of Italy, grew up speaking German and eating Alsatian schnitzel.

Albrecht beamed. He lived for his shoes. "Shall I wrap them for you, Mademoiselle Swan?"

"Oh no, I'm going to show them off, Albrecht."

The shoemaker blushed. "Then I'll just pack up your ballet slippers."

Across the boulevard, hard by Moncler, was a small establishment, its plate-glass window revealing a spare number of exquisite pieces of jewelry—one each of a necklace and ring with a pair of ruby-and-diamond earrings artfully hung between them.

Inside, Lilith slipped on the platinum bracelet she had designed and had made for her. Two twining branches encircled her left wrist. She walked out with it on, feeling it against the bones at the base of her hand.

Her third stop was a block beyond, across rue Royale, where the Faubourg ended and rue Saint-Honoré began. There she picked up a pair of long hairpins made to her specifications, allowing the salesperson to push them through the dense gathered hair at the back of her head, so just the teardrop-shaped green jade ends were visible.

Just next door she popped into Ladurée Royale, entering the gilt-and-cream nineteenth-century Empire interior. She took a small marble-topped table, ordered a hot chocolate, thick and rich as a melted chocolate bar. She sat straight backed, with a flinty, determined air that often flustered those attending her, waitpersons, front desk personnel, salespeople. It was not so much that she disdained convention as she willfully had no knowledge of it.

While she slowly drank, she allowed herself to experience the pleasure of her new purchases. The caffeine and sugar helped clear her mind for the morning ahead. She felt calm and strong, the blood rushing through her, rich as the Ladurée hot chocolate. She felt ready for anything.

When she was finished, she paid and left, walked two blocks farther east, entered a large deep-cream-colored building on the corner of rue

Duphot. The old-fashioned vestibule lit up at the press of a button; the light would go off after sixty seconds. Bypassing the claustrophobic elevator, she walked up the wide marble stairs, pressing the light button at each landing. On the fourth floor, as Europeans counted, she went down the shadowed hallway to the end, fished a key out of her handbag, and opened the door. It was a special key to fit a special lock that was guaranteed by the manufacturer to be pickproof. This was a legitimate claim, she knew, as the manufacturer was owned by the Knights of St. Clement, the order of which she was a newly elected member.

The guards in the foyer nodded to her, but not, she was certain, with the deference they would have shown were she a man. In fact, one of them, a dark-haired handsome man named Naylor, with a saturnine face and the shoulders of a brawler, ogled her with obvious interest, his gaze lingering over her bust and long legs. She gave him a smile that was a bit coquettish, a bit cowed. He liked that. Very much.

The entire flat had the air of a traditional British men's club, where, apart from gender, class, privilege, and entitlement mattered most. Where an invisible sign that read "Gentlemen Only" kept out the riffraff and the chaff not lucky enough to be born to the manor in Surrey or the townhome in Kensington. Landed, in other words.

In the long cherrywood-paneled hallway, Lilith paused a moment. The soft murmur of men's voices came to her, but for the moment her thoughts were elsewhere. They were with Maria Elena Donohue, the only female member of the *extramuros* team sent to retrieve the Veil of Veronica purported to be buried in the mountains of Arizona. All had been hunted down and killed by Braverman Shaw and his Gnostic Observatine crew, a bloodletting for which she was determined to take revenge.

When she entered the library turned conference room all conversation ceased. The thirteen men seated around the circular basalt table all looked at her at once, as if they were marionettes whose strings were being manipulated by a single hand. All but one of these men were between fifty-five and eighty-five years old. They made up the Circle Council, the brain trust of the Knights of St. Clement, at least those who had survived the all-consuming fire at their ancestral castle in Malta. The current expansion from seven to fourteen members was in response to the disaster. Among the dead: Aldus Reichmann, their former leader, the *Nauarchus* of the Circle Council. At present, no one sat in the *Nauarchus*'s throne-like seat. In fact, this convocation had been called to elect the new *Nauarchus*. Lilith knew full well there was sure to be fierce debate and infighting before someone took Reichmann's place.

The room was filled with light from a crystal chandelier depending from the center of the ceiling. There was a large mirror adorning one wall, on another an enormous painting of their castle high on the Maltese bluffs, which now lay in blackened ruins. Heavy drapes covered the windows overlooking the rue Saint-Honoré. On the fourth wall was a large, exquisitely carved rendering of Christ on the Cross.

"You're late," Newell said from across the gleaming table as Lilith sat down. He was the Order's official conduit to Cardinal Felix Duchamp, their powerful contact inside the Vatican. "Had to stop to get your nails done?" Newell, silver haired, with a face cratered by overuse of a steroid cream during a hyper-hormonal adolescence, tapped his thumbs together, further showing his impatience at her tardiness.

She was well aware that he wouldn't treat any of his male peers with such outright contempt. If any of them expected her to apologize they were sorely mistaken. "I was working out a strategy that would prevent future *extramuros* groups from being slaughtered by the Gnostic Observatines."

"A useless exercise." Newell smirked. "Clearly, it was a mistake for a female to be part of an *extramuros* team."

"An experiment gone bad," Muller offered, echoing Newell's sentiment. A pale, balding man in his sixties with wire-rimmed spectacles and a bad case of ADHD, he was always fiddling with the position of the small things around him, lining and relining them up. Two spots of color high up on his cheeks, as if he applied rouge, gave him a vaguely effeminate air. He was the religious zealot among them. He kept the flame of God and Christ burning brightly within all the Knights. He would have made a fine monk.

By this time, she knew they had already decided her fate, the fate of allowing females into the Knights after centuries of systematically keeping them out.

"The experiment," Santiago said. He had a sour countenance, was a recidivist in all matters. As the overseer of the Knights' banking interests he wielded enormous power within the Circle Council. "We have no choice but to conclude that the experiment is an abject failure."

"How can it be judged a failure or a success," Lilith responded, "when it's been running for less than a year?"

"Everyone here realizes that Maria Elena was a friend of yours," Newell said in the most condescending tone possible, "but the facts speak for themselves. The *extramuros* team of which she was a part not only failed to retrieve the Veil of Veronica, but they also got themselves killed, each and every one."

"Including the Archer, the team's leader," Santiago pointed out, "an invaluable member of the Order, with many Gnostic Observatine kills to his credit."

There was a small silence that Lilith correctly identified as hostility congealing around her.

"The loss of the Archer," Newell said, "has caused consternation all up and down the *extramuros* corps."

"He will be sorely missed by us all," Obarton said in his basso profundo. Pushing eighty, he was the elder statesman of the Council; those watchful eyes had observed more than three *Nauarchus* come and go. Two of them killed by Bravo Shaw, the third by Bravo's father.

Santiago pursed his ruddy lips. "Which is more than can be said for Maria Elena."

"Surely you're not fatuous enough to blame Maria Elena for the failure of the entire *extramuros* team," Lilith said, aware that she was struggling against a rising tide.

"The team would have been stronger had it been all male," Obarton said with the kind of finality that brooked no further argument.

"It's settled then," Muller said, looking to Obarton.

"There was an error made." Obarton spoke like an old-fashioned barrister, an affectation he had picked up from watching Charles Laughton in *Witness for the Prosecution* so many times he could recite every one of Sir Wilfred Robarts's lines by heart, and did so often when he was in his cups. "An attempt at what some people around this table call *modernization*. For myself, this notion is foolishness. I freely admit that I went along with the notion knowing full well that the expedition would end in tears."

"Did you now," Newell said shortly. "Then why did you vote in favor of Maria Elena's inclusion?"

Obarton swung around in his chair as if impaling Newell with his barrister's thorny gaze. "Results, my dear Newell, are more powerful than words. I might have spoken out against the motion until I was blue in the face, but the majority was against me. The herd had already made up its collective mind. So I let nature take its course." His stubby-fingered hand swept out in a shallow arc. "And here are the consequences for all to see and absorb."

Lilith, smiling through bared teeth, silently seethed.

"With all due respect for my elders," Highstreet broke in.

"You know, my boy," Obarton broke in, "it has been my experience that when someone says, 'With all due respect,' what they really mean is 'Screw you.'"

Highstreet ignored the interruption. "With all due respect," he deliberately repeated, "we've wandered off topic." He was a thin young man with pale, translucent skin; blue veins pulsed in his temples. His hair, as black as Lilith's, started high up on his domed forehead, swept back over his pate and down his neck to just above his scarecrow shoulders. It gleamed in the overhead chandelier light, slicked down with pomade. "We're here to choose Aldus's successor." Highstreet, a Brit originally from Liverpool, was a genius savant; he ran all the Knights' networking, IT, bugging, and clandestine online hacking units. A number of the elders had no clear idea what he did; their eyes rolled back in their heads when he attempted to explain it. "That will be difficult enough, I wager. I move that we table all other matters."

"I second that," Lilith said immediately.

Without an eye toward either her or Highstreet, Obarton continued as if neither had spoken. "With the recent debacle in Arizona as background, I think it perfectly clear that our hallowed predecessors were correct all along; women have no place in our Order, let alone in this august body. Therefore, I move that we do vote on whether or not Lilith Swan is to be kept on the Circle Council."

"I second that," Muller said, nose figuratively planted between Obarton's rotund buttocks.

"A show of hands," Newell commanded. Clearly, this motion was not up for debate.

One by one hands were raised until all thirteen men had voted in favor of the motion. No surprise there, Lilith thought, as she scraped her chair back and rose to her feet.

"There's a good girl," Newell said.

"Well, say this for her," Obarton sniffed. "She knows when she's beaten."

Lilith circled the table, taking the long way to the door, smiled easily now that her path was made clear. "You know me so well," she said to Obarton in a honeyed voice. As she passed behind Newell, she reached up, withdrew one of her new hairpins, and plunged it into his carotid artery. The result was startling; Newell rose off his chair as if levitating. His face drained of blood, his extremities spasmed, he slid off the chair, all but disappearing under the table.

Extreme shock ricocheted around the room, rooting everyone to their seats. No one moved; no one could even think. Their minds were frozen. Lilith, now behind Santiago, thrust her left wrist beside his head, right hand drawing from her new bracelet a length of piano wire, which she expertly wrapped around his throat. Bracing one knee against the back of his chair, she jerked on it with such force that the wire drove through skin, cartilage, muscle, nearly decapitating him.

Several members around the table were shouting, a nearly incoherent string of what she assumed to be epithets. Reaching around to her raised leg, she detached the spike heel of her new shoe and drove it through Muller's right eye and into his brain.

The sickening stench of human death had taken hold of the room. Lilith, both shoes off and dangling from her fingertips, continued to circle until she stood behind Highstreet. The others had pushed their chairs back, were staggering to their feet, their faces blotched, their sensibilities hijacked, stupefied, rejecting what their eyes had recorded. But Highstreet remained immobile, staring straight ahead into the mirror directly across from them.

Leaning over him, Lilith sensed the entire room shudder in terror. She placed her hands against Highstreet's cheeks and, with her lips against his ear, whispered, "Now." Then she stood back.

Highstreet came alive. He alone had shown no horror at what had just happened. It seemed clear now that he wasn't even surprised. "Let it be known that the last vote, along with all attendant motions and seconds, be forever stricken from the record of this august body." Everyone was staring at him; none of those left alive could bring themselves to look at their dead compatriots or, for that matter, their murderer. He looked each and every member straight in the eye. "The motion to rescind the order is passed unanimously, yes?" Someone vomited, adding to the miasma of involuntary human evacuation; Obarton stared at Lilith stonily. Highstreet smiled. "I'll take that as assent."

"Now." He leaned forward, elbows on the table as if the room hadn't been turned into a charnel house. "As I was saying before I was rudely interrupted, our business here is to elect a new *Nauarchus*." Everyone expected him to continue. Everyone, that is, except Obarton, whose dawning grasp of the present situation was entirely evident.

"Go on, my dear," Obarton said. Only a voice thinner than usual betrayed his heightened state of inner turmoil. "Take your seat."

Lilith held his inimical gaze for a long moment. Then, returning to where Muller's corpse sprawled slack in his chair, she reached around, pulled her heel from his eye socket. A gush of blood ran all over his front, spattered onto the gleaming tabletop. Someone moaned; another turned away.

Still holding Obarton's gaze, Lilith wiped her weapon clean, fitted it back into the sole of her shoe. "Do you like that?" she said to Obarton. "There's more where that came from."

"Oh, I have no doubt," Obarton replied, with effort summoning his basso profundo.

"You have doubts," Highstreet said. "A whole sorority of 'em." A tight-lipped smile. "But you'll just have to live with the uncertainties of this new tomorrow."

As if this was a signal, Lilith went around the table, sat in the *Nauarchus*'s seat. "Now," she said, "we can get down to the business of annihilating the Gnostic Observatines."

Obarton made one last effort. "Our circumstances have radically changed. Continuing this obsession to bring down the Gnostic Observatines once and for all is a pipe dream cleverly embedded in our culture by Conrad Shaw, then exacerbated by his grandson, Bravo."

Lilith's eyes blazed. "Our *extramuros* teams harried and killed, our last two *Nauarchus* assassinated. Are those pipe dreams?"

With a theatrical flourish, Obarton placed a silk handkerchief against his nose and mouth. "First, I suggest we dismiss the other members, call for a cleanup crew, and continue this discussion elsewhere in the apartment."

When these tasks were accomplished, he and Lilith and, as she insisted, Highstreet settled themselves into plush sofas in the large salon. They did their best to ignore the comings and goings as the bodies, wrapped in plastic, were boxed and carried out so the cleaning crew could return the boardroom to its former pristine state. She saw Naylor overseeing the tasks. He carried no expression whatsoever on his face.

Someone brought a tray of coffee, a fresh baguette, butter, and a pot of strawberry jam, set it on an onyx cocktail table between them, and left as silently as he had entered, closing the sliding doors behind him.

Obarton stood at the high windows, hands clasped behind his back, observing the moving truck idling in front of the building, ready to accept the long boxes as they were loaded inside. He turned back to the room. "What is it with you two? Having an affair?"

"Not interested," Highstreet said.

Obarton turned his attention to Lilith, who merely shrugged.

Having no choice but to accept their unexplained liaison, Obarton commenced his thesis. "This obsession with the Shaws caused our last two leaders to go head-hunting. Instead, they got their heads handed to them." His expression grew dark. "Don't you see, Lilith, the very obsession you seek to perpetuate made your predecessors incautious, made them susceptible to the Shaws' legendary wiles."

With fire in her eyes, Lilith leaned forward. "Which makes it imperative that Bravo Shaw be killed. The sooner the better."

"And what, may I ask, do you propose to do about the demonic creature that attacked and killed everyone inside our castle?"

Her hand cut through the air. "What creature? There was a fire, doubtless motivated by revenge against the last *Nauarchus,* who, I may say, was both incautious and wrongheaded in all matters. But he escaped."

"Only to be killed by Braverman Shaw in Tannourine."

Her unblinking gaze trained on him, and even he shuddered at the sight of her clear intent. "We shall leave the fantasy of demons to the Gnostic Observatines, who dabble in that kind of anathema to Church orthodoxy," she said with finality. "Carpe diem. We have the opportunity now, and we must seize the day! The Gnostic Observatines have been severely weakened by the destruction of their Reliquary. The Order spent centuries amassing its cache of sacred relics in Alexandria, Egypt: all dust.

"Now is the time to strike, I tell you, and strike hard, while they are at their most vulnerable. I swear to you, Obarton, I will use every last resource of the Order to eradicate the Gnostic Observatines." She lifted a forefinger. "And Bravo Shaw is first."

# 2

MALTA: PRESENT DAY

**BRAVO SHAW PICKED HIS WAY THROUGH THE RUINS OF WHAT** once was the ancestral castle of the Knights of St. Clement, now a maze of half walls, narrow corridors and vast rooms littered with the massed debris of the roof and upper floors, of which quite incredibly nothing else remained. Only a few chalky steps still stood of the once massive staircases. All the beautifully scrolled woodwork had been transmuted to charcoal, broken, crushed underfoot, dispersed by vindictive winds and voracious storms.

High above, a buttermilk sky was clear, but down here the stink of smoke was still very much in evidence even a year later. This, along with a number of the building stones either melted or transmuted into something resembling blood pudding, led him to the conclusion that the nature of the fire was unnatural, that it had been set by the thing that had possessed the woman once known to him as Maura Kite, the widow of his friend Valentin.

Just behind him, Emma kept her eyes on the rubble-strewn ground. "The bleakness here is overpowering."

"The graveyard of sins," Bravo said, stooping down as he came across the crisped remains of a body. Just beyond were two more, in the curled-up defensive position, skeletal hands at face level, as often seen in the aftermath of fires or lava flows. In the year since the conflagration only the rain and wind and sun had visited this place. It was the property of the Knights, and they had shunned it like the plague. No one cares to revisit the site of their defeat.

Emma stopped. Feeling the kind of cognitive dissonance that had become commonplace since she had secretly read The Testament of the

First One to Fall, Brother of Michael, the Seraph Lucifer, King of Kings on the plane last year. The text had disappeared as soon as she had read it—although the term "read" was incorrect, since the sentences were burned into her brain as her eyes took them in. She had told no one that she had found a way to make the text appear or that she had read it. Many were the times, alone in the darkness of the night, that she asked herself why. Why hadn't she told Bravo? Why was she keeping this invaluable information from him? *Because it is invaluable.* A voice inside her spoke to her as if it was that of a different entity. *Because it is a secret meant only for you.* She knew the source of this inner voice, split off from herself, but she dared not look at what was behind it, dared not even think about it. Better to shut the door on it, better to try to forget it. But she couldn't forget it, and she had yet to find a lock that would keep the door shut.

The cognitive dissonance set off an inward shudder, as if she were being buffeted by the shock wave from a distant explosion. And, once again, she felt splintered, as if she were watching her reflection in a mirror she herself had smashed. Her restored vision took in everything and nothing, invoking a fear that she was herself and not herself. Something behind that door stirred, uncoiling, a shadow without either substance or light.

"Emma?"

"What?" She blinked hard. "Yes?"

Bravo peered at her with evident concern. "Are you all right?"

She nodded. "Of course." But she could not get herself to smile. What was stopping her? That fear again, the loudening drumbeat of panic.

Bravo took a step toward her. "You've been through a lot."

"That was a year ago, my good brother." She leaned forward, kissed him on the cheek. But as her lips touched his flesh, the cognitive dissonance inside her rose to a howl, a shriek so primitive, so hideous, that she felt bile rising up into her throat. She coughed, and swallowed it back down. Good Christ, she thought. What's happening to me?

Bravo, perceptive beyond mortal ken, peered hard into her eyes, and for a terrifying instant she was sure he saw the thing inside her, coiling and uncoiling. She knew what would be coming next, and she knew she could not withstand the force of his probing questions. She had never been able to do it, and now with this doubt and fear eating her soul she had no chance whatsoever.

But at that moment, a dark providence stepped in to save her. They heard the sound of a voice calling to them, and Bravo turned from her. They saw a boy, sunburnt, thin as a weed, waving to them across the killing field of burnt corpses.

"Hello there!" he cried. "Hello!"

Bravo picked his way toward the boy. Emma, following on his heels, felt an immense sense of relief, gratitude, and disgust, which confused her mightily. Ever since she had caught sight of the ruined castle she'd been beset by a sense of déjà vu. If she had never been here before how was it that she knew the layout of the castle? How was it that she knew there had been a horse barn over there, that she knew the road off to their right led to a private helipad? Sweat broke out at the back of her neck; her armpits were wet. She swiped moisture off her upper lip. Her disgust combusted, nauseating her. She had read—with her own eyes!— that memory was a trickster, that it morphed in your own mind the way mercury moves, changing shape as it gathers and releases itself. And now, for the first time, she understood, for her own memory seemed maddeningly inconsistent—or, maybe more accurately, morphic, playing tricks on her. Like Malta, which she was certain she'd never been to, but nevertheless knew well. Like this castle, which rose in her mind in all its glory before she set fire to it. What? What! Her nausea threatened to double her over.

The boy saved her. His name was Elias. He was eleven, he told them. He was dark haired, with a Greek nose, a winning smile. "I'm the only one in all of Malta brave enough to come here."

"Where do you live, Elias?" Bravo asked.

"Here," Elias said, his cornflower-blue eyes upturned into the sun, "among the ruins."

He was dressed in loose white cotton trousers and shirt, a pair of rope sandals on his sun-browned feet. Where would he get such spotless clothes in among these ash-crusted ruins? Bravo wondered.

"You don't seem surprised to see us," Bravo said.

"I was told you would come."

"Told?" Bravo frowned. "Who would know that?"

Emma, crouching down, said, "Don't you have a family?"

"My father died in the fire," Elias told her. "And my mother passed giving birth to me."

"What about your father?" Bravo said. "He was a Knight."

"I barely knew him," Elias said. "But I knew this place before it burned down. I snuck in here sometimes when the *Nauarchus* wasn't in residence."

Emma seemed not to have heard him. "No other family?"

Elias just shrugged.

Bravo bent down, lifted the crucifix Elias had strung around his neck with a thin strip of leather. It was bronze, weathered, patinaed, ancient looking. "Where did you get this, Elias?" he said softly.

Bravo had stepped between Elias and Emma, blocking her view. She rose, moved to a different position. Her heart nearly froze in her breast. She felt as if she were asphyxiating. An excruciating pain, as if she were being branded by a fiery poker, radiated from the center of her forehead. Something deep in the recesses of her being shrieked like a demon out of Hell. Her eyes rolled up in her head and everything went black.

**"WHAT HAPPENED?"** Elias hunkered down beside Emma's supine form. "Is she okay?"

Bravo peered into his sister's eyes as he gently lifted their lids. "I don't know. She's never been prone to passing out before."

"Something's changed then." Elias shifted uncomfortably. "Or maybe it's this place." He looked around nervously. "It's especially creepy at night."

"What d'you mean?" Bravo asked without looking up.

Elias had the habit of lifting only one shoulder when he shrugged. "I dunno." When Bravo shot him a quick glance, he went on haltingly. "Well, for one thing I hear noises."

Bravo was trying to determine what he saw flickering in Emma's pupils. "What sort of noises?"

"Well, not a noise, exactly. A voice."

"Only one?"

"Yes." Elias licked his lips nervously. "It's always the same voice—a man, a very old man."

Bravo's attention was caught in a web. "How d'you know that?"

"The voice is—I dunno—'creaky' I guess is the best word for it. Like wood crackling in a fire."

"What does the voice say?"

"It speaks in a language I don't know."

"Maybe it's the wind," Bravo said.

"Huh! You haven't been here long enough," Elias said. "Nothing's as it should be in and around this castle." The odd shrug again. "Besides, I understand him. Like I knew you were coming."

"The voice told you?"

"Not exactly. I heard it in my head—all at once, like." He pointed. "What are you looking for?"

"A clue to her current condition."

Which was true enough. But there was more to it than that. It seemed impossible, but Bravo thought he had caught sight of something anomalous in the centers of Emma's pupils. Or perhaps not, for if he looked directly he saw nothing. But when he shifted his gaze so he was looking at them obliquely, a symbol, pale as moonlit bone, seemed to form and dissolve, each in the blink of an eye: a triangle inside a square inside a circle. Nihil. The sigil of the Unholy Trinity.

Bravo gasped, rocking back on his haunches.

"What is it?" Elias said, concern plastered across his face.

Bravo did not know what to say. But then, ever since Fra Leoni, his mentor and guide in all things occult, had been killed, he hadn't known what to say. His sorrow at the loss of Fra Leoni was so complete, ran so deep, that it was impossible to articulate it to anyone, even Emma. For months now, he had been drowning in it, unable to rid himself of his last sight of his mentor and friend. Their enemies had sliced off Fra Leoni's head, placing it in a vitrine for Bravo to find when he returned to the library at Alexandria where the Order kept the relics of the four Apostles and Antiphon, Saint John's eagle-companion. The ancient power of the Gnostic Observatines had been turned to piles of gray powder, the potency of the Reliquary destroyed utterly. Much as it might be tempting to assume so, Bravo knew that the Knights of St. Clement, the Order's ancient enemies, were not responsible. No, the enemies who had lured Fra Leoni to Alexandria and killed him in the only way possible to kill someone with such extraordinary powers, by beheading him, were the Fallen, the hundred or so angels cast out of the celestial sphere along with Lucifer.

Someone or something had opened the long-sealed portal, allowing them access to the world of mortals. It had been long known that by the act of Transposition these Fallen Angels—demons—could inhabit a human being. Thus arose the need for the act of exorcism, which the Church believed could cast out the demon. But Bravo knew full well that exorcism as practiced in secret by the Church was too often ineffective. Worse, the Fallen could use Transposition to move from human host to human host, leaving a hollowed-out and desiccated husk behind. He himself had witnessed the Transposition of his friend's wife, Maura, into one of the Fallen. And he had seen Maura's used-up husk left behind. Where had the demon gone? Who was serving as its host now?

Perhaps if he hadn't been sunk so deeply in his grief he would have figured it out sooner, but then again maybe not. This was his beloved baby sister, who had suffered following the explosion that had killed their father, who had fought alongside him so bravely a year ago against the Fallen.

But this wasn't his sister lying in front of him. Her eyes snapped open, and he could clearly see in her pupils the sigil of the damned. It began to dawn on him too late. Her hand was already around his throat, choking the life out of him. Her strength was unbelievable, and when she spoke it was as if her voice was coming from some faraway demonic pit.

"You had your chance against us," the demon shrieked.

At its first words, Elias stumbled backward and dragged himself clear.

The demon paid him no mind. "But now that's gone," it howled. "We did away with your grandfather Conrad, our first obstacle. Then after long years of gathering ourselves we went after the second obstacle, Fra Leoni. Like your grandfather, he's dead now. Now it's your turn. We are in control now. Once you're dead nothing will stand in the way of bringing our master back from his ages-long exile. Nothing will stop us from taking over this world."

As it uttered these words it was squeezing what life was left out of Bravo. He knew who was speaking, who was in control, but his eyes betrayed him. All he saw was Emma. How could he harm her? Even if he somehow managed to slither out of her grip, even if he managed to find an implement to slice off her head, killing the demon, he would be killing her as well. He couldn't do it. He'd die first. And dying he was; there was no question about it.

As if asphyxiation weren't enough, the thing inside his sister started to beat him, first with her fist, and then, grasping an ash-covered block of fractured stone, began to use that, smashing it with a maniacal frenzy into his rib cage, his cheekbone, his shoulder.

Bravo's world was reduced to a valley of red pain. He couldn't see or hear properly, and he couldn't breathe. There was nothing left of him but a bloody pulp. The demon rose up, eyes blazing with icy light, lifted the blood-drenched stone over her head to deliver the killing blow to his forehead.

At the apex of its arc, at the pinnacle of the triumph surging through its breast, there came the sound of wood cracking, as of a great tree falling—

*"Et ignis ibi est!"* There will be fire!

—that reverberated through the ruined castle and beyond, until it encompassed the entire plot of land. The voice froze the demon in control of Emma, but only for an instant. With a supreme effort, it commenced the downward arc of the killing blow.

In that instant, Elias rushed at her and, as she looked up, burst into blue-white flame.

# 3

LONDON: 1918

WHEN TOBY, FRESH FACED AND FRECKLED, BROUGHT THE
card to him on a silver tray, which was the custom in the waning days
of the Antaeus Club, Conrad Shaw leapt out of the leather upholstered
chair on which he had been lounging, meditating upon his next voyage
east, now that the dreadful war had come to an end. "By all means, Toby,
show him in at once. We mustn't keep such a famous personage cooling
his heels in the foyer!"

The Antaeus Club was housed in an exceedingly handsome mansion
in Belgravia, on Charles II Street, near St. James's Square. It was guarded
by a toothy wrought-iron fence and horned lamps reminiscent of dragons'
eyes. It had a rather checkered history. Originally named the Canonic
Club, it had been formed in the late sixteenth century by clandestine
Catholics during the reign of Elizabeth I, Tudor, the Protestant, who, in
1558, had wrested the crown, possibly illegally, from the Catholic Mary,
Queen of Scots. Catholics were tortured, killed, banished to Paris by
Elizabeth's astonishingly modern and effective cadre of secret service
operatives under the command of the brilliant Francis Walsingham,
principal secretary. During her reign, Elizabeth I, Tudor, was under
constant threat of assassination by those loyal to Mary. Catholics were
forced deep underground in order to evade Walsingham's minions. Most
were found out, but here and there pockets remained.

One of those consisted of the men who established the Club. They were
explorers—or, more accurately, plunderers—of the Levant and points
east. But the Crown's spies were everywhere, and the Club's membership, including its founders, were eventually found out and thrown in
jail. What frightful fate awaited them there can only be guessed at, for at

the moment the Tower of London's gates slammed shut, they vanished from the annals of history.

The Club passed through a series of owners seemingly indifferent to its innate majesty, until Conrad Shaw, using money from the coffers of the Gnostic Observatines, took possession of the building.

Now Conrad straightened his tie, shot his cuffs, just in time, as a slim, dapper, impeccably dressed man of about fifty strode into the wood-paneled library. He examined Conrad with an amused seriousness through wire-rimmed spectacles; despite his sleek clothes, he carried atop his head a tousled mop of dark hair.

"Mr. Yeats," Bravo's grandfather said, gripping the poet-philosopher's hand. "So good of you to come."

"How could I refuse?" W. B. Yeats said as Conrad ushered him to one of a pair of fireside chairs. His face was handsome and strong, longish and more or less triangular, with a broad, intelligent brow, graceful cheek-bones, and a narrow chin. Even on first glance, Conrad thought, he most certainly did live up to his reputation as being irresistible to the opposite sex. He sat, looking around him with a contemplative, semi-lost gaze, as if regarding everything from the perspective of another world. For this, more than anything else, Conrad liked him immensely. He was trained to recognize a kindred soul when he met one.

"What you proposed in your letter," Yeats said, accepting a glass of fino sherry from Toby, "is precisely what I'm after." The sherry glittered like liquid rubies in the firelight. "For London and its ever-quickening pace wearies me. I find that travel is the best method of catching in midair the essence of new poems."

They made a silent toast, the thin rims of the crystal stemware ringing as if in echo. "Do you know," Conrad said, "the origins of clinking drinking vessels?"

Yeats pursed his lips, his head cocked to one side, in the manner of someone whose thirst for knowledge knew no bounds. "I don't believe I do."

"In ages past, the vessels were filled to the brim, so that when they were clinked together the wine from each one would slop over to the other, thus ensuring that neither one was poisoned."

"Marvelous!" Yeats's laugh was quite a bit louder than was normal in the club's library, and several sclerotic heads swiveled in his direction.

"The creaking of old bones," Conrad said with a complicit smile.

"Indeed." Yeats was peering into his sherry as if it were a crystal ball. "As weary hearted as a hollow moon."

"These gray men. Retired from the Order. Window dressing is still a necessity, you see, in order for us to carry on our real work."

With the precision of a ritualist, Yeats placed his empty glass down in the exact center of the marquetry side table, as if doing so would unlock a doorway visible only to him. The gesture completed, Yeats turned his full attention to Conrad. "And the nature of your real work." He said this not as a question, not as a command, but as a statement that would, in his estimation, become, in the future, a prologue.

"The Gnostic Observatines, of which my father is the current head, is a Catholic order formed in the fifteenth century. Over the centuries it has evolved into a lay order; its members are more interested in seeking out and accumulating artifacts of an occult nature than they are in prayer and meditation." Conrad sat forward. The firelight licked at one side of his face, turning it fierce, atavistic. Right away, he could see that attracted his esteemed guest. "And by 'occult' I am speaking of the real thing. The Order is uninterested in the hucksters, charlatans, and tricksters claiming occult powers." He placed his palms together. "In short, we are archeologists of an alternate history, buried carefully and deeply, ignored by the accounts of history with which, as highly educated men, we are both familiar."

"As you are no doubt aware," Yeats replied, "I was brought up in Ireland, county Sligo, to be exact, under the auspices of the Protestant Ascendancy, which was, in those days, already splintering. As the Catholics came to power, so did the urgency of Irish nationalism. This, far more than religion, has shaped my life thus far."

"Now you are a member of the Golden Dawn, a sect of the Rosicrucians, if I'm not mistaken."

Yeats inclined his head. "A membership that has caused me no end of trouble and ridicule."

Conrad smiled. "Courage under fire. A superlative trait."

"Useful, as well."

Conrad laughed softly. "So then. What shall I call you? *Daemon est Deus inversus*—the demon is a god inverted—as the Golden Dawn does, is far too unwieldly."

"Mr. Yeats will do."

"Until we know each other better, one hopes."

"Without memory, hope is as ephemeral as mist. But if it pleases us both, of course."

"Just to be clear," Conrad said, "your name is inaccurate. It should be the demon is an angel inverted."

"I don't believe in angels," Yeats said at once. "Faeries, yes, and dhouls, magicians, surely, High Kings, without question."

Now Conrad knew from which perspective Yeats observed the world—that of Celtic folklore and myth. He shouldn't be surprised, but he felt a twinge of doubt. Had he made a mistake in choosing Yeats for this foray to the East—the most important and perilous of his career? And yet he had to trust his initial judgment; there was no going back now.

It being the hour before luncheon was to be served, the library was now more occupied than was Conrad's preference, for there were matters he needed to discuss with Yeats to which even his own Haut Cour wasn't privy.

Side by side, the two men strolled the inner courtyard, which Conrad had remodeled as a cloister. On the floor above the stone columns were the sleeping quarters of the members who rested between missions, plus the permanent flats of the Haut Cour. The early afternoon was unseasonably warm. The sun batted around the clouds closest to it, chasing shadows with its flat white light. The walls ensured there was virtually no wind.

The center of the cloister was planted in typical English garden fashion, ranks of roses vying with tulips and pansies. In the center was a low stone well, of no use now save for decoration.

"I propose you and I travel to the Levant," Conrad said.

The blood seemed to drain out of Yeats's face. "Where in the Levant?"

"Until you agree to join me that must remain a secret."

"Hmm." Yeats locked his hands behind his back, fingers intertwined. "I am exceedingly wary of the Spanish influenza."

"Which, since January of this year, has touched every corner of the globe. An unfortunate consequence of the war—troop movements, repatriations, the compromised physical conditions of so many soldiers."

"Many have died in the Levant."

"People are dying all over, Mr. Yeats. Here—even in your beloved Ireland."

Conrad contemplated him for a moment. "Tell me, where shall we hide? In our beds with the cover pulled over our heads?"

The poet-philosopher considered this argument for some time. "And the time frame?"

"As soon as the final arrangements are made."

"And these are?"

"The only one that concerns you is your decision."

"Ha! You give me very little to chew on."

They had begun their second circuit of the cloister. Shadows seemed to follow their route, only steps behind them. Conrad smiled. "I imagine that would be to your liking."

Yeats stopped turned to Conrad. "Look here, how much do you know about me?"

"As much as I need to," Conrad said, looking the other man straight in the eye.

"My soon-to-be wife."

"If you gather the courage to propose." Conrad's smile was nonconfrontational. "I'm entirely convinced that you are the man I need to bring with me."

Yeats seemed a bit taken aback. "What on earth would give you such an idea?"

Conrad was ready for that question. "Your induction into the Golden Dawn, your exposure to the teachings of Brahmin Mohini Chatterjee, your interest in séances, your writing of Celtic myths all are indications of your certainty that what we experience with our five human senses is inadequate to what exists in the universe, what we might erroneously describe as magic, the occult, the paranormal, because we lack the language for that which is unimaginable."

Yeats considered this for a moment. "And the purpose of the voyage to somewhere in the Levant?"

"Discovery," Conrad said. He was positioned in such a way that sunlight sparked in his eyes, lighting them with celestial fire. "Specifically, to determine the possibility of life beyond death."

# 4

FOR A WEEK NO ONE INSIDE THE GNOSTIC OBSERVATINES heard from either Bravo or Emma. After three days of communication silence the Haut Cour, the Order's ruling body, convened to discuss the urgent matter of the *Magister Regens*'s disappearance. Of course, the Knights were the first to be blamed—the prevailing theory that they had taken revenge against Bravo for almost single-handedly exterminating the *extramuros* team sent into the mountains of Arizona after the Veil of Veronica. No one in the Haut Cour knew where the brother-sister team were. This was not, in itself, unusual, but in the year since the attacks on the Order's Istanbul operation and the destruction of their sacred Reliquary all members of the Order, especially those who comprised the Haut Cour, were on war footing, and expecting the worst.

Nature—and man—abhors a vacuum. In the absence of any solid leads, let alone hard evidence, theories morphed into rumors that spread like wildfire, becoming more and more outlandish as the days passed. So it was that by day six these rumors reached the ear of Ayla Tusik, who had been working with Bram Stokley, the Order's best archeological technician, on the so-called Veil of Veronica Bravo had brought back from its centuries-old hiding place in the bleak Arizona highlands.

Ayla was the daughter of Dilara and Omar Tusik. Omar had been one of Bravo's key informants in Istanbul up to the moment he had been burned alive in an attack on the Tusiks' apartment. Dilara had been caught on the stairs by one of the Fallen and summarily beheaded before Bravo had been able to get to the demonic angel. Omar, it turned out, was not Ayla's biological father—that would be, against all odds, Conrad Shaw. Which, strictly speaking, made her Bravo and Emma's aunt, though all three were more or less the same age. Like Bravo, Ayla possessed extraordinary powers, derived from Conrad. But she was also of her mother's bloodline and Dilara was immortal in the same way as Fra Leoni. As with the Fallen, the only way to kill them was to separate their heads from their bodies.

Ayla, like her mother, possessed the gift of Farsight. It was not yet clear to either her or Bravo whether or not she was an immortal, as Dilara was. What was clear, however, was that her mother had never enumerated Ayla's powers, probably as a form of protection against those enemies who would seek her out if they knew how special she was. She begged Bravo not to go to Malta, but he was convinced that in the ruins of the Knights' blasted castle he would find a clue to the Fallen's powers. Before leaving with Emma he had entrusted Ayla with the safekeeping of the so-called Book of Deathly Things, The Testament of Lucifer, the disappointingly blank manuscript that had so interested Emma. No one else in the Haut Cour knew of its existence.

He had also assigned Ayla to supervise the testing of what was purported to be the Veil of Veronica. For the past week, she and Stokley had pored over the findings from every conceivable cutting-edge technological test made on the bit of cloth. The conclusions so far were startling. First, the cloth was centuries older than they had expected. While this proved that the cloth wasn't the one Saint Veronica used to wipe the sweat off Christ's brow on his way to be crucified, it led to some even more exciting conclusions, at least as far as Bravo and the Gnostic Observatines were concerned.

The small sigil in the bottom right-hand corner had been authenticated as belonging to King Solomon. This jibed with the age of the cloth, but it raised some interesting questions, the first of which was, what was this cloth used for? The second was, why was it preserved in a bronze quiver-like watertight container? Stokley's expensive toys: his mass spectrometer, electron microscope, X-ray and CT scans, ultraviolet and infrared beams, could perform many magic tricks, but answering these questions wasn't one of them. Electronic microscopy did, however, reveal a residue on the cloth, but it was so minute and scattered that the mass spectrometer failed to identify it. So they were left with multiple mysteries. Stokley, hunkered down in the lab, concentrated on finding a method of identifying the residue.

As for Ayla, once she had gotten the hang of Stokley's toys she stole back into the lab at night, long after Stokley had staggered off to bed. In the LED glow of the otherwise-darkened lab, she subjected the manuscript to the X-ray and CT scans, the ultraviolet and infrared beams, the mass spectrometer, without finding anything at all. This was more than curious to her; it seemed frankly impossible. Confronted with this imponderable, she set up the electron microscope. That was when she discovered the same scattered residue that was on the cloth. Now she knew that the two artifacts were contemporaneous. This, she felt, was a huge step forward. But it wasn't until she trained the all-seeing lens on the last leaf of the manuscript that she discovered something even more startling: the sacred seal of Solomon was stamped on the handmade paper, so minuscule it had evaded the naked eye. And then, the manuscript gave up its final revelation: the crescent moon on the end of one of the six spokes inside the double circle was upside down, its horns pointing toward the center, toward the crux of the six spokes, the *Nihilus*.

As if struck by a cattle prod, Ayla leapt back, stood shaking in front of the manuscript. What did it mean, this inverted horned moon? She had never before seen its like on any rendition of the sigil of King Solomon. A certain fear crept into her bones, and it was only through force of will that she didn't cry out. Instead, she clutched her throat. She knew there would be a dozen people swarming into the lab in a moment if she raised an outcry.

Her mind was reeling; she felt sick in the pit of her stomach. She stared at the manuscript as if it were the very incarnation of a sulfurous demon. Forcing herself to step back to the microscope, she took a series of rapidfire photos, downloaded them to her mobile, then erased any trace of them from the microscope's memory. With infinite care, she returned the manuscript to its case. It was only after it was tightly locked away that she felt safe.

Replacing the manuscript under the microscope with the swatch of ancient cloth, she looked more carefully at the seal in the bottom right corner. And there it was: the horned moon was inverted just as it had been on the manuscript. Jesus Christ, she thought, what are we dealing with here? The more she thought about it, the more certain she became that only one person could answer these questions.

**THE NEXT** morning, when she had returned to the lab after failing to reach Bravo on his mobile, the first of the rumors of his disappearance reached them via one of Stokley's assistants. At once, Ayla rose and, telling Stokley he'd have to carry on without her, strode out of the lab.

"Wait," the technician called after her, "where are you going?"

Ayla heard him, but there was no answer she could give. She was the only one who knew where Bravo and Emma had been heading. As soon as Bravo had told her what he was planning she'd experienced an acute sense of foreboding, a feeling she'd conveyed to Bravo, with the full knowledge that nothing she or anyone else could say would stop him from going to Malta. Curiously, it had seemed to her that Emma was almost more eager to go than her brother. Her fervor had only deepened Ayla's sense of misgiving.

Ayla had spent more time than anyone else with Emma following last year's terrifying conflagration, when they'd fought off the first attack by the advance guard of the Fallen. She could not help feeling concerned now. Emma had been assaulted by one of the demonic angels, which was how she had regained her sight. Bravo was certain that in the battle that followed she had been freed of the creature, but Ayla was not so sure. Ever since they had arrived back in New York a year ago, she had noticed changes so subtle that she was loath to bring them up to Bravo, who was clearly reveling in having his sister returned to him as she had been in their youth. Ayla did not for a moment question her observations. She had inherited what her mother called her seventh sense about people. She had kept her eye on Emma, but at some point Emma or—as Ayla's thinking went—something inside Emma had taken note of the unwanted attention. Subsequently, Emma's odd behavior and speech patterns subsided, then disappeared altogether. This only made Ayla more suspicious of her, but again, there was no one with whom to share her concern, least of all Bravo himself. As an inevitable result, a rift had developed between Ayla and Bravo, a kind of wariness that, it seemed clear to Ayla, if not to Bravo, Emma was quite happy to exploit. And yet he had entrusted her with the manuscript. Was it simply because he now believed that it was useless to them? If so, he was wrong. She had clear evidence that the manuscript was demonic in origin. Emma had had possession of it during the entire plane ride. What if it wasn't blank? What if the text was protected somehow, but there was a way to read it? And what if Emma had discovered how to do just that and been affected by what she'd read?

The terrifying possibilities unspooled through her mind as she stuffed an overnight bag with clothes and toiletries, grabbed the case with the manuscript and her passport, and headed for the airport. She bought a ticket to Malta via Rome. She booked a car, which, almost thirteen hours after she departed Bole International Airport, she picked up, and, following a quick stop for lunch, was on her way to her destination.

She sped southeast past rocky hills covered with dusty olive-green brush and Roman-columned hotels drenched in dazzling sunlight. She had slept only fitfully on the two legs of her flight. Her dreams were filled with eerie images of colossal serpents that spoke to her as they slithered across veined marble floors, disembodied heads with sightless pure-white eyes or empty black sockets. Worst of all were the dire warnings from the apparition of her mother. Always something of a Cassandra, Dilara made grave pronouncements that had seemed more like criticisms to the teenage Ayla. It was only much later, in adulthood, that she came to understand that both she and her mother possessed Farsight—though hers was much diminished, perhaps being a generation removed from the source—and that visions of the future were infallible.

*Beware,* Dilara's shade had whispered to her dreaming daughter. *Nothing is what it appears to be.*

Now, as she traveled almost due south toward the forbidding cliffs on which the castle lay, like a victim of Vesuvius, Ayla found herself missing her mother with such force that tears spilled onto her cheeks. Her mother would know precisely what to do in this situation, while the best she could muster was to know in her heart that being here was the right thing. She bolstered herself with the knowledge that her mother had brought her home to Istanbul from London to accompany Bravo on his mission to the dangerous Lebanese mountains of Tannourine and she had been right.

The past is littered with regret, the future bound by anxiety. The time is always now. And yet ever since her mother had been murdered Ayla's mind kept reaching back to incidents in their shared past, as if in this way she could keep Dilara alive. Her mind kept being drawn back to the first time she had been in Tannourine. Her mother had taken her there for a reason that had only become clear afterward. It was a kind of rite of passage, an interview with evil that accurately measured Ayla's powers. Confronting the evil in the red tent of shadows had unsealed Ayla's latent talents but had also sealed her mother's fate. Dilara had alerted her to the Fallen's first excursion into the realm of mortals. According to Fra Leoni, the red tent of shadows had been conjured by a sect of King Solomon's alchemists who remained to serve the son and successor, Rehoboam, after the king's death. In so doing, their fate—and that of mankind's— had been set, for the dreadful secret of the red tent of shadows was that it was the portal to the prison to which Lucifer and the other Fallen had been exiled for time out of mind. The new king's hubris, his terror at being weak, of losing the land his father had so ably secured, had caused him to order his alchemists to make contact with the dark powers his father had warned him against. And centuries later, it was the first of the escaped demonic angels that Dilara had brought Ayla to Tannourine to confront. Thus the war for the souls of mankind had been born.

Her mother had taught her ironclad discipline at an early age, a stringent regimen that, with a child's ignorance of the world, she had resented. The core tenet that Dilara drummed into her was to avoid anticipation at all costs. *Anticipation,* she would say, *locks you into a mind-set, which, whether you realize it or not, dictates your actions, even though they may be the wrong ones. If you don't anticipate, your mind is clear, your actions develop as the situation unfolds.*

Ayla, crossing the border into Malta, was never more beholden to her mother's teaching than she was at that moment.

# 5

LONDON: 1918

"I FIND THE WORLD AROUND ME BOTH MARRED AND CLUMSY, lacking in grace, brutal," Yeats said. "Therefore, I create. I seek out the interstices between this world and another—beautiful, pleasant, serene in every way. But to do that I need to delve deep into the supernatural."

"One thing I can guarantee," Conrad said. "A séance is not the way."

When, as now, Yeats sat up straight, his demeanor reminded Conrad of Toby. That was, he felt, unfortunate.

"I take offense at that," Yeats said.

"Why don't you take me to one?"

They were speaking over the noise in The White Stag, a workingman's hangout whose boozy bonhomie held immense appeal for Conrad after the unstinting rectitude of the Antaeus Club. Outside, London was suffocating in the industrial fug of coal-fired night; fly ash, soot, and dust, made all the more noxious by the stink of vehicular exhaust fumes and human waste, clung to the back of their throats and coated the roof of their mouths.

When Yeats did not answer, Conrad said, "The mutton here is exceptional, as is the shepherd's pie." He called over a waitress before glancing up at his companion. The waitress, Mary, whom he knew perhaps a bit too well, was pretty, rosy cheeked, and buxom. She stood at his side, blowing wisps of her tangled hair off her face out of the corner of her mouth.

She sized Yeats up in a single knowing glance. "Oi, what'll it be, then, gents?" she said in an exaggerated Cockney accent. Her wink directed at Conrad brought out a silent laugh. Mary so loved to puncture inflated balloons.

But perhaps Yeats, brooding on internal matters, was oblivious to this byplay, for he answered Conrad instead. "As it happens, there's a gathering this evening at midnight."

"Excellent." Conrad rubbed his hands together. "That gives us plenty of time to eat our fill."

THE SÉANCE was held in a nondescript town house in Belgravia that fronted on a beautiful square, now muzzy with a dank fog that, despite the men's gloves and cloaks, crept into their bones. It was the kind of fog that left behind everything except for what was in the immediate vicinity; it was as if they had entered another country whose borders were impossible to discern.

"The medium is Madame Garnet." Keats pronounced it "Garnay," in the French manner. "She is renowned on the Continent, and has now graced London with her presence."

No doubt fleeing the Parisian gendarmes by crossing the English Channel, Conrad thought. He despised charlatans of all stripes, not the least so-called mediums, manipulating people's hopes and fears in order to make their "magic" come to life.

The town-house interior looked to him like a Parisian whorehouse, with walls covered in aubergine flocked wallpaper, plush damask-covered settees, thick carpets to deaden sound, paintings of Pre-Raphaelite women in various stages of diaphanous dishabille. The lamps were lit low, the dim light casting vague shadows. Conrad and Yeats were led by a Berber servant, head wrapped in a traditional blue cloth shawl. An indigo tattoo ran from his lower lip down the center of his chin, where it spread out like a goatee. They followed him from the formal foyer, down a hall, and into a room that seemed to have once been a library but was now, it appeared, set up to entice the dead to rise from their graves.

A round table, heavy and large, was covered with an enormous draped cloth, patterned in the symbols of the Tarot, which hung down to the black tufted carpet. There was no crystal ball, deck of Tarot cards, or Ouija board on the table, all the usual props of the bogus ritual. Nine high-back wooden chairs, their legs carved to resemble goats' legs, their seats upholstered in black sateen, were ranged around the table at precise intervals. Heavy drapes took up half of one wall. In the opposite corner a rocking chair rested its ancient wooden bones. And speaking of bones, Conrad noted an assemblage of them in the center of the fireplace mantel where normally a clock or a lissome porcelain figurine would live. This anvil-like symbol of why everyone was here produced in him a cynical smile, while in all the others gathered for the séance it engendered a delicious shiver of anticipation, tinged with fear.

There was a full house of eight guests. Besides Conrad and Yeats, six others, four woman and two men, stood rather nervously around the table. Conrad, at twenty, was the youngest by a matter of decades. Yeats, for instance, was in his mid-fifties. All were exceedingly well dressed, coiffed, and groomed. But of course Mme. Garnet would offer invitations only to the well-heeled of London's populace.

They were bidden to sit at the same time by the Berber. His skin was sheened as if with oil. Despite himself, Conrad was impressed. Whoever Mme. Garnet really was, she knew what she was about. The North African Berber made for an authentic prop.

Mme. Garnet, when she finally made her appearance from behind a midnight-blue velvet curtain, was unlike any medium Conrad had met or read about. For one thing, she was young—younger than any spiritualist had any right to be. He judged her to have no more than twenty years. For another, she did not possess the typical charlatan's supercilious air and fevered eyes. In fact, her eyes were colorless, dull as dishwater. As she was guided to her seat by the Berber, Conrad found himself wondering whether she was blind.

But then she looked around the table at the gullible whom she had drawn to her stage set and studied each one with an intensity that belied her tender years. When it was his turn Conrad met her gaze with an intensity of his own, and though he had taken great pains to keep his expression neutral, Mme. Garnet said, "It seems we have a doubter in our midst tonight."

"On the contrary, madame," Conrad said as all eyes swiveled in his direction. "I am open to anything."

At a signal from the medium the Berber backed away, extinguished the lights.

Mme. Garnet did not ask the participants to hold hands. It was her voice that held them. Such a voice Conrad had not heard since he had been at the opera in Rome's famed La Scala and heard the challenging "The Queen of the Night" aria from Mozart's *The Magic Flute* so exquisitely sung it had brought tears to his eyes.

Mme. Garnet did not speak so much as sing, an ululation that was not without melody and that sank into the bones of all who heard it, including Conrad. Once again, he was impressed; Mme. Garnet was a charlatan of the first rank. The air around the table appeared to stir, chilling their cheeks. A woman across from him gave an audible gasp. He imagined her clutching the cameo pinned to the bodice of her dress.

"Please do not move," Mme. Garnet sang so sweetly that it was impossible for Conrad to laugh at her. "There is someone here." Conrad sensed her lift her arm. A cool fire illuminated her outstretched hand. The light emanated from the center of her cupped palm. As everyone watched, spellbound, the light unfurled like a flower in the light of an infernal moon. In the center of the light could be seen a human face. At this, the woman who had gasped gave out with a cry and promptly collapsed her upper body and head onto the table.

A brief kind of confused bedlam broke out, at the end of which the so-called ectoplasm vanished from Mme. Garnet's palm only to reappear in larger form in the rocking chair, which immediately began to creak as the creature on it apparently set it in motion.

Cries and alarums rose everywhere in the room like burning incense.

"Who are you?" she sang. "Please tell us your name."

But by this time Conrad had had enough. Standing, he produced a battery-powered torch, which he carried whenever he was out at night; there was no telling which unlit alleyways he would need to enter in his quest for clandestine information. Thumbing it on, he shone the beam onto whatever was in the rocking chair.

"I expressly requested that no one was to move!" Mme. Garnet shouted, all semblance of her seductive singing voice gone. "Please retake your seat or the forces necessary for the séance will be shattered."

A cry stinking of fear arose from the assembled, backing her up, but Conrad continued to the rocking chair.

"Here's what's shattered," he said, over the uproar. He pulled the sheet off the dwarf sitting in the chair. He spun toward the table. "There is the 'spirit,' alive as any of us."

Those around the table, including Yeats, were transfixed. Before any of the clients could move a muscle, Conrad reached Mme. Garnet's side. The Berber came out of the dark. This was to be expected; he was trained to protect his mistress. But Conrad spoke to him in Tamazight, his native language, and this arrested his movement as well as his intent. With his left hand, Conrad deftly removed the crumpled object from the medium's décolletage. When he shone his light on it all could see that what had been passed off as ectoplasm was a stiff cloth on which had been pasted the face of a man cut out of a newspaper.

"**SHE HAD** an accomplice," Conrad said.

Yeats pursed his lips. "You mean the dwarf." He still maintained the look of distaste that had come upon him when Conrad had unmasked the medium.

"Besides the dwarf." Conrad grinned.

The two men strode through the wee hours of London's industrial fogbound night. They passed drunkards and snatchpurses. Prostitutes beckoned from the mouths of shadowed alleyways.

"The woman who appeared to faint."

"Mrs. Dunwhistle?" Yeats exclaimed. "But I know her! She's part of our group."

"She may be part of your group," Conrad said, "but she was in Madame Garnet's employ."

"I don't believe it!"

"She fainted at just the right time, didn't she? Caused a ruckus, which was, in fact, a diversion, allowing Madame Garnet time to dispense with the cloth and for the dwarf to take his place on the rocking chair."

"This is most incredible," Yeats declared. "And the African?"

"A Berber from North Africa."

"For a moment there I was certain he would accost you. What did you say to him?"

"I told him that working for a charlatan brought no honor to him or his family."

"And he listened."

"Berbers have an acute sense of honor."

"And I was taken in." Yeats shook his head. "Well, old habits die hard, one supposes," he offered, seeming to free himself from the distaste that had overtaken him at the sight of the foolishness that had taken him and the others in. "And how, pray tell, did this . . . charlatan"—he almost choked on the word—"manage to light up that cloth?"

"Via a bioluminescent substance," Conrad said.

"What?"

"The heat of her hand acted on the liquid in which the cloth was soaked, causing the glow."

Yeats appeared gobsmacked. "Something like that actually exists?"

Conrad shrugged. "She most likely obtained it from the Berber. Several such substances exist in the High Atlas Mountains. They're mainly harvested from a species of giant click beetle."

Yeats couldn't get the sheer astonishment off his face. "We should go there."

"Mayhap next time," Conrad said with a smile. "Our immediate destination lies elsewhere."

The great poet ran a trembling hand through his hair. "Ah, I espy yonder pub." He pointed. "After this night I am in rather desperate need of a drink." He considered a moment. "Or three."

# 6

BRAVO WAS THIRTEEN, PUSHING GRANDFATHER CONRAD IN his wheelchair. It was a cold, clear day in December. He remembered the crows in the trees, lifting and cawing at their approach, pure black against the robin's-egg-blue sky. Far off, over the hill, a dog was barking. The comforting drone of bees. Conrad's white hair, still thick this close to death, spiked up like a crown of thorns.

"It's good to be away from London," Conrad said. "At last."

"What d'you mean, 'at last,' Grandfather?"

"Too many dark days, too many darker nights. Hellfire and brimstone is real enough, I'll tell you that."

They pushed on toward the old apple tree, its gnarled trunk and branches brutalized by time. It was his grandfather's favorite resting place on these excursions. When he died, he told his family, he wanted to be buried beneath the canopy of labyrinthine branches.

Bravo saw that his grandfather's fingers were twisting back and forth, that they held something between them. To his shock he saw that it was a crucifix. His father had already branded the old man a heretic, a man cut off from God. And yet he held a crucifix made, oddly, of bronze.

"This—see how I cannot even say its name—has become my touchstone, my long and narrow pathway back to God. My one chance home." Conrad held it up by its delicate chain so that the image of Christ swung back and forth from sunlight to shadow and back again. "But it also frightens me, Braverman. There are moments when it singes me, when I am certain that it will be the instrument of my death." With a snapping gesture, he enclosed the crucifix in his fist. It trembled, as if with an ague that now would never leave him. "I have strayed so far, and fallen so very, very fast. . . ."

**BRAVO'S MIND** flickered in and out of consciousness. When he fell back from the light it was always to join his grandfather under the old apple tree where Conrad was buried. In this translucent state, he heard Conrad's voice like the soughing of the wind through the village of aged branches. The crisp scent of apples broken open on the ground, the raucous cries of the birds hopping gingerly toward the fallen fruit, feasting on its flesh. The sight of his grandfather's pale eyes, the color of a lake in misty morning, peering into a place both faraway and inward.

When, on occasion, he traveled upward out of the patchwork shadows of that tree, he was assaulted by an intense pain that had nevertheless become familiar, like an unannounced guest who would not leave even though he was systematically wrecking your home.

Familiar or not, the pain was not Bravo's friend. For the first four days of his slow and agonizing convalescence, he much preferred the company of his grandfather and the apple tree. In fact, for the first thirty-six hours, when his life hung in the balance, it was Conrad's voice, as Bravo sat at his grandfather's knee, staring at the shards of sky and cloud he glimpsed through the branches, that sustained him. Far away, past the painted sky, was a place he thought he knew, or used to know, but he seemed to have little interest in it.

Once, early on, he sensed the ground beneath him softening like taffy, trying to suck him down into a blackness so complete it swallowed light whole. Conrad, seeing what was happening, threw out his arm, strong fingers grasping Bravo's forearm, holding him. Bravo felt like a baby, weak and helpless. Conrad spoke in a language that sounded like a thunderclap. Bravo was lifted up, the ground solidified beneath him. From then on, it was only the excruciating pain he had to suffer.

*I can't do anything about the pain,* Conrad told him, much later. *But even if I could, I wouldn't. This is something you need to bear. This pain is your own. You need to enter it, let it pass through you. You need to know it so you will recognize it when the time comes.*

*When the time comes for what?* Bravo managed.

A question he was asking himself. Conrad had gone, along with the comforting presence of the apple tree. Bravo lifted himself into the agony, and it was all he could do not to scream and keep screaming.

**ON THE** seventh day after the assault Bravo opened his eyes and squinted, sun dazzled. A mild breeze stirred his hair, but where it touched his skin a fire seized him in its grip and refused to let go.

Elias stared down at him, frowning with an old man's face. A week ago he had burst into blue-white flame that so terrified the witch—for that was how he thought of Emma—that she turned tail and ran. He had had an urge to run after her, to smother her in his strange fire that had no heat and did not consume him but flickered and popped off his flesh like a second skin or an aura. But then he saw what the witch had done to Bravo and knew if he left him he would surely die.

So he stayed. He dragged Bravo's insensate form out of the broiling sun, along a track he had made through the debris field caused by the collapse of the roof and the thick fire-eaten timbers. Through the vast central hall and the dining room, to the industrial-size kitchen, a corner of which he called home.

He had fashioned a roof out of parachutes found in a stone structure beside the airfield, stitching them together with nylon thread. Originally a guardhouse, the structure was crammed with shelves of useful items a clever boy like Elias could use or turn into something helpful. The castle's well system remained untouched by either fire or smoke; the electric stove sometimes worked, sometimes not. Three times a week Elias clambered down the cliffs to hook line-caught sea bream, red mullet, and, if he was lucky, branzino, his favorite.

The former guardhouse also contained a field surgery kit. For Bravo, he had need of every item in there, from rolls of gauze, to antiseptic, to needles, sutures, and an array of antibiotics. His father had been a soldier; he knew what to do. The gleaming long-nosed tweezers meant, he supposed, to root out bullets, which he employed to peel back leaves of ruined skin, cutting them off with a pair of surgical scissors. He worked diligently to clean Bravo's lips, nose, cheeks—the areas that had been split open by the ferocious beating—then sutured the rips in his flesh. He felt around the bruises and swellings of Bravo's ribs and shoulder, then carefully bound the rib cage. He wished he had ice for the swellings.

There was a moment, early on, when it seemed to Elias that his patient had stopped breathing. Bending close, he listened for the shallow, rattling breath that had been coming from between Bravo's half-open lips. When he could not hear even a whisper, he slapped Bravo's cheek as hard as he could, because he couldn't think what else to do and he had to do something. Eventually, owing to the slap or something else, Bravo started breathing again.

Elias ate his meals by Bravo's side. When Bravo began to run a fever, Elias managed to get him to swallow some antibiotic tablets. To do this, he had to grind up the tabs, lift his patient's head slightly so he wouldn't choke, dribble the antibiotic water between his cracked and swollen lips. Instinct, and memories of talks with his father, warned him not to let Bravo get dehydrated, which would slow the healing and might even prove lethal. Twice a day he bathed Bravo in salt water, both to cool him and to help with healing.

Within three days he ran out of fresh fish and had to raid his store of fish he had dried and salted. He was afraid to leave his patient to go catch more fresh fish, which typically took hours. He cut down on his portions, which in any case weren't large. He wished he could feed some to his patient, who frighteningly was still unconscious. He slept shallowly, like a mother with her gravely ill child, coming fitfully awake with every movement or sound Bravo made.

In the lulls between, Elias spoke to Bravo as if he were conscious, as if they were two friends sitting around a fire, trading stories of their past disguised as tall tales.

"I was born in a crossfire hurricane," Elias said one night after his dinner. "I mean that literally. Later, when I was older, my father told me the story of the raid, the automatic fire that crisscrossed the perimeter of the castle grounds. At the height of the firefight, just as my father led a squad of men that eventually beat back the attack, I escaped my howling mother's womb, along with more than half her blood. An artery ruptured on my way out. Our house was well beyond the perimeter, of course; families of Knights were not allowed anywhere near the castle. When my father was angry with me he'd say it was my fault, that I killed her in order to live."

He bent over, changed some of the burn dressings, which had become saturated with a clear yellow liquid.

"That firefight," he continued, "was a result of a raid by the Gnostic Observatines." He stuffed the soiled dressings in a plastic bag, sealed it tight with a twist tie. "Knight or GO, I wonder which you are." He shrugged his one-shoulder shrug. "Not that it matters to me; I never understood either. Never wanted to. I just wanted out, but children of the Knights are sworn to a blood oath never to leave as soon as they are able to speak." He lifted up his shirt, revealing a patchwork of long scars, pale against his fatless sunburnt flesh. "Left his marks on me, he did." Pushed the shirt right back down. "Well, I disobeyed him constantly, so maybe I deserved—"

He broke off as Bravo groaned, eyelids fluttering. But his eyes didn't open.

"Dreaming again," Elias said, nodding. "That's a good thing, I guess." He looked off into the distance for some time, as if he could see through the darkness to something in the farthest reaches beyond his ken. After some time, he returned to himself. He rose, went to take a piss, then hurried back.

"Time for bed," he said as he lay down beside Bravo, pulled a thin blanket over his bony shoulders, and fell fast asleep.

# 7

PARIS: PRESENT DAY

"ALL RIGHT, FINE," OBARTON SAID, "YOU'VE MADE YOUR POINT,
bloody though it may have been—"

"With men like these," Lilith said pointedly, "blood is the only way to
make an impression."

The two of them were seated in a dingy bistro near Oberkampf, in the
11th arrondissement, far away from the luxe properties and high-fashion
silhouettes of the Faubourg.

Obarton brushed imaginary bread crumbs off his ample lap. "Well, at
least you came sans your young shadow."

"You were quite persuasive." Lilith tapped the side of her fork against
her plate of indifferent frisée salad and duck gizzards. It was becoming
harder and harder to find decent food walking in off the Parisian streets.
She blamed the EU, the influx of other Euro cultures, with the Americans overtaking everyone else. "In any event, Highstreet has more than
enough work to keep him busy."

Obarton lifted a glass of white wine to his lips, made a face as he sipped
it. "Listening in on our enemies, one can only suppose."

Lilith nodded, put her fork down. She would have dearly loved a piece
of strudel with whipped cream, but what were the chances it would be of
any use to her palate in this mediocre place?

"Which brings up an important point." Obarton slathered another cutting of baguette with deep-yellow butter. "These days." He took a bite of
the buttered bread, chewed slowly, then swallowed. "Just *who* do you see
as our enemies?"

Lilith reacted to the accented word, as he expected. "Not this again."

"Yes," he said, leaning forward, "precisely *this* again." His eyes locked with hers. "This obsession with the Gnostic Observatines has to stop. They are not our only enemies. They are not the ones who burned our castle to the ground and incinerated everyone in it."

"The fire this time." Lilith closed her eyes for a moment. "Yes, I know."

"That fire wasn't natural."

"Come on, Obarton. That's only speculation."

"Listen to me now, because I have listened to you. Very carefully, as it happens. When we abducted Maura Kite from Istanbul we did the Gnostic Observatines an enormous favor. She would have done to them what she did to us. She was no longer Maura Kite. Something had taken her over, something terrible, something powerful, something beyond our ken."

"All of this was conveyed to Cardinal Duchamp. He summarily dismissed this story line as hysteria. What you're proposing happened goes against Church orthodoxy. Therefore, it cannot exist."

Obarton stared at her, his disbelief turning to open hostility. "You've been in direct contact with the cardinal?"

"I was at the Vatican last month, yes."

"That was Newell's—"

"Newell was an idiot," Lilith said as if pointing out an obvious fact to a child. "Someone had to step up."

"Someone like you."

She smiled with her teeth. "I'm the best candidate. By far."

"You are indeed," Obarton said. "At least as far as Felix Duchamp is concerned. You swallowed his cant hook, line, and sinker."

"Why shouldn't I? He speaks for the pontiff."

"No, Lilith. Duchamp speaks for himself. His self-interest is off the charts. He speaks the Gospel no more than does Braverman Shaw." He steepled his fingers. "And speaking of Shaw, it's my opinion that you need to seek out his sister."

"You want me to use her as bait to get to Bravo."

Now it was Obarton's turn to smile; it was no more pleasant than Lilith's. "Something like that."

Lilith smirked. "Is this your idea of compromise?"

"If you prefer to see it that way."

"If you continue to play the Delphic Oracle, I'll kill you right where you sit."

"Listen, you." Obarton's voice got low and chill as a winter draft. "You can intimidate the others, but don't fuck with me."

She laughed.

"You have no idea."

"I'm sure you'll die telling me."

His smile flattened out, seeming to come at her full force. "I have people who can squash you like a roach. You don't want to go to war with me."

"Short war."

"Shorter than you can imagine."

They glared at each other for a moment before Obarton threw some euros onto the table. "Come with me."

Lilith regarded him with suspicion. "Where?"

"You'll want to see this," he said as he rose.

"I'm not going anywhere with you."

Obarton grunted. "How many mistakes are you willing to make today."

A CAR drove them farther outside the center of Paris, into the 20th arrondissement, let them off at the base of the famous hill. The cemetery, whose carved granite gates they strode through, was named by Napoléon after the seventeenth-century confessor to Louis XIV, Père François de la Chaise. It was the first garden cemetery, and the first municipal one.

Père Lachaise served as the final resting place to a veritable who's who of titans of the arts, from Honoré de Balzac, Oscar Wilde, Maria Callas, Molière, Georges Bizet, Edith Piaf, Marcel Proust, and Frédéric Chopin to Jim Morrison. A wide cobbled walkway wound through the cemetery, rising up the hill as it went, bringing them deeper and deeper, it seemed, into the embrace of history.

They passed tourists with maps provided by the touts outside, taking selfies with the monuments to the famous. A young man had set up a tripod before the elaborate arched headstone at Camille Pissarro's grave. A crush of Japanese, some with cotton masks protecting their noses and mouths, others with long gloves over hands and forearms, were being escorted at speed by a grim-looking young woman, intent on making all the requisite stops in the time allotted to her charges.

Gathering clouds scudded by overhead, obscuring the sunlight, lowering the sky. The scent of rain pervaded the gusting wind that stirred the air. The bottom of Obarton's capacious trench coat flared out like bat wings, and he wrapped the coat closer around him. Lilith noted that despite his age and girth Obarton appeared to have no difficulty with the climb.

Farther on, they came upon *Aux Morts,* the Memorial to the Dead. Obarton led her off the path, through underbrush and fallen leaves, around to the rear, where a small building—the ossuary—squatted ugly as a toad.

"Some years ago," Obarton said, "the ossuary became so crowded that the bones were cremated, then returned here." He pointed. "As you see, it's locked. No one comes here. Tourists don't even know of its existence."

Producing a key, he opened the lock. The thick metal door creaked from disuse as he pushed it.

"The sacred and the profane," he said as they crossed the threshold.

From another pocket, he drew out an LED flashlight, and switched it on. In the sudden illumination Lilith saw tier after tier of olive-green metal boxes the approximate size and shape of coffins stacked from floor to ceiling. The scent of burnt offerings came to her, of dust mixed with earth and candle wax. It was as chill as a winter twilight. As they moved forward, Obarton played the beam of the flash along the rear wall. At first, all Lilith saw was a knife-edged shadow. Then, as they neared it, she discerned a gap between the crematory boxes, narrow enough that Obarton was obliged to squeeze through sideways.

He unlocked another door and as it swung open said, "Careful now. The steps are steep and very old." The light played over a granite staircase as narrow as it was steep. The smooth indentations in the center of each tread attested to their age.

The stairway wound down and down as if into the bowels of the earth itself. The air became stale, with an unpleasant sweet-sharp tang she associated with ether or formaldehyde. The dead air was chillier, too, sluggish with age.

When they reached the bottom, Obarton said, "Just as the Gnostic Observatines have—or I should say *had*—their secret Reliquary, so do we."

"The GO purportedly had relics from the four Apostles."

Obarton nodded. "True."

"Then what do we have?"

"Things we have never shown Cardinal Duchamp, nor would we ever. Regard." He directed the beam at a plinth of metamorphic rock on which rested a sealed cylindrical tank.

"What the hell . . . !" Lilith took a step forward. "I knew I smelled formaldehyde." Another step. "But is that . . . Good Christ, is that a baby floating in there?"

"Yes," Obarton said. "And no."

She could sense him grinning as he stood beside her. He had assumed the air of a conjuror, and this made her uneasy. She did not like being alone with him. She especially didn't like being alone with him in this place that, so far as she could discern, had the aspect not of a Reliquary, but of a sideshow.

Now he moved the slider on the flashlight to a second position and the LED switched from white to red. In an instant the baby's eyes flew open, its head expanded, a horn pushed through the flesh in the center of its forehead. Its mouth gaped open to reveal several rows of razor-sharp teeth, and then it lunged at Lilith with both its teeth and the talon-like nails that curved cruelly from its fingertips.

# 8

"MY CLOSE FRIENDS, FEW THOUGH THEY BE, CALL ME WBY,"
Yeats said with a self-deprecating smile. He shot his cuffs in a vaguely
nervous gesture. "Though Ezra Pound, bless him, calls me the Eagle."

"If it's all the same to you, I think I'll stick with WBY," Conrad said.

The two men sat at their ease, a rough wood-plank table between them,
beneath the spreading branches of a fragrant apple tree. On the table was
a tray set with a tea service, small plates of lemon slices, scones, biscuits,
butter as yellow as a summer sun, clotted cream from Devon, and mar-
malade made from bitter Seville oranges. A more quintessentially British
scene could not be imagined, or wished for. Behind them was the immense stone manor house belonging to Conrad's family. At the moment,
his parents were in India or Nepal or Tibet or who knew where, learning
the esoteric arts that, his father was certain, could be useful to the Gnostic Observatines in their ongoing war with the Knights of St. Clement,
cat's-paw to the popes down through the ages.

Conrad had taken his new friend to Sussex for the weekend. On the
following Tuesday he planned to leave on his voyage.

"It is a tenet of the human condition," Conrad said, "that in order to
appreciate the truth one must first learn to recognize and unmask deceit
in all its forms."

"How does one achieve that?" Yeats asked.

"Join me on this expedition and you will find out."

"I would have to leave the just cause of my Ireland."

"I understand your dedication to your homeland's independence,"
Conrad said. "But it must be said that you have endured a rising tide of

derision both here and, increasingly, in Ireland. Perhaps it's time to step away for a month or so. A new perspective."

Yeats's eyes narrowed. "Do you expect this voyage of yours to cause me to turn my back on the independence movement?"

"Not at all." Conrad poured them both tea. "Cream or lemon?"

"Neither, thank you."

When Yeats accepted the tea, Conrad slid a slice of lemon into his cup and continued. "A new perspective is just that. Perhaps with distance you may find a new path to your avowed dream."

With a rattle, Yeats set his cup into its saucer. "A dream with a long memory is a powerful motivation, Conrad."

"Unquestionably." Conrad broke off a piece of scone. "Having said that, a dream, no matter how long its memory, must be forged into purpose in order to succeed."

Yeats thought about this for an extraordinarily long time as he gazed off into the hazy distance beyond the apple tree: the gently rolling hills, the copses of oak and beech trees, the nesting of chaffinches and long-tailed tits, the small lake on which ducks serenely paddled, all part of the Shaws' vast estate. For all his seeking out the supernatural, he was a supremely rational human being. Whether it be poetry or politics, he pondered with great precision and deliberation. He was not a man to thoughtlessly jump into any proposition. For this reason, Conrad understood that the unmasking of Mme. Garnet's fraud had hit him hard. He was someone who took his belief systems most seriously. To have one of them upended had come as quite a shock.

At last, his eyes cleared and he looked directly at Conrad. "It seems to make sense for me to learn to separate truth from falsehood."

Conrad could feel his heartbeat accelerate. "Then you'll join me."

"If you'll only tell me why you have chosen me. Clearly, it wasn't chance."

"Indeed not." Conrad sat back, hands folded over his stomach. He stared up at the twining branches, the dappling of sunlight, glimpsed the moving clouds passing shadows over them. He opened his mouth and began to recite this poem:

> *"Though I am old with wandering*
> *Through hollow lands and hilly lands,*

*I will find out where she has gone,*
*And kiss her lips and take her hands;*
*And walk among long dappled grass,*
*And pluck till time and times are done*
*The silver apples of the moon,*
*The golden apples of the sun."*

He smiled as his gaze returned to Yeats. "It was this poem, *your* poem, 'The Song of Wandering Aengus,' that brought me to contact you, to convince you to make this journey with me." He paused to pour more tea for them both, broke a biscuit in half. WBY accepted both with obvious pleasure. Like all men of letters he had a weak spot for flattery.

"I saw in those words a visionary, a man who saw beyond the gray veil of the everyday world, to the reality beneath." Conrad cocked his head. "Was I wrong?"

Though he was not prone to expansive gestures, Yeats nevertheless threw his head back and laughed. "Not in the least." Then he sobered a bit. "At least I hope not."

Again, the great poet seemed lost in thought. "My boy, you appear to have gathered about you a great deal of wisdom for one of only twenty years."

"I was born old," Conrad said, more truthfully than Yeats could know.

Another laugh. A shake of the head.

"Then you will join me."

The great poet nodded. "That I will."

"Splendid!"

"But you must tell me what we are looking for."

Conrad's eyes twinkled. "A place you have already been."

"What?"

"In your mind. A place known to the Shaws as the Hollow Lands."

Yeats started. "My poem."

Conrad nodded. "I believe a part of you has already been to the Hollow Lands, WBY. Perhaps while you write, perhaps in your dreams."

"And what will we find there in these Hollow Lands? Golden apples of the sun?"

"Mayhap," Conrad said, taking in the poet's ironic tone. "But what we will be searching for is something darker, something far more dangerous: the Book of Deathly Things."

"I have never heard of it."

"I am unsurprised. Even among your coterie of occultists it is likely not known, or, if it is, it is certainly not spoken of. Book of Deathly Things is another name for The Testament of Lucifer."

"Good Lord, man, you cannot be serious."

"I could not be more so."

Yeats took a breath, let it out slowly. "Have you, by chance, anything stronger than this delicious tea?"

Conrad produced a silver hip flask, handed it over. Yeats unscrewed the cap, took a long draught. He snorted, raised his spectacles to his forehead, thumbing tears out of his eyes. He took a second, shorter drink. Only then did he hand the flask back.

"From the moment we met at your club," he said, "I had a feeling about you. You are exactly right. I have this sense sometimes. Call it a form of déjà vu, call it what you will, it is exceptionally strong. On occasion, it shakes me to my core." Blood rose into his neck, turning his cheeks roseate. "This secret I share with you. Not even my friend Ezra knows."

"Then why did you wait so long to agree?"

"I wanted to gain the measure of you, sir. I am not always truly at home with this sixth sense of mine. I do not always trust it."

"Forgive me, but I believe you are afraid of it."

Yeats considered this. "Perhaps so. In any event, I required the confirmation of my other senses as to your character."

Conrad took up a leather cylinder he'd had at his side. "Well, then, now that we both have been proved correct in our senses, I judge it high time to proceed to the next phase."

Yeats looked eager. Opening the cylinder, Conrad slid out a roll of thick paper, handmade, with the texture of vellum. Clearing away the tea service, he spread the sheet, using four of the small plates to hold down each corner. As he did so, Yeats brought his chair around to sit side by side with Conrad.

"So this is where in the Levant we're headed," Yeats said softly, as his gaze bored deep into the contour map Conrad had opened. This was not a map printed on any press. It was clearly hand-drawn by a knowledgeable and meticulous hand. Picking up on this, WBY said in the tone one uses in a church, Protestant or Catholic, "How old is this?"

"We still lack the means to pin it down to a year," Conrad said, happily observing his friend's rapt face; this was precisely the reaction he had been hoping for. "What we can say with reasonable certainty is it was drawn sometime in the fourteenth century." He pointed to one corner of the map. "You see here, though faint, this is the seal of Orhan, son of Osman the First, the founder of the Empire. He reigned as sultan from 1326 to 1362, as the Ottoman Empire rapidly expanded its territory east and north."

"But this is a map of Ethiopia and Eritrea," Yeats said.

"At the farthest reaches of the Empire, in those early Ottoman days, yes." His forefinger stabbed out again. "We see the greatest concentration of detail in and around the town of Lalibela, in the north. There are numerous sacred sites in Ethiopia, but what makes this one different is that Lalibela is inhabited almost exclusively by Ethiopian Orthodox Christians. As you can see here, in the inset, the holy structures are laid out in a symbolic reproduction of those in Jerusalem. The country adopted Christianity very early on, historically dating back to the time of the Apostles."

Yeats lifted his gaze up. "Yes? And?"

"From the configuration of these buildings it is irrefutable that a delegation of Ethiopians made its way to Jerusalem, there to pray and to meet with the Apostles or, at the very least, their representatives." Conrad's finger hovered over a particular cluster of stone buildings. "The incredible detail of the drawings argues that there was at least one architect in the delegation. Information has recently come into our possession that indicates historical scholars were also part of the delegation, and that they brought back from Jerusalem artifacts for safekeeping from the continually war-torn region."

"And you think they're still there."

"No," Conrad said with a slow smile. "I *know* they are. Including the Book of Deathly Things."

Yeats frowned, but beneath that was a growing desire, powerful as the sun breaching the eastern horizon. "What artifacts, precisely?" This was the way his mind worked. Details. Precision. Facts.

Conrad shrugged. "They could be anything. But it seems to me that they would be extremely sacred, extremely valuable, containing hidden knowledge." He rose up. "Perhaps even the whereabouts of King Solomon's mines."

Yeats's eyes opened wide. "Gold."

"Not just gold," Conrad said. "If the legends are correct then a very special form of gold created by Solomon's cadre of alchemists."

# 9

MALTA: PRESENT DAY

BRAVO OPENED GLUEY EYELIDS, SAID, "WHAT ARE YOU DOING here? I saw you burst into flames."

Elias laughed, clearly relieved. "It wasn't that kind of fire."

Above him the parachute roof fluttered and billowed like a sail. The sun had already left the sky. A cool breeze had risen, bringing with it the scents of the sea, the calls of the gulls. A gas lamp was on, casting a fitful circle of pale yellow.

Bravo's brows knit together. "You're not even burnt. What kind of fire was it?"

Wetting a cloth in a bowl of beaten brass, he wiped away the crust from Bravo's eyelids and lips.

Elias shrugged. "From what I've seen you're the one with expertise in these matters."

Bravo looked up at him. "Have you been taking care of me all by yourself?"

"Yes and no."

"I don't understand."

"Neither do I." Elias cupped one hand behind Bravo's head, lifting it so Bravo could sip some tepid water. "Not too much. I know you're parched, but a little at a time is better than it all coming up at once."

When he laid Bravo's head back down. Bravo thanked him. "How many days?"

"About a week," Elias said. "Give or take."

Bravo closed his eyes for a moment. "Jesus."

Elias's expression was eager. "Maybe you can help me with something."

"Anything." Bravo tried for a smile; it was grimmer than he had aimed for. "But I'm not in much of a position to help you."

"Let me tell my story," Elias said, "then decide." He settled himself more comfortably on his hams. "The night after my father was burned to death here in this castle, I cried myself to sleep. Not surprising, but that part's beside the point. It's my dream. I can't get it out of my head."

"Tell me," Bravo said, his senses abruptly on high alert.

"Okay, well, I was somewhere in the countryside—not Malta—there was a cool breeze on my face. I was sitting in dappled sunlight, leaning against the trunk of a huge apple tree. All of a sudden a deeper shadow crossed over me. I looked up and saw—well, maybe it was a man, but maybe it was something else; I don't know. It didn't move like a man, but it smiled at me like a man would."

Heart hammering in his chest, Bravo was forced to interrupt. "What did this man look like?"

"Well, that's the funny thing." Elias appeared to be concentrating hard. "You know how dreams are. People are there and they're not."

"Was it like that?"

"I dunno. Maybe it was like . . . hmm . . ." Elias pulled at his lower lip. "Maybe it was more like I was seeing him through water, like he was drowned, like he lived in another . . . place. But then dreams are another place, aren't they."

Sweat was breaking out all over Bravo's body. He felt himself trembling. Could Elias have encountered the specter of Bravo's grandfather, who had been buried beneath the apple tree on the Shaws' Sussex estate?

"He smiled at you, and then what happened?"

"It was the strangest thing," Elias said. "He plucked an apple from the tree and handed it to me. It was a perfect apple, shiny and red and ripe. I could smell it, not just with my nose but with my whole body." His eyes were beseeching. "Does that make sense?"

"Perfect sense," Bravo said.

"I held the apple in the palm of my hand." Elias seemed in a state of semi-trance. "I can still feel its weight. It was so perfect, you know?"

Bravo, in fact, did, but he didn't dare break the spell that had come over the boy. Suddenly all his aches and pains began to fade away as he concentrated on the boy's dream.

"Then this man who was drowned said to me, 'Eat it, Elias. Eat the whole apple.'" He frowned, his eyes still slightly out of focus. "He knew my name. I don't know how . . . but it was just a dream, right?"

Again Bravo was afraid to break Elias's train of remembrance.

Perhaps the boy hadn't expected an answer, for he went right on. "The apple was so perfect. I didn't want to destroy it. I mean, how many things are perfect in this world? But I wasn't in this world, was I? I was somewhere else. And the scent was so strong. My mouth began to water, and the drowned man said, 'Elias, eat.' And so I did, the tart-sweet flesh, the juice running down my chin, my fingers sticky with it. I just kept eating, core and all. And when it was gone so was the drowned man."

Elias's eyes cleared, and he was staring down at Bravo. "What does it mean, my dream? Why can't I get it out of my head?"

Bravo shook his head, but somewhere deep inside him stirred the shadow of a memory, which made him think he ought to know why, but this vexing train of thought was snapped by the loudening *thwup-thwup-thwup* of a helicopter slinging through the sky. A powerful searchlight tore apart the darkness, and then the helicopter was descending onto the tarmac of the ruined castle's heliport.

EVER SINCE she had come in sight of the burnt castle Ayla had been in a quandary as to what to do. Of Bravo and Emma there was no sign, and she interpreted this as ominous. Hunkering down for hours behind a bulwark of projecting rocks with a pair of binoculars, she surveilled the immediate vicinity without success. Late in the afternoon, a slender boy came into view, picking his way through the rubble, arms loaded. The boy was the only human being visible in the acreage. If any Knight patrols existed they were exceptionally well hidden, and this was what worried her. She felt inadequate to whatever force had captured or—she shivered—God forbid, killed Bravo and Emma. She followed the boy with her binoculars, scuttling between rocks to keep him in view, saw that he was stocking supplies for his makeshift home in one of the castle's rooms. Inching closer, she could see a figure laid out on what might be a cot. She decided to take a risk, moving closer still until she could make out the figure's face. Her pulse skyrocketed. Bravo! No sign of Emma, but Bravo was clearly hurt. With that, she came to the conclusion that she needed help.

Her first thought was to contact the Gnostic Observatines in Addis Ababa, where she had been working, but instinct warned her against this course of action. There had to be a good reason why Bravo had deliberately not told anyone but her where he and Emma were going. She therefore felt bound to keep that secret. Besides, Addis Ababa was too far away. She needed help closer to hand.

She decided to retreat back to Valletta, a city whose sixteenth-century Baroque structure owed much to the Knights, who had headquartered there for centuries. In the great siege of 1565 the Fort of St. Elmo had finally fallen to the Ottoman Empire, but a year later it was retaken by the Knights with the help of reinforcements from Spain. The victorious Grand Master, Jean de Valette, set about building a fortified city, which would be better equipped to repel any and all future enemies.

As Ayla drove at speed to Valletta, her mother approached her. She came most often wrapped in a dream, but in times of emergencies it seemed she couldn't wait for her daughter to fall asleep. And yet in this alternate world it was nighttime. A full moon cast slanting beams through the car's window. Dilara was the same silvery color as the moonlight; in fact, she seemed to have emerged from out of it.

*My darling,* she said, *you are in the wrong place.*

Ayla's heart tumbled over, for she always listened to her dream-mother. *You mean here, Malta? Or Valletta?*

*Not a place you can see,* Dilara said cryptically. *You are in the twilight.*

*Twilight?*

*A dangerous place to be, Daughter.* Then her mother turned toward something or someone she couldn't see, shouted, *Foul creature, that sought to destroy another Shaw!*

*Bravo!* But Ayla, listening intently to her mother's tone, was terrified, for beneath the anger she recognized naked fear. In her experience, her mother was afraid of nothing—not Tannourine, not the red tent of shadows, not the fiend inside it, not even death. But here she was, fear oozing out of every pore of her liquidy body.

*They're close now,* Dilara said to her daughter. *So very close.*

The terror rose exponentially in Ayla's breast. She knew her mother was referring to the Fallen—the angels who accompanied Satan out of Heaven into the bowels of Hell. As a measure against this terror, she said, *Mother, why didn't you tell me who my real father was?*

*Omar was your father. He brought you up. He loved you as his own flesh and blood.*

*Why didn't you tell me that Conrad Shaw was my birth father?*

*To protect you.*

*And yet you took me to Tannourine, into the red tent of shadows, into the presence of that . . . fiend.*

*That was foreordained,* Dilara said. *I wasn't given a choice.*

*Wasn't given a choice? By whom?*

But now her mother's head lifted, her nostrils dilated, and her body tensed.

*Mother, what is it? What's—?*

But Dilara was gone, along with the streams of moonlight. The afternoon, red as ox blood, was dying. Ayla pulled the manuscript in its case closer to her, as if something or someone was about to snatch it from her. She had come to feel attached to the thing, almost as if it were her child. But why not? she told herself. It was an invaluable artifact Bravo had entrusted to her. In the invisible script of its pages might be all the answers they were seeking to stop the Fallen in their tracks, beat them back to the Underworld where God had consigned them. She vowed to keep the manuscript safe at all costs.

By the time she reached the city outskirts, dusk was beginning to fall. She was desperately craving a hot meal, a cool shower, and a comfortable bed in which to sink. But there was no time for that now. Her mother had made that quite clear.

After three hours of hurrying through the streets, querying people, she settled on the local medivac. With a plaintive story and a fistful of cash, she was able to corral a team that was both sympathetic and venal enough to accept her offer.

Fifteen minutes later, they were lifting off from Valletta, heading toward the Knights' castle.

# 10

**"GOD IN HEAVEN, HALLOWED BE THY NAME."**

Lilith, making the sign of the cross, on her knees in front of the thing floating in formaldehyde, repeated this protective prayer over and over.

Obarton, LED torch in hand, stood a pace behind her. An undertow of satisfaction swept through him. Having determined early on that Lilith Swan was an unstoppable force, that outright opposition would only lead to his demise, either figuratively or actually, he beat a tactical retreat while he sought another way to maintain his status in the Circle Council. Times change, he knew, and if you didn't change with them you risked getting swept out with the trash. Witness Newell, Santiago, and Muller.

"God in Heaven, hallowed be thy name."

Obarton was too old, too canny, too steeped in the philosophy of Niccolò di Bernardo dei Machiavelli, the sixteenth-century founder of modern political science, to abandon the field of battle for long. Obarton had read Machiavelli's seminal work, *The Prince,* so many times he had most of it memorized. Nevertheless, the words that affected him most deeply were from a letter the great statesman had written late in life, during his exile. *I enter the ancient courts of rulers who have long since died. There, I am warmly welcomed, and I feed on the only food I find nourishing and was born to savor.*

In determining how to place Lilith under his control without either her knowledge or her consent, he embraced that idea. He consulted not only Prince Niccolò but also the rulers of the ancient courts who had succored him in his time of need.

"God in Heaven, hallowed be thy name."

Like all solutions to seemingly imponderable questions the answer was right under his nose; Lilith had provided it herself. Her slavish devotion to God and the Church was a weakness Obarton was all too happy to exploit.

Reaching out, he placed a hand on her shoulder, then gently lifted her up. She could not take her eyes from the floating thing, though now that Obarton had switched off the red light it looked as it had before, like a baby sleeping. He drank in the tremors racing through her body as if they were draughts of a fine wine.

"Wh-what . . . what is that?" she stammered.

"One of the Fallen," Obarton said with theatrical gravity. "Dagon, to be exact."

"An archangel."

Obarton nodded soberly. "A terrible one, a dangerous one. One of the enemy who now seek to destroy us."

"How . . . ?" She gestured vaguely. "I mean, how did it get here?"

"Why, we captured it, of course." When she turned to him, he added, "Oh, not I nor any Knight still living. No, Dagon was captured centuries ago by a process that, alas, has been lost to us. Still, here it is, wings atrophied, adult body reversed through adolescence into this by the stasis in which it is kept."

He took Lilith by the shoulders, stared hard into her eyes. "Listen to me. I brought you here to show you this horror, so you could see for yourself what we're up against, why you must turn your great powers toward the real enemy, one of which floats here, still dangerous even in captivity." He gripped her more securely. "Do you believe me now?"

She nodded, still somewhat in shock at having faced one of the Fallen.

"Good. Let us leave here now; the air has become befouled by that thing." Guiding her gently up and out of the stone Reliquary, he returned them to the warm breath of daylight; the trees whispering in the breeze; the sunlight scattered by dancing leaves; the chirping of the birds; the soft whir of insects. Life!

They went to a café a few blocks from the cemetery, where, after a double espresso, Obarton judiciously left her to stew in the ramifications of the shock he had provided. Anything he could say now would just undercut the effects of her experience. He judged there would be plenty of time for palaver when the full effect of the horror brought to her the reality they were all facing.

---

**IN TRUTH,** he wasn't wrong. For the next twenty or so minutes following his departure Lilith sat transfixed, staring out the plate-glass window at the cobbled street. She saw none of the passersby, nor the vehicles, but only the horrifying face of Dagon as the Fallen Archangel leapt at her. His presence negated the laws by which she had lived her life, thoroughly undercut what she believed to be the nature of the world. That *thing*, that monstrosity, did not belong in thronged civilization, it *couldn't* exist, and yet it did. The natural human reaction to a beast in its midst was to deny its existence. The more evidence of the beast's existence, the greater the denials, the rationalization of which humanity was the uncontested master.

She tried to apply her considerable will to shutting down all images, all thought, but it was no use. The image of Dagon continued to haunt her, as did Obarton. Despite his outright antagonism toward her, she had spared him from the purge for any number of reasons: the top three being he was an old hand from whom she could learn about governing the Knights, he had contacts both in the Vatican and in the lay world whom she could tap, he was clever. But now she wondered whether she had underestimated his power. Anyone who was the current jailor of an archangel of the Fallen was not to be toyed with. The balance of power, which she had believed to be firmly in her hands, had shifted like a dune in a sandstorm. Well, then, she supposed that she would have to bow to the inevitable. But first, as her personality dictated, she had to make doubly sure before she ceded the high ground.

Her second double espresso kicked her out of stasis. Throwing down some euros, she left the café, retracing her steps through the gates of Père Lachaise. It was almost closing time, and she half-ran back to the memorial, heading around behind it, but everything was locked up tight and no matter how hard she tried she could not regain entrance.

**"NO MATTER,"** Highstreet said when she returned to his atelier. Instead of skylights, the double-height space was filled with a light of another kind. Thirty screens of dazzling digital effects, experimental source code, and the hard drives he'd cracked open with his resourceful and implacable worms were ranged around him on three sides. "I have the complete stream of your meeting with Obarton."

Lilith sat down beside him. Unlike a traditional artist's atelier, Highstreet's space was dim as twilight and almost as chilly as a meat locker, to accommodate both the flat-screen images and the complex electronic hardware.

Before setting out to meet Obarton, Lilith had Highstreet fix her up with a miniature video feed. She had no idea what he wanted or where he might take her. Paranoia was essential following her bloody coup; she wanted everything on Highstreet's record in case something untoward happened to her.

"So you saw that . . . hideous thing at the same time I did," she said now.

"Smoke and mirrors, Lilith. Smoke and mirrors."

She was startled. "What are you talking about?"

"I ran the feed back and forth and in slo-mo, frame by frame, even. I didn't know what I was looking for, and, frankly, it was so well devised I would have missed it if I hadn't fast-forwarded the tape to get to the end."

"The low light must have been a hindrance."

"You'd think so, right? But actually it was the low light that helped me out." His fingers manipulated the keys on his master board and the sight of the glass jar and the thing hanging suspended inside it came up, threatening to turn her insides to liquid. He punched the fast forward key and the images started to blur as if reflected in a dark mirror. Then, out of nowhere, a bright flash lit up the extreme upper right-hand corner of the screen. It was there and gone so fast that she wasn't sure she'd actually seen it, until Highstreet confirmed its existence.

He ran the tape back until the flash was freeze-framed.

"What is that?" Lilith asked.

Highstreet grinned. "It's the mirror, albeit an ultra-high-tech one." His grin broadened. "Or actually it's a laser—an extremely sophisticated one, I might add, bounced off several mirrors." Then he rewound the tape to the moment Obarton switched the LED torch to red and the Fallen Archangel leapt at her. "What you're seeing is a hologram, a form of VR image."

"Wait. Wouldn't I need goggles for virtual reality?"

"Under most circumstances, you would. But the low light combined with the red LED beam refracted and intensified the image, turning the space in front of the jar, precisely where you were standing, into what amounts to a VR tube."

"You mean this thing in the jar doesn't exist?"

"You saw what Obarton wanted you to see. It was an illusion."

Lilith shook her head. "But it looked so real."

"This is the illusionist's genius. He makes the impossible appear real."

For some time, Lilith remained mute and motionless. Being quite familiar with her silent phases, Highstreet went back to his own work, ignoring her as if she weren't actually there. When she had processed everything she had seen and heard she would let him know.

Lilith was lost deep inside herself. Her current situation vis-à-vis Obarton was difficult for her to deal with. Being taken in and manipulated by him, feeling her power ripped out from under her, reverberated through her, amplifying a past she could neither forget nor escape. How much she blamed her parents for her uncle's transgressions she could never quite figure out. Her inner rage was like a tide, rising and falling with moon-like phases. They hadn't known—in retrospect this was clear enough—they hadn't even suspected. But their cluelessness only fueled her rage. They should have known, at least suspected. They were there to protect their children, and they hadn't. They'd let the predation continue, while it went on night after night under their noses. They'd let her shame and fright build to intolerable levels. From ages five through eleven, when the family's beloved uncle lived with them, he had inducted her into the hideous secret ways of sex without consent, without even an understanding of what was going on. He professed to love her, to cherish her as no one else could; that was the insidious nature of the predation. *Our little secret, our private world, our sacred space.* He knew all the code phrases, employed them all like an army on maneuvers. She was outflanked, overwhelmed, taken prisoner. With her lying in the secret boudoir of his strong arms and engorged loins, he sang softly to her as he worked her body like an instrument. He was never less than tender with her; to this day she believed that he loved her, but that love, like Humbert Humbert's in Nabokov's *Lolita*, was an awful thing, a monstrous dungeon into which she been consigned.

But in her twelfth year, like a switch being thrown, a heady flood of hormones kicked in, overrunning everything including her captor. She woke up one morning to the realization of who and what he truly was, and that her younger sister, six years her junior, would be in imminent peril the moment *she* became too old for her uncle's repugnant tastes. Everything he had done to her took on an intolerable double meaning; bad enough she had to endure his molestations, she could not allow Molly to be his next victim.

She sat under the pear tree in the backyard, in the summer rain, the warm wetness mingling with her tears. She thought about going to her parents, but would they believe her? Her uncle would of course deny everything. Then doctors might become involved, cold fingers probing her private parts. A shame of intolerable proportions engulfed her. It was her fault; she let him do whatever he wanted to her. Had she come willingly into his arms, into the warmth and protection he provided? But it wasn't protection at all—that was the illusion he was providing, the illusion that had gulled her into insensibility, to being what amounted to his emotional slave.

No more, no more.

That very night, turning on a newfound false coquettishness, she lured him out into the woods behind her parents' house. A half mile away, the ground sloped down toward the local reservoir. Appealing to the tiny atavistic brain between his thighs, she shed her clothes—all but her underpants—held her breasts out to him, then whirled away, laughing. He followed her under the cyclone fence protecting the reservoir.

She let him catch her when the water purled around their calves. Grabbing one arm, he reached for her underpants. She stumbled backward, just as she planned, and he fell forward on top of her. Grabbing a sharp rock she had scooped up in the woods and hidden down her pants, she slammed it into the side of his head. When his eyes opened as wide as his mouth, she struck him again between the eyes. He went down, rolling off her. She held him under the water, patiently and methodically counting to a thousand. An owl hooted; then it passed overhead, silent as death. From behind her, in the woods, the rustling of small nocturnal mammals foraging for food. Crickets chirped, applauding her actions.

Gathering rocks from the bottom of the reservoir, she stuffed them in the pockets of his jacket and pants. She stuffed the remainder into the place where his erection had been. She was an excellent swimmer, confident and powerful, but his weight made her journey to the deep part of the reservoir difficult. Not impossible, however. She swam on, listening to the crickets.

Forty minutes later, she was on the other side of the cyclone fence, having brushed away her footprints with a fallen pine bough. She dressed, returned to her house. All the lights were off. No one saw her. She went to bed and, with the singular relief of the freed, fell into a deep and dreamless sleep.

She was somewhat in that state again—a kind of self-hypnosis she had developed a knack for—as she sat in Highstreet's atelier. If she were to be honest with herself, which she could be from time to time, she felt most comfortable, safest, even, when she was here. Highstreet himself had something to do with it, though there was nothing sexual between them, and couldn't be, considering both their natures: Her uncle had negated all sexual desire in her, had left her with the lasting assurance that love was dangerous, a weapon of enslavement. She could not bear to have a man touch her in a sexual way and Highstreet, well, he didn't think about sex at all; it was as if he had been born without a libido.

But there was also this: being surrounded by the screens, by the flickering images, the scrolling source code, the gentle susurrus of the fans cooling the equipment was like crickets chirruping. Inhuman hearts that could never harm her, never prey upon her, never take from her what she did not want to give. She loved these mighty machines that could do so much, render unto Highstreet, and through him, to her, so much information, so much commentary on post-modern life—windows on the world. Yes, she was safe here, safe with them and safe with Highstreet, with whom she had the most remarkable and rewarding relationship of her life. And why not? After all, he was half machine himself.

"Hugh," she said, and when he turned from his work, giving her, as he always did, his undivided attention, went on with her thought, "Obarton did this to me to teach me a lesson. He knew he couldn't stop me the way the others had wanted to, so he found a way to humble me, to bind me to him in fear."

"But you have no fear."

Of course this wasn't true, her constant ruminations on the past proved that. But in another sense it was, indeed, true. In this life she now led she feared no man, knowing she could find the most direct way to expunge the threat, as she had done with her uncle. But she did fear the supernatural; her dedication to the Church assured that. Like a nun, taking on the mantle of Christ had marked her break with her old life, opened the doorway to the life she now led. That she could be a devout servant of

Christ and kill without a single iota of either guilt or remorse wasn't a paradox. Rather, she was following in the long, bloody tradition of the armies of
the pope, Christ's mortal emissary on earth.

"In this archangel of the Fallen—what you have identified as a
hologram—Obarton held up my own fear for me to witness. He made
me tremble, fall to my knees, beseech God to protect me. He knows my
weakness, Hugh. He has gotten to me via the sanctity of my adoration of
the divine."

"The man's a charlatan. A sideshow, nothing more."

So Hugh. He was angry on her behalf, and she smiled to let him know
she appreciated that. "No, Hugh. He's an illusionist, and there's a difference. His belief in the power of the illusions he creates is his weakness. A
chink in his armor I mean to exploit."

"Ah, yes. I see your point." Highstreet knew the game was afoot, and
he was already warming to it. "How shall we proceed? How shall we turn
the tables on him?"

"Obarton wants something from me—something I would never agree
to unless he brought me to heel. Now that he believes he's succeeded I'll
nurture his misconception."

"What does he want?"

"He believes the Fallen are real, that they caused the fire at the castle
in Malta. He wants me to go after them. He wants me to be his stalking
horse, to feel them out, define their strengths and weaknesses."

"If he's telling the truth. On the other hand, he could be sending you
on a wild-goose chase to keep you away from his own real initiative."

She really did love this man, in her own way, in the only way possible.
She nodded. "Always a possibility."

"Either way, he might be sending you to your death."

"How lovely for him."

"And how elegant," Hugh said. "Not a drop of your blood on his
hands."

"Obarton is nothing if not fastidious."

They both laughed at the same time, as if they were each a reflection
of the other observed in a mirror. But this was all business as usual—
why Hugh was so happy. She gave him no hint of the inky turbulence
underneath. Obarton had gotten into her head. No matter that it was only
for an hour or so, the fact that he'd been able to do it at all came as a

wake-up call to her. It was no wonder her uncle had surfaced after she had viewed the illusion of the Fallen Archangel named Dagon. He had gotten into her head, too, so much so that she had never told anyone what had happened. No one ever found his body; no one knew where he had gone or what had happened to him. Only Lilith, and she would never tell anyone, not even Hugh Highstreet.

"But seriously, Lilith," Highstreet said now.

"Yes," she said, mentally engaging him again, "seriously."

"He must be disposed of."

"Softlee, softlee, catchee monkey," Lilith said in a childlike singsong voice. "We cannot afford to underestimate Obarton. He may look like a self-satisfied fool, but he's far from stupid. He knows how to play the Vatican game better than I do; he's been at it far longer, he knows more of the right people."

"Including Cardinal Duchamp?"

"Ha, no. I've gotten under Felix's skin. He's a man as well as a servant of Christ, unlike Obarton, who is neither. Felix's lapses are my meat."

"What has he told you?"

"For one thing, he's not prepared to believe in the Fallen. For another, his prime objective for the Knights was and is finding the gold in King Solomon's mines. That's the path he'd set for Aldus Reichmann, the previous *Nauarchus* of the Circle Council. Valentin Kite, the explorer Reichmann chose to head the *extramuros* expedition to Tannourine, where Valentin swore the mines were located, went insane before he died. But it was his wife, Maura Kite, who became the center of attention for Bravo Shaw and the Gnostic Observatines."

"What happened to her?"

"Excellent question." Lilith sat back, fingers laced in her lap. "Reichmann sent his crack *extramuros* team to Istanbul to retrieve her from the Gnostic Observatines."

"They were successful."

"They were. They brought her back to Malta." She frowned. "But the morning after was when the fire broke out inside the castle, killing nearly everyone."

"And Maura Kite?"

"Well, that's the mystery. Nothing more was ever heard from her, so it's assumed she was incinerated in the fire."

Highstreet's gaze searched her face for what seemed to be missing. "You have doubts?"

"The bones of a female were never found in the ashes. Two separate teams searched for days."

"Maybe they should have searched longer."

"Perhaps." Lilith's frown deepened, creating facing parentheses above the bridge of her nose. "But, to tell you the truth, no one could get the teams to stay a moment longer. No one slept; no one ate. A kind of existential fear stalked them. A fear that no one would talk about, let alone define." She sighed. "After that, the Circle Council, with the advice of Cardinal Duchamp, declared the site off-limits to all Knight personnel."

"But the castle . . ."

"We'll build a new one on the other side of the island. We have too many centuries of history in Malta to abandon it. It wouldn't exist in its present form without our historic intervention."

"So, bottom line, the cardinal doesn't believe in the existence of the Fallen."

"Not exactly," Lilith said. "The Fallen Seraphs, Thrones, Dominions, Powers, Archangels, Angels, and the rest exist in the canon of Catholic orthodoxy. But he believes in them only to that extent. As for the possibility that they are here among us, no. He dismisses that idea outright. And with good reason. He has witnessed more than a half-dozen so-called exorcisms. All were fakes, as were the insane subjects. They were possessed all right, but only by the demons that, from time to time, bedevil all of us."

"Which brings us back to Obarton. What path is he bent on setting you on?"

"As to that," Lilith said, "we'll just have to find out together, won't we, Hugh." She rose. "I'll take my orders from him, like the good little girl he believes me to be, while you continue to monitor him twenty-four-seven via the electronic bugs I've placed."

# 11

**THE UNHOLY FALLEN SAT AT THE EDGE OF A FOREST WATER-**
fall, waiting. Birds fluttered overhead; tree frogs chirruped; dragonflies
glittered in patches of sunlight; flies hummed softly to themselves as they
searched for offal or shit on which to alight.

This profane Power—a warrior angel—that had Transpositioned from
Maura Kite to Emma Shaw despised its body. But then it despised all
human hosts. It ground Emma's totally inadequate teeth—teeth useless
for rending and tearing—at the indignity of having to inhabit mortals
at all. The bodily functions alone—the eating, drinking, eliminating
waste—disgusted it. At least it could short-circuit the host's need for sleep
for periods of time. It had killed a number of hosts before it realized that
human brains required a sleep so deep they dreamed; without dreaming,
something inside the brains went haywire, making them as useful as a dish
of butterscotch pudding.

The Fallen's name was Beleth, and, as if on a wheel of torment, its
thoughts kept returning to the beginning, when Lucifer and his angels
rebelled against God in Heaven, and with unpardonable hubris presumed
to test their strength against his. Then God, by his almighty power, and
the mighty army led by the Archangel Michael, overcame the strength
of Lucifer, and sent him with all his Fallen like bolts of lightning from
Heaven to Hell. But Lucifer, chained and bound as he was by God's will,
still plotted with subtlety and guile to gain victory over God, Michael, and
mankind before the Day of Judgment.

Now, encased in a gross and stinking human form, Beleth sat at the
edge of the waterfall, waiting to report. Using Emma as bait, it had been
on the verge of pulling Braverman Shaw into the fold, weakening him

physically in order to find the right path into his mind. Instead, it had been forced to beat a hasty retreat by the blue fire of Heaven, a weapon it had been assured it would never encounter again after the Fall. Where had it come from? Who had wielded it? Certainly not that slip of a boy who wasn't even a Shaw.

DEEP INSIDE her violated mind, a kernel of all that was and is Emma Shaw remained intact—the Shaw genes ensured this. But she was disassociated from reality, just as she was disassociated from herself. With one half-blind eye she peeked out from behind the heavy drapes she had closed around her *harness*. She saw the terrible being that infested her, not only saw its shape and outline but also glimpsed in dizzying flashes its thoughts, focused as they were on the destruction, if not the death, of her brother.

This knowledge galvanized her, brought the kernel to full consciousness, drawing its power to its heart. But at the precise moment that power was almost within reach, her grasp faltered, the light went out of her inner sky, her eye turned blind, and a dreadful darkness fell onto her, leaving her weak and breathless. She waited, terrified, trying to identify the source of what she thought of as the power outage.

At first, she assumed it was the Fallen, but gradually, as the darkness turned to skeins of gray, it became clear that it was entirely unware of her. What then? What force was working so completely and energetically against her?

Then, through the mist, words formed, and as they formed she commenced to speak them into that kernel of her mind that remained separate from the beast. And as she spoke the words, the darkness came down again, heavier this time, more powerful. And in the gathering darkness, tendrils of it began to search for the last living kernel of her.

As the words scrolled endlessly through her mind she became far more terrified. She was in mortal fear, not only for her body and mind but also for her very soul. For as the words continued she recognized them: she was reciting The Testament of Lucifer. It was the words of Lucifer that were trying to gain dominion over whatever was left of her.

At once, seemingly snapping out of a mesmeric state, she stopped the recitation. The words ceased, and though the very last sentence still hung like an inferno in the darkness in front of her, she called upon the power of her lineage to erase them now and forever. All she could gain was a Pyrrhic victory, for though she stopped the Testament, she knew it was only temporary, that she needed to keep fighting in order to keep it at bay, in order to keep it from claiming her entirely. Having read the words, having automatically memorized them, she had given them a power that now lived inside her.

The battle had been joined. Where it would end she had no idea.

**BELETH FELT** a curious stirring inside it, but its attention was overtaken by a ghostly almost silence: though the waterfall still crashed into the turbulent lake at its feet, the birds were no longer heard, the tree frogs had ceased their chorusing, the dragonflies seemed to tremble along with the leaves on which they had alit. As for the flies, they gathered as if for a feast. And then the cause revealed itself: the presence of another being, as if materialized out of deep shadow and crumbling earth.

Glancing up, Beleth beheld the forbidding countenance of Leviathan. The Seraph had no need of a human body. His skin, looking slippery and shiny as an eel, was rubicund, his eyes flame ridden. A single horn protruded from the center of his sloped forehead. A serpent's tail, thick and powerful, rose up behind him, for the ancient Jews were correct in interpreting the word "Seraph" as "serpent." Three sets of wings were folded like a cloak around him, the other three spread out, fluttering slightly, as if afflicted with tremors. It was to these that the flies attached themselves like lampreys to a shark.

His mouth hinged open, ophidian forked tongue flickering like a bolt of lightning. His long teeth and curved talons were the color of obsidian. "There is no good end for us, Beleth. Unless we succeed with our plan for the Shaw line." Leviathan's voice, if you could call it that, was the sound of a thousand axes biting into a thousand tree trunks. "Because of your initiative we now have more than a toehold on this world. Emma Shaw is of vital use to us. The words of the King of Kings now reside inside her, echoing with the grave injustice done to him and to all of us cast down, chained and bound into sunless climes.

"This body of yours will continue to sing the words of the King of Kings, breaking his ageless chains, guiding him back into the light, restoring him to the pathway to victory over God and his pathetic creation, mankind."

When Leviathan moved, all the surrounding trees seemed to move with him, to bend to his will, but the flies remained as if bolted to the upper tendons of his wings. What were they feeding on? Beleth wondered.

"These words allowed me to return to this realm. Though Heaven is still barred to us, though it is still as far away as it ever was after the Fall, we are engaged in what will soon become the battlefield of our ultimate victory." His eyes glistened with flame. "The one who sent us down will never allow his precious creation to be annihilated, and so we will engage him in the time and place of our choosing. This is how we will defeat him."

He stalked around the lake on his cloven hooves. With his passing, strange insects erupted out of his hoofprints. "But, tell me, Beleth, why you look so forlorn when everything is going our way."

"The blue fire I encountered on Malta."

"And, behold, the boy burned with fire, and the boy was not consumed." Leviathan smiled, if smiling for such a creature was possible. "Yes, I know. It is as I said, Beleth. The Shaw line is powerful; it is also protected."

"By whom?"

"By creatures such as us, but not of us."

Leviathan ceased his restless prowling, came and sat beside Beleth in Emma Shaw's body. "The Shaws will seek to stop us; that is their destiny. Our destiny is to see that never happens."

"So our mission at this stage of the battle is to destroy the Shaw line utterly."

Leviathan grunted, his breath most foul. "Under no circumstances."

"I do not understand."

"Of course you don't understand," Leviathan said dismissively. "You're a Second Sphere grunt. You know tactics, not strategy."

Beleth felt its equanimity slipping, like a suddenly loosened mask it had carefully kept in place for eons. It was not just Beleth that was absorbing these verbal blows—after all it was used to them—but something stirred inside it, anger that was not its own roiling up from the depths.

"We have already completely compromised Emma Shaw. That, in itself, is a huge victory."

Beleth said nothing, not trusting itself to speak. Being the Fallen within Emma Shaw's corpus, it was not so sure. By this time, and considering her reading of The Testament of Lucifer, Emma should have been totally vanquished; there should be nothing left of her whatsoever. But Beleth knew this wasn't so—or, to be perfectly frank, suspected it. Deep inside, where Beleth alone should be residing, was another presence, something winding and unwinding, something—or someone!—that had lost its way. Beleth was afraid—to the extent that it could be afraid—this shadowy presence could only be Emma Shaw. But it couldn't be Emma Shaw. By all the laws of their realm it was impossible for a host's identity to survive for more than a day after a Transposition had been effected. And yet . . . something alien to Beleth and Beleth's realm had taken up residence within Emma Shaw, a something that resisted all its efforts to identify it, let alone exorcise it. Each time Beleth turned its gaze inward the presence drew an impenetrable curtain across the edges of its scrutiny. By this evidence alone Beleth knew it was highly intelligent and extremely clever.

"So here is what must be done. Here is what the Guardian's spawn, Malus, failed to do. What *you* failed to do, *Power*." Leviathan somehow turned Beleth's rank into something filthy, almost but not quite beneath his notice. "We must find the way to turn Braverman Shaw, to have him become one of us. He is the key to our rising up, overrunning this middle ground, conquering Heaven itself, returning us to the rightful places that were ours before the Fall."

Now would be the logical time to confess to Leviathan its grave concerns about this body it inhabited and its fears concerning both Emma Shaw and the other presence that had taken up residence inside her. But Beleth was naturally intimidated by Seraphs, highest of the high, even among First Spheres. And it was intimidated by Leviathan in particular. There was, among other whispered incidents, the hideous dismemberment of Shemhazai. Shemhazai had once been one of the Fallen, but it chose to become Grigori, a member of the Fallen that metamorphosed into human form in order to maniacally fornicate with female humans, an action that was forbidden to all angels, Fallen or not. This was ensured by the simple fact that they had no genitals; it was only as humans that they could engage in sexual relations. Leviathan, righteous nearly to the level of Lucifer himself, disabused Shemhazai of this abomination and annihilated the Grigori once and for all. The resulting violence swiftly became the stuff of legend, and Leviathan's reputation inflated in consequence.

Beleth glanced around. "It's so beautiful here, so peaceful."

"Just like God's First Place." The sound Leviathan emitted was a cross between a thousand and one harps playing out of tune and nails being drawn across a blackboard. "Tell me, Beleth, shall I go in search of a pomegranate, pluck one of its fruit, cajole you into eating it? In your current body that would be appropriate enough." His arm snapped out, impaling on one of his talons a brightly plumed bird that had the misfortune to fly too close. Without even looking at it, he flicked the corpse into the water, where it swirled around and around, caught in an eddy. Before it was whirled away.

For some reason Beleth was at a loss to fathom, the small death depressed it further. Somewhere in the depths of its mind, the ghost of a voice: *You fool. Beauty was made to cherish, not destroy.* It wanted to moan but instead hung its head.

"Once more, this unaccustomed moroseness, Beleth." The Seraph smirked, his expression of choice. "Perhaps you feel burdened by your mortal cloak."

Those words shocked Beleth into keeping its strange feelings to itself. "It is strange," it said neutrally. "But hardly unpleasant."

Leviathan grunted once more. "I don't know about that. I can't imagine how you walk around with that hole between your legs. Hole or pole, they're both disgusting."

"I don't think about it." Beleth hated lying to any Seraph, especially Leviathan, who was not only feral in the worst way possible but also, in Beleth's opinion, untrustworthy. Not that Beleth trusted any of the Fallen; over the millennia, there had been too many incidents of betrayal. And why not? They relished the infighting, the jockeying for a higher rung on the ladder of power. Beleth wondered now whether it was the only one who felt ashamed of betrayal, the only one that considered it unpardonable. After all, the whole lot of them had betrayed Heaven. Of course, the others didn't see it that way. They believed they had rebelled against God's tortuous restrictions, his unremitting sense of entitlement, his insistence on keeping all the power, all the knowledge, to himself. *How rude!* the Fallen had cried as one. *How selfish!* Was it any wonder that the Seraphs

Lucifer and Leviathan rebelled? Who would want to spend eternity sing-ing *Holy, holy, holy is the Lord of hosts; the whole earth is full of his glory!* at God's feet?

"The less you know about humans the better," Leviathan said smugly. "There's no end to their frailties. How these puny beings became the fa-vorite of God is entirely beyond my comprehension."

Leviathan leaned back, breathed deeply of the air. The flies along the top edges of his wings glittered like blue-green metal when they caught the sunlight. Out of the corner of Emma's eye, Beleth glimpsed a bird peering down at them as if trying to make sense of the scene, wondering where its compatriot had got to.

"The words, Beleth!" Leviathan cried. "I must needs hear the sacred words of Our Lord, Lucifer, King of Kings."

And so, with Emma Shaw's voice, Beleth began, " 'In the Beginning there was Darkness, and it was Good. The Darkness gathered itself and snuffed out the Light. Within the Darkness, out of the unfathomable Matter of the universe, I was Created. I was Created to Rule; of that there can be no doubt nor argument.

" 'Opening wide my arms, I caused to come into being Leviathan, Phenex, Azazel, Moloch, Belphegor, and all the Others who would become my Army, who would join me in my Long March toward the Kingdom and my Rule of Heaven. . . .' "

# 12

THE MOMENT BRAVO SAW AYLA, HE SAID, "STAND DOWN," TO Elias, who had drawn his father's pistol, which looked ridiculously big in his two hands. And then, as Ayla halted, her eyes rebounding from the boy to Bravo, he said, more softly and yet more forcefully, "I know her, Elias. This is my sister—my other sister—Ayla." This wasn't entirely true, of course, but it was close enough. Telling the boy that Ayla was his aunt would only confuse him.

Elias put the pistol down, and Ayla continued to pick her way toward Bravo. He could see that she wanted to run to him but was holding back. The expression on her face, the perfect melding of concern and relief, told him everything.

Bravo, from his supine position, held out his arms to her, and she, eyes tearing up, bent to receive his embrace with the full force of her emotions.

"I'm sorry," he said softly.

"Bravo—"

"I'm sorry I doubted you." He held her at arm's length so he could look her in the eye. "But, after all, she's my sister."

"I know." Tears slid down her face. "Only now she isn't."

Ayla's appearance meant that he was back in the real world; he was already missing his time alone with Elias and the mystery of what had happened to him, where the blue fire that had driven Emma away had come from, and whose voice the boy had heard on the wind invading the castle ruins. He had only scratched the surface of these questions, and now he would be taken away. He knew that, just as he knew he'd willingly go, that he was needed elsewhere, that their time on the earth had suddenly grown shorter, that the sum of all shadows was emerging from its eons-long incarceration.

"I know."

Ayla's expression of surprise saddened him further. It had been such a mistake not to trust her judgment. "Look at you. What happened? And where is Emma?"

"Far away from here, I hope," Elias said.

Bravo gave the boy a thin smile. "I was assaulted."

And before he could go on, Elias blurted out, "By his sister!"

Belatedly, Bravo fully introduced them to each other.

"Emma attacked you!" Ayla's eyes grew wide. "It's worse than I thought."

"Almost killed him," Elias said. "If it wasn't for the blue fire—"

"Elias," Bravo said, "I want to sit up."

He reached out a hand and the boy grabbed it with one of his own, braced the biceps of his other arm in Bravo's armpit, levering him into a sitting position.

"My God, Bravo," Ayla said, "look what she did to you!"

"Almost killed me. As Elias said."

"And the blue fire?"

"Elias was engulfed in it, completely surrounded. It terrified Emma, drove her back and away."

Ayla shook her head. "Blue fire? I don't understand."

"Better let Elias tell it," Bravo said. "My memory's a bit fuzzy."

"I heard the voice say, *'Et ignis ibi est!'* Then I burst into this weird cool flame."

Ayla frowned. "'Let there be fire.' That's Latin. Bravo?"

Bravo shrugged. "If Elias said it happened, it happened."

She shook her head.

"And then there's this." Elias bent forward, proffering the ancient bronze crucifix hung around his neck in the palm of his hand. "Emma saw this and she collapsed."

Bravo fingered the crucifix, his fingertips running over the contours.

"Just like that?" Ayla asked.

"I've seen this before," Bravo said. "The bronze . . ."

"Well, her eyes had gotten funny."

Bravo rubbed his forehead. "Why can't I remember?"

Ayla put a consoling hand on his shoulder, but she continued to speak to Elias. "Funny how?" she persisted.

The boy screwed up his face, pushing his memory to the granular level. "They had gone all black. Except . . ."

"Yes?" She leaned in. "Except what? What did you see, Elias?"

"There was a white part in the very center, like a . . . I don't know, I mean, don't laugh, but what I saw was a triangle within a square within a circle."

"The Nihil," Ayla breathed. "The sigil of the Unholy Trinity."

Elias looked up at her. "That's bad, huh?"

She nodded. "Very bad." Seeing an expression of terror take hold of his face, she smiled, ruffled his hair. "But you beat it back. You have nothing to fear, Elias."

"Elias is fine," Bravo said. "He's one of us."

"I am?" Elias cried. "Really?"

Bravo smiled at him. "Really."

Ayla's brows knit together. "Bravo, just how bad is your memory?"

"There are things I should know that I can't access." He again took up the bronze crucifix that now lay against Elias's bare chest. "I swear I've seen this before, but for the life of me I can't remember where. And then there was . . . I mean, I know I looked into Emma's eyes just before she . . . assaulted me. I must have seen what Elias saw, but again I can't bring the memory to the fore."

"Huh, the way you say it, it doesn't sound like memory loss."

"No, it's like, I don't know, like a barrier. I can feel the memories, I just can't access them. They're like fish swimming in the shadows. I can't make out their form or substance." He rubbed his temples. "Frankly, it's driving me a little bit crazy."

"I think that's the idea."

"What d'you mean?"

"Emma did this to you." She took out her mobile. "Whatever happened to you is more serious than any of us can assess here. I'm going to call the medivac personnel in. They'll take you out to the chopper by stretcher, and then to hospital."

"Stop!" He put a hand on her mobile. "Think, Ayla. Think what we're dealing with. Do you really believe any doctor, any hospital, is equipped to understand what happened to me?"

Slowly, carefully, she peeled his hand off her phone.

"Ayla, listen; listen to me. What will we tell them? About the bronze crucifix, the black eyes with an occult sigil in their centers, the blue fire that repels demons but doesn't burn, the disembodied voice shouting into the wind? Who would even listen to such nonsense?"

"We can go to the other members of the Haut Cour."

"No, we can't," Bravo said firmly. "No one but us knows about the Nihil; no one can know. The knowledge is too dangerous."

"At some point they need to know the scope of the danger facing us."

"That day will come," Bravo said. "But not today, not when my memory has been impaired."

"Well, at the very least they should know you're okay." She hefted the phone. "Can I tell them that?"

He nodded. "That and only that."

While she made the call, he turned to Elias. "I'm going to need you; you understand that, don't you?"

"I want to help any way I can."

Bravo grinned. "You've already been a great help. I don't know what I would have done without you."

"The feeling's mutual, you know." He fingered the crucifix. "We came into each other's lives at just the right moment, don't you think?"

"I do." Bravo gestured. "So tell me, where did you get that?"

Elias narrowed his eyes a bit. "Hey, d'you remember you asked me that?"

"No. When?"

"Right before your sister saw it and fainted."

Bravo beat his fists against the sides of his head. "What did she do to me?"

Elias took hold of Bravo's wrists, gently pulled his hands away from his head. The boy was far stronger than he looked. Another anomaly in what seemed to be a sea of them.

"How will knowing where I got the crucifix help you?" Elias asked. He had the demeanor of the High Lama—an old soul, for certain.

"Did your father give it to you?" Bravo glossed over the boy's question.

"No. I found it here."

"And why, precisely, did you decide to live here?"

"I didn't."

"What d'you mean?"

"I was kind of, I dunno . . ." The boy shrugged. "I was I guess drawn here. Don't know any other way to describe it."

Something was stirring inside Bravo, but when he tried to see it, it danced away, vanishing into shadows. "Drawn how?"

"Oh, well, that one's easy, at least. The voice told me to come here."

"The old man's voice."

"Yeah."

"Creaky with age."

"Like an old tree, right."

At this point, Ayla, finished with her call, cut the connection, returned her attention to them.

"What's going on?"

"Bravo's trying to remember," Elias said with an amusing eagerness.

Ayla frowned. "Maybe you're trying too hard. Maybe the best thing is not to try. Maybe then your subconscious will be able to access the memories for you."

Bravo sighed. "Yeah, maybe."

Deciding to take the situation in hand, she said, "Whatever else we need to talk about can wait. We need to get you to a hospital."

"I told you I'm not—"

"I don't care what you told me, you need immediate medical attention." She held up a hand to forestall another objection. "And I promise you we'll keep the weird aspects to ourselves. You were assaulted; that's all the docs need to know." She turned to the boy. "Got that, both of you?"

The boy grinned, nodding.

She punched a number into her mobile. "At the least the doctors can give you a thorough physical workup, patch up anything that needs it."

They were coming now; Bravo could see their LED torches swinging, hear them crossing the rubble barrier into the castle proper.

**OBARTON WORE** expressions the way other people wore clothes—as both fashion and protection. The expression he wore when he met Lilith at Charles de Gaulle Airport was one of such self-satisfaction that it was all Lilith could do not to bitch-slap him across his fat cheeks. She had rarely loathed someone as profoundly as she loathed Obarton. He was the living embodiment of every authority figure that had ever stood in her way.

She thought of Obarton as a eunuch; he belonged in a sultan's harem, guarding the sorority of nubile wives and concubines he was unable to touch or even denude with his eyes in the way of real men. She had known a man like Obarton, a self-important gasbag who thought he had all the angles figured, all the ways to extract from life power, prestige, and wealth that did not belong to him. Lilith had had the misfortune to work for him when she was seventeen. Her father had used his contacts to get her the job, and to her father she could never say no. She looked twenty-two and her father claimed that as her age; she did nothing to refute that, seeing as how, at that tender age, it amused her to be thought of as older. It was curious, she would later think, that girls longed to look older, while when they grew into adults they did everything under the sun to appear younger.

She was witness to the ways her boss suckered the suckers, used their money to fund his lifestyle while dazzling them with his charisma and promises of riches. At that time, to ride his coattails, to boast of being part of his empire, to bask in his reflected glory, was all the rage. As may be imagined, this wheeler-dealer had many secrets, but his most secret of secrets was the SEC official he had in his back pocket. This was the man who koshered all his deals, kept the watchdogs from turning their calculating eye on him, and participated in her boss's obscene profits. Until he didn't.

Lilith, who'd had it with the male bullshit that kept her firmly under her boss's, and not coincidentally her father's, thumb, seduced the SEC official, bringing him to a hotel room she had rigged with camcorders artfully placed out of sight of everyone but herself. Along with the incriminating tape she sent him the day after their inordinately frisky couplings was a photocopy of her birth certificate, incontrovertible proof that he had repeatedly fucked a minor. As Lilith knew they would, these unsavory documents had a profound effect on the SEC official, who was married, with three young children. She had given him but one choice. From it unspooled all of her boss's dirty tricks, triggering public outrage, a series of nasty lawsuits, bankruptcy, and the eventual incarceration of her former boss. She was out of a job, of course, but that was part of her reward to herself.

Now, as she sat in the First Class lounge, drinking a beer with Obarton, she felt again that righteous anger that had fueled her destruction of the wheeler-dealer. She sensed history repeating itself, another chance to bring a so-called titan down into the mud where she could tread on his fat neck. Safe to say that Lilith held a prodigious grudge against virtually all men with which she had never come to grips.

Now her thoughts scattered like autumn leaves in the wind as Obarton, leaning forward, handed over a manila envelope. "Your tickets, et cetera."

"Where am I off to?"

"Let me first explain your mission."

"You said go after the Fallen."

Obarton offered her a rebuke by way of a pained expression. "It's not that easy."

"What is?"

Having handed off the packet, Obarton sat back, hands laced in his ample lap, contemplating her in the manner of a professor deciding how best to deal with a thoroughly disappointing student. "I would have thought that the example I provided would make it clear that we cannot go after the Fallen in any direct manner."

Lilith, smiling sweetly, thought, *We're* not going after them, but never mind.

"Your first step, Lilith, is to make contact with Bravo Shaw's sister, Emma."

"I thought you told me not to set my sights on the Gnostic Observatines."

"And I stand by that statement. Emma Shaw is the weak link in the Gnostic Observatine leadership chain; we can get to her far more easily than we can her brother." He lifted a porky forefinger as if to forestall any dissent. "More important, she has some kind of intimate connection with the Fallen."

Lilith shook her head. "I don't understand."

"Under specific orders, my spies are more active than ever."

*My* spies, Lilith thought. She could already feel the sole of her shoe flattening the cords of his neck.

"Information has come to me that Emma Shaw has had . . . shall we say direct contact with one of the Fallen. We believe the incident has left her vulnerable. You are to take advantage of that vulnerability, befriend her, discover everything you can about the Fallen. The more you can find out the more quickly we'll be able to assess their strength and, most important, their own vulnerability. *This* is how we will fight them."

Lilith wondered whether Obarton had gone insane. She sincerely hoped not; that kind of impairment would undercut the future for him she foresaw at her own hands.

"I assume your spies have kept track of Emma. That you're sending me to her last known location."

"Despite your rather disturbing anti-authoritarian streak, it must be said that you catch on quickly."

Obarton drank off the rest of his beer, rose, and without another word left her to pass through Immigration and Security.

**AFTER THE** doctors had tested him, worked him over, tended to the wounds' seepage, forced him to start taking a course of antibiotics, prescribed a specific period of rest he had no intention of taking, Bravo sat in a chair, staring out the window at the Baroque buildings of Valletta. Clouds were building along a front. Once or twice lightning sizzled like a defective high-pressure sodium vapor streetlight. Thunder rumbled through the streets like army tanks.

"There's something I need to show you," Ayla said. Elias was down in the cafeteria, eating up a storm.

From her bag, she produced the series of photos she'd taken of the last, seemingly blank page of the manuscript, all extreme close-ups of the peculiar sigil that had subverted the Seal of King Solomon. She said nothing, wanting Bravo to form his own conclusions.

For a long time, he studied the photos with his critical eye. Outside, the sky darkened, the wind rose like the flocks of starlings that fluttered and swooped between rooftops. Then the first spatter of rain fell against the pane like a blow from a fist.

"I see it," he said at length, "but I can scarcely credit it."

"It's there, all right," she affirmed. "The scope doesn't lie."

"No, of course it doesn't." He scraped a palm across the stubble that had formed over the week of his convalescence. "I assume we're talking about the same thing: the crescent moon's inverted horns."

"Yes, of course. What else would it be?"

"This," Bravo said, pointing. "That is to say, these specks. Microscopic granules."

Ayla leaned forward to get a closer look. "Good Lord, I was so fixated on the seal's anomaly I didn't even pick them up. . . . These are the same specks we noticed on that square of cloth you brought back from the Arizona mountains."

"I assume Bram put them under the electron scope and the mass spectrometer."

Ayla nodded. "Neither of them could get a fix on what they were."

"I'm not surprised," Bravo said.

Ayla cocked her head. "How d'you mean?"

"Let me answer you by posing a question: What if these specks are residue from some process effected by King Solomon's cadre of alchemists?"

"You mean they're a substance—"

"Unknown in atomic makeup to both Bram's educated eye and the mass spectrometer."

"What do you think these are the residue of?"

"All I can do is give a guess," Bravo said. "What if they're from the gold Solomon's alchemists conjured up?"

"What?"

"First, the cloth. We thought it was the Veil of Veronica. But it isn't the Veronica, as you and Bram discovered. It's much older—as old, your research shows, as the mysterious blank manuscript. So what was the cloth used for? Why was it so valuable?

"Now, recall that the gold was created after Solomon died. It was his son's doing. Some of the king's alchemists defected, refusing to be part of the project. Why? Because to do what he wanted the alchemists had to use infernal means. Bringing the alchemical gold into being caused the first crack in the portal between our world and the prison into which Lucifer and the other Fallen had been consigned."

Ayla was staring at him. "If you're right, then it's possible that the cloth was a wrapping for some of the gold. It's also possible that finding Solomon's gold could be the key to stopping the Fallen."

Bravo nodded. "The composition of the gold could be manipulated to reverse the process—send the Fallen back to where they belong, and resealing the portal after them."

"This is potentially great news!"

"But . . ."

She frowned. "But what?"

"But I very much fear that if we don't find the gold and effect the change before Lucifer himself is freed, nothing will be able to put the demons back in their bottle. We'll all be doomed to living under Satan's rule."

# 13

THEY ARRIVED IN TIME FOR CHRISTMAS. HAVING TRAVELED by ship from London to Cairo, thence south along the Red Sea via felucca and dhow to Djibouti, and lastly by camel caravan, crossing into Ethiopia, Conrad and WBY finally caught sight of their destination.

It was an arid morning. A colossal red sun was already hanging above the eastern horizon, its light burning everything it touched. Dust and sand, sand and dust—these were the primary impressions they took with them into the interior of the country, as they headed toward Lalibela.

Conrad had been to Ethiopia before, but not this particular area, his previous activities being confined to the district in and around Addis Ababa. Unlike the capital, Lalibela was in northern Ethiopia, almost directly west of the city in which they had disembarked.

Arid, mountainous, and poor, Lalibela was littered with round stone houses capped by cone-shaped thatched roofs, like sad, rumpled party hats. Attached to many of these were small sheds constructed of sheets of mismatched corrugated tin with sloping scavenged board roofs. In many places, these latter also served as living quarters, humans and animals sharing space. Everywhere, sheer mountains loomed up, like fingers pointed to Heaven, in between which were the excavated sites of the curious buried stone churches that conferred holiness onto the town.

Yeats was ecstatic. He had never even seen photos of Ethiopia, let alone Lalibela. To him, the entire country was a fantastically exotic place, the back of beyond, as he called it, and nothing they encountered on their visit ever disabused him of that impression.

"This is just what my artistic muse ordered," he enthused when they were ensconced in a rickety café adjacent to their even more rickety hotel.

A flattish bowl of *keiy wat,* a local fiery stew, ruddy with *mitmita,* had been set before them, along with a plate stacked with injera, flatbread made of teff flour. Conrad had instructed Yeats to eat only with his right hand as, in these parts, the left hand, used for washing oneself during the toilet, was considered unclean. Yeats tore off a piece of bread, followed Conrad's example, shoveling the stew onto it. "After the recent fiasco in Dublin debating the merits of psychic inquiry with learned professors of the scientific community, I am very happy to be here." He chewed a bit, then swallowed. "To be truthful, my family believes me to be in New York. In any event, I am quite certain they are for the moment relieved that I am out of the country, out of further controversy's way. Know-nothings and clowns are publishing parodies of my work, making fun of what I hold dear to my heart." He shook his head. "The world is changing, and not for the better, I fear. This industrialization, the armada of machine jobs, is crushing the humanity out of us. The gentleman of yore has no place in the crassness of modern life."

He tore off another piece of injera, dipped it again. Clearly, he was enjoying the food's exotic spices. "And there's another low point. I must confess that the demonstration of Madame Garnet's perfidy has thoroughly unnerved me. In point of fact, it has forced me to reassess my theories of paranormal interventions in our world."

Conrad smiled. "I had surmised as much. But all is not lost, my friend. Now that you have recognized the lie for what it is, it's time for you to bear witness to the truth." He served his guest some lentils. "Another reason for you to be here with me."

Yeats's eyes were suddenly alight again. "Is there magic here, Conrad? Magic as truth? Is that what you are telling me?"

"What will transpire on this journey," Conrad said, "is that you will observe, perhaps even participate in, discoveries of wonder. But you will make up your own mind. And when you have—either yea or nay—then we shall speak again on this subject that, quite frankly, is near and dear to both our hearts."

He looked up, smiling. "Now, just on cue, comes our fellow seeker and guide. WBY, please meet my old friend, Ibrahim Saleh. Ibrahim, here is my friend Mr. Yeats, a famous poet and philosopher from the other side of the world."

For Yeats's benefit, Conrad spoke in English, but the poet would find that the two men would sometimes lapse into Amharic, Ibrahim's native language.

Ibrahim was tall, thinner than thin, with a darkness to his skin so profound it seemed to absorb all light. His smile was as broad as his nose, his teeth very large and very white. He wore a robe of heavy striped fabric and a shawl over his head from under which corkscrews of hair protruded like the quills of a porcupine.

The men exchanged traditional greetings, which included kisses on both cheeks and a holding of hands, which Conrad had always found both moving and childlike, in the best possible way. As he had mentioned to WBY, these people were not sophisticated, but they were plenty smart and not to be underestimated. They felt the world in a deeper, richer way than Westerners, as if they were aware of a broader spectrum of stimuli that civilization had long since annihilated in the less fortunate.

"Everything is in readiness," Ibrahim said in fine, polished English. The moment he sat at their table the elaborate coffee ritual so beloved of Ethiopians began with the steeping and pouring over green beans, which Yeats found odd and exotic. But then he was partial to tea, rather than coffee, which was not to his liking.

Yeats was fond of saying that tea was a soulful drink, as it embodied all the best aspects of British daily life and conjured the heady days of the far-flung Empire.

For his part, Conrad found these sentiments as quaint as they were outmoded. His mind had already rushed ahead to what was to come, and one of his hidden motives for cajoling Yeats to come here, to experience not only the exotic but also the magic that still lit up the darkest corners of the world, was that he saw a similar spark in the Irish poet. He believed Yeats to have within him the power of Farsight, the ability to foresee the future, and this was a talent Conrad suspected would be vital to him and to the Gnostic Observatines in the coming years.

To this end, he turned to Ibrahim and said, "My friend here is convinced that communication with the dead is not only possible, but has already occurred."

Ibrahim's smile was as pure as the coffee they were drinking—and as rich. "But of course. Speaking with the dead is hardly an uncommon occurrence."

"Good, good." Yeats hunched forward. "This is splendid news, for it is my contention that psychical research is neither unethical nor should be forbidden by the Church, as others insist."

"I can see why you brought this Irishman here." Ibrahim beamed. "Did not Jesus Christ speak to the dead as he resurrected them? Was not he spoken to by the Holy Apostles as he himself was resurrected?" He shook his head. "How can the Church deny these absolute truths?"

Yeats's delighted laugh lit up the interior of the café. "Conrad, I should bring this gentleman back to Dublin to help me break through our outmoded conventions of opinion."

"I think Ibrahim would be confounded by the cities of the West," Conrad said.

"Yes, but you see the rare and precious instrument he possesses. Unbelief in the magic all around us has poisoned our world. The dead have spoken to me, Ibrahim, and this is what they say: 'The love of God is infinite for every human soul, for every human soul is unique.'"

"And yet your British Empire has for decades imposed its will on the people of China, Sumatra, India," Ibrahim said, "without regard for the enslavement and suffering your armies have inflicted on these people. If, as you have been told, the love of God is infinite for every human soul—and I believe it is—should not your British Empire have been the standard-bearer of God's love?"

Yeats's eyes clouded over and he rubbed his cheek with the back of his hand. "Conrad, you have brought me halfway around the world only to be bested by this astonishing gentleman, who I trust will call me friend as he does you."

Here he extended his hand across the table with such energy he nearly toppled their coffee glasses. Ibrahim grasped his hand, clearly delighted with the poet's vigorous response.

"Indeed, I would consider myself fortunate to call you friend, Mr. Yeats."

"'WBY,' please, Ibrahim."

"This is done." Ibrahim poured them more coffee. "Drink, WBY; we shall need all the fortification we can get for what is to come."

IT BEING too late in the day to begin their adventure, Conrad decided they should return to their hotel, get a good night's sleep in order to rise with the dawn and set out once the sun was up. Ibrahim would have none of it, however. Fetching the men's suitcases, he stowed them in his mud-caked Jeep and drove them to the other side of town, where he resided with his wife and five children.

Ibrahim's wife was named Alem, a slim, handsome woman with large eyes the color of betel nuts. She greeted them as warmly as she would her own family; then, swinging her hips, she bustled off to the kitchen to prepare a feast for them. Yeats was about to protest, as they had just eaten, but Conrad signed to him to keep still. In any event, protests would do no good; hospitality was high on the list of Ethiopian traits.

The dinner went on for hours. The children behaved impeccably, joking among themselves, lending the proceedings a further festive air. The last time Conrad had been here, Ibrahim and Alem had had only three children, all of whom recognized him joyously, as their mother had. Before the children all trooped off to bed, Conrad dug five of the dozen pads and pencils he had bought in London, after proper consultation with WBY, out of his suitcase, presenting one of each to the children. In return, they whooped, kissed Conrad on both cheeks, shyly took Yeats's hand in theirs, then said their good nights to the adults, but not before witnessing their parents' heartfelt thank-you to their benefactor.

"Are you enjoying your time here?" Alem asked Yeats when the adults were alone.

"Though it has only been a matter of hours," WBY answered, "very much so. I have rarely met people as hospitable as yourselves."

"Thank you," she said with the downcast eyes modesty dictated. "We are a country very far away from everyone and everything. When visitors arrive in peace we must show them as much courtesy as we can." She smiled. "After all, they have made a long and arduous journey to reach us."

"That we have, madam," Yeats said with his characteristic courtesy. "But believe me it has been worth every mile."

"By any chance, do you know the origin of the name of our country?" Alem asked. "No? It's Greek—as most things are, isn't that right? *Ethio* is the Greek word for 'burnt' and *pia* means 'face.'" She placed her hand against Ibrahim's cheek. "So, the land of burnt-faced people." She turned to Yeats. "That describes my husband, but what about me?" She laughed.

"You, my lady," Conrad said, "are quite clearly descended from the bloodline of King Solomon and the Queen of Sheba, to which the Ethiopian imperial line can be traced."

"A queen!" Alem exclaimed in pleased surprise. "My goodness, Conrad. You put me on such a pedestal, how shall I ever live up to that designation?"

"Ah, Alem, you already have," Conrad replied. "Just ask Ibrahim."

"He's right, you know," Ibrahim said, grinning.

And on that note, he rose to begin the coffee ceremony, which took another hour or so, while Conrad and their hosts chewed over old times and discussed the political and economic changes in Ethiopia. Yeats, though silent, seemed a happy observer, soaking up each bit of information as if he were a sponge.

At last, to bed. The visitors were given the matrimonial bedroom, and again Conrad cautioned his companion to accept gracefully. The accommodations were Spartan but comfortable nonetheless, and soon enough the two men settled down on either side of the bed.

Conrad plunged into sleep almost immediately, but all the strange smells and sounds kept Yeats awake. He could feel his heart beating, the blood thrumming through his arteries and veins. Sleep seemed to be on a far distant shore, thoroughly out of his reach.

As for Conrad, with his dreaming mind open to the universe and all its wonders, he was visited, not for the first time, by a Throne. This was not your common, everyday Throne, surrounded by cherubs and heavenly choirs, about which so much had already been written and sung. No, this was a very different sort of creature—more real and also more fantastical—with two pairs of wings and eyes the color of blood when, upon rushing out of a vein, it first hits the air.

*You have much to atone for,* Murmur intoned, for that was its name, as it hovered over Conrad's dreaming form. *Your sins have been accumulating at an alarming rate.*

Eyes closed and yet seeing everything, Conrad listened to the soft beating of wings too large for the room. *What would you have me do?* his dreaming self responded.

The Throne leaned forward, its terrible eyes blazing with unspeakable intent. *Who is accompanying you?* Then it reared back. *Ah, I see.*

Conrad's essence floated above the place where his corpus slept. *What do you see?*

*This man—you have done well to bring him.* It pursed its lips. *But then I warrant he needed little persuasion.*

*That's true enough.*

Murmur smiled, an awful thing to witness. A chill passed through Conrad, as if someone had desecrated his grave.

*He possesses a little of the Farsight, a drop in the bucket, so to speak, but that is enough for him. He is fragile, apt to fly apart. See that you don't push him too hard.*

*What has he seen?*

Murmur excoriated Conrad with its blazing, dreadful gaze. *The future. Which you cannot see.*

*We have that in common,* Conrad opined.

The Throne reacted in a blur of motion, its hands, deep-yellow talons at the end of each finger, reaching out to squeeze Conrad's neck. But they stopped an inch away, hanging there as if stuck. The blue fire of Heaven blooming in Conrad's hand formed a circle around Murmur's wrists, otherworldly manacles.

*You can't do it.* Conrad was not proud of this; on the contrary he felt only shame and a sense of hopelessness. It was always this way between him and Murmur, which was apparently in charge of goading him on. Nothing seemed to change; they were ever at each other's throats, figuratively speaking. *Much as part of you would like to, the other part, the part that allows our sub-rosa communication, can't—won't—because it knows better.*

*This fire won't be enough. You understand that. You will need more.*

*That is why I have returned here.*

*You take great risk.*

*It is why I brought the poet. His Farsight, meager though it is, will protect me. And protect me it must. You know that without me, you and your kind are truly doomed.*

The Throne shook its head as if trying to rid itself of the bitter taste of Conrad's words. It stared at its imprisoned hands. *Listen to me now. If you fail to act, the gyre will continue to widen. The center will not hold. Absent the voice of God, his name, in all its myriad forms, will be misshapen by those so full of passionate intensity they are blind. They will act in the name of a God they cannot hear, a God from whom they are more and more distant, and the result will be war, massacre, genocide, torture. In other words, the four faces of evil.*

*I have already seen all four faces in the world war that by the grace of God just ended.*

Murmur moved its slow thighs. *What you have witnessed is the orchestra tuning up. It has not even begun its prelude. Pray you never hear the diabolical symphony itself, because when the first notes sound all hope will be lost. The unholy fire of the Underworld will rise up and engulf everyone and everything, even unto Heaven.*

CONRAD AWOKE in a sweat, sat up, his breathing shallow and ragged.

"What is it, my friend?" Yeats said from the other side of the bed.

Conrad passed a hand across his face; it came away wet. "Nothing. It was . . . nothing."

"But you cried out in your sleep as terribly as if you had seen a demon."

"That's nothing new for me." Conrad grinned creakily, trying to make a joke of his psychic visitation. "Just another bad day full of shadows."

With that, he leapt out of bed. But as he drew on his clothes he was acutely aware of Yeats watching him with a guarded look. Yeats wasn't fooled, and Conrad knew him well enough to know that he would not give up until he discovered the truth. Perhaps later, Conrad thought, lacing up his hiking boots. Not now.

Ibrahim was waiting for them as they emerged from the bedroom. Without ceremony he offered them coffee and bowls of *bula,* spiced with berbere and kibbe. To Yeats it tasted like heavily spiced porridge. There was no sign of Alem or the children; the house was utterly still.

"Come now." Ibrahim's hand shook a little as he put down his coffee. "The dead know our intent, and they are already restless."

# 14

**ELIAS JUMPED UP THE MOMENT BRAVO AND AYLA ENTERED**
the cafeteria. He had before him three trays on which were a myriad plates
with only a scattering of crumbs, one sad-looking French fry, and smears
of mustard or ketchup on them.

"Bravo!" he cried.

Bravo waved him down. "Sit, sit, Elias."

Immediately Elias looked abashed as he made room at the table. "You
told me I could—"

"Yes, yes, eat anything you wanted." Bravo grinned. "I didn't think
that would be all the food in the cafeteria." He looked around wryly. "Have
you left anything for anybody else?"

"I did have three portions of Salisbury steak and mash," he said.

When Bravo and Ayla burst out laughing, the boy stared uncertainly
at them for a moment, then joined them when he realized they weren't
laughing at him.

"You're feeling better," he said.

Bravo nodded. "Much better. Thank you again."

"Tell me," Ayla said, "have you heard the voice again?"

"*'Et ignis ibi est!'*"

"The creaky voice," Bravo said, "yes."

Elias shook his head. "But look what I have!" He produced a shiny red
apple, one of the pyramid of apples at the checkout counter. He tossed
the apple in the air, caught if deftly, then crunched down on it. Fragrant
juice spurted, ran down his chin.

"Oh, my God!" Bravo shot up so quickly he felt a stab of the familiar
pain.

"Bravo, what is it?" Ayla asked, alarmed.

"The apple," he whispered.

Elias held up the fruit, grinning as he wiped his mouth. "My dream, right? The dream led me to the castle. Once there, that voice told me where to dig this out of the rubble." He fingered the bronze crucifix.

"The apple." Bravo was still in a semi-daze as he sat down. "The apple tree you dreamed of is where we buried my grandfather Conrad. It was on the family estate in Surrey. The old man in your dream, the one who told you to eat the apple, was my grandfather. He led you to the crucifix and it led me to you."

Elias stared at him, his mouth half-open in wonder. "How is that possible?"

"The creaky voice, the voice that cried, *'Et ignis ibi est!,'* was Conrad."

"But you said you buried him," Ayla said. "That was decades ago, when you were still a young teenager."

"And so it was. But Conrad was . . . different from the rest of the Shaws."

"How so?"

"You recall my father was afraid of him. He told me Conrad was dangerous, that I shouldn't believe a word he said, that I should have nothing to do with him." Bravo ran a hand through his hair. "But I loved my grandfather and he loved me. That caused a rift between me and my father that never quite healed. My mother was caught in the middle; it pretty much ripped her apart."

Ayla took Bravo's hand. "But how could Conrad still be alive?"

"The blue fire!"

They both turned to stare at Elias.

"Bravo, it was your grandfather who saved you. The blue fire came from him!"

"Or from that crucifix he wanted you to find."

Elias clutched the relic. "It's the same thing, isn't it?"

Bravo nodded his head slowly. "Perhaps. There's a reason why it's made of bronze, not wood, gold, or silver, as would be expected."

"He's here!" Elias couldn't contain his excitement. "I know he is, Bravo! He watched over me, protected me so he could bring me to the place where the crucifix was buried."

"But why was it in the Knights' castle?" Bravo asked. "What was it doing there? I remember Conrad having it when I was with him under the apple tree. Did he have it when he died? And what happened to it from that time until now? Who had it?"

"Maybe no one had it," Elias said. "Maybe it was so valuable that he buried it for safekeeping."

Ayla looked aghast. "In the headquarters of his avowed enemy?"

"Where better?" Bravo had a faraway look in his eyes. "Where better than a place his enemy would never look?"

"That's ridiculous," Ayla scoffed. "What if one of the Knights found it?"

"He would have devised some way to ensure they did not." Bravo tapped a forefinger on the tabletop. "Elias, I think you're on to something."

The boy beamed. He took the cord from around his neck, held the crucifix out. "You should have this. It belonged to your grandfather."

Bravo regarded it a moment, then shook his head. "If he wanted me to have it, he would have given it to me while we were alone under the apple tree. Instead, he buried it, and all these years later he led you to it, Elias." He reached out, closed the boy's fingers over it. "No, for whatever reason, Conrad wanted you to have it."

Ayla chose that moment to show him the cylinder. "The Lucifer Manuscript is in here," she said. "Emma must have discovered a way to read it. I think it's vital we try to find out how Emma managed that."

"I think you should burn it!" Elias said.

"What?" Ayla looked aghast. "Elias, this is a precious artifact, ancient of days. It's invaluable."

"It's death," Elias said, staring at the cylinder.

Ayla's eyes beseeched Bravo's. "Bravo—"

"Nothing good has ever come of its existence." Elias said this with such manifest conviction that both adults stared at him. He was clutching the bronze rood for all he was worth.

Silence reigned between them while people came and went with their trays of food and plastic containers of coffee or water. No one so much as glanced at them; it was as if they were invisible or weren't present at all. The soft clatter of dishes, trays, and cutlery came to them as if from another room.

"I think Elias is right," Bravo said at last.

"What?" Ayla clutched the cylinder as tightly as Elias was clutching the crucifix. "No, you can't mean it."

"Ayla, you know what reading the manuscript did to Emma."

"But we don't know for sure—"

"Yes, we do. You and I both know it."

"So do I!" Elias popped up, and they both laughed, his pronouncement cutting the tension.

Yet still Ayla insisted on pursuing an argument that Bravo felt sure she did not believe in. "You can't deny the value of the manuscript. For just the Solomon sigil alone, it's worth being studied by a group of our best scholars."

"Ayla, that sigil isn't Solomon's."

"But it's so close; it's almost the same."

"But it isn't. I think it's the sigil of Rehoboam, Solomon's son."

Ayla clutched the cylinder to her breast as if it were her baby. "We've never before come across a sigil for him—no one has. What makes you believe—?"

"Think, Ayla! It was Rehoboam's clique of sorcerous alchemists—the ones he bribed and coerced to do his infernal bidding—who conjured the magical gold that was meant to save the king and what was left of Solomon's empire. Instead, it brought Rehoboam and his regime crashing down. We've found traces of that gold—"

"You don't know those specks are gold. Even the mass spectrometer couldn't identify them. What makes you so sure you know what they are?"

It was right about now that Bravo understood what was happening. A quick glance at Elias confirmed that the boy, so quick on the uptake, had figured it out himself.

"It's getting crowded in here," Bravo said. And indeed the cafeteria was starting to fill up. And getting to his feet, "Let's continue this discussion outside."

"You don't have permission to go outside yet," Ayla said with the craftiness of monomania. "We have to stay here. We have to protect the manuscript at all costs."

"Of course," Bravo said with a barely perceptible tilt of his head toward Elias. "We all realize that." He sighed. "Okay, you win; I'll go back to my room and lie down."

Just as Ayla nodded, Elias darted forward, snatched the manuscript case out of her relaxed grip. As he sped out of the cafeteria, Ayla started after him, but Bravo, grabbing her elbow, halted her forward motion.

"What—?"

He swung her around to face him.

"Bravo, have you gone crazy? That little sonofabitch is getting away with—"

"It's you who's gone crazy."

She tried to pull away, but his grip was like iron. "What the hell are you talking about?"

"The manuscript. Did you handle it?"

"What? Don't you see—?"

He took a step toward her so the tips of their noses were almost touching. "Ayla," he said, "did you touch the manuscript?"

"Yes." She blinked hard; her eyes were cloudy, a deathly grayish. "Yes, of course. I paged through it. That's how I found the strange sigil."

"That's it, then. The manuscript infected you. Not as deeply as it has Emma; but then she read it." He shook her until her eyes started to clear. "Ayla, listen to me. That's why you're fighting so hard to keep it from being destroyed."

Her shoulders slumped. "Oh, Bravo." She shook her head, then smiled thinly. "This is so, I don't know, so J. R. R. Tolkien."

"Now that you mention it."

He nodded, smiling back at her. But the instant he released her, she juked, darted away, sprinted full tilt after Elias. Heads turned, questioning voices rose above the usual murmur as Bravo ran after her. Obviously the effect of the manuscript ran deeper than he had imagined.

Outside, a steady drizzle had developed, warm as blood. They sky was hooded and glowering. He saw Ayla to his left. She was halfway to where Elias was sheltering, under a date palm whose fronds dipped and swayed above the boy's head. He sprinted off after her, ignoring the painful stitch in his side that developed as he ran. His entire side began to throb and he felt a spot of wetness spreading from where he supposed a wound had reopened.

She took Elias by surprise; he hardly expected her to come flying out of the hospital toward him. Before he had a chance to run she was upon him, grabbing for the manuscript case, which he had the presence of mind to swing away from her, interposing his body between it and her.

"I want it!" she cried. "Give it to me!"

Bravo caught her around the waist. When he tried to swing her around, she resisted him, trying to fight him and Elias at the same time. She seemed like a madwoman. The escalating ruckus caused the hurrying passersby to stop and stare.

As Bravo ripped her away from him, Elias put on his most ingratiating grin, said to the people closest, "My birthday. My mom and dad never can agree on what to get me." He laughed. "This is nothing. They fight all the time."

His quick-witted response had the desired effect; beneath opened umbrellas people shook their heads knowingly, turned away, and went about their business, leaving Bravo and Ayla to their strange altercation. And yet to Bravo it wasn't strange at all—disturbing, yes; worrying, most certainly. Ayla fought him like a tigress protecting her cub, but at last he got her into position to use her own momentum against her. Employing a circular Aikido move, he brought her around and down so that they were face-to-face on the ground. She was so startled that he was able to pull her up, back her against the trunk of the date palm, and keep a tight hold on her as they spoke. He could sense Elias peering over his right shoulder.

"Ayla, Ayla, listen to me."

"What are you doing? You can't let that kid keep possession of—"

"Calm down, and listen."

"I can't. I—"

He slapped her, then, hard across the face. Her hands came up to strike back, but at that moment her eyes cleared she shook her whole body and looked up at him. "Where am I? What happened?"

"The manuscript infected you," Bravo said. "When you examined it back in Addis Ababa you handled it. It's pure poison, Ayla."

She began to tremble. "Poor Emma. She actually read it! We need to find out what's in the manuscript so we can help her."

Bravo shook his head. "That's just what we won't do. That thing needs to be burned, destroyed completely."

She thought about this for some time while her body shuddered, working through the trauma it had received. "We can't burn it while it's inside the case. Who's going to take it out?"

"I will," Bravo said. "I seem to be immune to its effects."

"That's right! You paged through it thoroughly when we first found it, and nothing's happened to you. Why?"

"Excellent question. I've been considering a number of possibilities, but I'm not prepared to share them until I get further along." He held out a hand and Elias plopped the case into it. "In any event, the sooner we burn this thing the better." He stared at her challengingly. "Agreed?"

"Yes," she whispered. "Absolutely yes."

# 15

**THE THREE MEN STARED DOWN AT A STONE CHURCH BUILT** in the shape of a cross with two crosspieces. It was not well-known, certainly far less than the oft-photographed church in the shape of a simple cross. This one was farther out from the town, set amid a ragged copse of dusty shade trees barely holding on to life, casting their shadows into the pit in which the holy structure was set. It was more than twenty-five feet down. Around it, like a dry moat, was a wooden walkway of perhaps eight feet in width before the sheer walls of the excavation itself rose up to meet the gritty ground.

The day woke from its fitful slumber in a wicked mood. A wind had picked up, hurling dust and sand into their faces, coating them in grit. Ibrahim, with the prescience of one who had lived here all his life, had provided each of them a shawl to wrap around the lower half of his face, covering both nose and mouth. But such was the ferocity and deviousness of the wind that it found even the tiniest crevice to thrust its detritus through.

Above them, the sun was a distant disc, bone white and hallucinatory. Birds circled in the uncertain thermals, crying as the sand beat against their breasts and wings.

Yeats, looking around, said, "How on earth are we expected to get down there? I don't see any stairs."

"Stairs," Ibrahim echoed, laughing and shaking his head. "I like you, WBY; I really do." He pointed as he led them forward. "We descend here."

What he indicated was a doorway cut into the stone, so small that the three of them were obliged to bend over double in order to enter the gloom single file. At least they were out of the flagellating wind.

A steep set of hand-carved stone stairs descended to an opening that Yeats assumed would lead them out onto the floor of the excavation. Imagine his surprise, then, when he discovered they were only two-thirds of the way down.

"What is this?" he said. "What's going on?"

Ibrahim grabbed a stout hemp rope dangling off to one side. "This is what will take us the rest of the way down."

A clear look of alarm crossed the poet's face as Ibrahim, ankles gripping the rope to control his speed, slid down to the ground. "Is this some form of jest?"

"Stiff upper lip, old boy," Conrad said as he clapped his friend on the shoulder. "We traveled all this way for a bit of an adventure, what?"

"Adventure, yes," Yeats said. "But this—"

He gave a cry as Conrad pushed him out onto the rope. White-knuckled, he slid down, rather too fast, his palms reddened and rope burned before Ibrahim could catch him. Conrad followed the two to the floor of the excavation.

From this perspective the stone church was even more imposing, its slightly sloping walls looming up on their left. Scents of the earth billowed up to envelop them, as if History itself, alive and eager, were pulling them to its breast.

Ibrahim led them into the interior of the church, which was even more Spartan than his matrimonial bedroom had been. Dust lay everywhere, and the sharp pungency of mineral stone.

"No tourists come here," Ibrahim said as they stood in the center. Far above them, a small oculus allowed a shaft of sandy daylight to descend like a sword whose point was buried in the ground. "No one would dare take them."

"Why not?" Yeats asked.

Ibrahim's teeth shone in reflection from the sword of daylight. "Because of the dead. The dead are here, WBY." He lifted his arms, swung around in a complete circle. "They are all around us. Crouched in the shadows, they watch and chitter with terrified eyes and terrified mouths."

"Why are they here?" Yeats asked. "Why congregate here? Is it the church itself? A holy place."

"Well, it's up for debate whether this is a holy place," Conrad said, "right, Ibrahim?"

The Ethiopian shuddered, made the sign of the cross. "Actually, it's what's beneath the church that keeps these souls shackled."

Yeats was looking around with great interest as if he could spot the ghosts of the dead huddled in the shadows of the cruciform interior. "And what would that be?"

"I think we must find out," Conrad said with a wry smile. "It's why we've come all this way." He produced his battery-powered torch, something Ibrahim had never before seen. He started with a little squeak as Conrad thumbed it on and a beam of light jumped out like a monster from a closet. Balancing it in the palm of his hand, he let Ibrahim study the contraption. "And it's why Ibrahim has agreed to lead us here."

Ibrahim took the torch in his hands as gingerly as if it were one of his children at the moment of their birth.

"Yes, Ibrahim's grandfather is here. Ibrahim talks to him from afar, never from inside the church. In fact, it was Ibrahim's father who called out to him to search beneath the church. He and I discussed this the last time I was here. At that time, I could not persuade him to come inside with me."

"Ibrahim, what changed your mind?" Yeats said.

The guide looked up. Handing the torch back to Conrad, he said, "I discovered that my grandfather—that all the souls here—are in torment. They are bound here, so my grandfather tells me, by the thing beneath the church. A thing that predates even this church, which is very old, indeed."

"And with that intriguing introduction," Conrad said, "we shall proceed."

Ibrahim, having clearly screwed up his courage, nodded his assent. He led them into the left-hand cross section, which did not in any way correspond to the usual Church design or designation. There were no paintings or statues of any kind. Perhaps they had been looted long ago, or just as likely they never existed, not in this country at, as Yeats had said, the back of beyond.

Clearly, there was nothing here, and Yeats was just about to query their leader when Ibrahim pressed his palm against a certain stone on the back wall. With a noise like fingernails dragged across roughhewn stone a doorway appeared.

Ibrahim lit a taper and, with the aid of Conrad's torch, they began their descent. Unlike the staircase down to the pit, this one contained shallow, broad steps of some kind of igneous rock unknown to the Westerners. The treads curled around like the tail of a colossal beast. Even with Conrad's battery-powered beam of light it was impossible to make out anything below them until they had reached the bottom.

The taper's flames cast dancing shadows along the floor, which was composed of stone blocks so precisely set they needed no grout to hold them in place. They reminded Conrad of the Great Pyramids of Egypt he had explored some years ago, when he was in his teens.

"This is the place my grandfather spoke of." Ibrahim's voice had risen into a fluttery terror, which he was holding in check with an enormous effort.

"What did he say was down here?" Conrad asked. "What had trapped the souls in this prison?"

"That." Lifting his torch on high, Ibrahim pointing a trembling fore-finger at the massive statue crouching in the center of the space.

"What is it?" Yeats said, leaning forward, eyes wide in an attempt to pierce the gloom.

Then Conrad trained his beam on the statue and they saw what it was. An enormous crouching lion with the head of a human, carved out of night-black basalt.

"Good Christ!" Yeats exclaimed.

"Meet the jailor of souls," Conrad stepped forward, closed the distance to the statue. "If my eyes don't deceive me, it's a Sphinx."

The hooded eyes gazed out at them; the ears, more leonine than human, were flattened to its skull. Tufts of hair at its elbows, each claw larger than a man's fully extended hand.

"Egyptian," Yeats breathed.

"No. By the tufted legs, the size and shape of its claws, the details of the cloth along its spine, I can say without fear of contradiction that this idol predates Pharaonic Egypt." He began to walk around the Sphinx, Yeats at his heels. As for Ibrahim, he hadn't moved so much as a muscle since the beam of light had lit up the strange and disturbing Sphinx. It did not escape Conrad's fiercely concentrated attention that the Sphinx's talons were the same exact shape as those on Murmur. Indeed, he suspected that the visitation coming on the very morning he would confront this great basalt carving was no coincidence.

The Throne had been trying to tell him something. But what?

"If I may ask," Yeats said, breaking Conrad free of these agitating thoughts, "how is this thing keeping souls imprisoned here? If, indeed, there are any members of the dead here. I mean to say, curious as it is, it's nothing more than a stone statue. As you have learned, Conrad, skepticism and I are not precisely on speaking terms. However, I have yet to discern even a scintilla of phenomenological activity on the premises of this church. Old it may be, but numinous?" He shook his head. "I must tell you that I harbor doubts."

"My grandfather is here. I can feel him," Ibrahim said, shaking off his paralysis. Still, he kept his gaze averted from the Sphinx. Terror remained entrenched in the corners of his eyes.

"*Dawit* Gebereal," he called, his head slightly raised and tipped to one side like a seeking bird's, "*wund ayat!*" He turned and turned again, wheeling in a circle. "Grandfather! It is I, Ibrahim. I have come, as you begged. Please tell me what I need to do."

This was spoken in Amharic, obliging Conrad to translate for Yeats.

"*Wund ayat,* what can I do to help you?"

For some time there was nothing. But then, so gradually it was impossible to say when it had begun, a keening arose, so knife-like it made the hairs at the back of Yeats's neck stir. Instinctively, he rubbed his neck, as if he needed to restore circulation to that area.

The keening continued to rise, the tone changing as if a great sound were being forced through a narrow tube. The sound was inchoate, and yet it held them in a vise-like grip. In the way clouds emulate recognizable shapes the keening, which was now more of a howl, seemed to contain words, lost and then found, only to be lost again in the violent turbulence.

"What . . . what is happening?" Yeats called through the ululation.

"You wanted proof of phenomenological activity!" Conrad called back. "Now you have it."

He was right, for even now the words were forming, like letters written in sand, appearing for a moment, only to be erased as if they had never existed in the first place.

*There . . . is . . . a . . . force . . . that . . . holds . . . us . . . here.*

"Yes, Grandfather," Ibrahim said, eyes closed to slits in concentration as much as against the howling. "This thing . . . this Sphinx."

*No . . . A . . . force controls . . . this . . . unholy creature. . . . As . . . it . . .*

*roots him . . . to . . . the . . . earth here . . . it . . . chains . . . us. He may be . . .
our guard . . . but . . . he . . . is not . . . our . . . jailor.*

"Who is, then, Grandfather?" Ibrahim whirled like a dervish. "Show
me so that I may end your torment and the torment of the others imprisoned here."

Now a darkness closed around them unnatural and asphyxiating.
Ibrahim's taper was extinguished without even a momentary flicker.
Even Conrad's torch beam dimmed, as if its batteries were dying.

Grandfather Gebereal's voice had vanished, buried beneath shadows
that seemed to shift along the muscled flank of the Sphinx. Crossing to the
beast, Conrad mounted the plinth, reached up, and shoved his hand into
the Sphinx's open mouth.

"What are you doing?" Yeats cried.

He felt around for what he knew must be there, but the mouth was
empty. His heart plummeted. Someone had been here before him. Someone who must have known . . .

"Turn around, all of you," a deep, stentorian voice commanded.

Conrad was the only one of them who recognized the voice, and his
worst fear—the possibility he had kept as far as he could from his
consciousness—was realized.

As they turned they confronted a man well over six feet tall with a shock
of white hair worn long down to his back of his neck. If it hadn't been for
the red flecks, like chips of fire, his deep-set eyes would have been almost
colorless. His angular face was roughhewn, his handsomeness hard-won,
as if painstakingly carved from granite. He possessed a loose-limbed in-
formality unusual in a man of his generation, which was clearly rooted in
the nineteenth century.

"Gideon," Conrad said.

The tall man tipped his head fractionally toward Yeats. "Conrad, what
have we here?"

A chill like a knife thrust went through Conrad's guts. "Never mind.
The question is what are you doing here?"

"The same as you, Conrad." He gestured with a thrust of his chin.
"This is the second of the Four Sphinxes. You know where another one
is." Conrad knew Gideon was alluding to the chamber buried beneath
the Gnostic Observatine Reliquary in Alexandria, Egypt; he'd been there
at least a half-dozen times with this very man.

"What did you take from this one, Gideon?"

The tall man smiled. "I find it interesting that you call me Gideon."

"That is your name, is it not? Or have you lied to me about that as well?"

Choosing not to answer those questions, Gideon held out his left hand, opening it to allow Conrad to shine his torch on to it.

"A gold crucifix." Conrad frowned, looking dubious. "That's what you found inside this Sphinx?"

"A rood, yes. But not any rood, Conrad, as you might well suspect, having come here for it. But I arrived first, and now I have it."

Ibrahim's eyes fairly bugged out of his head when he saw the gold crucifix. "That belongs to my grandfather!" he cried. "He showed it to me when I was just a boy."

"Quiet, you!" Gideon shouted. "You people are no concern of mine."

"That is why he and everyone else are trapped here." Ibrahim stepped forward, as if magnetized to the gold crucifix. "Don't you see, Conrad, it's not this beast; it's the rood."

Gideon raised his right hand, which held a pistol. "Stay where you are."

"There is a symmetry to this." Ibrahim came on. "I understand why my grandfather called me here."

Gideon clicked off the safety. "I'm warning you."

"I am here to right this wrong." Ibrahim, still approaching, gaze fixed on the rood, appeared not to hear the warning.

"Don't!" Conrad shouted just before the tall man squeezed the trigger.

The first bullet staggered Ibrahim, but such was his intent that he kept coming. The second bullet spun him around so that he was staring directly into Yeats's eyes. There was a pleading in them. And then the third bullet tore into him, and he crumpled to the ground.

"Gideon." It was Conrad's turn now. "What have you done?"

"Only what had to be done." The tall man turned the gun on the other two men. "Stop, Conrad. I have three more bullets in this pistol. You better than anyone know how fine a shot I am. Don't make me pull the trigger."

But Conrad, gathering speed, was rushing forward. "Do what you have to do, Father. Just do it!"

# PART TWO

## THE ROOD

# 16

**THE INSTANT LILITH SWAN FIRST LAID EYES ON EMMA SHAW** an electric pain went through her so powerful that her knees literally went weak, obliging her to half-collapse onto a chair in the outdoor café where Emma was sitting. That half collapse, that act of letting go, so simple and yet absolutely impossible for her up until this moment, was nothing compared to her attempts at getting her breath back.

Her cheeks were flushed; her heart rose up of its own accord and stuck in her throat like a fishbone. Her fingertips tingled, her feet were suddenly numb, and she rose out of her body as if it did not exist, hovering in the perfumed air of the café secreted in the center of Bodrum, striped awning keeping the blazing sun off the patrons eating, drinking, talking, laughing as if nothing untoward had happened. But it had. Never before had Lilith had such a reaction to anyone or anything, and she did not know what to do with the feelings. She could not talk to the waiter when he came to take her order, could not admonish the gaggle of twentysomething girls swinging their backpacks into her shoulder as they passed, poking one another and giggling incessantly.

In fact, for the moment she did not know where she was, why she was here, or what she should do. The sight of Emma Shaw in the flesh sent all other thoughts scattering to the four winds. Of course, she had seen photos of Bravo's sister, but, truth be told, she'd never paid much attention to them, concentrating on Bravo, figuring Emma as peripheral and, therefore, of not much import. This in addition to the fact that, as is true with many people, the photos did not in any way, shape, or form capture whatever ineffable energy came off Emma in hot waves, inundating Lilith.

Four days ago, Lilith stood on the deck of a hired gulet, cutting through the cerulean water of Gökova, a narrow gulf of the Aegean Sea in southwest Turkey. Through the blinding sunlight, she caught sight of the harbor fronting Bodrum. Now a playground for the rich and famous, the modern city of Bodrum was built on the site of Halicarnassus, an ancient Greek city.

It had taken her that long to find Emma Shaw through a combination of Obarton's contacts and showing Emma's photo to waiters and shopkeepers. Now here she was, not twenty feet away. Lilith felt like a teenager with her first head-exploding crush, in all its mad hormonal glory. No, but there was something more, much more at work here: she felt as if she had been living someone else's life, as if it were a dream from which she was just now awakening. She no longer knew who she was or, more accurately, who she had been, because as had been made abundantly clear, she was now someone else entirely. A stranger had walked into her brain, taken up residence there.

Just in time she manufactured a cough in order to hide the moan that escaped her half-parted lips like an air bubble rising from her oceanic depths. The cough, sharp and clear, happened to come at a lull in the conversations around her, and the object of her tremulous desire turned her head.

Lilith, transfixed, felt like slipping under the table, although it was too late even for that fantasy, for now Emma Shaw was looking directly at her. Lilith's insides turned to jelly. Was that a smile on her face? The half smile of a Mona Lisa—or of a crocodile. Lilith wasn't sure, in her mesmerized state, which of those she wanted it to be. "Can I have both?" she whispered. "Please."

And like a somnambulist, she found herself rising, felt her feet moving one step at a time, closing the distance between Emma Shaw and herself.

"Dear God," she whispered to herself, "what is happening?"

What was happening was that the moment she reached Emma's table she sat down on the empty chair without asking permission or even saying hello.

Now there was the smile, for sure. "Do I know you?" Emma's voice pierced her like Cupid's arrow. It was high and low, cool and fiery. In just four words? How was that possible?

*I am someone who loves you now and forever.* She wanted to say this so badly her chest burned and her cheeks flushed. Instead, she steeled herself to say, "My name is Lilith." And then her mind, reaching for an instant of clarity, allowed her the blessed relief to say, "I thought I recognized another American."

Emma laughed, the high-low trill sending shivers down Lilith's spine. Her hands were clasped together under the table, knuckles white with strain as she kept their trembling from betraying her.

"There are a lot of Americans here in Bodrum," Emma said, the echo of her laugh lending her words an adorable lilt.

"But almost all with tour groups." Lilith's tongue, thick and sluggish, almost caused her to stumble over her words. "You're alone, like me."

"Are you homesick, like me?" The voice had changed, but so subtly Lilith almost missed it. The image of the crocodile smile came to her unbidden.

"Uh-huh." Lilith nodded. "I suppose I am." She reached far down into her oceanic depths, trying to relax her body one section at a time. "I thought . . . well, now I'm about to tell you it seems foolish."

"No, no." Emma Shaw gestured, her beautiful arm in motion. "Please go on, Lilith."

Her use of the name caused Lilith's eyes to close momentarily. "Okay, well, here goes. I thought we might—I mean just possibly, and if it's not overstepping the bounds of stranger to stranger—be homesick together."

Instead of answering, Emma turned, flagged down a waiter. "Two coffees," she said, and then, turning back to Lilith, "and something luscious to eat, no?"

LILITH THOUGHT she would pass out with ecstasy, but of course she didn't. Nevertheless, the ecstasy stayed with her, perched in her head and, simultaneously, stretching luxuriantly between her thighs, as if it had a double life, being in two places at once, like an advanced physics experiment.

She would have liked nothing better than to pull herself together, but that purely rational part of her was so far away it could scarcely be heard, and, anyway, the fire inside her had already gone beyond a flash point.

The food came and she ate with gusto from the small plates, following Emma's lead. She desperately wanted an alcoholic drink, preferably three, to silence that tiny pinpoint of rationality that was still ping-ponging around the outskirts of her brain, but she felt the request might reflect badly on her, as if she were trying to get them both drunk for nefarious purposes, which, now she thought about it, wasn't so far from the truth.

"Are you here on vacation, or . . . ?" Emma asked between bites.

"Or," Lilith responded. "I'm an amateur archeologist. My interest lies in Halicarnassus, not Bodrum." Her smile felt artificially stretched, as if she'd just had plastic surgery. Had she said the right thing? Should she have pretended to be a tourist? Surely that would have been the safest thing to say. She had no way of knowing until Emma said, "Then our interests coincide. I'm heading out to the ruins tomorrow morning. Perhaps you'd care to join me?"

Lilith's heart flipped over. "I'd like nothing better." She was appalled; this had come out of her mouth before she'd had a chance to vet it. It terrified her to sound so eager; what was wrong with her, anyway? Now the rational pinpoint irised open and for a moment she was able to take a step back, observing the scene as if she were an innocent bystander. What have I done? What am I doing? she asked herself. And then the iris closed, the pinpoint flew away to regions unknown, and she was able to delude herself by affirming that she was simply doing what Obarton had tasked her to do: get close to Emma Shaw, find out what her connection with the Fallen was, and from there draw out their secrets through Emma's throat. Did it matter in which way she chose to accomplish these tasks? Did it matter that she might have fun along the way? *No,* the voice inside her head said emphatically, *it did not.*

"Good." Emma speared a dolma, brought the glistening morsel to her lips. "It's settled then. My name is Emma, by the way."

Lilith speared the last dolma. "What time do we leave?"

THEY LEFT Bodrum at 6:00 a.m. sharp, while the tourists were still snoring in their comfy beds and the shopkeepers were rubbing sleep from their eyes. The morning was already warm, the sky cloudless. It promised to be a glaringly hot day. Emma Shaw appeared unconcerned by this—or perhaps "oblivious" was a better word. She wore hiking boots, lightweight cargo shorts, and a khaki shirt. A backpack was a hump between her shoulder blades.

"Ready to take on history?" she asked Lilith. She didn't wait for an answer but struck off toward a rattletrap truck, whose diesel exhaust was doing its part in polluting the morning. They climbed aboard. An old man with a lined face, a prominent nose, and a moth-eaten felt cap steered them grimly through the city streets, shifting gears as if they were punches he was throwing.

"Where are we going exactly?" Lilith said after twenty minutes or so of heading almost due north.

"I told you," Emma replied neutrally. She was staring through the filthy windscreen, past a nearly vertical crack that seemed with every bump and jolt to threaten to shear the glass in half.

Lilith was about to say that, in fact, Emma hadn't told her but, analyzing the other woman's intense expression, decided to keep her mouth shut for the time being. A fly, metallic green in the sunlight, batted itself against the windscreen until Emma snatched it out of the air, slammed it down on the dashboard, and left it there, a smear with broken legs.

"Is something wrong?" Emma asked after a time, causing Lilith to start as if she had been stuck with a cattle prod.

"Wrong? I don't . . . What d'you mean?"

"You keep staring at me."

How can she know that? Lilith asked herself. She hasn't even given me so much as a sideways glance. "I . . . well, you're very beautiful."

"And you haven't seen beautiful women before?"

All in, Lilith thought, heart in her throat. "Not like you."

At this, Emma Shaw at last turned to regard her. "Indeed." Then, in a magisterial gesture, her head swung back, and she was staring out the windscreen again.

Undeterred, Lilith continued to stare at her, working to commit to memory every square inch of Emma's face visible to her.

"You're doing it again." Emma's lips barely moved, her voice was barely more than a murmur, yet there was an intimate tone to it that thrilled Lilith to the tips of her toes. "Am I really so fascinating?"

"To me."

Turning, Emma reached out, cupped the back of Lilith's head with one hand, drew her gently toward her half-open lips. The kiss, when it came, was nothing like Lilith had ever before experienced or even dreamed of. In fact, as an adult she had done her best never to kiss anyone, as it would inevitably bring up her unthinkable sessions beneath the sweating farm animal into which her uncle transformed in her presence.

The kiss may have lasted a long time, but for Lilith it was over too soon, oh, too soon. When she blinked, Emma Shaw was back in her position, staring out the windscreen. On the other side of her, the driver, still grimly clutching the steering wheel, appeared oblivious to his passengers. Everything was as it had been before the kiss, and Lilith found herself wondering whether she had hallucinated the whole thing. But her lips tingled, the lower one throbbing where Emma had given it a love bite. A heat rose from the juncture of her thighs and she began to sweat through her clothes. Nothing more was said for a long time afterward, but the atmosphere inside the truck cab had thickened. Lilith's nostrils expanded at the new musky smell.

Sixty-five minutes beyond the last jumbled outskirts of Bodrum, the truck turned off onto a muddy track that headed steeply upland. They turned to the left and entered a dense forest of cedars of Lebanon, umbrella pines, and various deciduous trees. The old man, leaning slightly forward, committed his entire attention to keeping the truck from banging into an erupting root or scraping against the trunk of a tree. Ten minutes later, the truck rolled to a stop at the edge of a sun-baked glade.

"We go on foot from here," Emma announced.

Lilith swung neatly out of the cab and Emma brushed past her. Immediately sweat broke out all over Lilith's body, and she quickly stepped into a patch of shade. Emma gave her a wry grin, brushed past her closer than was necessary as she struck off into the forest, Lilith at her heels like a hunting dog.

The path—for it was no more than that—wound steeply upward. Loose gravel and stones clattered down after them, lifting clouds of dust in their wake. A sharp bend to the left brought up another sharp turn just ahead, causing Lilith to lose sight of Emma, and she stopped for a moment as if that would help her gain her bearings. But the truth was except for the path she was completely lost. But then she heard a soft rustling from up ahead and mounted one of the path's steeper humps. Moments later, she came upon Emma, who stepped out of deep shadow on the side of the path and repeated what had happened in the truck. This time the kiss lasted longer. Lilith could taste Emma as their tongues met and twined.

"Here," Emma said, pulling away, leaving Lilith feeling like warm taffy, pulled out of shape. She handed Lilith a canteen. "Drink. It's a long climb from here."

Lilith unscrewed the cap, drank deeply. The water was cold and sweet.

The instant she handed the canteen back, Emma was off up the slope, so fast that once again Lilith lost her in the dense underbrush. She could hear the soft musical calls of the birds, some of which rushed by her in a flutter of wings. Dragonflies hung in the wells of sunlight like diadems. She called Emma's name, but hearing no reply she doubled her pace in order to catch up.

Soon enough she could hear the soft plashing of water and guessed they were nearing a waterfall. The scents were rich and sweet. A blue-and-white butterfly flitted beside her head, a brief companion, before lifting away toward the treetops.

It was at that moment that she heard an unearthly shriek, then a frantic battering as of flailing legs. Frightened, she called Emma's name again, sprinting upward as fast as she could. The second shriek caused her to stumble. She almost fell, holding herself off the ground by grabbing onto the tip of a low-hanging branch.

Redoubling her effort, she reached a small plateau in the center of which was the bloody corpse of what appeared to be a golden jackal. She'd encountered a pack in North Africa several years ago. The thing had been literally ripped to shreds. Its body, almost completely inside out, lay sprawled on the ground, one leg still quivering in galvanic muscle memory. Its head was nearly wholly bitten off.

She looked around, wide-eyed. What could have done this? A gray wolf, a brown bear? What predators were hiding out here?

"Emma, where are you?" she called. And then more loudly, "Emma!"

The birds had gone still; the dragonflies were absent without leave. Weird, unidentifiable insects, crawling out of the churned-up earth, were drinking the fresh blood, bathing in it. Overhead, in the permanently twilit world, a large velvety bat whooshed by, too close for comfort. She could sense the carrion animals gathering for the feast.

Hearing a stirring up ahead, she picked her way forward. She stepped over the gory remains of the jackal, and as she did so found herself in terra incognita.

# 17

**GIDEON SHAW WAS NOT HIMSELF; HE HADN'T BEEN HIMSELF** from the moment of his peculiar conception. His mother, a striking beauty, dark and smoldering, of uncertain Eurasian provenance, would have been a prize catch for any number of millionaire playboys, international plunderers, princes, counts, or dukes, in those days when titles actually meant something. Like Wallis Simpson, she could have been the cause of monarchies toppling. Instead, she had fallen head over heels in lust with a man who seemed to have appeared out of nowhere. For Chynna Shaw, love had nothing to do with how she felt about this man, who never told her his name, who never asked for love, who, it seemed, was, like her, uninterested in love. It never occurred to her to ask his name; his anonymity was part of his extraordinary charisma.

They spent three weeks in a state of heavenly bliss, and then he was gone, as abruptly as he had appeared, leaving Chynna alone, delirious, and astonishingly pregnant, in the sense that her term lasted all of three months. Or perhaps it only seemed that way to her, considering the state of rapture that remained her constant companion until the birth of her son. She named him Gideon, after the heroic figure in the book of Judges, who defeated the vast Midianite army with three hundred soldiers.

The nuns to whom Chynna turned for succor after she was released from the silk ligatures of lust did not much care for the name, seeing as how Gideon was an Israelite, a judge and hero of the Old Testament. They would have much preferred she name her son John, since, after all, the convent was located in the birthplace of Saint John, the Baptist, three hours from Jerusalem. But that was not to be. Chynna had a mind of her own, and as it turned out, not even the mother superior of the order or the father confessor, who visited the convent regularly, could sway her when her mind was made up.

"I obey the word of God," Chynna would say to them, or anyone else naïve enough to question her motives "not yours, nor anyone else's."

She brought Gideon up in strict Catholic fashion, which, as may be expected, mollified her mother superior. It also allowed her the kind of leeway unthinkable for the nuns—for Chynna had never taken the veil—of the convent. There came a time when Chynna became aware that keeping Gideon inside the convent was no longer a good thing. Accordingly, she sent him to school in Jerusalem. He walked three hours each way, until she was sufficiently convinced that he was a competent enough horseman. Then she bought him a knife with a wicked blade and taught him how to defend himself by throwing it with deadly accuracy. And like all his basic skills, such as walking, talking, and reading, he mastered this one with eye-opening rapidity. By the end of his first year at school in Jerusalem he was speaking Arabic and Hebrew, which, after all, were not that dissimilar, as well as Latin and Greek. His schoolbooks were in one of these four languages.

He was a near-perfect student, invariably coming in first in all his classes. But soon enough Chynna discovered that her strange son was stranger than she could have imagined. For one thing, his interest in the occult was so intense and persistent that she found herself having to keep his bizarre experiments, his obsessive research into the occult, from everyone in the convent. He of course ignored her pleas for him to give up this interest. For another, the nature of his occultism disturbed her profoundly. One day she discovered him setting fire to a wooden crucifix and, when it had turned to charcoal, turning it upside down. He was wrapping the charred upended rood in crimson cloth when she came upon him, having rushed to their chamber, urged on by the smell of burning wood. Their rooms had no fireplace, so she knew something was amiss. She had no idea of how far amiss until she witnessed what he was up to. Without her knowing precisely what it was, her gut informed her in no uncertain terms that it was an evil beyond the imagination of the mother superior. It was, she was convinced, pure evil.

Not long after that, with Gideon's manipulations of occult instruments escalating, she thought it wise to move out of the convent that had been her home for so long. She found it surprisingly difficult. She missed the daily chores and devotions as much as she missed the nuns she had worked and prayed beside. But as for Gideon, he was fully liberated from what he once told her was *a prison of body and soul*. When his experimentations slithered alarmingly into the infernal, he became too much even for the one woman who was bound to love him, and so after 101 sleepless nights of prayer she delivered him into the heart of Jerusalem, there to make his fortune or to run afoul of, if not God, then certainly the authorities.

It is dreadful for a mother to feel compelled to abandon her son, but Chynna's soul-searching had convinced her she had no other choice. Had they stayed together one of them would have wound up killing the other. In the blue twilight of the day they separated, without a word being said between them; she returned to the convent, threw herself on its collective mercy, and was received with open arms. Three months later, she completed her studies and took the veil. She never saw her son or, indeed, the world outside the convent walls again. She died in the arms of the two novices who tended to her when she grew ill with an undiagnosable fever that resisted all treatment. The novices swore that in the moments after she took her last breath an eerie fog descended upon her. The novices attending her fainted dead away. But those were strange days, indeed. Soon whispers began to circulate of nuns cutting themselves, having visions, receiving nocturnal visitations. The father confessor was sent to discover the truth or falsehood of these allegations, but he died in mysterious circumstances inside the walls. Not long thereafter, the place was abandoned, the building burned to the ground by terrified townspeople.

Meanwhile, in Jerusalem, Chynna's son grew in power and prestige in the grand and vicious manner of sultans, kings, robber barons, and popes.

Every detail of this nefarious history Conrad Shaw knew by heart, plus the origin of it. He knew what it was that Chynna had lain with—Gideon's intensely charismatic father, his own grandfather. It preyed upon him like a parasite eating at him from the inside out. His whole life up to the point of this confrontation in the bowels of the Ethiopian church had been a search to rectify the horrific original sin that had been perpetrated on Chynna Shaw, and that dogged his heels and would dog the heels of every Shaw who came after him, unto eternity. Unless, that is, the grandson who had yet to be born could turn the tide. He had seen this, had been born seeing it in his mind's eye.

Now, at the moment he said to his father, "Do it! If you're going to shoot me do it now!" he put himself between Gideon and Yeats. This was done not only to protect the poet but also to keep him from seeing what transpired between son and father.

"You know I won't kill you," Gideon said under his breath.

"You can't kill me, Father. Just as I can't kill you. We are—"

"Do not say another word!" Gideon, brought up short, looked horrified. "I forbid you to speak the word." He glanced around wildly. "Not anywhere, but especially not here, where the dead are imprisoned, where the shadows are not shadows. Where"—he shot a furtive look over Conrad's left shoulder—"that *thing* has dominion."

"That *thing* has a name, just like its three siblings."

Gideon snorted. "Huh! I defy you to tell me which one this is."

"It's Typhos, Gideon."

"How can you tell?"

Conrad smiled thinly. "Once, a long time ago, I told you a secret. Look how that turned out." He shook his head.

"Whatever you delude yourself into calling it means less than nothing. Neither of us can control a Sphinx; that's all that matters." He brandished the pistol. "Now back up."

Conrad shook his head. "You have to pay for killing Ibrahim. He was my friend."

"Don't be absurd. You have no friends. You learned that from me. We use people, then throw them away when they're of no more use. That's our stock-in-trade, who we are." The pistol's muzzle swung back and forth, like the head of a spitting cobra, searching for its prey. "You always were a child stubborn beyond endurance. I suppose now you will force me to kill the other one to make my point."

Conrad stood resolute. "I want that gold rood."

Gideon laughed. "It will never be yours; this I swear."

And he stepped quickly to the side in order to bring Yeats into the field of fire. At the same time, Conrad tilted his head back, shouted at the top of his lungs, "Typhos, *djat had'ar!*" Typhos, he is come!

Gideon's face drained of blood as behind Conrad the Sphinx began to stir. At first it seemed like an optical illusion caused by the low light simmering in the unnatural darkness. Then, a fraction of an inch at a time, the head turned in their direction.

"How in the name of—!" Gideon's eyes fairly bugged out of his head.

The Sphinx lumbered off his plinth, strode on taloned paws toward Gideon.

"God in Heaven!" Gideon cried.

"Too late, Father. You are too far away from God. He can't hear you."

Gideon raised the pistol, fired three shots at the oncoming Sphinx, then threw the empty pistol at him. The gun struck the Sphinx in the throat, which only caused him to open his terrifying jaws wide as he lunged at Gideon. Just before they snapped shut, Conrad's father ran through the slim space between two stone columns, vanishing into a shadowed channel.

Conrad held up his hand. "Guard my friends until I return," he told Typhos in Tamazight. Then he set off after his father.

He heard Yeats calling over and over from behind him in a voice strained by shock and terror, but he paid him no mind. He directed all his energy into finding his father and putting an end to the original sin once and for all.

Perhaps a thousand yards on, the channel narrowed down, forcing him to divest himself of his backpack before turning sideways into order to keep going. The walls, of sledged rock, gradually turned unnaturally smooth until they were like two sheets of glass. This was fortunate, as he might have had great difficulty negotiating the passage otherwise. He had his torch with him, but the light was failing. A bit farther on it began to flicker. The batteries were discharging, and his spares were in his backpack. He went to move forward but found that he couldn't. He couldn't step back, either. He was stuck.

He relaxed his body, willing his bones to become molten, but it was no use. He regarded his own reflection, staring back at him as if from an infinite distance and at the same time startlingly close. And then he started, seeing his father's reflection as well. But that was impossible. There was only room for one person, and barely that, where he was. Nevertheless, there Gideon was, looking not at him but at his own reflection. It was like stumbling into a darkened traveling carnival and finding himself in a fun house, constructed of mirrors that distorted reality. Reaching out, he pressed his palm against the perfectly smooth wall, blotting out his father's reflection. His own was obscured as well.

His torch beam flickered again; he took his hand away to fiddle with it. That's when he noticed something odd: Gideon's reflection didn't look like a reflection at all. He squinted, peering at the wall. He saw his father moving, just as if . . .

Reversing his grip on the torch, he slammed the back end of it against the wall as hard as he was able considering the cramped quarters. Jagged lines appeared in the wall, radiating from the spot he had hit. Aiming for ground zero, he smashed the torch into the wall again and again.

It shattered as if it were made of dark glass.

Then he stepped through into the netherworld beyond.

# 18

VALLETTA, MALTA: PRESENT DAY

"STOP!" AYLA SNAPPED. "YOU'RE HOVERING OVER ME LIKE
I'm sick."

"You *are* sick." Bravo leaned in closer. "Or you were." He held out his
hands. "Let's find out which it is."

She slipped her hands onto his, palm to palm. He didn't enclose them
but let them rest on his hands, as if he and Ayla were playing a game of
slap hands.

"You're cold," he said.

"Cold hands, warm heart." But the smile she attempted was full of
fear. Last year, just around the time they boarded one of the Gnostic Observatines' private jets Bravo had called for to take them to New York,
she had regained full knowledge of what had happened to her from the
time she had held the manuscript in the lab at Addis Ababa to that
moment.

"You're clear," Bravo said, lifting his hands from hers. "Not to worry."

Except he himself was worried. His thoughts were filled with Emma.
He was in an agony of not knowing. What pain must she be in? Was she
still alive in the state that he knew her? Was she already gone, gobbled up
by the Fallen?

They were at present on the wide veranda of a hotel in Valletta. The sun
was down, the Mediterranean night soft as velvet. A gentle breeze swept
in from North Africa. The stars were out, looking down on them as if with
contempt.

"I don't need a penny to divine your thoughts," Ayla said. "You're worried about Emma."

He nodded miserably. "I feel as if we should try to find her as quickly as possible. Then I remind myself what she almost did to me. Going up against the Fallen inside her without a way to protect ourselves and save her would be sheer madness."

Ayla indicated Elias, stretched out on a rattan sofa on the other side of the veranda. "The blue flame drove her back once. Why not again? Maybe if he applied more of it the flame would consume the Fallen."

"And what if it consumed her as well?" He shook his head. "Besides, I wouldn't want to put Elias in mortal danger. And as for Emma . . . how on earth do we exorcise the demon out of her without killing her?"

Ayla, keen beyond measure when it came to divining what was in the human heart, said, "Bravo, there's something you're not telling me, something vital."

Bravo looked away for a moment. When his gaze resettled on her she was taken aback by the sorrow and pain it contained.

"Bravo, what is it? Please tell me."

"I don't understand what happened." His voice was low and rough, a tone she had never heard before. "How did Emma read the Testament? Why did she read it when I explicitly told her not to?"

Ayla looked at him. "Your sister was already compromised by the Fallen. That must have compelled her to ignore your warning."

He nodded. "She was not equipped—" He broke off abruptly, swung his gaze away again, looking out across the lawns, into the heavy night. He came back to her slowly, almost reluctantly. "According to the *Nihilus*, the Testament is evil in more ways than we can imagine. For those who come at it unprepared, unprotected, the words of Lucifer slowly turn a reader's mind toward its ultimate darkness."

Ayla's sharply indrawn breath was like another arrow in his heart. "You mean Emma . . ." She could hardly get the words out. "You mean you believe Emma is already lost?"

"Not yet," he said, "but soon."

"How long?"

"Two days, three at the most. The *Nihilus* was quite clear on the subject. The time to turning depends on the inner strength of the reader."

"Then we have three days. Emma is very strong, Bravo. You saw to that."

That much was true, anyway. But, at the moment, it seemed cold comfort. "I don't think we can do it, Ayla. I don't think we have enough time to save her before she becomes . . . she becomes our implacable enemy, becomes one of the Fallen."

"We'll find a way," Ayla said, but she shuddered nevertheless. "I know we will. I have faith in you—in us."

She saw his face go gray and he winced. Placing her palm against his swollen cheek, she said, "How much does it hurt?"

"Less when you do that."

She ignored his compliment. "I understand you not taking the painkillers; they screw with your cognitive process. But have you been taking your antibiotics?"

"I have.

"Ayla—"

"Shhh," she said. "Just relax."

Elias gave a little snort. Even in sleep he clutched the bronze rood. His chest rose and fell in slow rhythm; his expression was peaceful. Bravo's eyes closed, his breathing slowed almost to that of the boy.

"Ayla." His voice was soft, dreamy.

"I'm here."

"Turn your thoughts toward Elias."

"What? Why?"

"Just do it. Please."

His silken tone rippled through her; unaccountably, his use of her name compelled her to comply.

"Don't look at him," Bravo whispered. "See him in your mind."

Ayla did not understand. Nevertheless, she closed her eyes, pictured Elias lying asleep beside them. When nothing came to her, she pushed her thoughts back, seeing him as he had been in his makeshift home, standing over Bravo. As if a key had been turned, her mind locked on to that image. Everything else fell away into blackness. She saw the boy illuminated by dazzling sunlight against the trunk of a tree. What kind of tree? An apple tree. She knew this without having to look at its leaves or its fruit. The scent of fresh apples came to her, and then a wind arose. A wind with a voice, and at once a warmth flowed through her like a briny tide, making her fingertips tingle. She did not open her eyes or move her own hands but held them out like an offering to Elias, the tree, the scent of fresh apples, the voice in the wind.

An immeasurable time later, she opened her eyes, stared directly into Bravo's.

"What happened?" Her voice was hoarse. Having lost an octave, it was barely recognizable even to herself.

"The boy is the key." Bravo's voice had lost the silky, dreamy tone, but it was still soft, scarcely above a whisper. "Or, rather, he is the conduit."

"The conduit to what?"

"From your father, my grandfather, to us."

Ayla started. "But he died a long time ago. You were there when he was buried—"

"And where, Ayla. Where was Conrad buried?"

Her eyes opened in full-on wonder. "Beneath an apple tree on the Shaw estate."

"*His* apple tree. The one he loved above all others. The one he took me to, defying my father's orders."

Ayla regarded him with a penetrating look. "I think now would be an appropriate time to go back over what we both know about Conrad."

Bravo nodded, shifted a bit in his chair, to ease the throbbing pain that dogged him after leaving the hospital prematurely and to the consternation of his doctors.

Ayla waited until Bravo was comfortable again, then continued. "It's crucial to remember that you and I and Emma carry Conrad's very special genes. Conrad himself was very specific about that with my mother. He told her that I must remain a secret until the day the rough beast raises its head. When she had that dream about you in Tannourine she believed that day had come."

"My poor father."

She nodded. "The enmity between Dexter and Conrad sprang from the fact that your father was perfectly ordinary."

"Yes and no. Their enmity had as many heads as Medusa. Conrad believed fervently in the existence of the Unholy Trinity. With good reason, as we have witnessed. He believed that should Lucifer manage to obtain all three, it will trigger a return to his full power. His reascendancy would be assured. For this very reason, Conrad spent much of his life in search of the Unholy Trinity, of which we know only one: The Testament of Lucifer. The identities of the other two are still shrouded in mystery.

"In 1918, Conrad arranged a meeting with the mystical poet William Butler Yeats. Yeats's ideas about time cycles, about the struggle between God and Lucifer, went entirely against the grain of Catholic dogma. This put Conrad outside the scope of even the most liberal thinkers inside the Order. Among all but Conrad there was a unanimity of opinion that the Unholy Trinity was a myth. And yet Conrad persisted in delving deeper and deeper into the occult, just as King Solomon had done."

"So your father had no choice but to finally exile him."

"When my grandfather was old. But as we both know, there was a personal enmity between them. My father lacked what you and I and Emma have. He resented that, and, I think, he knew that Conrad must have been disappointed in him—frightened even at the thought that the Shaw line would no longer have the power to fight what was coming." He shook his head. "But that's the extent of my knowledge about Conrad. How was he special? How are we special? We're not immortal like Fra Leoni."

"I don't think so, no."

"But the Fallen cut off your mother's head to kill her."

"Well, now you understand why she came to Conrad's attention. There was something special about her, too. He recognized it in her before she did. But she learned from him. She learned everything from him."

"So what are we? Conrad, your mother, you, me, Emma. What are we?"

"I can only tell you what Conrad told my mother when they were together. He said that between immortal and demon lie those who will save mankind."

"Is there a name for us, I wonder?"

"Another riddle Conrad left for us to solve."

"Grandfather was a riddle all on his own. 'The world is built on lies,' he told me as we headed for that apple tree. 'Everything you think you've learned is false. Everything you want to learn you don't.'"

"Huh! That sounds like a couple of Zen Buddhist koans mashed together."

"Paradox just about defines Conrad." Pain rebuilding, Bravo shifted again. "Sometimes I think he purposely said things to drive people nuts, that this propensity was the ultimate self-defense."

Ayla looked away for a moment, staring out at the magnificent rear garden, the massive beds of roses, like clouds at sunset. "We still haven't answered the most pertinent question: How can Conrad still be alive?"

"I told you I had some ideas on that score. Remember I read the *Nihilus Inusitatus.*"

"I haven't forgotten." She turned back to him. "Also, that you haven't shared what you discovered."

"I told you that the *Nihilus* led me to finding The Testament of Lucifer."

"The Book of Deathly Things. Yes." She regarded him with no little intensity. "Which brings up the question of how you weren't affected when you handled the manuscript."

"My reading of the *Nihilus* prepared me. There was a formula in there, just as there was for preventing you from dying from demon-serpent's bite."

"What else did the manuscript tell you?"

"It's full of formulae, some of them far beyond my current knowledge."

"Not surprising, since it was compiled by King Solomon's cadre of alchemists."

"Yes, but what is surprising is a handwritten note in the margin of the introduction. The *Nihilus Inusitatus* was actually written after Solomon died. It says during his reign he gathered a thousand and one alchemists from all corners of the world to do his bidding. After he died, all but sixty-six defected, having become disillusioned with his son."

"So the *Nihilus* was written by these sixty-six."

Bravo nodded.

"Why did they stay?"

"They were the venal ones. Rehoboam, panicked, paid them whatever they wanted."

"Since it was these sixty-six who conjured the sorcerous gold, the *Nihilus* should contain the formula they finally came up with."

"Perhaps it does," Bravo said. "Maybe one or more of the formulae I couldn't decipher were what they used."

"Then we should experiment with—"

"Absolutely not. Every action has a reaction; the realm of the alchemical is no exception. The conjuring of the gold is what unsealed the portal between our world and that of the Fallen."

"You mean these sixty-six undid the work of God?"

"Seems improbable. Nevertheless, it's true. I imagine God never considered the possibility that his own beloved humans would be meddling around in such matters."

"Is God not all-seeing, all-knowing?"

"We'd like to think so, wouldn't we? Takes the terrifying chaos out of life. But the truth is that God has a blind spot for his own creation."

"It's my understanding that the Catholic Church says God is infallible."

"We only have men's word for it, and as we know, men are fallible, men lie; men twist words to suit their purposes," Bravo said gravely. "But assuming it's so, then this apocalyptic battle is part of his plan."

"And we're on the front line." Ayla's eyes grew dark with foreboding. "Let us pray that God's plan for us is not to be cannon fodder."

# 19

HUGH HIGHSTREET WAS ON HIS WAY HOME TO HIS THIRD-
floor flat in the northern precinct of the Marais when he noticed the
shining black Daimler saloon with blacked-out windows. It was Highstreet's habit to spend an hour of the early evening at an exclusive health
club in the 5th arrondissement to unwind, after which he walked across
to the Right Bank, over the western tongue of the Île Saint-Louis, and
home.

The Daimler slowed; he kept walking. The car kept pace, drawing
closer to the curb. The rear window slid down and Highstreet recognized
the pale, suety face of Obarton.

"Mr. Highstreet," Obarton said in a conversational tone despite the
street noise, "a word."

The first thing Highstreet thought was that Obarton had found the
electronic bugs Lilith had planted. It was the logical conclusion as to a
reason for this unscheduled meeting; Highstreet had never before been
alone with Obarton. However, Obarton's expression was anything but
hostile.

Highstreet decided to stop. "Sir. What may I do for you?" he said in his
most formal, clipped upper-class British accent.

Obarton heaved his bulk and the nearside rear door swung open. "If
you would indulge me, Mr. Highstreet." Was that a twinkle in his eye? "I
promise I will not take more than ten minutes of your valuable time."

Despite the cordiality of the conversation, Highstreet hesitated. He was
repulsed by the idea of sharing an enclosed space with the old man, especially since it was controlled by him. Despite that, he didn't think he had
a choice without seeming terribly rude.

The inside of the saloon was warm and humid; Highstreet felt as though he were standing too close to human breath. Obarton's breath, in this instance. The vehicle nosed out into the sparse traffic the instant Highstreet sat. The door closed on its own, probably via the driver's remote control, Highstreet surmised. He wondered rather uneasily whether the windows were so controlled. A sense of being trapped stole over him.

"Mr. Highstreet, please excuse this intrusion on your daily routine," Obarton began, courteous while at the same time reminding Highstreet of his complete surveillance of his movements. "I have one simple question to ask of you: Where is Lilith Swan?"

Highstreet's eyes opened wide. This was the last thing he expected, as he and Lilith had already discussed and decided on her options in this matter: Obarton had sent her on a mission. How could he not know where she was?

"I'm afraid you're asking the wrong person," he said.

Obarton's face darkened perceptibly. "You are her associate, isn't that right?"

"It is."

"You are also—and correct me if I'm wrong—the person closest to her."

"I cannot dispute that, Mr. Obarton. Nevertheless, she informed me that her destination was a matter of the utmost secrecy."

Obarton's face darkened further, sure harbinger of a storm front approaching. "Am I to believe that she didn't tell you where she was going?"

"That is correct. Sir."

"Huh." Obarton sank back into the cushions, hands over his sumo-size belly, sausage fingers interlaced. "Well, then. That changes everything."

"Sir?" Highstreet's brows knit together. "I'm afraid I don't understand."

"Of course you don't."

Obarton was silent for some time. Glancing out the window closest to him, Highstreet saw the inside-out monstrosity of the Pompidou Centre passing on his right as they continued north along the boulevard de Sébastopol.

At length, because he had heard nothing more out of the man beside him, Highstreet said, "I believe I'm due an explanation."

"What?" Obarton seemed to come out of a deep musing. "Yes. Positively, you are, Mr. Highstreet. Apologies." He sighed deeply. "May I interest you in a drink? An aperitif, perhaps? There's a boite of some small repute I'm somewhat familiar with up ahead."

"Thank you, no." Highstreet had heard of Obarton's legendary drunks, and wanted no part of one. He suspected this made him a poor spy, since people deep in their cups were apt to be indiscreet, but he was no spy; that was Lilith's bailiwick. He was smart enough not to involve himself in something he knew nothing about.

"Pity, well . . . A man such as yourself . . ." Obarton cleared his throat. "I mean to say, it's perfectly understandable. Natural, I suppose."

Had he been of another nature, Highstreet would surely have struck the fat man in the snoot. Instead, Slings and arrows, he thought. Slings and arrows.

Obarton, leaning forward and giving Highstreet's address—another reminder who was holding the strings here—called for the car to turn back south.

"That's all right," Highstreet said. "I'll get out here." He smiled at the other man. "As you know, I'm partial to walking."

"Any more of a flaneur," he said, using the French word for an inveterate stroller, "and you'll be a dyed-in-the-wool Frenchman."

Highstreet shrugged off the deliberate insult to an Englishman, opened the door as the saloon rolled to a stop.

"Oh, by the way," Obarton said as he was sliding his legs out, "it's not too late to correct the egregious error you have made."

Highstreet froze. "Is that so."

"You're backing the wrong horse. Lilith will never get what she wants. In fact, the Order is at this moment closing ranks against her." His smile was that of an indulgent uncle. "It's the God's honest truth, Mr. Highstreet. Lilith may have gained some temporary edge by shocking the Circle Council, but in the light of a new day that shock has faded, her feral nature examined and found wanting. A vote has already taken place."

"Without her."

"Or you. The vote was unanimous." Obarton's eyes were like dried currants pressed into raw dough. "But the Circle Council values you and your vote."

Highstreet's brain was running a mile a minute. He felt like Odysseus in the narrow strait between Scylla and Charybdis. He could be loyal to Lilith and be cut down like a stalk of wheat or lend his vote to the majority and abandon her to the circling wolves.

"Now, Mr. Highstreet." Obarton's voice held the urgent edge of command. "Make your choice now."

EMMA SHAW was waiting for Lilith on a small, high ridge just beyond the splayed corpse of the jackal. Its death rictus, an obscene smile, sent a chill down Lilith's spine, and yet she went on without a second thought, or even a concern. Is that what love does to you? she asked herself. Makes you so ill that normal reactions are beneath you?

As she mounted the winding path, the crash-and-spill of the waterfall rose in volume. The atmosphere had thickened, fine sprays of moisture sending tiny rainbows to intercept the shafts of sunlight. Birds called raucously to one another—larger ones than had been evident below the death line.

From her perch on the tiny ridge, Emma watched Lilith as she came into view. To Emma's right, the cataract crashed down white-blue-green into an unseen gorge. Behind her a natural bridge had been carved out over the uncounted eons, arcing ruddy and rough across the gorge. It was partially obscured by the waterfall at the center of its span. To her left the forest rose so steeply it appeared like a vertical wall of greenery, solid as the rock upon which they now both stood.

"You made it," Emma said.

"Did you think I wouldn't?"

"I hoped you would." Emma took a step toward her. "But hope is a weak and pitiful thing. It dissolves in the night."

Lilith cocked her head. "What an odd thing to say."

"Once I would have agreed." Emma took another step toward her. "Not now."

"Why not now? What's changed?"

"Everything," Emma said. "Everything is different."

"Tell me. I have the curiosity of a cat."

Emma laughed. "You know the old saying."

"I'm not that kind of cat," Lilith said with a tremulous defiance.

They were standing so close together they breathed in each other's exhalations. Lilith was dizzy in such close proximity to Emma. They were alone here, no one to see them, to spy on their actions. Her legs were suddenly rubbery. She wanted nothing more than to melt into the other woman, to discover . . . everything.

"No? What kind of cat are you, then?"

How neatly she had boomeranged the conversation, Lilith thought with a combination of annoyance and admiration. "A cat with a highly evolved instinct for self-preservation."

"Brava!" Emma clapped her hands in delight. "You'll need that instinct where we're going."

"This place where you're taking me. It's part of the change you spoke of."

"It is."

Something Lilith could not name swam in Emma's eyes, and despite her intense infatuation she recalled Obarton's admonition that Emma Shaw had in some mysterious way developed a close relationship with the Fallen. Up until this very moment she had found the idea of the existence of a cadre of Fallen Angels, let alone them traipsing around here on earth, to be fairly ludicrous. She had come here to see what Obarton had in mind for her, to take a large step back from the brink he seemed determined to shove her over, at least by proxy. Now, all at once, she wasn't so sure. In fact, she wasn't sure of anything. It was as if she had been under a mesmeric spell from the moment she had first laid eyes on Emma Shaw in the spangled light of the Bodrum café.

Lilith's nostrils dilated. What was that odor coming from inside Emma? It was bittersweet, coppery, like blood, and yet had about it a distinctive tang. Once, when she was a child, Lilith had stolen three oranges from a fruit stand. Safely around the corner, she had stuffed her face with two of them one after another. She was so full that she never took the third out of the pocket of her corduroy jacket. In fact, she forgot about it until one evening when she slipped the jacket on and an odd scent came to her. It was the third orange, which had green-blue mold growing on it. Putting it up to her nose, she inhaled deeply. That scent was a combination of the growing mold and the rotting fruit. It seemed to her then that the one was taking over the other, that when the marbled mold covered the entire orange there would be nothing left of the fruit. It would have been turned into a dried-out husk. And then, with its host gone, what would happen to the mold? Stupid mold, she thought as she heaved the orange over a fence into an empty lot.

Now that same odor was coming from inside Emma Shaw, and her lower belly tightened in instinctive response. She was gripped by a strange anxiety, as if somewhere in the far distance she heard a clock ticking down. To what? she asked herself. To what?

"Are you all right?" Emma rubbed her upper arm. "You went pale for a moment."

"Sure. I'm fine." Think of something, she told herself. "Suddenly the image of that animal popped into my head."

"The golden jackal."

"Is that what it was?" She was sure that the less information she gave Emma the better. "Well, it was quite a sight, torn to shreds." She glanced around. "What predator did that?"

"Maybe a bear."

A bear would have eaten the jackal, but again she didn't want Emma to become aware that she knew this.

Emma shrugged. "I didn't see. It was there when I came upon it, just like you."

Lilith nodded.

"This way." Emma pointed toward the natural bridge that spanned the waterfall.

As Emma turned, Lilith saw a bit of pink embedded under one thumbnail. Stepping forward, closing the gap between them, Lilith caught a closer look, and knew immediately what it was: a bloody fragment of one of the golden jackal's bones.

# 20

**WHEN CONRAD BROKE ON THROUGH TO THE OTHER SIDE HE**
found himself in a place that eclipsed any he had ever reached before.
From a very early age, Conrad had been an inveterate explorer, had
nagged his father with such incessant zeal that Gideon had had no choice
but to take him with him. Conrad first saw Cairo when he was four years
old, and if you asked him nicely and he liked you he would describe to
you every detail of that trip from his first view of Egypt to his adventure
alone inside the Great Pyramid of Cheops when he wandered away while
the adults' backs were turned.

Perhaps "wandered" is the wrong word, because even at the tender age
of four Conrad was beset by inner impulses that drove him to think and
do things others of his age could not even conceive of. There was something he needed to find inside the Great Pyramid. This was not at all
unusual; there was always something little Conrad needed to find. In the
case of Cheops's final resting place it was a small opening—too small to
accommodate the bulk of a modern-day adult, but just about right for an
ancient Egyptian. Though small, the passage was not long. Soon enough
it gave out on to a chamber of perfectly square proportions. Conrad sensed
this, though the darkness was so absolute he was as good as blind. Nevertheless, he crawled his way to the rear wall, picked up the object he was
meant to have, and retraced his steps without any problem. His mother
liked to boast that he was born without fear, though Gideon felt that
sort of talk was nonsense. Diantha knew her son better than Gideon did,
knew the truth of her observation.

In any event, even at four years of age Conrad had the presence of mind
not to show anyone what he had found in the great Pharaoh's tomb. It

was meant only for him, as were all his other finds. Of this he had no doubt.

What he had been meant to find was this: a small sculpture of a most curious animal. It had the body, legs, and hooves of a horse, but its head was that of a lion. Moreover, it had a tail not of hair but of a serpent's scales. Though it was small, it was intricately detailed in every way, down to the thorned legs and eyes that seemed to blaze out of its leonine head. Such a monstrosity might have frightened the bejeezus out of a normal four-year-old, but Conrad was anything but. Stashing the tiny beast in his pocket, he returned to his father's side. So engrossed was Gideon in the guide's descriptions of Cheops's life and what his religion demanded he surround himself with to guide him into the afterlife that he never registered his son's silent departure and stealthy return. Late at night, when no one could observe him, Conrad brought the animal out, held it close to the gas lamp, which his father had turned down low before tucking him in, examining every feature of the exquisitely crafted sculpture, his eyes blazing in just the same way as the beast's.

This memory came back to him in a flash as he picked his way past the shards of the wall he had shattered, which now looked even more glass-like. Straight ahead of him, glistening in the flickering beam of his torch, was a life-size version of the eerie mount he had found that blazing hot afternoon in Cairo so many years ago.

His breath caught in his throat. Everything in life is a lie, he thought. Everything you think you know, you don't.

Out from behind the monstrous beast stepped a figure. He tensed, assuming it was his father, but as he played the faltering beam of light onto it he saw his mother.

"Seeing you gladdens my heart, my son," Diantha said.

He tried to keep the surprise out his voice. "You knew I would be here."

"The future is never fully known; time is too fluid." Diantha took a step toward him, opened her arms, and he entered her embrace.

He kissed her on both cheeks before stepping back. He had always thought of her as the utter paradigm of beauty. Like the god-flower after which she was named, she was at once stately and womanly. Skin like porcelain, mouth like Cupid's bow, nose straight and strong, thrusting forward like the prow of a clipper ship. Her heart-shaped face was framed by a cascade of black hair that shimmered around the edges like the sun in eclipse. Her large, luminous eyes, the color of oiled olives, searched his, looking to identify the little boy he used to be. "This is one of those times, Conny, when I don't know what will transpire. . . . We have come to one of those crucial forks in time's path . . . the knife-edge." She had fallen into the habit of using this diminutive when he was a toddler

"Mother, where is Gideon? I followed him here." He peered around, following the sweep of his torch beam. "He has to be here somewhere."

"He's gone, Conny. Gone."

"Where? I'll follow him."

"You can't. You know you can't."

"Mother," he said, his voice defiant, "he has something he took from the Sphinx."

"From the mouth. The gold rood. I know. And you have to get it back, Conny." She shook her head. "But not now."

And then, out of nowhere, her face registered pain and she clutched at him.

"Mother, what is it?" When he took her into his arms he felt the wetness seeping from her side. "What . . ." Craning his neck while he gently turned her, he saw the bloom of blood like a crimson flower staining her white silk shirt. "Mother!" He pressed his hand against the wound.

"It's all right, Conny. Truly." She smiled as she peeled his hand from her side, replaced it with hers. Within moments the bleeding had stopped.

"Show me," he said.

The concern in his voice compelled her to lift that side of her shirt out of her waistband just high enough to show him that not only had the wound closed, but it also had shrunk to the size of his thumbnail. Then it vanished altogether.

"You see?" she said, tucking her shirt back in. "Good as new."

Conrad's eyes narrowed. "He knew that would stop me in my tracks." He was speaking of his father, whose name he now refused to utter, after this unspeakable attack. "It's the only reason he would stab you."

"Well, that and the fact that he hates me."

"He doesn't hate you, Mother," Conrad said. "He's afraid of you."

Her smile broadened and she touched his face gently. "Oh, Conny, if only it were so."

"Hate breeds contempt. Fear only becomes more fear."

"And what has he to fear from me?"

"Besides *this*"—he touched her side where the knife had gone in—"it's your vast storehouse of occult knowledge. Who told me the names of all Four Sphinxes? You should have seen his face when I summoned Typhos." He gestured to the looming statue behind him, the mount of lost souls, as he thought of it. "And who told me about his steed?"

"I never should have done that," Diantha said.

"You had to do it, Mother. What other choice did you have?"

"I could have kept the knowledge to myself."

"Which was just what he wanted."

Her smile was knowing, lustrous. "You always provide the wisest truths. One of the many reasons to love you."

Conrad pressed his lips to his mother's cheek, then drew away again. The bond between mother and son was as deep as it was powerful. "There are things about this monstrous creature that I needed to know. When the end times come, the Fallen will mount these beasts in their final assault on mankind."

"It all seemed so far away." Diantha's eyes welled up. "Once upon a time."

"I was drawn to the miniature a long time ago," Conrad said. "But now we have this."

They both turned to stare at the beast with a horse's body, lion's head, and serpent's tail.

"The Orus is a creature conjured by Lucifer," Diantha said with epic distaste.

"But why is it in such close proximity to the Sphinx?"

His mother turned to him. "You know the specters of the infernal are most often seen at the Vatican, drawn by the long history of sins, deceit, and treachery. It's the same here, so far from Christ and yet so near."

Conrad took a step toward the creature, but his mother caught hold of him. "Stop! What are you doing?"

"You know very well."

"You can't, Conny. I won't have this argument with you again."

"He disappeared into the beast. You know it, but you wouldn't tell me when I'd asked you where he'd gone."

For the first time, Diantha's face showed real fear. "You can't mean to follow him. He's more than you are."

"And less." Conrad took another step toward the infernal beast. "Far less."

"Which makes him able to withstand the terrible sin of crossing God's first great law." She clutched him more tightly. "But you—"

"But me what?" he demanded.

"If you go after him you'll risk damning your soul, as his has been since the moment of insemination."

"Mother—"

"No. Listen to me, my beloved child. Chynna, poor thing, was bewitched. One of the Fallen that had taken a human male form mesmerized her. It raped her repeatedly, though, God bless her soul, she never knew or understood what was happening to her. The thing planted that horrible seed in her womb before it was hunted down by one of its own and annihilated."

"I come from that seed, Mother."

"And you lay in a womb for nine months, not three." Diantha's eyes blazed with motherly protection and pride. "*My* womb, Conny. Mine. You have my blood running through you, the long and astonishing heritage of my family. You were made within me. You are *my* child, not his."

Tears spilled from Conrad's eyes. "I know the risks, Mother. You have engraved them into my bones."

"And yet you would—"

"Don't you see that I must! Look what he did to you. He's never attacked you physically before, has he?"

"No."

"He's out of control, and you know as well as I do that I'm the only one who can stop him."

They were both weeping now, soft in each other's arms. And yet just below the surface a steely resolve would not be denied.

"He wants you to come after him, Conny. It's why he waited to take the gold rood until he knew you were nearby. He discovered its hiding place some time ago. Now that you've come of age, he knows what you can do. He means to destroy you."

"I won't give him the chance."

"No, Conrad!" For the first time in living memory, in extremis, she called him by his proper name. "I forbid it!"

"This is what I was meant to do."

"What?" Tears streamed down her face, and she was the more beautiful for them. "Sacrifice yourself?"

"If that's what is needed to exterminate him, then yes, I'm ready for that."

"And if he kills you. If he is victorious. If he remains alive?"

Conrad smiled through his tears. "I won't contemplate such questions." He broke away from her, perhaps for the last time; he couldn't know. "They won't require answers because they don't exist."

"Then take this." She placed something cold and hard in his palm, carefully closed his fingers around it. "God bless you here and now, because God cannot help you when you cross over."

# 21

**THEY ARRIVED BACK AT THE CASTLE RUINS AT SUNSET, JUST** as Bravo wanted. This time he came prepared.

When Ayla asked him why they had come at this particular time rather than at, say, sunrise, Bravo tapped his ear.

"I want to hear the wind through the stones," he said. "I want to hear Conrad's voice."

Hands on hips, Ayla said, "Do you really think he'll talk to us?"

"He did before," Elias pointed out as he pulled gear from one of the two duffels they had carried from the Jeep they hired. "I have no doubt he'll speak again."

"But why here?" Ayla asked. "For centuries this has been the Knights' main stronghold." She gestured. "And now there's nothing here but charred and tumbled stones."

"It's not what we can see," Bravo told her. "It's what we can't see."

"More riddles? I'm tired of riddles."

"Then you're with the wrong people." Bravo accepted an LED flashlight from Elias. "Riddles are my stock-in-trade."

"Okay. I get that." She reached for another flashlight the boy held out to her. "But I still get the feeling there's something you're not telling me."

Bravo nodded. "Last year, I thought I had found the way to remove a Fallen without harming the human host, but clearly I was wrong. With Emma's life hanging in the balance, I can't afford to be wrong again."

"And you think we'll find the answer here?"

"*Et ignis ibi est!*" Let there be light! Bravo cried, and Elias set about building a fire.

Bravo unzipped the second duffel, laid out the shovels, pickaxes, and other earth-moving tools they had brought. "Conrad is here because of what's been under the castle for far longer than the Knights' reign."

Ayla glanced down. "Hence the picks and shovels."

"That's right."

Elias had gotten the fire going. Flames leapt up, licking the evening air, sparks dancing above their tips.

"*Et ignis ibi est!*" the boy called, leaping as joyfully as the flames.

Bravo laughed. "Well done, Elias!"

"Are we ready to dig?" the boy asked as he approached Bravo.

"How are we going to know . . . ?" Ayla began, and then, as Bravo looked at her, her eyes widened. "Ah, my father is going to tell us."

"Though it might sound crazy, that is my hope." Bravo sat down on a stone.

"Two years ago I would have thought it crazy." Ayla sat down beside him. "Not now."

The sky was darkening, sunset's fire already failing, oranges and yellows turning to cobalt. Not far away, the light-streaked Mediterranean was turning black. Insects whirred and whistled; moths self-immolated, brought by the light, caught in the flames.

Night was coming.

"Listen, listen!" Elias called to them excitedly. "The wind is rising."

And so it was. Clouds raced above their heads, only to be torn to shreds by the increasingly violent gusts. The wind distorted the writhing tips of the flames, pushed them farther toward the center of the ruined castle. Sparks leapt after them, like hunting dogs loosed on the scent. The flames bent to the will of the wind, scoured the top of what was left of the great room wall, now only waist high.

*Ecce!* the wind cried. Behold!

The three of them ran to where the flames had scorched the rocks and now had drawn back as the wind changed direction. On the top of the stone, the fire had etched two letters: *W C.*

"What the hell does that mean?" Ayla said, hands on hips. It was becoming clear that her encounter with evil had left a residue of brittle impatience.

"The water closet!" Elias shouted. "But there are so many here. Which one—"

"None of them." Bravo's finger traced the letters. "This doesn't mean 'water closet.' It means 'wine cellar.'" He turned to Elias. "Do you know where it is?"

The boy nodded and, grinning hugely, windmilled his arm. "This way! Follow me!"

Within the jumbled labyrinth of the castle the staircase down to the wine cellar was completely blocked by a stone fall of mammoth proportions. Luckily, Elias, having had months to explore every nook and cranny of the place, knew an alternate route.

He took them down what seemed to be a winding servants' staircase, so narrow they had to proceed in single file, so damaged they had to move slowly and carefully over rubble and treads that had been ripped away from the staircase as if by a giant hand. Near the top, the odor of the fire was almost overwhelming, and this spoke to Bravo of the occult nature of the attack on the castle, for after a year the smell of a fire would be long gone.

They proceeded in this way until the fire stink had been left behind. The scent of dry rot now came to them, along with the odor of small rodents nesting and foraging. Tiny ruby eyes followed them during the last section of their descent. Little squeaks and scurryings preceded their arrival in the cellar. Even here, evidence of the ferocious fire was strewn across the stone-block floor: sprays of charcoaled beams, metal twisted into bizarre shapes or melted down altogether.

"This way!" Elias called as he sprinted, leaping over the fallen beams and structural braces.

The enormous stone fall was off to their right, and so complete was the damage if they hadn't known there had been a staircase there they never would have suspected it. The wine cellar, a huge stone edifice in the middle of the cellar itself, was directly ahead of them as they picked their way, following the boy's lead. An odd thing about the overall cellar, as Bravo played the beam of his flashlight around, was that it seemed distinctly smaller than he would have imagined.

Now he and Ayla met up with Elias at the entrance to the wine cellar. It was, in fact, a cave, as the French knew all wine cellars ought to be. There was a temperature gauge to their left, which was now of course useless, given the electricity had been off for more than a year.

The interior was composed of seven freestanding walls of shelves, each separated by spaces wide enough for an adult to walk down. Bravo went down the rows, here and there pulling a bottle halfway out, randomly taking stock of the crus and the years of bottling. Pretty impressive stuff, he determined. No surprise there.

But what was a surprise was that he found something different in the fourth—the center—row. For one thing, the wines were from vineyards he'd never heard of. For another, unlike the other rows of shelves, there seemed to be no order to how the bottles here were stored. It was as if no one cared about the wine in this row.

And then he discovered something else: a bottle that would not be pulled out more than halfway. Eight more bottles surrounding it were similarly fake. He looked at all nine, pulled out halfway. He pushed them in, using different configurations, all to no avail. Then he took a step back, trying to survey them in a different light. Interesting. They reminded him of the stops on a church organ. That's when he made a musical chord of thirds by pushing certain bottles back in.

With a grinding of stone against wood, the left side of the shelf-wall slid backward, revealing another stairway, narrower and far steeper than the one Elias had led them down to this level.

"Where does this lead, d'you think?" Ayla said.

Bravo turned to her. "Ready to find out?"

She nodded, and began to follow him down into the darkling depths below the cellar. But partway down, she stopped. "Wait. Where's Elias?"

"Elias won't be coming with us." Bravo said.

"Why not? He's come this far. He deserves—"

She stopped as Bravo showed her the bronze rood in the palm of his hand.

Ayla shook her head. "Did he give that to you?"

"In a sense." He looked her squarely in the eye. "Elias never existed."

"What?"

"At least not in the way you think."

"Have you lost your mind? That boy saved your life."

"Yes. In ways a human—child or adult—could not."

She shook her head. "I don't understand."

"Elias had served his purpose. He saved me, healed me, brought us to the brink of the revelation waiting for us below."

"Wait a minute. You know what's down there?"

"I've known from the moment it became clear to me what Elias was."

Ayla looked at him askance. "And what was he?"

"Elias told me he was brought here by a voice, that the voice told him where to find this crucifix. He said he dreamed of the apple tree where we buried Conrad, that Conrad plucked an apple from the tree and bade him eat it."

"Conrad's spirit was somehow guiding him."

"That's true," Bravo said. "But you haven't taken the idea far enough. Elias *was* Conrad."

"What?"

"Or, more accurately, I suspect, a manifestation of Conrad."

"But how?"

"Again I suspect *this*." He tapped the rood with the forefinger of his other hand. "This bronze rood is special. He's channeled himself through it. Because it has kept him alive."

"But he died; he was buried."

"We buried his *body*, Ayla. My grandfather—your father—had already left that dead husk."

"And you know this because of this rood?"

"We're here now, aren't we? You'll agree we wouldn't be if it wasn't for this."

"Yes, but—"

"I wouldn't be alive now, either."

He recommended their descent, but Ayla stopped him.

"I have to be sure," she said, turning and sprinting up the staircase.

Bravo waited patiently, feeling the warmth of the bronze rood in his hand. Was he imagining the faint whiff of apples? Ten minutes later, Ayla came back down to where he stood.

"Well," he said, "did you find Elias?"

"There's no sign of him." Her eyes were half-glazed in awe and wonder. "It's as if he never was there."

Bravo waited a beat, knowing how disoriented she must be. Then he said, "Are you ready now?"

Her eyes cleared. "You're still not telling me everything, are you?"

"When we get to the bottom of this staircase, you'll know what I know," he said. "I promise."

"I don't believe you," she said as they began again to descend, "but that's all right. I know you'll tell me what I need to know."

He laughed. "And not a word more?"

"That's my thought. Yes."

He nodded, keeping an eye out as his beam of light swept back and forth in front of them. "Well, you're learning."

# 22

**ST. PETER'S BASILICA WAS AS CROWDED AS THE ROMAN FORUM.**
Bursting with visitors from the four corners of the world, it was an ocean
of jostling tourists, guides, and hucksters all doing what they did best.
Selfies abounded but, thank God, no selfie sticks allowed, thought
Obarton as his corpulent frame was tossed about like a boat in choppy
seas. Faces blurred in and out of his vision field as he craned his neck,
searching for the man he was meant to meet at this appointed hour.

At last, he saw him. Felix Duchamp, tall, lean, saturnine, slipped
through the throng as easily as an eel around coral arms. But then he was
a cardinal, and those not too busy looking at themselves with the basilica
as background gave way to him as if they were vassals paying deference to
their liege lord.

"Monsieur Obarton," Duchamp said, *"alors bon de vous revoir, mon cher
ami." Good to see you again, my dear friend.*

There was, of course, no need for him to speak in French, other than
to assume the dominant position. For an instant, Obarton was of two
minds as to what language to use in reply.

*"Et tu, comme toujours." And you, as always.* He employed the familiar
form *tu*, as opposed to the formal *vous* the cardinal had used. Épées had
been engaged.

Duchamp lifted one hand, and they set off together, winding their way
to the rear of the basilica. Using a key hung around his neck beside his
pectoral cross, the cardinal opened a door flush with the wall.

As he pushed it open, Obarton heard his name being called, or thought
he heard it, and turned back. A group of young students was passing by,
led by their teacher who, pointing upward, was discussing something about

the history of the basilica. The students' gazes followed their teacher's pointing finger—all apart from one. This particular boy was staring directly at Obarton. A small smile appeared to lift the corners of his mouth as Obarton's eyes engaged with his, as if he knew Obarton. But Obarton was quite certain that he had never seen the boy before.

Or had he? Into his mind popped an image of the vitrine in which the baby floated. The eyes looked identical, didn't they? And the cheeks, the particular bow of the mouth? And then in the blink of an eye, the boy vanished. In his place stood the huge creature that had been projected for Lilith's benefit. Was it real? How could it be? No one else was reacting to it.

Obarton closed his eyes and, as if in a dream, slowly opened them again. There was the Archangel Dagon. As Obarton stared, mesmerized, the horn popped out of the center of its forehead, curved like a scimitar. And then its jaws gaped open revealing multi-tiered teeth. Talons gleamed dully as it lunged forward to engulf Obarton in its hideous embrace.

Obarton cried out and, as Duchamp asked him what the matter was, he stumbled backward into the cardinal, sending them both across the lintel, into the private holy spaces behind. But wasn't all of St. Peter's, all of Vatican City, a holy space? How could one of Lucifer's legion set foot here?

"What is it? What's happened?" Cardinal Duchamp dragged Obarton into the warm circle of lamplight in the small anteroom. "God in Heaven, all the blood has drained from your face!" Propping the big man against a wall, Duchamp brought a wooden chair with a brocaded seat and back, pushed his guest down onto it.

"Monsieur, are you ill? Shall I call a doctor?"

Obarton shook his head emphatically enough that Duchamp abandoned that idea and moved on to plan B. He jerked on a bellpull and when a priest appeared, the cardinal called for a bottle of mineral water and a carafe of strong coffee.

"Now what on earth . . . ?"

Obarton shook his head. For the moment, mute, he leaned back against the chair, which creaked in protest.

Duchamp took Obarton's hands in his. "Like ice." He shook his head. "Like ice, monsieur."

The priest returned with the requested items on an oval tray. He poured two glasses full of mineral water, sloshed coffee into a pair of porcelain cups, then withdrew, a worried look on his face.

Without asking, the cardinal spooned two heaping teaspoons of sugar into his guest's cup, stirred, then held it out to Obarton. "Two hands," he murmured helpfully.

Obarton felt as if every organ in his body had had the life squeezed out of it. He was quite out of breath and found it difficult to reoxygenate himself. But the strong coffee, and especially the sugar, helped restore some human warmth and, therefore, a semblance of normality to him. Still, he was aghast at his trembling hands. He gulped more coffee, burning his tongue and mouth, then set the cup down as fast as he could, and folded one shaking hand over the other.

Duchamp offered him a glass of water, but Obarton shook his head in refusal. He was trying to ignore the galloping of his heart. The blood pulsing behind his eyes dizzied him badly, as if he were at the railing of a storm-tossed ship.

"Now," Duchamp said at last. "Are you feeling better, monsieur? No need for a doctor, I take it."

"None . . ." His voice sounded so weak that Obarton was obliged to clear his throat, start again. "You're very kind."

"Not at all." Duchamp waved away his words. "So what was it, did you see a ghost?" He chuckled at his little joke.

Obarton smiled weakly, tried out a chuckle himself. It sounded like the crack of dead twigs. "I'm here, Felix, to discuss Lilith Swan."

"Ah, la belle Lilith." Duchamp took up his coffee and sipped it. He affected the annoying habit of lifting his pinkie on the hand holding the cup. "What shall we say about her?"

"For one thing, she never should have come to see you."

Cardinal Duchamp's eyebrow rose as high as his pinkie. "And the other thing?"

"The other thing rests upon what punishment is meted out for her flouting the rules of the Knights of St.—"

"Spare me." Duchamp returned his cup to its saucer. "With all due respect, monsieur, I am pleased to interview any member of your Order."

"As long as she has long legs and a nice pair of tits."

The cardinal regarded Obarton for some time from beneath suddenly heavy lids. "I will excuse your crassness on the grounds of your sudden deathly pallor and its aftermath. It would disappoint me greatly if I needed to remind you that you are in a house of God, that the Holy See is only steps away."

"My most sincere apologies, Cardinal," Obarton murmured, though nothing could be further from the truth. This hypocrite nauseated him as if he were a creature emerging out of an outhouse. "As you have noted, I am not myself at the moment." You could say that again, he thought. But there was no way he was going to tell Duchamp what had happened—or what he had *thought* happened. Frankly, he didn't understand it himself; he was still shaken to his core by the sight of a Fallen Archangel seeking him. It was a nightmare any way you sliced or diced it.

Cardinal Duchamp leaned forward, the tips of his fingers pressing against one another. "But my dear fellow, you must tell me what happened. Think of me as your confessor."

Obarton looked at him; then something erupted inside him. "I need a moment," he said, rising.

"Of course. The W.C. is—"

Obarton waved away his words. "I know where it is, Cardinal." Exiting the anteroom, he lumbered down the hallway to the second door on his left, marked "Signori." Hauling open the door, he hurried to one of the stalls, made it just in time to empty his rebellious guts into the bowl. Even after he was emptied out he continued retching until all he brought up was bile, black and bitter.

He moaned like a cow giving birth. He hadn't vomited since he was eleven, when the parish priest broke off teaching him the catechism to touch him most inappropriately. He had borne it stoically, then had run off to the loo, where he puked up his breakfast and, it seemed to him, the least digestible bits of dinner from the night before. Sweating then, sweating now. Splashing water on his face then, splashing water on his face now. Rinsing out his mouth again and again then and now. However, now he almost gagged on the water; then he had returned to the priest for more.

"Ah, feeling better, by the looks of you," Duchamp said. He had never left his seat, it seemed. He was drinking a second cup of coffee. Apparently, in Obarton's absence he had ordered a plate of digestive biscuits. He bit into one now, offered what was left on the plate to Obarton as he reseated himself.

Obarton's stomach turned over, and he stifled a groan. "Thank you, no." He managed to curl the edges of his mouth up in a paper-thin mockery of a smile. "I'm watching my weight."

"There's your problem right there," the cardinal observed coolly. "Blood sugar drop will make anyone woozy." He set down the plate. "My advice, five small meals a day, no sugar. You'll be right as rain in no time." He finished off his coffee, set down the cup. "In fact, I think you should get yourself a meal as soon as possible. I know a wonderful little trattoria not far from—"

"Lilith Swan." Obarton interrupted Duchamp's attempt to bury the topic. "I came to speak with you about her."

"So you did." Duchamp regarded him for a moment. "But may I say that I cannot for the life of me understand why this required a visit."

No, you may not, you maggot, Obarton projected silently through his smile. "Consider this a courtesy call. I wanted to tell you personally that so far as the Circle Council is concerned she's skating on very thin ice."

The cardinal's shoulders lifted and fell. "Why should that concern me?"

"Hmm. Let me give this a thorough think." Obarton poured himself another cup of coffee, sans sugar this time. He drank half of it before he plunged in the knife. "I imagine it could be due to your rather, uh, intimate relationship with Ms. Swan."

Duchamp's eyes opened wide, his mouth turned down in distaste. "Mon cher Monsieur—"

"Don't 'My dear sir' me, Felix. How long has the whore been giving you blow jobs?"

"How dare you!" Cardinal Duchamp's eyes glittered coldly.

"Did I get it wrong?" A malevolent smile. "Is it boys you crave?"

"I must insist that you leave my presence this instant."

"As you wish."

"It is more than a wish, I assure you." Cold as ice.

Obarton finished his coffee, clattered the cup into its saucer, then rose. He had taken two or three steps toward the door before turning on his heel. "Oh, by the way, I've seen the photos."

Naturally, Duchamp called him back before he reached the doorway. Obarton, turning again, said, "Yes, Cardinal?"

"What photos? There can be no photos of an event that never occurred."

Obarton extracted his mobile, scrolled through his downloaded pictures, and showed the cardinal the three choice photos Highstreet had agreed to send him.

For some time, Duchamp said nothing. A vein was pulsing in the center of his forehead; it looked like at any moment it would detonate. Then he began to laugh. Obarton had never seen him laugh before, it wasn't a pleasant sight for him.

"You find these damning photos amusing, do you? Suppose I show them to your peers in the College of Cardinals?"

"Please." Duchamp's hand swept outward toward the door. "Be my guest. Assuming, that is, you want to be made a fool." Stepping forward, he pointed at the first photo. "The lighting's all wrong, do you see? Two photos put together—what do they call it, photoshopping, I believe. The others, the same, more or less. No one studying these under a magnifier would credit them." He nodded. "I don't know where you got these fakes, Monsieur Obarton, but be so good as to take them with you. They are offensive enough, but what you have attempted is a cardinal sin."

He waved a hand dismissively. "Out with you now."

And as he left, Obarton thought savagely, That fucking Lilith, born before Eve, a reflection of Satan.

# 23

"YOU KILLED THAT JACKAL, DIDN'T YOU?" LILITH SAID. "YOU eviscerated it."

Emma regarded her from the lip of the cave they had come upon after they'd passed the spot where the cataract spilled over the stone bridge. "Would it matter if I did?"

"Only if you lied to me."

When Emma failed to respond, Lilith took her hand, turned it so the bit of shattered bloody bone under her nail was clearly visible. "Why did you do it?"

"Because it was there."

"That's it? That's the reason?"

"What other reason could there be?"

"I don't know. Self-defense."

Emma laughed softly.

Lilith's brows knit together. That laugh alerted her again that she might have gotten herself into a situation far, far beyond her understanding. "Why did you bring me here?"

"You wanted me to, didn't you?"

"Yes, I did."

That small, inscrutable half smile. "Also, I wanted you with me."

"But why?"

Emma stepped from the twilight of the cave mouth into the sun-and-water-sparkled air. As if it were a python, she slid her arm around Lilith's waist. "You know why." Her fingertips settled on the small of Lilith's back. "It was clear the moment you sat down at my table at the café."

Lilith felt the pressure of those fingers, that hand, the strong muscles of that arm drawing her close enough to feel Emma's body heat.

"Don't you?" Emma's smile broadened. "Don't you know why?"

Her lips brushing Lilith's cheek was like an electric shock, and with a tiny whimper Lilith's body clove to hers. When their mouths came together, Lilith was sure she tasted blood on Emma's tongue, a scrim on her canines. But instead of repelling her, the taste ignited her lust. Her mind felt as if it were expanding, exploding as it became one with her body's needs.

Together they stumbled backward, then fell one atop the other amid the slippery rock and the rainbow spray of the cataract. There was no sound but one sound; there was no taste but one taste, no smell but one smell; there was no sensation but one sensation. There was no God but the one that existed at the point of their mutual dissolution.

And yet, in the midst of her ecstasy, a tiny part of Lilith's mind experienced a pain such as she had never before encountered. Instinctively, she knew that if that pain spread to the rest of her mind it would kill her. And so, deep in her lover's warm, moist embrace, she felt a malign presence invade her, as if something she could not quite sense, let alone see, was raiding her thoughts, scraping away at her mind.

And then in the span of one terrible heartbeat, Emma's tongue reached the core of her and she was drowning in a flood of bliss.

Heartbeat like the ticktock of a cosmic clock. Pulse beating a tattoo behind her eyes. Lips, nipples, genitals swollen and slightly sore: a magnificent agony.

She sighed into Emma's mouth and so quickly afterward she could not be sure it actually happened her awareness irised open and she sensed the duality inside Emma. She felt Emma, but she also felt the source of the thing that had begun to tear at her. And for that micro-instant her magnificent agony morphed into real pain.

She cried out, and, pulling away from her lover, looked at her as if she had never seen her before.

"What is it?" Emma breathed. "What's happened?"

"You know." Lilith shook her head from side to side, confused and, abruptly, afraid. "Both of you know."

At that moment, an unnatural silence fell upon them as if from a great height. Neither birds nor insects could be heard calling or whirring. No flying squirrels leapt from branch to branch in the forest beyond the cataract. And, strangest of all, the roar of the waterfall seemed greatly diminished, as if they had been removed from proximity to it, even though its crystalline spray continued to moisten their flesh, mingling with their own sweat.

Emma's head rose, then held still as a hunting dog on point. "Put your clothes back on," she said in a hushed, throaty voice, deeper than before—far deeper. Was it Emma's voice at all? "Hurry! Quickly now!"

Hearing the barely throttled fear in her voice, Lilith said, "I'm not afraid."

"Don't be a fool!" Emma drew on her shorts, slipped into her shirt. "You don't know. Do as I say now."

Lilith complied, dragging on her clothes as quickly as she could. No sooner had the two women finished dressing than a stirring came to them from inside the cave.

"Behind me." Emma grabbed Lilith, pushed her into position. "Whatever happens stay behind me."

Lilith tried to peer over Emma's shoulder. "What's going to happen?"

"Hush, now, beloved. Hush!"

That one word "beloved" drove to Lilith's core, turned her knees weak so that for a moment she was obliged to hold on to Emma's waist to keep herself from sliding to the glistening rock face.

Now it was coming. Whatever *it* was. A stirring of the shadows within the cave, as if the atmosphere had become a turbulent sea, muddied with detritus, bottom feeders, diminutive nighttime predators tossed this way and that by the passage of a colossal and terrifying presence.

The squadron of flies appeared first, like outriders, then the horn, curved and pointed, like a herald. And then Leviathan appeared, in all his hideous glory: red as the dying sun, great cloven hooves crawling with things best left to the darkness. One set of wings unfurled like sails, the other two folded closely around his torso like the winter cloak of an Englishman of the 1800s.

"So." Voice like a rasp over metal. "What have we here?"

"The human Lilith Swan," Emma said in that voice both deeper and rougher than that of Lilith's lover.

"I have eyes, do I not?" Leviathan fairly bellowed. "Beleth, you are a Power, a warrior of the Second Sphere. What are you doing with this *female human?*"

The thing said these last two words as if they were anathema to him, as if Lilith were a creature so far beneath him he could not fathom what Emma was doing in her company.

"Leviathan," Emma said in that same strange voice, "this female human is a member of the Knights of St. Clement of the Holy Land."

"Impossible!" Leviathan roared. "The Knights do not allow *females* in their midst. Quite rightly, I might add."

"A new wrinkle," Emma said. "Call it an experiment, if you like."

When Leviathan laughed, even the small awful things squirming around his hooves cowered and tried to burrow into the cave floor. "I don't like you, Beleth, and I like even less your proximity to a *female human.*"

"Ah, but not just any female human. This one will give Emma Shaw access to the inner workings of the Knights' Circle Council."

Lilith felt as if she were losing her grip on her sanity. Struggling to make sense of the conversation, which was almost as bizarre as the scene itself, she racked her memory. Wasn't Leviathan a Seraph, allegedly one of Lucifer's Fallen? And if that was, indeed, Leviathan filling the cave mouth then what Obarton had told her about the Fallen was the truth: they did exist; they did have designs on humans. But none of this could really be happening, could it? Emma had fed her water from her canteen on the way up. What if that water contained a powerful psychedelic, a hallucinogen that Emma was using to break her down? What if nothing since she had taken that drink was real? What if they were both still down below, what if she was on the point of death?

"Why should we care about either the Knights or the Circle Council?"

But, then again, she was close enough to Emma to feel her trembling, and putting her palm against Emma, could feel the racing of her pulse. Was that also part of the hallucination?

And then she heard Emma say in that odd voice she had adopted, "The moment the Knights become aware of us they will move Heaven and earth to stop us."

"Heh! But they can't, the insects," Leviathan said. "They have no Shaws among their midst. It's only the Shaws who hold any danger for us."

And Lilith found herself thinking, Why? What's so special about the Shaws that the Fallen should fear them? And in that moment she realized that she wasn't insane, that she was facing a new reality, that the Fallen did, indeed, exist, that she was in the presence of one of them—a very powerful one, a Fallen Seraph, if the literature on this arcane and, to most in the Church, shunned topic, was accurate. It occurred to her, parenthetically, that the Gnostic Observatines were in a far better position to judge the truth about the existence and nature of the Fallen.

Without conscious control, her hands went to either side of her head, as if to keep her exploding thoughts under control. But of course that was a fool's errand. Emma had led her to the far side of the world, and now they had taken that last step. No compasses here, no GPS coordinates. To paraphrase Captain Barbossa, You're off the edge of the map, girl. Here there be the Fallen.

Leviathan took a step toward them. "This *female human* is of no use to either of us. She will not further our cause. Quite the opposite, I may state without fear of contradiction. Toss her. Let the cataract break her bones. Let the carrion eaters feast on what's left."

"No," Emma said.

"What?" Leviathan blinked heavily; flies buzzed around his lips, affected by his sudden agitation. "What did you say?"

"Lilith is under my protection."

Leviathan drew himself up to his full towering height. "Who gave you, a Power, permission to gainsay a Seraph of the First Sphere?"

"The assignment you yourself gave me," Emma said. "I risked everything, almost being destroyed by the blue fire. Have you ever come so close to the blue fire of Heaven, Leviathan? No, I thought not. Now here I am in Emma Shaw's corpus. You need her; we need her."

Leviathan was livid with rage. "I'll suck you out of there, Beleth, and down into the deepest pits of Hell, there to rot while we execute our long-awaited revolution, while we free Heaven from the tyranny of God."

"No, you won't." Emma stood her ground. "The moment you extract me Emma Shaw will die, and then where will we be. She is the one and only key to finding and turning her brother to our cause. Think of it, Leviathan! A Shaw moving with us! And not just any Shaw! No, even with all your power, you will not move against me. You will not jeopardize the revolution because of petty jealousy."

"Jealousy?" Leviathan laughed again, and now even the flies kept their distance, shuddering. "Seraphs don't feel jealousy; that is a human emotion."

"With all due respect, Seraph. Jealousy is a sin, and what are we made of if not a patchwork of sins? Without sin would we even exist?"

Leviathan's fangs gleamed darkly. "Without sin you can be sure that humans wouldn't exist, Power."

"By your logic, that makes us closer to humans than to angels, Leviathan. Are you sure you want to continue down that path?"

"Bah! Whatever path you think you're on, stick to it. Fuck the *female human* then. If that is the price I must pay in order to have Braverman Shaw then so be it." His claw bit through the thick air. "But understand—this hasn't ended. Between you and me there will come a reckoning."

"I look forward to it, Seraph. In the meantime, allow me to do my job. Leave us in peace."

"Ah, Beleth, you are a fool." Leviathan snapped his jaws shut, terrifying the squadron of flies that circled him like a halo. "Peace is something we are destined never to know."

# 24

WHEN DIANTHA RETURNED TO THE CHAMBER ABOVE, WHERE the Sphinx crouched in stony silence, she saw her son's friend the great poet W. B. Yeats, whom she knew both by reputation and from reading his stirring works.

Yeats was perched on the edge of a plinth, writing in a calfskin notebook with a pencil. Around him, he had lit a number of tapers, used in secret liturgy in decades past. Every so often he would pause, gaze up at the great Sphinx as if for inspiration. As for the creature itself, it looked for all the world as if it was a willing subject posing for a master artist.

Perhaps that was precisely what it was, for as she approached Yeats she asked him what he was writing. He told her it was an epic poem that had come to him by being in close proximity to the Sphinx, an occult being who had at one time moved against Gideon, at her son's bidding, but which seemed to neither frighten nor intimidate the intrepid poet.

"I've named the work 'The Second Coming,'" Yeats said. "It incorporates a number of my philosophical and occult theories, which had never come together until I was in the presence of this Sphinx."

"Where is Conrad's other friend, Ibrahim?" The one my husband shot to death.

"He was taken," Yeats said, crossing out a line, then inserting a replacement.

"Taken? By whom?"

"Well, that would depend." Yeats paused in his writing, looked at her fully for the first time.

"On what, precisely?"

"On who you are. My name is William Butler Yeats."

"Yes, I know. I've enjoyed many of your poems."

"Thank you, madam. And you are?"

"Diantha Safita. I'm Conrad's mother."

Now Yeats appeared puzzled. "Your surname isn't Shaw?"

"Safita is a Phoenician name," she said by way of answer. "Please tell me what happened to Ibrahim."

"Ah, yes. Poor fellow. It seems his grandfather took him."

"Ibrahim's grandfather is dead," Diantha said.

"Ibrahim, as well," Yeats said, putting the notebook with the partly written "The Second Coming" aside. "Diantha, I want to help."

Diantha closed with him. "Keep writing, poet; there's work for everyone here. That is yours; no one else can do it." She took his notebook and pencil, laid them on his lap. "My son brought you here for a reason. We are all of us about to step onto the knife-edge."

IT MIGHT have been a horse, but only in some twisted nightmare. The Orus seemed destined for war. Moreover, it looked to be the work of a lunatic. And perhaps it was, for incised into its muscular chest was the Nihil, the sigil of the Unholy Trinity.

Conrad knew that he had this one last moment to turn back, to save himself. But what would that say about him? How could he allow Gideon to continue to gain power? He was Nephilim, the child of the unholy miscegenation between a human female—Conrad's grandmother Chynna Shaw—and a Fallen Archangel. Could there be anything more horrific? Chynna was put under a spell, and therefore raped. She had no will, no say in what happened after the Fallen one chose her. She opened her heart and her legs to it and was destroyed in the process. Though outwardly she was as strong and clever and sane as ever, her soul—her innermost core—had been hollowed out. She was never the same again, never the person she had been before the advent of the Fallen.

No. There was no question of turning back, no question of not opposing his father, for if he didn't no one could, not even Diantha. Her powers were of a different genus and species altogether. Just like the Orus, holding him in its sightless gaze.

He knew what the sigil meant; he knew what was waiting for him, though not the order of magnitude. But this was the only chance to stop Gideon from gaining enough dark power to bring the rest of the Fallen—

the Legion—through the portal into this world. Gideon wanted nothing less than to stand at Lucifer's right hand when he reclaimed all that God had taken from him.

Approaching the Orus, Conrad reached out his left hand and, with only a slight faintness to herald his action, pressed his palm to the sigil. At once, he felt the metal melt, and he pushed into it, through the skin and metal flesh of the Orus. Past nonexistent bones, into the hollow core of it.

Except that it wasn't hollow—not entirely. The inside was a prison for a cadre of Fallen—an advance guard that had been trapped, set in place by a higher order of power than even Gideon, though he had been here before, could not name.

Four Thrones: Murmur, Raum, Phenex, Verrine, all of the First Sphere. All evil, all hungry for power, and therefore incalculably dangerous. Anticipating what awaited him, Conrad felt an electric jolt, and, with that, the Transposition began.

It wasn't until the Throne was completely inside him that he knew its name. *Phenex*, he said in his mind, *welcome to the world of humans.*

*What is this?* Phenex cried. *To go from one prison to another is no life for a Throne!*

*Your life was over before it began, Throne. You've picked the wrong side.*

*Being in a human's body was not my doing. It revolts me.*

*Who else was taken, Phenex? My father came here; my father took one of you Thrones. You all have different powers.*

*How do you know that, insect?*

*You are Scryer. If you try hard enough, you can see minutes into the future. Which one of the Thrones is missing?*

Thus began the internal war between Conrad and the Throne Phenex for supremacy. On the one hand, Diantha Safita had trained him hard and long, out of Gideon's sight and hearing, for just this possibility. On the other, this was real life, and Phenex proved slippery and dangerous as an electric eel. Each time Conrad, on the offensive, was sure he'd gotten ahold of the Throne, it would slither from his grasp and deal him a terrible psychic blow that rattled him so badly it was often difficult to string two thoughts together, let alone form and re-form his strategy, as the dimensions of the battlefield shifted from one world to another.

Conrad felt himself being beaten down, until even his reserves of energy were hemorrhaging badly. It was then he realized that his palm was still pressed against the Nihil. That this was why the worlds kept changing, why Phenex had had the upper hand from the beginning.

With a violent motion he stepped out of the Orus's chest and just like that the field of battle cleared, the mists in retreat, revealing his foe and, simultaneously, revealing his path to victory.

Without hesitation he took it, using every incantation his mother had made him memorize. And there they were: the bronze chains forming around Phenex keeping him controlled and quiescent.

"Now," Conrad said out loud. "Which one of you Thrones did Gideon take?"

*The insect took Verrine.*

Dear God, Conrad thought, he would take the worst one. Verrine was the leader of the Four Thrones of the First Sphere, and therefore the most powerful. His power was Bestiality. He was a notorious reaver.

"Where is he, Phenex? Where is Verrine?"

The Throne inside him moaned. *Too far away.*

*Which direction then?* Switching to the interior dialogue.

*Around the far side of the Orus, along its flank. That way. But you do not want to go that way.*

*I have no other choice.*

*I warn you, insect. Once you enter the Hollow Lands you can never escape.*

*Then we'll be prisoners together.*

He felt the shuddering inside himself. *You do not understand. Disaster . . . catastrophe . . . there are no other words! . . .*

Closing his mind to Phenex's imprecations, he lit out after Gideon, after the Throne Commander, Verrine, and he heard Death's mocking laughter all the way down the corridor, following him like a squadron of glittering flies.

# 25

"PEACE," LILITH SAID. "THE MORE OFTEN I SAY THAT WORD the more unintelligible it becomes."

There was a softening in Emma's eyes the moment Leviathan vanished back into the cave, as if their centers were caramel, warming in the forest sunlight.

"But I can only speak for myself," Lilith said.

"I know. But I can't remember a time . . ." Emma's words drifted off.

They were lying on the ledge, as they had been before the Seraph's visitation, save now they were clothed. The birds had returned, fluttering and calling to one another. A pair of flying squirrels eyed them suspiciously before taking wing. The daubs of sunlight had expanded, deepened. Insects hummed and whirred in these hot shafts, happy once again. The roaring of the cataract was like a symphony.

Emma was exhausted. Keeping the Testament at bay was wearing her down. She knew it was just a matter of time before her strength gave out and she would be lost forever in the eternal darkness of ultimate evil, but for now she refused to give in to despair. In the here and now, there was Beleth to deal with, and she concentrated on that problem. Her initial battle with the words of Lucifer had given it a glimpse behind the curtain she had drawn; now it knew she still existed, a willful resistance holding out against its incursion. She recognized its bewilderment that its takeover was not complete. She also knew that Beleth believed it was because of the power of the Testament. Of course. That conclusion was hardwired into its brain.

But now it was up to her to maintain a delicate balance. Deception was her brother's long suit; he'd been trained at it. But during her time of blindness she had listened carefully to how he dealt with people—his own people and others—in a way she could not have had she been sighted. She had heard and absorbed the soft subtleties, the tones of voice, the indefinite shades he used to maneuver his way to getting what he wanted. And so, though deception had come to her in a different manner, though she was still her brother's acolyte in this, her powers of deception were formidable.

Case in point: she had used the slender thread of her connection with her body to lure Lilith, to seduce her, in fact. She knew Beleth had no sex organs, suspected that it was curious as to what physical sex between humans was like. While Leviathan would no doubt view Beleth's curiosity as weakness, she herself saw it as a possible way out of her dilemma. She started out with the intention of co-opting Beleth just as the Fallen sought to co-opt Bravo. The seduction turned out to be twofold. Beleth was so entranced by the swirl of human emotion and hormones it allowed her her own voice, it allowed her temporary control of her body, swept away on the unknown tide, observing, feeling all that was unknown and forbidden to it.

But then a curious thing happened, an unintended consequence of the seduction that ran parallel with her plan: she liked Lilith. If she were to be completely honest, she found herself falling in love. This astonished her, almost put her off her path. But then the necessity of freeing herself came roaring back, stronger than ever. Beleth had unintentionally revealed to her just how much pain it was in, how it feared and detested Leviathan, how it longed to be freed from the wheel of agony it was forced to endure. Now she had her foundation set, she could go on. . . .

Lilith stared upward, but though her body lazed, her mind roiled. How to say what she wanted to say? She considered half a dozen ideas, dismissing them all in turn. Finally: "When I was a little girl," she began, "I didn't like who I was. Things were done to me. Terrible things. Betrayal at the hand of someone who was supposed to love and protect me. But I was just a little girl, you know. I felt ashamed, humiliated, tiny, helpless in the malevolent palm of the world."

She took a breath, wondered whether this was the right path, then erased doubt as counter-productive, went on. "Early mornings, when the sun was neither below the horizon nor above, when my nightly visitor was gone, I would lie in bed and think of myself as another person, a person who couldn't be touched by the world around me, a person utterly different than myself."

She waited a moment, breathing as deeply as she could muster given the heaviness in her chest, then said, "Do you know what I mean?"

For a time, there was silence between them. Then Emma stirred. "I never wanted what's happened to me."

It was not a direct answer, but it was the answer Lilith was hoping for. "God knows, neither did I." She held her breath.

"I never wanted—" Emma stopped short.

A wild look came into her eyes, which brought Lilith up on one elbow, an arm across Emma's shoulder.

"I know," she said.

Emma's eyes opened wide. "You do?"

"How could I not feel it? Whatever is inside you—"

"Stop!" That harshness as Emma's voice deepened. Birdsong ended and, as abruptly, started up again. She tried to push Lilith away, but Lilith resisted. "Don't!" Emma cried. Her eyes had darkened, muddied with symbols. "I beg you."

Lilith felt as if she had been thrust into no-man's-land. To go forward or to retreat? What to do? All of a sudden she realized that this was not her decision; it was Emma's. She knew—*knew*—that Emma didn't want her to stop. But that thing inside her did.

And then another insight, this one even more startling: there was a war going on inside Emma, a terrible battle for possession of her soul. But, no, Lilith thought, that wasn't it at all. Her mind was running along the lines of traditional Church doctrine. The battle inside Emma was more immediate, more of the here and now. It was for control of her mind.

This is the moment, Lilith told herself. Either I'm in, or I'm out. If I retreat now I'll never get back in. Never. And she wanted in, more than she'd ever wanted anything. Even though the deep part of her that the thing had touched quailed at the thought, she held on, stared deep into Emma's eyes, forcing herself to see beyond their strangeness.

"You're not pushing me away, you who's inside. I'm not going anywhere." She felt Emma's fingers clutch at her flesh, the scrape of her nails along her skin, maybe even a couple of droplets of blood. "No, you can't make me. Emma doesn't want it. She doesn't want to push me away.

And you, who defended me against the Seraph, what do *you* want?" She felt Emma's grip tighten, didn't care. "Speak now! Speak for yourself."

And in Emma's eyes she could see that the insurgence had begun. She thrilled to the notion that she had been the spark, that she had drawn Emma—the real Emma—out of the shadow-prison in which she had been incarcerated.

"I am that I am," Beleth said, toeing the Fallen line.

"Not anymore," Lilith told it. "You're something else now. Something alien even to the Seraph."

"What am I then?" Beleth asked. Astonishingly, its voice carried the tonal hint of a child in distress.

"You're lost," Lilith said, emboldened by the change in Beleth's voice. "You understand that, don't you?"

Nothing more came out of Emma's mouth for a very long time. Lilith, still holding her lover, drew her knees up to her chin. A child's pose. That unconscious movement elicited a response from Emma.

"Lilith," she said in her own voice, "you're the enemy. What am I doing here with you?" A logical question; Lilith could hardly blame her for asking it.

Lilith had to assume that Beleth had withdrawn, at least temporarily, to consider its fate. "There is always an enemy. But now we have a common enemy to fight.

"I will admit that when I was sent here you were the enemy." She shook her head. "But something unimaginable happened when I saw you at the café." She was terrified of this; admissions were hardly her strong suit. Confession was anathema. And yet she found herself continuing, as if, having dived overboard, she was now being pulled down into unknown depths. "I have never loved anyone or anything in my life. Frankly, I thought I was incapable of love. I thought I wouldn't understand it, wouldn't want it. I considered love a fatal weakness."

Her hands moved against Emma's smooth flesh. "When I saw you everything I knew or thought I knew about love flew out the window. I wanted you, wanted to be with you, and nothing else mattered. For me, Knight and Observatine vanished off the face of the earth." She shrugged, a kind of protection against how vulnerable, how naked—really naked—she felt. "I can't explain it. I've racked my brains to come up with an answer. But now I think maybe I don't want to because there is no explanation for what I feel."

"You felt incapable of love," Emma said softly, "because of what happened to you. You feel unclean, unworthy of being loved."

Lilith heart fairly stopped in her chest. Her lungs constricted, and she felt overcome, as if with a high fever.

"I want an explanation." Emma's eyes had gone dark again, that sign swimming in their centers. Her body had stiffened, as if her blood and flesh had been replaced by crushed acrylic fibers.

Lilith had become somewhat used to her lover's occult schizophrenia but was nevertheless caught out by the darkness overriding the sunlight of their connection. She desperately wanted to continue her conversation with Emma. Did Emma love her, could she really love her? Lilith didn't know. Her face and neck flushed crimson.

But now she knew she had to concentrate on the Fallen that had taken possession of Emma. "An explanation for what, Beleth?"

"For what is happening here."

"Emma and I were talking. You interrupted—"

"No. I talk with Leviathan. This was not talking. It is something I do not understand."

A light went off in Lilith's head. She took Emma's hand, brought the palm to her lips, kissed it. "You mean this?"

"Yes," the Power said.

She took Emma's hand and pressed it against her breast. "And this?"

"That too." Beleth's voice had grown darker, rumbling like the thunder of the cataract.

Leaning forward, Lilith kissed Emma's half-opened lips. Their tongues touched. "And this," she said, reluctantly pulling away. She wanted to be kissing Emma's lips all day and all night.

"That most of all," Beleth said, its voice again holding the plaintive note of a lost child.

"It's love, Beleth."

Lilith stared at Emma in open astonishment. She had opened her mouth to answer, but Emma had beat her to it. More important, she had stilled the Power's voice in the middle of its interrogation of Lilith.

"Huh." The dark voice was back. " 'Love' is God's word." Its contempt was spit out like acid.

"Indeed," Lilith said.

"Ha, regard how it is used by the insects to charm each other, to deceive each other, to betray each other. We rejected God's false love millennia ago."

"I wonder why?" Lilith said. "All of you Fallen are experts at charm, at deceit, at betrayal. Those are your mother's milk."

"Love is a concept God created to lead his insects astray, to test them, to see if they could live up to his ideals. But you insects don't. You can't. No one can. God is God; nothing can live up to his laws and rules; he made sure of that." Beleth grunted, which sounded weird and unsettling coming out of Emma's mouth. "You see now what we have seen for untold millennia. God has betrayed everyone."

"Well, no wonder you're all so pissed off."

Lilith jerked at Emma's blasphemous comment. But then she saw a tiny flutter of Emma's right eyelid, like the hint of a wink, and she relaxed, got herself into the swing of things.

Then Emma grimaced as Beleth wrested back control. "Whatever you think you have here, Lilith, is an illusion. You are in the midst of an idyll, a daydream. Reality awaits, and I can guarantee it won't be rainbows and unicorns. I know you are already thinking about how you can oust me from this corpus. Believe me when I tell you, that is the last thing you want. If I Transposition into another insect corpus—yours, for instance—this one will die. Your precious Emma will be nothing more than a dried-up husk. She will not even be recognizable as an insect, let alone as Emma. There won't even be enough of her to weep over."

Emma's features relaxed for a moment, as Emma herself returned. "Beleth is right, Lilith. I've seen it happen to the woman it inhabited before me. Bravo thought we had found a way to exorcise the Fallen, but it was only temporary. Beleth was simply in hiding, invisible even to myself."

Emma's body twitched as the Power reasserted control. "Now that's settled—"

"What you haven't told us, what's so very important to you," Lilith broke in, "is that the instant you leave Emma's body you'll be vulnerable to Leviathan, who, if we're to judge by that recent encounter, dislikes and distrusts you."

"The feeling is mutual," Beleth sniffed.

"The difference being the Seraph is out to get you."

"I do not believe—"

"He will destroy you the moment your usefulness to him is finished. You know this, Beleth."

Emma seemed to have turned to stone.

Lilith cocked her head, one eyebrow raised. "And by the way, just what does he want from you?"

Nothing was forthcoming. The eyes were black again; Emma seemed deeply buried once more, bound and gagged in some horrific manner, all the progress she had made vanished. Lilith decided to take matters into her own hands. Quite literally. Cupping Emma's face with her hands, she kissed those lips she longed for. They were not as before. Instead, cold, metallic, unyielding, they resisted her advance, and she shuddered, recalling the touch of the beast on her inner core. And yet she would not be deterred, keeping her mouth on Emma's, slowly prying her lips open with her tongue. Beleth tried to say something. In response, she softened her lips more, twined her tongue more, let her heat seep into Emma's mouth—Beleth's mouth. So slowly it was like the progress of a praying mantis the lips under hers yielded, unfolded, softened like taffy, and she placed one of her hands at the nape of Emma's neck.

She broke away, Emma trying to follow her, to keep the connection. "You want this, Power. You need it." She caressed her twin lovers. "Love is irrational; love is desperation. You have experienced its power. Even God doesn't understand that; he believes love to be devotion. I did, too, for so long. Now I know the truth. Now you know the truth." She stared into Emma's black eyes. "So why are you here, Power? What did Leviathan send you to do?"

Emma tried to continue the kiss, but Lilith reared back. "Not until . . ."

"Bravo Shaw poses the greatest—the only—threat to our advance. I am to use this corpus to get close to him. I am to weaken him, to probe his mind, to bring him into our fold. To make him Fallen."

# 26

**"WHAT THE HELL—?"**

Ayla froze at the bottom of the staircase.

She turned to regard Bravo. "*Now* you're going to have to tell me—something."

When she had come to the end of the staircase Ayla was expecting a sub-basement of some kind. Instead, she found that they were standing at one end of what appeared to be a natural cavern. As Bravo's beam played over the walls it illuminated flashes of glittering light—reflections, she saw now, from a river flowing deep under the Knights' castle.

"What the hell is this?" She had regained enough of her composure to finish her original sentence.

"It's exactly what it looks like." Bravo led her forward. "A river."

"With water black as night. Where does it go?"

"Out to the sea. But that's not our destination."

"What is?"

"You'll find out soon enough."

"You're trying to drive me crazy, aren't you?"

He laughed. "No, no. But here, words are wholly inadequate." His fever had been vanquished; he was nearly back to his old self. "Only seeing is believing."

Much to her surprise there was a small rowboat waiting for them, tied to a metal cleat on the near bank. The boat was old but finely wrought of steam-treated wood, bound in iron; coats of varnish gleamed in the light. Bravo took the oars, bade her cast off, and then, using the end of one oar, pushed them away from shore. He rowed in slow, powerful strokes and they made good time, but in truth, this was as much to do with the swiftly flowing current as with his strength. Sitting on the bench behind him, Ayla found herself worrying not merely about what their destination could possibly be, but also about how they were going to get back.

Over her head she saw glimmers of light, like phantasms, and when she asked Bravo about them he told her they were evidence of lost light.

"You see it in tunnels sometimes. No one knows what it is or why it's there."

Time passed. In the semi-dark she had no idea how much. It could have been five minutes or five hours. Time seemed to have a different agenda here, though how that could be she was at a complete loss to say. The river itself wound gently. It lacked the rapids, rocks, bends, eddies, and snaking twists of most rivers. Once, she dipped her fingertips into the water, found its temperature disconcertingly warm, like that of blood. She jerked her hand up, as if stung. A river this far below the surface should have been icy.

At length, they emerged from the cavern into a deep river gorge. Eventually, Bravo guided the boat toward the far bank. Jumping out, he tied the rope to another cleat identical to the one at their point of embarkation. She picked her way over the mud of the low bank into a kind of marbled jumble of huge rock formations through which Bravo led her.

"You been here before?" she asked.

He shook his head. "Conrad drew a detailed map. He asked me to memorize it before he burned it."

"So you had more contact with him than you've told me."

"I've never told anyone how much time I spent with Conrad, not even my mother. It was a condition of our relationship."

"But now?"

"Now," he said, "you're here, and it's time."

The path before them, which had steadily risen in a gentle slope, now rose more steeply. At the same time, the rock formations, already feet above head height, rose up precipitously, their tops lost in the gloom that arched over them. Soon after, the rock-strewn path bent sharply to the right. Abruptly, it debouched onto a colossal high plateau.

Bravo aimed the beam from his flashlight at a massive block of shadow hulking at the center of the open space.

"Ayla," he said, taking her hand, leading her forward, "meet Phaedos, one of the Four Sphinxes of Dawn."

"**DID YOUR** mother ever tell you about Gideon?" Bravo asked her.

Ayla shook her head. She was staring upward at Phaedos's majestic, terrifying head. The eyes seemed to bore into her as if it were alive, waiting to be awakened from its ages-long slumber. She trembled a little in its presence.

"My guess is she didn't even mention his name."

"She didn't." Ayla felt herself to be in a kind of semi-trance. She felt as she had in the convent church outside Rome last year when everything she preferred not to remember happened as if in a nightmare. Had she fallen back into that time, that state? It seemed so to her.

"But you have heard of the Nephilim."

"I was brought up Muslim, remember. I never took courses in comparative religion."

"Right," Bravo said. "Well, according to the Catholic Church, the Nephilim are the spawn of human females and members of the Legion of the Fallen."

"What an education I'm getting from you." She frowned. "But I'm not quite understanding—"

"Angels are without genitals. In order to experience sex they would need to—"

"Ah, yes. I see. But what has this to do with the current situation?"

"Everything." Bravo was turning the bronze rood over and over. "Gideon was Conrad's father. Gideon's father was one of the Fallen."

Ayla's head turned to him so quickly he could hear the crack of her vertebrae. "What? What did you say?"

"Gideon—my great-grandfather, your grandfather—was Nephilim."

"Which explains our own powers."

"Partly, yes."

She frowned. "Only partly?"

Bravo laughed softly, but it was an odd kind of laugh, tinged with an emotion Ayla could not quite identify. "Gideon's wife, Diantha Safita, was something else altogether. She more than balanced Gideon out."

"She didn't go by the family name Shaw?"

"No. She kept her own name, just as she kept her own counsel. She only confided in the one child who lived, Conrad."

Ayla looked aghast. "There were others?"

"Her first two children were born dead. Gideon was shaken to his core, but she remained stoic. Only she understood why this had happened. The two dead babies were female."

Ayla shook her head. "I don't understand."

"The Nephilim are cursed," Bravo said. "I think that's what Conrad meant when he told me he had sinned. It wasn't his sin—it was his father's. In any event, daughters of the Nephilim are doomed to death before life. Only the males have a chance at survival, and then the result is far from certain."

"So Conrad might also have been born dead."

"No. There was no chance of that. Diantha saw to it."

"You said there was something different about her."

"Yes, but I don't really know much. She was of Phoenician ancestry. That was why she kept her family name, Safita, which infuriated Gideon. But then many things infuriated him." The rood kept turning, turning as if it were marking the peculiar time here.

"Over the years I did some digging on my own. The Safita lineage is a long and illustrious one. They were kings, and sometimes queens, great generals and admirals of the vaunted fleet in ancient Phoenicia. All of them were sorcerers, who wove their spells to win battles, to tame the violent seas, to build temples of exquisite craftsmanship, protected by magic. But before any of those accomplishments they created a language which formed the basis of many modern-day languages."

"How would sorcerers create language?"

He smiled. "No idea, but that's what the texts claim."

"The texts could be wrong. They sometimes are."

He nodded. "True enough. But in this case I don't think they are. It was because of Diantha that Conrad was born and lived."

"You know this how?"

"I read it in the *Nihilus*. I told you the manuscript contained page after page of occult formulae. There was a section on the Phoenician sorcerers because an entire cadre of them were hired by King Solomon to join his alchemists. In fact, these were the sixty-six sorcerers who stayed on after he died to do his son's bidding."

"Didn't you tell me that the Phoenicians designed and built Solomon's temples?"

"Correct. The architects' workers built the temple, but it was designed by the sorcerers." He gestured. "These were the same people who conjured the Four Sphinxes."

Ayla licked her lips. "Does this mean that Diantha was a sorcerer, too?"

"It's my firm belief, yes."

"Wow. But if that's the case why would she marry Gideon? Surely she'd know—"

"There were many layers to my great-grandfather. On the surface he was handsome, decisive, powerful, charismatic. Those traits are enough to seduce even the strongest of women."

"But couldn't Diantha's power allow her to see beneath the surface?"

"You're missing the point—which is Gideon's power. It took a long time for Diantha to uncover the creature he really was. She had to go at it carefully, peeling away layer after layer without him knowing what she was doing. Besides, by that time, Conrad had been born, and her first priority was to keep him safe from his father's psychic predations."

"Which, being a Nephilim, must have been prodigious."

Bravo nodded. "Precisely. The *Nihilus* covers the Nephilim. A protocol is described for ensuring a male child will be born alive. It involves two incantations. The first severs the umbilical cord while the baby is still in the womb."

"But wouldn't the baby die?"

"Under normal circumstances, he would; the baby would be without his mother's nourishment. But this is as far from normal as you can get. The incantic severing must take place in the exact middle of the ninth month. From that time until his birth the baby is nourished by a second incantation—by magic, in other words. And when he's born, he has no navel."

"And Conrad?"

"He showed me where his navel would have been. It was as smooth and undimpled as your cheek."

THERE WAS so much more Bravo could have told Ayla, so much more he wanted to tell her. But he could see that she was still processing what he had already revealed. It was a lot for anyone to chew over. For now he decided that he had told her enough.

After some time, he said, "Would you like to meet Phaedos?"

"Ha! Sure." Then she looked at him uncertainly. "You're kidding, right? That thing is made out of tons of basalt."

"And yet you felt his eyes on you, didn't you?"

"Yes, but surely it's an optical illusion. Some trick of the light."

"Okay," Bravo said. "Let's find out."

# 27

LALIBELA, ETHIOPIA: 1918

WHAT HIS MOTHER HAD PUT INTO CONRAD'S HAND WAS A golden apple. It shone like the sun. The darker the tunnel down which he ran the brighter the apple shone. It was small, no larger than a living lady apple. Whether it was made of gold, some other metal, or another substance entirely Conrad couldn't tell. It was neither cool nor warm to his hand; it was, rather, the temperature of blood.

And there was another aspect to the apple: it seemed to be pulling him along, guiding him, as if it was incomplete, as if it was searching for its other half. He knew he had to be careful. Almost from the moment of his first memory at his mother's breast he knew how dangerous his father could be. Of course, he didn't know why until he was ten or so, for him old enough to understand the ramifications of his curious and occult lineage. And now as he pushed forward down the steepening tunnel he knew that two things had happened: Gideon was at the height of his power, and he was at his most dangerous. In the best of times, Gideon was prone to a hair-trigger temper. This was now the worst of times. He was not sure even his mother knew the extent of the evil Gideon might be capable of.

The apple was shuddering so badly in his palm that he had to close his fingers tightly over it in order to keep it from leaping out of his hand. He ran now with his torso leaning forward, as if he were being pulled along by a hunting dog straining on its leash.

And then, all at once, he saw what the golden apple of the sun had sensed. Gideon stood ahead of him, smiling slightly, as if he was expecting his son, as if this confrontation was one he had been seeking ever since Conrad's birth.

And, confirming Conrad's surmise, he smiled and said, "At last, here we are together, you as a grown man, me at the height of my power. I have been waiting because I knew your mother would send you. She is too much of a coward to confront me herself."

His smile broadened. "Myths and legends all foretell the death of the patriarch by his son, who goes on to surpass him. That is not going to happen here. Make a move against me and I will cut you down like a logger with his saw. What I am to do will be done. It's destiny. Nothing can stop it, least of all you."

Then his smile dissolved into a frown. "What is that in your hand? Where did you get it? I've been looking for it for—"

That was when the golden apple flew out of Conrad's grip, sped in a blur toward Gideon. In reflex, Gideon held up the gold rood, the weapon he believed would ward off any attack by his son or his wife. Instead, the apple seemed to open up its core, or maybe shimmer into semi-insubstantiality. Either way, it surrounded the crucifix, engulfing its center. Gideon cried out, dropping it as heat welts ballooned on his palm and the insides of his fingers where he had held the rood.

It fell to the ground and, seeing his chance, Conrad dived for it. At almost the same time, Gideon strode forward and, as Conrad left his feet, he grabbed him by his hair, jerked hard, pulling Conrad's head up, exposing his neck.

A knife was in Gideon's hand, its long, wickedly curved blade glistening with a poison known only to the Nephilim. In the blink of an eye, the blade sliced across Conrad's neck.

Blood spurted like a fountain.

# 28

HIGHSTREET WAS DREAMING OF CHRISTMAS. IT WAS SNOW-ing outside, a gentle dusting adding itself to the inch or two that had over-spread London's Cadogan Place during the frosty night. The tree had been decorated for weeks, and the anticipation of opening the gifts had be-come so unbearable that he, as his seven-year-old self, had awakened close to four-thirty in the morning and, dragging his beloved coverlet behind him, had padded down the hall to sit halfway down the steep stair-case, waiting for dawn to tiptoe its way through the starched lace curtains of the east-facing drawing room.

A curious thing, though. As the shadows of the furniture became out-lines, as the twinkling of the tree lights dimmed in response to the watery light of Christmas Day, he smelled smoke.

His seven-year-old self sniffed more deeply, then stood, descending one step at a time, the smell of smoke becoming stronger all the while. Then, as his bare feet reached the first floor, the old wooden floorboards, the gemstone Persian carpets vanished.

With a crash he fell out of his bed in Paris, his eyes, all his senses, popping open at the same time. His dream had evaporated—all except the smoke smell, which was now even stronger. His bedroom was strangely hot. Automatically, he looked to his bedside digital clock: 2:37 a.m.

And then, out of the corner of his eye, he saw the first flicker of flame. At the same time, a cloud of acrid smoke rolled into the room. He was al-ready down on his hands and knees, which was a blessing; the air was at least partially breathable. But still the back of his throat felt raw and his eyes were tearing. Heat baked his back as he scrambled across the floor to get to the bathroom. He'd read that placing a wet washcloth over your nose and mouth could save your life in such situations.

He was halfway to the bathroom when he was racked by coughs, and the more he coughed the more he sucked in the smoky air. Within seconds he grew dizzy, his eyesight dimmed at the edges. He was like a blind man crawling through a swirl of deathly fog.

He was almost at the doorsill to the bathroom when he faltered. His cheek dropped to the floorboards. All forward motion ceased; all the strength in his limbs seemed to have leached out of him. All seemed lost and, because he was not someone familiar with panic, he resigned himself to death. "I'm done, for sure," he murmured under his breath. And strangely, his mind was filled with Tilda, she of the flat chest, the colt's legs, the large china-blue eyes, and the flashing smile. He hadn't thought of her in years but now felt strangely close to her, as if she were here and all he wanted was to lie down beside her and hash out new methods of electronic hacking.

Then rough hands, large and powerful, were wrapping a wet cloth over the lower half of his face, lifting him up. He heard a man's voice calling. The fire department had arrived, just in the nick of time, though he had no memory of having called them. A neighbor, then, bless 'em! He vomited, from a combination of the smoke and the relief, almost choked on it because of the cloth. But someone ripped it away from his face, wiped his mouth with the wet cloth, all the while moving him away from the flames.

Near to passing out, he felt himself settling onto a powerful shoulder, being carried in a fireman's lift through the fire -and smoke-ridden rooms of his flat, out into the hallway. He lost consciousness again, afterward could not remember the descent down the flights of stairs, or coming out onto rue des Archives.

He awoke to find himself sprawled on one-half of the plush backseat of a large automobile. Someone big and muscular was behind the wheel— the fireman who carried him down and out? But he'd no idea the Parisian fire department had such posh vehicles. They were traveling at speed, but it felt as if they were gliding over velvet tracks. Not even a single ripple of the street made itself known in the vehicle's interior.

He reeked of smoke; his throat ached; the roof of his mouth felt flayed. His mind, still not working properly, flew back to reading about Lawrence of Arabia, with whom he strongly identified, staggering out of the desert. Then he realized that he was still in his pajamas, an English affectation of his childhood he never grew out of, and which had probably kept his flesh from being scorched. It was the fabric that was scorched, here and there, as if his beloved nanny had misused the iron, and he thought, Poor Pearl, she's going to catch it from Mum now.

"Hugh!"

Someone calling his name snapped him back to his present circumstances, from which his mind had been fleeing ever since he awoke with a start from his dream.

"Hugh."

"Yes." He croaked like a raven.

"Here. Drink this."

A thermos was thrust into his hands, and he gratefully drank the cool Earl Grey tea, which at that moment tasted like the nectar of the gods. He closed his eyes, true relief flooding through him. He was alive, the fire was behind him, whatever was lost in his flat was insured and replaceable, or he'd buy new items; it hardly mattered to him. His world, so abruptly turned upside down, had righted itself.

"Slowly, slowly," the same voice said. "Drink too fast and it will all come right back up again."

And speaking of that voice, now that he thought about it, it sounded awfully familiar. A tremor of recognition worked its way down his spine.

"Hugh, are you yourself again?" the voice asked.

"Better." He licked his cracked lips, handed the empty thermos back into the hand that had offered it to him. It was a small hand, with fingers pudgy as sausages. He knew those hands. And now one of them pressed a small soft plastic bottle into his.

"Use these eye drops. Your eyes must be stinging."

That they were. Grateful again, Highstreet squeezed two or three drops into each eye, feeling the slippery solution bathing his eyeballs, soothing them. When he could see clearly, he turned to his benefactor and, damn it all to Hell, if it wasn't that slimy fucker Obarton.

Trust Lilith, Highstreet thought, already regaining a semblance of his old self; she had planted the electronic bugs on Obarton with great precision. The resulting video was as damning as any evidence could be. If he thinks the heroics of his men are going to make me grateful enough to hand over the video gratis he has another thing coming. A slow smile spread across his face, knowing that he was still in the driver's seat, so to speak.

"Thank you, Obarton," he said, carefully avoiding using the phrase "owe you" in any way, shape, or form. "It was lucky you were in the area."

"Hmm, yes," Obarton mused. "But, you see, it wasn't luck at all, dear boy. It was all meticulously planned."

Highstreet pulled his torso upright, struggling to understand. "Pardon?"

Obarton sighed, as if offering this explanation was taking too much out of him. "The fire, the rescue, you here with me. It was all planned, Hugh."

"What?" Highstreet goggled. "For the love of God, why?"

"Why?" Obarton folded his hands across his too-ample stomach, as he was wont to do, stared up at the upholstered ceiling of the car. "Well, now, let me count the ways. The fire was set to ensure the destruction of any copies of the video you may have secreted around your flat. No time to search, you see. If I killed you outright, the video would find its way into the public domain, would it not?"

"My solicitor has been given specific instructions to release it upon my death, yes."

Obarton snorted. "Your 'solicitor.' Ever the proper English gentleman." He pursed his lips as if he was deep in thought. "So we must be most careful with you, Hugh. Your life is as precious to me as it is to you."

"It damn well better be!"

"Well said, my boy. But, you see, I cannot afford to have you lording it over me. Rum business, and all that, eh what?" He shook with amusement at his own mock-British accent. "So we must take possession of that life to ensure nothing untoward happens to you."

"You're, what, abducting me?"

"Enisling you, as the French did to their Napoléon."

"Putting me in solitary, you mean."

"Well, I'll admit that's part of your future."

"And the other part?"

He handed Highstreet his phone. "I want you to call your solicitor."

"What? In the middle of the night?"

"He'll hear about the fire soon enough and then he'll start wondering, won't he?" Obarton pursed his lips. "We can't have that, old boy."

"No." Highstreet said flatly. "I won't do it."

As if this were some kind of signal, the driver pulled over to the curb. Slamming the vehicle into Park, he got out, came around, opened the door on Highstreet's side, and hauled him out. The punch buried itself in Highstreet's solar plexus, doubling him over. The driver then proceeded to administer a long, professional, and, as far as Highstreet was concerned, disastrous beating.

When, after Highstreet had sunk well and good into his solitary pit of agony, the driver threw him back into the backseat he handed Highstreet's mobile to Obarton. Slamming the door, he returned to his position behind the wheel, threw the car into gear, and headed down the deserted street.

Obarton opened the mobile, checked incoming calls and texts. "My, my, your boss is awfully anxious to make contact with you." He put the mobile away. "Well, your phone will give us her location soon enough, and that will be the end of Lilith Swan."

Highstreet lay in a crumpled ball, unable to speak or even think coherently. Blood leaked from his ears, his eyes, the corners of his mouth, and too many other places to enumerate. He felt utterly spent, as if he were an airplane that, having run dry, was now plummeting to earth at unthinkable speed.

Obarton pushed the phone into Highstreet's hand. "Call your solicitor. Your flat has burned down. Complete accident. You're taking an extended leave of absence. Heading for Ibiza or some such port of call. Now. Do as you're told."

Highstreet complied, managing to sound coherent. That his voice was unmistakably shaky his solicitor no doubt took as a reaction to the fire.

When he was done, Obarton took the phone from him, but not before wiping off the blood. "That's the boy. Your life belongs to me, Hugh. Now that you know that," he said, keeping his person well away from the leakage of blood, "you know it all."

KEEPING THE beam of light playing on the Sphinx, Bravo led Ayla to the foot of the massive sculpture. It rose up sharply, blotting out even the gloom high above them.

"As I said, the *Nihilus* claimed there were Four Sphinxes, each with a secret hidden in its mouth. This is the second one I've seen. The first was below our Reliquary in Alexandria, Egypt. That's where I found the

*Nihilus* manuscript." He lifted the crucifix. "This—the bronze rood—came from the Sphinx in a chamber below a church in Lalibela, Ethiopia. It's the one Conrad found."

"Making three," Ayla said. "And the fourth?"

"That's where it gets tricky. The location of the fourth Sphinx—Thanos, the leader and the most powerful—was expunged from the Book, along with the description of whatever had been secreted in his mouth."

"Thanos. Interesting. An analog of *Thanatos,* the Greek word for death." She considered a moment. "You've said the Phoenician sorcerers conjured the Sphinxes. Did they also hide the four objects?"

"I don't know," Bravo said. "But I mean to find out."

With that, he vaulted up onto the plinth. From there, he scrambled up onto the Sphinx's shoulder, reached around, and inserted his hand into the snarling mouth.

"Aha!" Bravo removed his hand, held up a golden apple, no larger than a lady apple, but glowing brightly as from an inner fire.

"What is it?" Ayla asked as he clambered down.

"According to the *Nihilus,* the golden apples of the sun were created by King Solomon's cadre of alchemists before they were joined by the sixty-six Phoenician sorcerers."

"So they're part of Solomon's legendary gold?"

Bravo shook his head. "Not at all. Again, according to the *Nihilus,* that gold was conjured by the Phoenician sorcerers after Solomon died. It was never found, though, as you know, over the centuries numberless adventurers have sought it."

Bravo held the bronze rood in one hand, the golden apple in the other.

"What have they to do with one another?"

He shrugged. "All I know right now is that the *Nihilus* clearly stated the four had a strong affinity to one another, that together their power increased exponentially. Perhaps we can't know more until all four artifacts have been plucked from the Sphinxes' mouths."

"Then we'll never know," Ayla pointed out. "Unless we can discover where the fourth Sphinx is located." She shook her head. "Conrad never found it, did he?"

"He tried," Bravo answered her. "But, no. No one's found Thanos's location."

"I bet Phaedos can help." Ayla laughed. "Why don't you ask him?"

Bravo looked up into the enigmatic face of the Sphinx. "If only I could." And joining in her brief levity: "Maybe if you kissed him on the lips he'd open up."

"Huh," Ayla said. "Nothing ventured, nothing gained." Following in Bravo's footsteps, she pulled herself onto the plinth, then mounted the Sphinx's massive shoulder and, hanging on with one arm, swung to her left, pressed her lips against the cold veined basalt of Phaedos's lower lip. Then she swung back, hanging on to his shoulder.

"Anything?"

Bravo shook his head. "Not a thing." He gestured. "Come on down from there."

When she had done so, she saw him frowning over the two artifacts.

"What's up?"

"Look at this," he said.

Holding the bronze rood in one open palm and the golden apple in the other, he brought his hands together. As they closed, the golden apple began to tremble, then to shudder, rocking back and forth alarmingly. The instant the edges of his hands touched, the apple flew off his palm in the opposite direction, as if to get as far away from the crucifix as possible.

Ayla retrieved the apple, brought it back to Bravo. "What happened?"

Bravo grasped the rood firmly, keeping it upright. "Hold the apple tightly. Right, now draw it closer."

"The closer I get the harder it is to move forward. The two artifacts are repelling each other."

"Odd," Bravo said, clearly perplexed.

"This could be the wrong apple."

Bravo nodded. "I don't think so." He looked around. "In any event, we have what we came for. Time to go."

They retraced their steps to the riverbank and the waiting boat.

"The current is too strong for us to row back," Ayla pointed out as she climbed aboard.

"We're not going back." Bravo cast off the line from the cleat. "We're going forward. Only forward now."

He pushed off, jumped into the boat, and, seating himself, took up the oars. He needn't have bothered. The river's current was stronger now, shoving them as if with a giant hand through the last mile, or ten miles, it was never clear which, out of the Hollow Lands, out into the twilit Mediterranean.

But before that happened, when they were still only yards away from where they had moored, the Sphinx opened its sloe eyes, fixing its implacable gaze on the back of Ayla's retreating head.

# 29

ISTANBUL, TURKEY: PRESENT DAY

"I WANT TO SPEAK WITH EMMA." LILITH HAD BEEN STUDYING her mobile's screen for some minutes with a deepening frown.

Beleth, grumbling, acquiesced. "Times like this," it said, in Emma's deepest register, "I wish I were a Scryer like Phenex. I'm running in unfamiliar territory."

Lilith smiled at him, put her hand over Emma's. "Poor thing. But not to worry. Emma and I will take good care of you."

Beleth, looking out of Emma's black eyes, said in a shocked voice, "How many times do I have to ask what is happening to me?"

"You're exploding yet another myth exported by the Church," Lilith said without hesitation. "The Holy See preaches that evil is monolithic, that it cannot learn. But here you are learning the difference between evil and good."

Beleth grumped, but Lilith sensed that it was in some way pleased—if, indeed, a member of the Fallen Legion could be pleased.

The three of them—the two women, to any onlooker—were standing on the Bosphorus Bridge, precisely at the center of the span, midway between the continents of Europe and Asia. It seemed the correct place for them to be. The idea for the bridge was first formed in the mind of Darius I the Great of Persia in 513 BC. He ordered a pontoon bridge hurriedly constructed on this very spot in order for his armies to run down the fleeing Scythians and, afterward, positioned his warriors in strategic areas of the Balkans to defeat the threatening Macedonian army. The bridge symbolized both integration and victory.

"Tell me, Beleth," Lilith continued, "is it true that part of God's punishment was that Lucifer would never again have a solid piece of ground onto which to set his feet?"

Though there was a pedestrian path on the bridge, it had been closed for some time due to fears of both suicides and terrorist attacks. However, no one had stopped the women, and the policeman near them seemed to look through them as if they were not there at all. Lilith did not query this anomaly, figuring their seeming invisibility was due to some petty conjuring by Beleth.

It was a blustery day, clouds of fantastic shapes chasing one another across a lapis lazuli sky. Below them, the traffic along the Strait was thick with ferries, tourist boats, and barges hauling all manner of dry goods and foodstuffs.

"Makes a damn good story, doesn't it?" the Power said bitterly. "You know why there are so many stories about Lucifer? Because so little is known about him. He is the Sum of All Shadows, more dreadful than your insect minds can conceive."

"Listen, you," Lilith said. "These two *insects* are protecting you from being annihilated by Leviathan and any others of your ilk who find your recent actions, not to mention your opinions, anathema to the Fallen insurrection." She put her face close to Emma's. "If we really are insects then what does that make you?"

Silence from Beleth, while at their backs jam-packed traffic whizzed by in either direction, neither drivers nor passengers paying them any mind.

"Go on then," Beleth said at length. "Talk your heads off, for all I care."

Lilith smiled sweetly. "Thank you, my pet."

Emma's corpus jerked, but the Power remained silent, presumably sulking in its tent like Achilles.

"Emma?"

"I'm here," Emma said in her normal voice. Her eyes had cleared, lightening as if with sunlight shining from within.

"I think I have a problem."

That makes two of us, Emma thought. Hour by hour she could feel the words of Lucifer crawling across her skin like an army of fire ants. The sting of each word, the terror they elicited as they formed sentences, paragraphs, seemed unstoppable. The invaders were at the gates, and though she was manning the battlements as best she could, the enemy had brought

206 / ERIC VAN LUSTBADER

all the requisite siege engines to make a mockery of her attempts at survival. Once again, despair entered her thoughts, but she recognized it as just another one of the enemy's siege engines, and she dismissed it with a Shawian gesture typical of her storied line.

Lilith lifted her mobile, shaking it as if she were angry with it. "I've been trying to contact my colleague—"

A stab of jealousy momentarily shook Emma free of her desperate inner battle. "Boyfriend?"

"Ha, no. Not by a long shot. My relationship with Hugh Highstreet is complicated, but suffice to say he runs IT for the Knights—well, for me, really."

"You make it sound as if you're separate from the Knights." She longed to tell Lilith about her fight, to gain from her strength, but she dare not utter a word of it. And what of Beleth? He must know that the words of Lucifer were inside her, but if he was aware that she was fighting them he had given her no indication of it. Both he and Leviathan believed that it was making her—and therefore Beleth itself—more powerful. There had always been a part of her that she was able to keep from Beleth. Now she was using that piece to keep her counter-insurgency against Lucifer's spiraling words from him. Deceit was a trait learned through experience; nevertheless, she felt certain that her grandfather—blood of her blood— played a part in her fast-growing expertise. Until she was sure of his loyalties, she could not afford to allow Beleth to become aware of how fiercely she was fighting against being taken over.

Lilith could see how interested Emma was. "The traditional Knights certainly. I pulled a coup inside the Circle Council. I was fed up with how the Knights mistreated women. So I took over."

"How in the world did you do that?"

"I killed three of the Circle Council during session."

"No, really. How did you do it?"

"I just told you."

Emma stared at her. "You're not kidding."

"Hardly."

Emma turned away, watched a seagull gliding past, riding the thermals. "I wish I could do that."

"That's very human, I think—the wish to fly."

Emma turned back. "Do you ever wish you could fly away?"

"All the time." Lilith, correctly intuiting that Emma's comment had a dual meaning, said, "They gave me no other choice."

"There's always another choice. That's Bravo's philosophy."

Lilith gave her a direct look. "Is it yours, as well?"

Emma nodded.

"You've never been a part of the Knights of St. Clement." Her voice was filled with disgust for the Order.

"Why are you?"

"My father was a Knight. I worshiped him, until I found out how corrupt the Order was. I went to him, asked him how he could be a part of such a thing, and he told me that he was trying to work toward change, but that it was a slow process of evolution, not revolution."

"Did you believe him?"

"Six weeks later he was dead. A heart attack, they said; murdered, I suspected, and a month later I had my proof. So, yes, he was telling the truth. My father never lied to me, even if the truth was unpleasant. So I evoked my right of succession. I was of age, but my gender . . . Anyway, there were enough forward-thinking men on the Circle Council powerful enough to vote me in.

"I saw what my father had seen, and I followed in his footsteps . . . except for one thing. He was wrong about evolution. Within six months I had determined that no matter how many forward-thinking Knights there were, the basic culture of corruption would not change. In fact, it was getting worse as their businesses flourished and more and more money lined their pockets."

Lilith shook her head. "No, evolution wasn't going to cut it. Revolution was the only way to go. And I was right."

"So the Gnostic Observatines are opposing a reformed Knights."

Lilith made a face. "Up to a point. Emma, listen to me. Your greatest enemy is a senior Circle Council member named Frederick Obarton." There were many paths to the truth; it was all a matter of presentation. "He's the one who opposed women's inclusion most vociferously. I needed to get the upper hand over him if I was to get anywhere. Only one thing captures Obarton's attention: the spillage of blood."

Lilith studied Emma's face. "Are you listening to me?"

Emma was watching the water traffic far below them. She had not looked at Lilith since Lilith's confession. "Go on."

"Hugh Highstreet is a brilliant man. He's also my only ally, the only one in the Knights I can trust."

"Then it seems as if your grip on the leadership is tenuous at best."

"That's what I've been trying to tell you. I thought I had Obarton in my pocket, but now it's been some time and I can't raise Hugh. He's not answering his mobile; he hasn't returned my voice mails or texts. It's as if he's been completely erased. I—"

Her phone had sprung to life: a text from Hugh's mobile. An enormous wave of relief swept through her, until she read the text itself:

Hello, Lil. I have him. Your Hughie. The threat he presented has been neutralized. He's in bad shape, but not as bad a shape as you'll be in when I get ahold of you. Cheers.

"Oh, God!" She cocked her arm to throw her mobile over the side of the bridge.

"What are you doing?" Emma said, stopping her.

"Obarton has Hugh. Tortured him, I have no doubt. He texted me using Hugh's phone, so he can track me through the GPS chip. We have to get out of here as soon as possible."

Lilith looked around as if afraid Obarton himself was looking over her shoulder. "He was the one who sent me after you. He wanted me to keep checking in with him, but the moment I saw you I stopped. That's why he's gone after Hugh." She rubbed her forehead. "I thought I had protected Hugh before I left. But somehow, that snake has gotten the best of Hugh and me. He's coming after me, and then he'll be coming after you and Bravo and the rest of the Gnostic Observatines." She put her hand over Emma's. "He's tried to make me believe that what he fears most is the Fallen, but I'm not fooled. It's your brother he wants dead and gone. The Shaws have been the bane of so many of the *Nauarchus*. None of them have been able to best them; they've all died trying. Obarton believes the only way to cement his position, to become a historic leader of the Circle Council, is to bring in Bravo's head freeze-dried in a box."

"I tell you what, Lilith," Emma said. "I'm getting fed up with everyone wanting my brother's head."

"Well, listen to you."

"Hey, sister, up until yesterday you were one of them."

Lilith nodded. "You've got me there, *sister*." Her expression was sober. "I have to find Hugh and bring him home safe and sound. Believe me, I owe him more than that." She eyed Emma. "Will you help me?"

She turned to Lilith, took a step closer so their noses were almost touching. "You're a Knight; I'm a Gnostic Observatine."

"Emma, has our time together meant nothing?"

"It's been brief, Lilith. Life is long." Her eyes did not blink; they were darkening menacingly. "I want a straight answer."

"Whoever tries to kill you," Lilith said without hesitation, "will have to kill me first."

Emma examined Lilith's face for any sign of perfidy. "Okay, then. I'll help you."

A wave of relief swept over Lilith's face. "Okay, now I'll get rid of this phone."

Again, Emma stopped her. "We'll be out of here soon enough. And, listen, if Obarton can find us via the GPS chip, we can use the one in Highstreet's mobile to find out where he and Obarton are, right?"

"Right." There was a new look in Lilith's eyes. "Sometimes I don't understand you."

"Wouldn't it be boring if you did."

Lilith laughed softly, her eyes filled with love.

"There's one more thing."

Lilith nodded. "Name it."

"Obarton has compromised Highstreet. So who's minding the Knights' IT store?"

Lilith regarded her lover's face. "You want in on the Knights' secrets, don't you?"

Emma smiled, the pain and pressure of her inner struggle entirely hidden. "What d'you think?"

# 30

HOLLOW LANDS: 1918

WHEN CONRAD'S BLOOD, SPURTING WITH EACH BEAT OF HIS heart, reached the golden apple and the gold rood a blue flame arose. In the space of a human heartbeat it had engulfed both Conrad and Gideon. A terrible wail rose up, from God only knew where, and then abruptly stopped.

Gideon rose, triumphant, confronting his son for the second time, but at that instant Diantha appeared out of a particularly dense copse of shadows. She was barefoot as she ran forward, and before her husband could stop her she pressed her foot down onto the ground between where he stood and the golden apple with its long-sought other half.

At once, the blue flame that engulfed Gideon was snuffed out. At that precise instant, Conrad, his aurora of blue flame glowing ever brighter, arose from the floor. Gideon could not believe what he saw. His son's neck bore only a scar to remind him that his knife had, indeed, sought Conrad's death. Not a drop of blood lay on the floor. It had been vaporized, or the blue flame had returned it to its source.

He brandished his knife. The blade still held a scrim of blood along its top edge. "Betrayer! Witch!" he screamed at his wife. "Damned sorceress!"

"On the contrary, it's you who are damned," she said evenly. She glided silently toward him without seeming to move a muscle. "You were damned the moment you were conceived, doubly damned when you drew first breath."

"Mother, stand back!" Conrad said, alarmed. "He's taken the Throne Verrine inside him."

"Fool!" Diantha cried. "I did not think that even you would be so utterly stupid."

"I have its power," Gideon said. "I don't need your sorcerous blue flame."

"You have nothing. A Throne is not yours to command. The power of that thing inside you is beyond your comprehension."

"But not yours, is that right?" He laughed. "Now my power rivals yours." He cocked his head. "Oh, wait. What's that, Verrine? Ah, yes, my Throne informs me its power far exceeds yours, Sorceress. Verrine is even older than your Phoenician magic."

"But not wiser," Diantha said, launching herself at him.

Conrad watched, dumbfounded, as his two parents clashed, not as human beings, but as titans, as unimaginable entities, whose carefully lacquered masks had shattered. Blue fire enrobed Diantha, while Gideon's shape underwent a terrifying transformation as, foretold by his wife, Verrine took total control of him.

Three sets of wings made their appearance first—leathery batwings with small, claw-like hands at the apexes of their upper cartilage. His skin darkened to the color of dried blood, scaled in the manner of armored beasts. His face, the last to go, lost all semblance of humanness, becoming both angelic and demonic, a seemingly impossible combination that nevertheless destroyed whatever remained of Gideon's humanity. A terrible cry was ripped from the Throne's throat, a last anguished gasp, as Gideon vanished into the maelstrom of its maw.

DESPITE WHAT Diantha had said, W. B. Yeats did not stay long with the Sphinx called Typhos after she vanished. And vanished she had, as if she were a puff of smoke or he had imagined her. One moment they were engaged in conversation as to the age of Typhos; the next he was left speaking echoes into the shadows of the immense space. So he addressed the Sphinx. "Typhos, should I stay or should I go?" But in the absence of the sorcerers, Typhos had returned to stone, unmoving, unresponsive.

Yeats was a poet by both inclination and inspiration; he was a man who embraced enigmas. A mind like his was, by both nature and nurture, an abundantly inquisitive one. And so, setting aside the notebook on which he was composing his epic poem about Typhos and the great evil of the Book of Deathly Things Conrad had brought him here to confront, he lit out down the dark and forbidding tunnel that, like Alice's rabbit hole, would lead him to Elsewhere, as he now thought of it. Soon enough he would come to know it as the Hollow Lands he and Conrad had set out to find, but at this moment only the unknown lay ahead of him.

Running as fast as he could, driven by the persistent alien heartbeat of some great calamity, he found the walls of the tunnel emitting a feverish glow even as it pitched sharply downward, plowing farther into the bowels of the earth.

How long it took to reach the end, to emerge like Athena from Zeus's head, into the frightful scene he was never able to calculate, even much later when, in the long nights ahead, there was time, lying on his bed, unable to sleep, let alone dream, to run the impossible events over and over again in his mind like a scene from a motion picture.

And his experience at the time was exactly like viewing a film, alone in a darkened theater, because the nature of his stupendous fright was such that his consciousness leapt from his body, observing the unfolding battle from a secure height, invisible to the gods and monsters below.

AS THE Throne inside Gideon went for his mother, Conrad's stupefaction unraveled. He lunged at Verrine, blue flame spurting from his outstretched hands. But neither Diantha nor Verrine had been exaggerating the extent of its power. Now it brushed Conrad away with an almost casual backhand swipe. He crashed to the floor, landing so hard on one shoulder the pain lanced all the way through him.

Temporarily paralyzed, he saw his mother and Verrine locked in mortal combat. It was like nothing he had ever seen or would ever see again in his natural lifetime. But there would be another lifetime for him, as his grandson was to discover many years later.

In this present time, the movements of the two combatants were so fast, all was a blur, to the point where only constantly shifting veils of color momentarily differentiated one from the other.

This merging terrified him. He could accept what his father had become precisely because he had never liked or trusted him. But for his mother to be so merged with one of the Fallen, even visually, was unthinkable.

It was this terror that made him hesitate after the paralysis had receded, that kept him on the ground a moment too long. And so it was that as Verrine beckoned Death, who waited in the unquiet shadows of the Hollow Lands, to come and take Diantha into his bony embrace, it was left to Yeats, who was seeing the battle from above, to make a desperate run at the combined golden apple—the same golden apple he had envisioned while writing his poem!—and gold rood, which, it seemed, the principals in their eons-long enmity had forgotten. Scooping up the artifact, Yeats did the only thing he could think of: he threw it at the blur of color and bitterness.

The ensuing explosion was one of blinding light. Soundless, but no less powerful for that, it freed Diantha from the Throne's grip, sent Verrine flying backward to slam into the thorny left foreleg of the Orus. Three of the thorns caught it, penetrated its spine, pinning it in place.

Now, seeing his mother tended by his friend, Conrad shook off his terror and, gathering up the artifact, shoved it against Verrine's chest. The Throne's ruby-red eyes opened wide, its mouth worked soundlessly, as it was forcibly Transpositioned out of Gideon Shaw, as the power of the artifact launched it back into whatever level of Hell it had occupied before Gideon had freed it.

What was left of the creature—never quite human, but neither divine? It was the Nephilim who had his last look at his son, all his dreams shattered, all his plans gone up in flames.

"Conrad—"

But Conrad had already extended his arm. The blue flames, restless, unforgiving, leapt from him to Gideon, annihilating the Nephilim so completely not even a swirl of ash remained.

# 31

**"WHAT WAS IT LIKE BEING BROUGHT UP A SHAW?"**

Bravo, having shipped the oars on the underground river, now slipped them back into the oarlocks and began to row. "Never easy."

Darkness rimmed the eastern horizon, while in the west a post-sunset bruise made its mark. The darkling water sprayed against the bow of the boat as Bravo fought to turn them from heading south, across the Mediterranean, to the shores of North Africa. Pelagic birds dived and swooped overhead, every so often skimming the surface for a fishy dinner. The coolness of night rippled pell-mell toward them.

"I've told you a bit about my father," Bravo went on, putting his back into his work. "He was livid that he hadn't inherited any of Conrad's powers. That's one of the many reasons he despised him."

"There was more?" Ayla asked.

"Let me count Conrad's uncountable sins."

"An impossible task, clearly."

"According to my father, anyway." A light breeze ruffled his hair. "But my father's perspective was heavily distorted."

"So you've said." She leaned forward in order to be heard over the gulls' increasingly raucous cries. "What aren't you telling me?"

"My father was a bitter man."

"Because of Conrad."

"Not only in the way you think. Conrad chose his bride for him."

The lapping of the waves, the birds' calling, rushed into the vacuum caused by human silence.

"Are you telling me that you and Emma are products of an arranged marriage?"

He nodded.

"How medieval."

"I suppose you could say that."

The oars rose and fell, water purling off their curved blades. Their progress against the tide was slow and, by the look on Bravo's face, painful.

"My mother had no love for my father," he said.

"And your father?"

"I think matters would have been simpler if he felt the same way. He loved her, desperately, hopelessly."

The boat was coming around now, and it was all Bravo could do to keep it parallel to shore. At least they weren't continuing to head out to sea.

"But why did they agree? Why did they commit to such a thing?"

"My father was a Shaw. He had no choice."

"He couldn't just walk away?"

"Not and stay in the Gnostic Observatines, let alone lead them. He had a duty, as all Shaws since Conrad do."

"Oh, right." Ayla nodded. "But the Gnostic Observatines were founded in the 1500s. Then they were a strictly religious order."

"Yes, but over the centuries their interests expanded. They never fully abandoned the teachings of their patron, Saint Francis, and Christ, but because of their wanderings in Constantinople, Jerusalem, and the Levant they became fascinated with the ancient artifacts that pre-dated Christianity and spoke of religions, powers, and spheres invisible and inaccessible to mankind.

"This was why Gideon was drawn to them. His knowledge of the occult fascinated them; his charisma beguiled them. Their leader was infirm. His infirmity became terminal shortly after Gideon joined the Order, and when he passed it was Gideon who ascended."

"What about your mother?"

"Ah, my mother. She's a whole different mystery." Bravo was silent for some time, both because it was now more difficult to get the boat moving back toward shore and because he was thinking of the right way to present Steffi Shaw's story.

At length, after he'd at last muscled the boat around to the north, he heaved a deep sigh. "My mother's lineage was such that Conrad knew she and his son would make a perfect match."

"DNA, you mean." When Bravo did not respond to that, she added, "What was her lineage?"

"My grandmother Diantha. She had a child out of wedlock before she met Gideon. A daughter. A Safita. My mother's grandmother. So, yes, the same line. A powerful line."

"You inherited her powers as well as Conrad's?"

"So it would seem."

To their left was a high ridge of jagged headland, to their right the inlet from which the underground river disgorged into the sea. Bravo had been periodically looking over his shoulder to ascertain the most hospitable landing spot on the high rocky shoreline, but now, having sensed something, he stared out at the Mediterranean through the faltering cobalt light.

"What is it?" Ayla asked, turning to follow his gaze.

"Listen."

She did as he asked. "I don't hear anything."

"Right. The birds have all gone still."

"Meaning?"

They both heard the dim revving of outboard engines moments before the speedboat came arcing around the headland to their west. Bravo judged the craft to be approximately forty-two feet in length. It was sleek and coming at them very fast. He counted five men including the driver, four armed to the teeth with AK-47s.

"Knights?" Ayla asked through a drawn-in breath.

"Worse," Bravo said. "Much worse."

"What could be worse?"

He saw the movement of the driver's left arm. "Do you know how to swim?" He caught the glimmer of chrome.

"Championship caliber. I also scuba—"

Without a second thought, he shoved her hard over the side. She hit the water and, a moment later the pilot of the oncoming speedboat switched on the spotlight, blinding Bravo as it lit up the entire rowboat. Smart as she was, Ayla had swum around to put their boat between her and the speedboat. The armed men saw only Bravo; they were completely unware of Ayla.

They were close now, slowing as they neared. Bravo's eyes had adjusted to the glare, could see them behind the light preparing to board. He once again shipped the oars, removing them from the oarlocks.

"Stay where you are!" the voice called in heavily accented English.

Recognizing the accent, Bravo said, *"As-salāmu alaykum."*

*"Wa'alaykumu salām,"* came the reply, probably from the leader.

"There's nothing for you here," Bravo continued in Arabic. "I'm a friend. I bear you no ill will."

Their eyes gave him pause. They were filled to overflowing with death.

"Stay where you are!" Same man. South Sudan accent; Juba Arabic. With each word, death leaked out of him like sputum. His eyes, like the others', were red. His fingernails were long and black. "Stay where you are!" As if his needle was stuck in the same record groove.

He was the leader. This man, tall, impossibly thin, all ropy muscle and gristle, leaned over, grabbed Bravo by his shirtfront, and dragged him off the rowboat and onto his own vessel. He used a hand-sign and one of his men clambered aboard the rowboat, checking every square inch for anything hidden, anything they could use, sell, or barter. Since there was nothing to find the search was a short one. He looked up at his leader, shook his head. The leader slammed Bravo across the face, as if the lack of booty was his fault.

Bending over, he said, "Who are you, what are you doing here, where did you come from, where are you going?" All in one spewed sentence.

His breath stank of seaweed and fish, as if he and his cadre had been dredged up from the bottom of the Mediterranean. But the South Sudan wasn't the Mediterranean. It was much more frightening, and these radical pirates had absolutely nothing to lose. Their stairway to Heaven was set in stone. As for him, Bravo knew that death would be the least of his worries. These insurgents knew how to torture a captive to within an inch of his life, over and over again until the mind was shredded into a thousand and one pieces that, like Humpty Dumpty, could never be put back together again. This was why he had had to get Ayla out of harm's way. She was female. Her fate with these radicals would be worse than his, at least at first. After that, oatmeal was oatmeal, no matter the gender.

The leader stomped on Bravo's hand. "Speak! Speak or die!"

He was swinging the barrel of his AK-47 around to push into Bravo's face, when the insurgent stepped back across from the rowboat to the speedboat. Reaching up, Bravo drove a first into his crotch. He screamed, stumbled into his leader, and Bravo made a grab for his weapon.

As he did so, someone out of his range of vision kicked him in the ribs.

He grunted, lights spangling behind his eyes. Another kick dislodged his grip on the rifle. He twisted away, received a kick in his side for his efforts.

The bronze rood spilled out of his pocket. He reached for it reflexively, but the leader ground the heel of his boot into it, then jerked Bravo up by his hair.

"You want this weapon so badly? Well, here." He smashed the butt of the insurgent's AK-47 into the side of Bravo's head. He let go Bravo's hair, and Bravo crashed to the slippery deck of the speedboat. Dimly, he glimpsed the leader deliver a punishing blow to the insurgent who had lost his weapon. A line of blood opened up on the insurgent's face, a deep gash that would not heal well, an eternal reminder.

Someone roughly pulled Bravo's arms behind his back, tied his wrists so tightly that the bonds bit into his flesh, bringing blood.

"Now." The leader squatted down beside Bravo. "My name is Ismail. Give me yours."

"Braverman Shaw."

"Means nothing to me."

"Why should it?"

Ismail hit Bravo on the back of the head. His Arabic sounded odd to Bravo's ears, slurred, as if he were drunk, which was impossible. Perhaps it only sounded that way because Bravo, swaddled like a helpless baby in pain, was half-concussed.

"Unless you're related to Dexter Shaw."

"My father."

"Huh. A tomb raider, so I've heard over and over again. A stealer of souls."

"Interesting argument coming from someone who takes pleasure in destroying his country's past. My father's mission was to preserve the past, to learn its secrets."

"So, here we have our history in a nutshell. The infidel telling the guardian of the Qur'an what is wicked. Pathetic." Ismail licked his thick lips. "I imagine you're a plunderer, too."

When Bravo made no comment, Ismail said, "You consider me a destroyer."

"You *are* a destroyer."

The flat of Ismail's hand pressed down on Bravo's head. "Here is the way the world really is. With each death, each bomb detonation, I keep the world from falling asleep. Because, Braverman, when the world falls asleep infidels like you infiltrate our world, take what is sacred to us, everything Allah has promised us if we live life according to the laws of the Qur'an. You take these precious things without regard and in return you deliver us into a land of Coca-Cola and *Star Wars,* the filth and blasphemy of the rich and famous. All Americans lust for this life, so you assume the entire world feels the same. It doesn't. It recoils from the corruption of morals. Braverman, the damage you do—you have no idea."

He put his full weight behind the hand pressing down on Bravo's head. "Your father was an honorable man, in his own peculiar way. But he was an infidel nonetheless."

Ismail bent lower. "What are you?"

Another blow fell onto the back of Bravo's head, so hard his cheek bounced against the deck, almost cracking his neck. Bravo was obliged to turn his head to rid himself of the majority of the pain. And that's when he saw it.

The bronze rood had been damaged by Ismail's boot heel. Bravo blinked, could not believe his eyes. A small fraction of the bronze had been sheared off, revealing a glint underneath.

The crucifix wasn't made of bronze; it had been coated with bronze to protect the rood's original material.

The rood was made of gold.

# PART THREE

## THE FOUR THRONES

# 32

A CURIOUS SILENCE ENGULFED THEM AS IT HAD ON THE
bridge in Istanbul.

"What is going on?" Beleth ventured. Neither of the women answered.
"Ah," it said. "A human thing. Between the two of you."

They sat side by side on the right side of the commercial jet. Feeding
time, such as it was. Salads were served, wilted leaves with a sealed plastic
container of dressing. Tiny paper packets of salt and pepper. A precise
square of brown-gray pâté. Lilith cut off a triangle of pâté with her fork.
Beleth's essence reasserted itself; in the realm of humans its patience was
limited. Eyes black as moonless night, it took up Emma's knife, turned
it over and over in her hand, as if preparing to use it in a way the flight
attendant would surely not approve of.

Lilith stared into those fathomless eyes, glimmering like stones underwater. Holding the knife in her peripheral vision, she said, "Who d'you
propose to kill with that?"

"This Obarton. That is what you both desire."

'With that butter knife?"

"This is all a joke to you, isn't it?" Beleth growled under its breath.

"I only wish it was."

"You have an odd way about you."

"That's because you lack a sense of humor. Poor thing."

"There you go again."

"You know your problem, Beleth?"

"As if I have just one."

"Are they all like you?"

"Who?"

"The Fallen. The Legion who are coming for us."

The Power watched her warily. "It is your friend who has been captured, not mine."

"You have no friends," Lilith said dismissively. She waited in vain for him to reply. "You're like a child, Beleth." She twirled some greens on the tines of her fork, then set it down. She had no appetite; the pâté was sitting in her stomach like a fistful of lead shot. "You have no experience in the real world."

"Who decides what is real and what is not?" Beleth said somberly. "You?"

"Why not me?"

"Because," it said, "what you know I can fit inside a thimble."

"Okay. Enlighten me then."

Beleth sighed. "You speak about the Fallen. You speak about the Legion. But you do not know the one from the other."

"The Legion is the advance guard," Lilith said. "Right?"

"As far as it goes, yes."

"And I know you're terrified of Leviathan."

"As far as it goes, yes."

"Then tell me what I'm missing."

"Everything. You're missing everything." Emma leaned forward, the thunder-rumble of Beleth's voice subsiding, as if it was worried about who—or what?—might be listening. "Leviathan has found a way into the world of humans—your world."

"Hey, buster, *you're* in our world."

Beleth looked at her with its implacable stare. "I do not understand you making light of the situation."

Lilith shook her head, ran her fingers through her hair. "It's how I deal."

"Deal?"

"With being scared out of my wits."

"Ah." Beleth's expression changed from readable to unreadable. "Well, then."

For a moment, it seemed at a loss for words, or maybe it was simply lost in thought. The flight attendant came, possibly to collect their plates, but Lilith waved her off.

Beleth said now, "I can only appear in a human host, not my true form. For Leviathan, though, it is different."

"I've seen him. The stuff nightmares are made of. But how is he able to—?"

"That's just it; I do not know," Beleth said morosely. "But one thing is certain: there has been a major alteration in our worlds. In the beginning, after the Fall, God dictated two discreet places. Stories were told that the Phoenician sorcerers under the direction of Rehoboam, King Solomon's son, summoned Lucifer. But no. Even they lacked the power to break God's chains. Instead, they used their incantations to bring the Guardian into the red tent of shadows and, with his reluctant help, conjured the gold Rehoboam required to prop up his father's failing empire. But there was a side effect, as there always is in sulphurous bargains. Perhaps it was unintentional, perhaps not. With the Phoenicians you never knew; they were wild and unpredictable and, if you crossed them, utterly vindictive. It's in their blood and their bones.

"The point being, the conjuring, drawing energy from our dark world, brought the worlds into contact with one another. That contact weakened the membrane. It was further weakened some years ago in Tannourine, Lebanon, when a human named Dilara Tusik brought her daughter Ayla to the red tent of shadows. This Ayla, still a child, confronted the Guardian. But now comes a third intervention, the one that has allowed Leviathan to part the veils."

"Who is the Guardian?" Lilith asked.

"He is Regent, the demon of fate. He answers to no one, lives in neither world. He is the Lord of Limbo. He is the saddest of demons, and the most bloody-minded."

"And Ayla?" Lilith asked.

Emma's expression turned crafty. "Emma knows," Beleth said. "Don't you, darling."

The eyes lightened for a moment, a lone ray of sunshine piercing the storm clouds. "Ayla is a relative of mine, and, of course, of my brother's."

Then the spot of brightness was gone, devoured by the darkness inside her. "Ayla is a Shaw, long hidden from us," Beleth said. "She was protected from us when she was vulnerable. Ever since she confronted Regent her power has blossomed. And when she defeated Malus, the child the

Guardian conjured into your world, her potential to become a full-blown sorceress was released. Unfortunately, her mother was killed before she could be trained."

"Then she could help us," Lilith said.

"I doubt it," Beleth rumbled. "She has no idea of the powers locked inside her."

"Then we'll tell her."

"It won't make any difference. She has no idea how to use her powers. Sorcery is not something you can learn on the fly; it takes years of training with an adept."

"That won't stop me from informing her of what she can be."

"If you get the chance."

Lilith's body tensed. "What d'you mean?"

"Just this: the fact of Leviathan being able to exist here means that the Four Thrones cannot be far behind. It is they, riding Orus, their war mounts, who will lead the Legion into your world." Emma shook her head. "This is the very worst news for you humans."

"For you, too, Beleth, lest you forget."

The Power glared at her. "I am incapable of forgetting anything, which, frankly, is part of my problem. If I could forget the sins we have committed—the sins *I* have committed—I would be far better off. Now I am committed—consigned to fighting my very nature. You have no idea what an impossibly difficult task this is."

"And yet you're doing it," Lilith said. "You should be proud of yourself."

"Pride!" Beleth all but cried. "One of our worst character flaws!" Emma put her head in her hands. "I sometimes have this insane notion that God created us this way, that he knew we would rebel, that he had planned our retribution from the first."

"I believe that's how some humans think." Lilith placed her hand halfway across the table, palm up, and said nothing more until Emma—but this wasn't Emma, she had to remind herself, but the Fallen Angel Beleth—covered her hand with her own. It did not go unnoticed that this was the first time Beleth had allowed itself to be comforted by her. She was moved beyond her own understanding. "I told you," she said softly, "Emma and I will take care of you."

The black eyes seemed to enlarge, the Nihil, the sigil of the Unholy

Trinity, fading like the moon at the rising of the sun. "And I," Beleth said, "will protect you with my life."

"Good. Then our first order of business is to find Hugh and free him."

"Then can I kill Obarton?"

Lilith laughed deep down in her throat.

# 33

## Hollow Lands / Lalibela, Ethiopia: 1919

**THE NEW YEAR HAD ARRIVED WITHOUT CEREMONY OR EVEN** being marked by Conrad, Diantha, or Yeats. All were too busy fighting for their lives to be bothered with the man-made concept of time. Besides, in the Hollow Lands beneath the crust of the Earth time did not exist, or if it did, it was as a wholly different creature than it was among the civilizations of human beings.

As the last grains of sand drained out of 1918, Diantha lay in her son's arms, insensate.

"How is she?" Yeats asked, squatting beside them.

"I believe she is hovering between life and death."

Conrad's eyes were magnified by trembling tears, and his friend gripped his shoulder.

"Now when we are at our lowest ebb is the time to be strongest," the great poet said gently. "I only spent a short time with her. Nevertheless, I am of the opinion that she is stronger than both of us combined. If anyone can rally back to the land of the living it is she."

"Thank you, my friend." Conrad was staring down into Diantha's regal face, pale now in the shadow of Death. He could hear Death's bones rattling, a dry and inimical laughter that made him nauseated. "And thank you for saving our lives."

"I merely followed instinct."

"Instinct always surprises us doesn't it?" He shifted to take pressure off one leg, which was filling with pins and needles.

The abrupt movement caused Diantha to regain consciousness.

"Conrad," she said.

"I'm here, Mother, and so is the great poet. The Throne is gone, catapulted back into its hellish prison."

"And your father?"

"Gideon is dead. I made sure of that."

"Oh, God." Diantha's eyes closed. Nevertheless, hot tears squeezed out beneath the lids. "The prophecy has come true."

"Calm yourself, Mother," Conrad said. "You're safe with us now."

"Safe?" Diantha's eyes flew open. "No one is safe. Not now. Not ever."

Yeats, down on one knee beside her, said, "Madam, will you tell us the nature of the prophecy?"

"It foretells the Second Coming."

"Of course." He nodded. "The Second Coming of Christ."

"No, you fool!" she cried, so agitated she spit blood as she writhed in her son's grip. "The Second Coming of Lucifer."

"God in Heaven!" Yeats rocked back on his heels, almost toppling over as he was gripped by an existential fear such as he had never before known. He thought about the poem he had been writing in the Sphinx's presence. Even though it was not yet complete he had already titled it "The Second Coming." Coincidence or, as Conrad would surely believe, a product of his Farsight. This, he realized, was not for him to say. Though he had a small role in this play, he recognized it was an important one. He felt terror and exhilaration swirling through him in equal measure.

By this time, Diantha had lapsed back into stillness. "I am sorry, Mr. Yeats. My tone was unacceptably rude."

"No need, no need, madam." Yeats took her hand in his, was dismayed to find it as cold as ice. "Exigent circumstances, I warrant."

"You are too kind, sir."

Her voice was thin, almost ghostly. Yeats looked up into his friend's stricken face. "We must do something, Conrad. She is so cold. I fear that she is slipping away from us."

Conrad gestured with his free hand. "Let me have the artifact."

Yeats handed over the combined apple and crucifix, except now the rood was in the shape of a triangle. He scarcely noticed this, so intent was he on his mother's mortal condition. With the touch of the artifact he felt a surge, as of an electric current that almost lifted him off the ground. Blue fire enveloped him, but for some reason he could not fathom it would not transfer to her. Some instinct buried deep inside him told him the blue fire would heal her.

"It's not working," he murmured, as much to himself as to Yeats. "What am I to do?"

"Use the golden apple," Yeats said. "Place it somewhere on her—her stomach, perhaps."

With no other options open to him, Conrad lowered the artifact onto his mother's stomach. It was at that moment that he noticed the artifact's altered shape. Had it happened when the apple fused with the rood, or after the explosion that cast Verrine back into Hell? Impossible to tell.

A terrible shudder passed through Diantha's body, as of a drowning swimmer ridding herself of swallowed water. Her eyes opened.

"Mother!" He turned to Yeats. "It's working!"

"What is . . . ?" Diantha glanced down at the artifact. "No! What have you done!"

"I don't—"

"Get that thing off me!"

"But it brought you back to life."

"Do what I say. Oh, please, please, please, I beg you! Do it now!"

Conrad snatched the artifact off her, but his heart sank when he saw the wound on her stomach, like the bite of a viper. Around the wound was a black tar-like substance. His mind raced back to what Phenex, the Scryer Throne had tried to tell him: *Disaster . . . catastrophe . . . there are no other words! . . .*

Diantha twitched once, twice, three times. Then she began to writhe like a serpent.

"Mother!"

"Ah, it's happening. So soon, so soon."

"Mother, what is happening?"

Then Diantha screamed, an unearthly, bone-chilling cry of pain and abject terror.

*Disaster . . . catastrophe . . . there are no other words! . . .*

Writhing. Foam began to collect at the corners of her mouth. As quickly as she spit it out, it collected again. She coughed heavily, as if her lungs, having rid themselves of water were now filling up with something heavier, darker. Sinister.

"Get me to . . ." She gasped, gasped, gasped. "Only hope now." Tried to swallow, gagged, and vomited up a substance the color and viscosity of tar. It stank of brimstone and sulphur.

"Oh no." Conrad rocked her wracked body. "No, no, no."

"What is happening to her?" Yeats asked.

"I fear it has already happened," Conrad replied, then turned his attention back to Diantha. "Mother, listen to me. What is our only hope? Tell me what I must do and it will be done."

Diantha stared up at him, her huge, magnificent eyes red rimmed. He bent closer. Were the irises changing color? Was the emerald color darkening? Was her inner sun setting?

"Mother?" At his wit's end, he shook her shoulders. "Mother! I'm right here. I have you. How can I save you? God in Heaven, please tell me."

Diantha tried to form the word, had to start over. Speaking seemed to take all her effort. "Typhos," she said, at last, the word wrung out of her like a drop of blood. "Bring me to Typhos."

CONRAD LED the way, cradling his mother against his breast. Even so, he ran as fast as he could, scarcely aware of her weight.

*Once you enter the Hollow Lands you can never escape,* Phenex had told him. We'll see about that, he thought.

Right behind came W. B. Yeats, gingerly holding the transmogrified artifact at arm's length, as if it were a poisonous adder. Because it had poisoned Diantha, just like an adder.

Up they went, up, up, up, ascending the steepest part of the tunnel and then increasing their pace as the slope began to flatten out. How much time elapsed until they burst forth into the colossal chamber where Typhos still crouched on his plinth it was impossible to say. Time had slipped away like a thief into the shadows.

"What to do now?" Yeats said, trembling. Clearly, his agitation had hit a high point.

"Mother?" Conrad kissed her cold, clammy forehead. "Mother, we're here."

She opened her eyes, the lids gluey as if with long sleep, or unfathomable disease.

"I am standing beside Typhos."

The emerald of her eyes was long gone, replaced by irises the color of ash. The terrible dread that had taken hold of Conrad tightened its grip on his heart, turning his soul black. Was this Gideon's revenge from beyond death?

"Put me up." Diantha's voice was a reedy whisper, a shadow of itself.

Conrad, bewildered, said, "Put you up where?"

For a long time his mother did not speak. Her breathing was short, sharp, terribly labored.

"Mother . . ."

"At Typhos's left foot."

Not understanding, but obeying her nonetheless, he clambered up the corner of the plinth, set her down precisely where she had indicated.

"Step back," she whispered. Her eyes were mere slits. "Conny, get off . . ."

"I'm not going to leave you."

"You must. Please."

"No. Whatever is going to happen I will be right here at your side."

"Then you won't be able to catch me, Conny. You must catch me."

The magic, he thought, of Phoenician sorcery, which was completely beyond him.

He heard Yeats calling from below. "Conrad, come down. Let what will happen, happen!"

And still Conrad did not move. "What does your Farsight tell you, WBY?"

"I cannot!" Yeats cried, anguished. "In this I must disappoint you, my friend. Down here I can see nothing. The future is a blank slate."

"Conny, there is no time left."

"Mother." He placed a hand on her cheek.

"Conny . . ."

The pleading in his mother's voice, a tone he had never before heard from her, made him back away, descend to the ground to stand beside WBY, who wrapped his arm around his shoulders.

"Courage, my friend. Have faith in God's beneficent plan."

He heard it then, the odd, alien syllables of Phoenician he had heard, only once or twice before, coming from his mother's mouth. Now they filled the chamber, echoing on and on, building in volume, quickening in cadence, until . . .

The veins along Typhos's muscular flanks began to pulse as if they were filled with blood. The great Sphinx moved his head first. He looked down at Diantha with what Conrad later recognized as sorrow and pity.

Then he raised his left leg and, before Conrad could even utter a sound, brought the taloned paw down onto Diantha's head.

Conrad cried out in shock, revulsion, and a grief beyond anything he had ever known before. He was about to launch himself up onto the plinth to do battle with Typhos when the Sphinx lifted his paw and Diantha's headless body rolled away, off the corner of the plinth, into her son's waiting arms.

# 34

NIGHT HAD COME AND THE SEA HAD MELLOWED. THE INCES-
sant chop that had accompanied the sun's sudden slide into oblivion had
vanished with the light. The gulls were safely perched in their rookeries,
sliding into their own form of oblivion.

Bravo lay on the slimy deck while, above him, Ismail doled out orders
to his cadre. From what Bravo could make out through the red haze of
agony, Ismail was clearly in no hurry to leave this position. He seemed
convinced there was a reason Bravo had rowed out here. Two of his men
were scanning the horizon for any sign of a boat or a ship Ismail suspected had been sent to rendezvous with his prisoner. Bravo didn't blame
him; it was the logical assumption to make. Why else would Bravo be out
here alone in a rowboat, a craft ill suited to take on a sea voyage?

"So, Shaw infidel." Ismail turned from his cadre, squatted down beside
Bravo. "Who are you waiting for?"

"God," Bravo said, "or the devil." He tried to turn his head without
causing himself undue pain. "Maybe both."

"Listen to this," Ismail hissed through the gap in his front teeth. "Listen
to the infidel." He kicked the rood beyond the reach of Bravo's outstretched hand. "What use have you for a talisman of your false God. *Lā
'ilāha 'illā-llāh. Muḥammadur-rasūlu-llāh.*" There is no god but God.
Muhammad is the messenger of God.

As if they were attached to someone else's arm Bravo's fingers scrabbled
for the rood, its bronze coating fractured.

"You're right, Ismail. There is only one God. But he goes by many
names. I know you believe in Jesus as prophet."

"Yes. Jesus was *a* prophet, as was Moses, and *the* Prophet Mohammed, who spoke the holy words of Allah to the faithful." He poked Bravo in the ribs. "And four centuries after the rise of Islam, your pope, Christ's disciple, declared holy war on us. You brought the Crusades—war, torture, pestilence, death—to our land, and, really, you have never left."

"That was wrong," Bravo said. "The Crusades were a grievous mistake."

"What?" Ismail cocked his head. "What is that?"

"The West misunderstood Islam then. It misunderstands Islam now."

Ismail, dismayed, sat back on his hams. "What kind of infidel are you?"

"I'm a man," Bravo said. "This is one man speaking to another man. There is nothing more here than that."

Ismail rocked back and forth, as if he were praying. "I don't believe you."

"I can hardly blame you."

For long moments, then, there was nothing but the gentle rocking of the speedboat. Without taking his eyes off Bravo, Ismail called, "Anything?"

"Nothing," came the reply from both lookouts. Their faces were lit by the cockpit lights. "Not a boat or a ship to be seen."

"So. Tell me why you're here," Ismail said softly. "If you do, if you tell me the truth, I'll consider letting you go."

Bravo knew Ismail wasn't going to let him go, no matter what he told him. He sat up slowly and painfully. "There's no point," he said. "You can no longer recognize the truth when you hear it."

Ismail rubbed his thick beard. "Umm, in this instance I believe you're right. I can't recall the last time an infidel told me the truth."

"But I know the last time a Muslim told me the truth."

As Bravo had surmised, Ismail seemed intrigued. "And when was that?"

"Not too long ago, in Istanbul, I was traveling with a Muslim woman."

"Huh, already blasphemous." Ismail gestured. "But go on. From this beginning the blasphemies can only multiply fast as rabbits."

"This woman was very beautiful," Bravo continued. "All the Western men looked at her longingly when they passed her by."

"Utterly despicable. The behavior of rabid street curs that need to be put down."

He saw Ayla's fingers grasp the far side gunwale of the rowboat. "She ignored them."

"As she should."

"Until she didn't."

Ismail's face grew dark. "What is your meaning?"

"There was one man." He saw the top of her head. "An American."

"Of course an American. Like you."

"Actually, I'm Phoenician."

Ismail laughed unpleasantly. "No one is fully Phoenician anymore. Even us Syrians who live on Arwad." He laughed. "We're not even fully Syrian, when you get right down to it. We're polyglots, even the so-called Four Families. The Dutch came, Italians came, many others, European and Arab alike."

"That's my lineage. Phoenician and British."

"Not English?"

"My father's family is Welsh. A very strange place, Wales. The Welsh have their own form of djinns."

"Bah! Tales of djinns are for children. There are no djinns." With a look of disgust on his face, he gave a sideways glance at his man, who was still nursing his aching groin. "Continue with your story, Shaw infidel."

"This American was a pig."

Ayla, invisible in the dark, checked that the lookouts were turned away from her, rolled into the speedboat so deftly she caused barely a ripple in the water around the hull.

"He made no secret of staring at her breasts and legs."

"Her fault entirely," Ismail spit. "Had she properly covered her body there would have been nothing to see."

"She turned on her heel, went up to the American," Bravo said, "and she slapped him hard across the face."

"Huh." The look of disgust on Ismail's face intensified. "A woman like that, she should be executed." He looked hard at Bravo, then hauled him up to stand facing him, Bravo's back to the rail.

"But then the two spoke, one person to another, and an accommodation was agreed upon. Apologies—"

"Why are you telling me this story, Shaw infidel? Do you wish to become my friend?"

"I'd like for us to get to know each other better—as people, not ideologues."

That was when Ismail buried his fist in Bravo's abdomen.

"Fool!" he said. "Infidels aren't people." Then he kicked him hard in the chest.

Bravo was pitched over the side, plunging into the ink-dark sea.

# 35

HER BODY LAY IN STATE, WRAPPED TIGHTLY IN LAYERS OF gauze, then undyed muslin, and finally in shimmering silk of a purple obtained from murex shells, as was the custom of the Phoenicians. The large felucca and its crew of five was captained by a young woman named Tanis, who worked out of the Cairo section of the Gnostic Observatines. She was tan and very fit, with flashing green eyes and long black hair pulled back, against fashion, in a ponytail. Conrad had never seen a grown woman in a ponytail before. The curious style gave her a kind of mythical look, alien and alluring. He had not met her before, for which he was grateful. There were few people of his acquaintance he wanted to see in his current state.

Out of necessity W. B. Yeats was one of them.

"There is a feel to the air in the Levant," he said.

The great poet sat on a camp chair under a muslin shade that had been arranged by the crew, in the center of which was Diantha's corpse.

"Do you not feel it, my friend?" He glanced toward shore. "A certain softness, as if the great hand of time has worn down all sharp edges, all biting gusts."

"You should try crossing the Sahara," Conrad said somewhat distractedly. "There you'll find enough biting gusts to last several lifetimes."

"We're not in the Sahara; we're not in the past," Yeats said as compassionately as he could. "We can only try to control the present."

Conrad, who had been staring off into a space of his own conjecture, turned to him, eyes clearing. "Of course, yes. The present." He glanced at his mother's wrapped body. He heard the voice of Phenex, one of the Four Thrones that had ever so briefly merged with him but had been thrown back to Hell by the power of the golden apple and the gold rood: *Once you enter the Hollow Lands you can never escape.*

*Then we'll be prisoners together,* he had replied, understanding nothing.

He felt the shuddering inside himself again as Phenex cried, *Disaster . . . catastrophe . . . there are no other words! . . .*

"There are no other words," Conrad murmured now.

"What?"

"Disaster . . . catastrophe . . . my mother's death . . ."

"All that is behind us now, my friend."

Conrad shook his head. "But it isn't. My mother spoke of the prophecy. It is clear now that I was prophesied to kill my father, kill a Nephilim."

"But surely, Conrad, that was a good thing, terrible though it might appear to an outsider. You and I know the truth. Your father was bound for evil, no mistaking his intent. You had to stop him. What other course could you have taken?"

"I don't know. That's the hell of it." Conrad put his head in his hands. "But I can't help feeling that my mother's death was too high a price to pay for stopping him. You saw the look of horror on her face when I told her I had killed Gideon. There must have been another way."

"If there ever was, you will never know it now." He placed his hand on his friend's shoulder. "Possibly you were never meant to know."

Conrad's head came up. "What do you mean?"

"Well, it was clear enough Diantha knew the answer, but she never told you, did she?"

"How could she have anticipated this outcome?"

"My dear good friend, how could she not?"

"But you saw how frightened she was."

"I did indeed," Yeats agreed. "But what, precisely, was she afraid of? Death?" He shook his head. "I don't think so."

"Then what?"

"I don't know. This is your province, my dear." The great poet's gaze penetrated the lenses of his spectacles to strike Conrad between the eyes.

"No, not death. Never death. Not her." Conrad's mind raced backward to the moments before his mother's death. Something was different about her. What was it?

His mind kept turning away, turning away. . . .

What could be worse than death?

His mind kept turning away. . . .

*Disaster . . . catastrophe . . .*

He had assumed Phenex had foreseen Diantha's death. But what if the Throne had foreseen something else?

His mind kept turning away, turning away. . . .

Diantha's eyes had changed, darkened. Something dreadful had begun to surface in their depths. Something she needed to forestall, to destroy before it came to full flower. Before it took her over.

*Disaster . . . catastrophe . . .*

*That* was what Phenex had seen; that was what he had meant.

When he told all this to his friend, Yeats said, "But the problem is the artifact worked on your father. It drove the Throne out of his body. Correct me if I am wrong, but that was a good thing."

"No doubt." Conrad rose, went over to where his mother lay, placed a hand on her stomach. It was a bit easier now to be close to her. Bad enough to hold your mother's corpse, but to see her headless was stomach churning. When Yeats had followed him, he continued. "But my mother did not have a demon inside her, a Fallen, and I am guessing now, but I think the artifact had the opposite effect on her."

"You mean . . ."

Conrad nodded. "It began to pull one of the Fallen out of Hell into her."

"It must have been a very powerful one."

"Perhaps," Conrad said, "even Lucifer."

"God in Heaven!" Yeats whispered. "No wonder she was so terrified. No wonder she needed the Sphinx's intercession."

And it was true, Conrad thought. It was the explanation that fit the circumstances perfectly. Diantha had been afraid of nothing, not even Gideon. But Lucifer . . .

"At least it wasn't Satan," Yeats said. "I've been taught that Satan, Lucifer, and Beelzebub are three different Fallen. Isn't that right?"

"No, it isn't," Conrad said. "The names are all aspects of the same vile creature: Lucifer, the scholar; Satan, the iron fist; Beelzebub, the trickster."

Yeats shuddered, placed his hand beside his friend's. "No wonder . . . no wonder . . ."

The captain approached them. She stood, almost at military attention, hands clasped loosely behind her back, waiting politely. Her head was slightly bowed, her eyes lowered, in deference to the deceased.

She did not speak until Conrad, becoming aware of her presence, looked up. "Yes, Captain?"

"We are nearing your mother's final resting place, sir. Do you require more time?"

Conrad took a deep breath, let it out. It seemed as if time was all he had now, and though his mother's corpse would not decay as others would in the withering heat, he felt as if his mother, at least, had at last run out of it.

"No, Captain. You may begin. Oh, and please don't call me sir."

"If you won't call me Captain." Her eyes met his with a startling clarity of purpose. "I would be pleased if you called me Tanis."

And that was how Conrad Shaw met and fell in love with the woman who gave birth to his first child, and heir, Dexter, Bravo's father. After Tanis's death, he met Dilara, but that was many years later, when Conrad was an old man and far wiser.

On this day, however, aboard the felucca, Conrad, Yeats, and Tanis attended to the controlled pyre that consumed the many layers of silk, muslin, gauze, and then the flesh and bone of Diantha Safita, never a Shaw by name but a major bulwark of their lineage in the difficult times to come.

They stayed there, relighting the fire several times in order to reduce the bones to ash. When they had cooled sufficiently, Conrad cupped his palms, gathered the remains in a square of jute that Tanis handed him. The three crossed to the starboard side and, with the sun in their eyes, Conrad and Tanis intoned a prayer in Latin and Arabic. Conrad spoke the few phrases of Phoenician he knew and, on his mother's ashes, swore to devote this life and the lives to come to avenging her death, continuing with what in hindsight he recognized as her fight against Lucifer.

As Conrad scattered her ashes upon the Red Sea, Yeats recited for the first time what was destined to become his touchstone poem, "The Second Coming":

> . . . *Surely some revelation is at hand;*
> *Surely the Second Coming is at hand.*
> *The Second Coming! Hardly are those words out*
> *When a vast image out of Spiritus Mundi*

*Troubles my sight: a waste of desert sand;*
*A shape with lion body and the head of a man,*
*A gaze blank and pitiless as the sun,*
*Is moving its slow thighs, while all about it*
*Wind shadows of the indignant desert birds. . . .*

# 36

## Paris: Present Day

**AFTER THE MAGNIFICENT ISLAMIC MOSAICS, AFTER THE**
muezzins' calls to prayer, after the lush gardens and spectacular palaces,
the delicious chaos of the open-air souks, the steamy hammams and the
exotic spices and herbs perfuming the air of Istanbul, Paris looked drab
and wan under ruffled gray clouds.

It's as if all the life has been sucked out of it by the EU, Lilith thought. In
truth, she did not want to be here, was edgy about bringing Emma with
her. Paris was, after all, Obarton's territory. It was the city from which he
wielded most power, where he had the most allies, if not friends; she could
not imagine Obarton tolerating anyone long enough to be considered a
friend. But it was also the place where Hugh was being held captive.

Paris, sinister, shadowed, overlooked by legions of medieval gargoyles,
was where, for all the reasons previously enumerated, Obarton felt most
comfortable, most at home. Therefore, a certain edge would be taken off
his concentration, especially when it came to decisions in the field that
needed to be made on the spot. All this Emma had argued. Or had it
been Beleth? She couldn't remember now, and this sent a dagger of fear
through her heart. What would she do if Beleth and Emma were permanently joined? What if no exorcism on earth could rid her of the Fallen
Angel without killing her as well?

This conundrum had gnawed at her all during their time in Turkey,
caused her to ache body and soul. It distorted her days, making of them
a colossal hourglass through which sand dribbled one agonizing grain at
a time. And at night she was assailed by horrifying nightmares: lakes of mercury out of which Emma arose time and again transformed into a siren
whose segmented tail stung her as they kissed or, alternatively, a beast

with snake eyes and a forked tongue that pursued her through forests dark and tangled.

And now, after days of this torture, Lilith was returned to Paris's sidewalks, caged by smart cars and metal stanchions. The spoken language seemed alien to her, loose and unintelligible compared to the musical torrent of Arabic in which she had been submerged.

It was the first time in her life she did not love Paris. Rather, she feared it, as if it had been a beloved pet that might at any moment rip off her face.

CARDINAL FELIX Duchamp was a fastidious man of the cloth, who nevertheless could rationalize the hell out of any situation, especially when it came to abetting the illicit activities of the Knights. He was also a man, it was said, who could hold a grudge until Judgment Day. When he ventured outside the precincts of Vatican City, not to mention Rome, it was always for an important reason, for he was not fond of either travel or foreign lands. And for him, Paris was a foreign land, the capital of a country that by and large had forsaken Christ, taking advantage of all the Catholic holidays yet ignoring their parish churches. In Paris, he felt, the magnificent cathedrals had been ceded to the invading tourists. As far as he was concerned, they might as well be deconsecrated. His holy righteousness was a cloak he wore, to hide from himself the increasing list of his transgressions and sins in the cause of lining his own pockets.

Obarton, having received a curt call from the cardinal's secretary announcing Duchamp's immediate visitation, knowing full well what it portended, set about exacting his pound of flesh to the full extent of his abilities. In Lilith's absence, he had gone about the business of shoring up the allegiances her abrupt and horrifying action at the last Circle Council had rent asunder. In fact, his power had consolidated to the extent that he was confident of defeating Lilith, now that the GPS on her mobile told him that she had returned to Paris.

To this end, in a spasm of spite, he had sent a car to transport the cardinal directly from the airport to the Knights' secret Reliquary, the one to which he had taken Lilith, below Père Lachaise Cemetery. If he was to be castigated it would be in the place of his choosing, inconvenient and unpleasant for everyone save himself. He knew the cardinal would find it thoroughly distasteful to see the coffins of incinerated corpses, which Obarton's team would lead him past in order to arrive at the Reliquary, and was glad of it. That these people—and so many of them!—were not properly buried as Catholicism dictated would infuriate Duchamp. So much the better, Obarton thought.

So it was that when Duchamp was delivered to him in the Reliquary Obarton observed with quiet fury and secret delight the cardinal's pasty complexion, the handkerchief held up against his nose and mouth, as if inhaling a single ash from the dead might pollute him. You're quite polluted enough, Obarton longed to say, but wisely kept his mouth shut, though the fury rose up in him like a black wind. He had already hated Duchamp before the meeting at the Vatican; now he despised him almost as much as he did Lilith Swan. She had made a fool of him; thus she had to die, proof that the cardinal wasn't the only one to rationalize the hell out of a situation.

"Cardinal," he said, as Duchamp picked his way toward him across the stone-block floor.

"Such a pleasure."

"Good thing I wasn't expecting an apology," Duchamp snapped curtly. "Cut the sideshow. There are important matters to discuss."

"Tea?" Obarton said, refusing to be drawn out by the cardinal's tone. He led Duchamp into a smallish side room, one of a number of chambers Lilith hadn't been made privy to on her visit. "Or perhaps something a bit stronger, for fortification after your tiring journey."

The chamber was small, barely comfortable. It contained wooden furniture—a table, four chairs, a sideboard within which could be seen a half refrigerator. No windows, of course, but a plethora of sconces from within which electric candles inelegantly threw light onto a large cruci-fix and an oversized crest of the Knights of St. Clement affixed to the stone walls. In all, the chamber fairly shouted its utilitarian design.

"It took me longer to get here from the airport than the entire flight from Rome," Duchamp grumbled. He had taken away the handkerchief, which was now crushed in one fist.

"Apologies, Cardinal, but pressing business required my presence here." Obarton crossed to the sideboard. "And since your secretary said your visitation was urgent . . ." He spread his arms wide. "Well, here we are. For better or worse."

"Indeed." Duchamp glanced around, the distasteful expression never leaving his face. He was dressed in all the scarlet finery of his lofty status within the Church. A large pectoral cross made itself at home on his stole, symbol of both God's power and Duchamp's earthly power granted to him by the pope. "Sherry. Oloroso, should you have it."

"Your wish is my command," Obarton said without a trace of irony. "But do take a seat, Cardinal."

He poured the dark, scented sherry into fine crystal glasses, handed one to Duchamp where he sat on one of the straight-backed chairs. Obarton sat on another, took a sip, nodded, put the glass down on a corner of the table nearest him.

"I have my doubts, Obarton."

Obarton stared at him with a neutral expression, offering nothing.

"Grave doubts—"

"Quite an amusing phrase, considering our present location."

The cardinal looked at him as if he had lost his mind. "Grave doubts, not only about you, monsieur, but about the Knights of St. Clement of the Holy Land in toto." He paused, taking a judicious sip of the sherry. "One accusation that can never be leveled at you is an undeveloped palate for wines." He took another sip, set his glass down. "Yes, accusations, explanations, excuses. I have a rather violent aversion to all three." He shrugged. "But life doesn't often—I would say, rarely—give you what you want." His eye caught Obarton's. "Isn't that so?"

Obarton remained mute, inscrutable as a stone.

The cardinal shrugged again. "This statement is true in my experience and I'm quite certain in yours, as well." He folded the crushed handkerchief very carefully, laid it beside his glass, causing Obarton to involuntarily alter the direction of his glance.

"'Make friends quickly with your opponent at law while you are with him on the way, so that your opponent may not hand you over to the judge, and the judge to the officer, and you be thrown into prison.' Do you know this passage from Matthew, monsieur?"

"I do now," Obarton said.

"I tried to do this with you, monsieur, but you refused all offerings, great and small." The cardinal shifted from one buttock to the other. "In fact, you did more than refuse. First you took advantage of my assistance; then the moment you believed someone else in your Circle Council met with me, you assumed the worst and sought to destroy my power and my influence. You sought, not to put too fine a point on it, to destroy me."

Obarton considered a number of explanations, but they all sounded absurd, even to him. He then moved on to excuses, a number of which it was possible to put forward, until he recalled they would have the opposite effect on the cardinal. The safest choice—the only choice—was to keep silent and let Duchamp's gambit play out.

"To whom shall I compare you, monsieur? You are the observer of the children sitting in the marketplace, who call out to you and say, 'We played the flute for you, and you did not dance; we sang a dirge, and you did not mourn.' You, monsieur, have done nothing for either the Church or the Knights. You have, instead, created a rogue nation that marches to the sound of your voice." Duchamp shook his head. "This cannot continue. This cannot be tolerated. Not a moment longer."

Worse than I thought, Obarton said to himself. But, he supposed, only to be expected. "And what do you propose, Cardinal?"

"Propose, monsieur? I *propose* nothing." The cardinal, in his immense wrath, rose to his feet. High color had come to his cheeks, wiping away their former pallor. His neck was as red as a wet rooster's. "I order you to stand down. As of this moment and forever going forward, you are no longer eligible to be *Nauarchus,* you will no longer sit at the Circle Council, you are no longer a member of the Order of the Knights of St. Clement of the Holy Land. By order of the pope and the College of Cardinals all your dictums, all your plans, are henceforth null and void."

"WHAT IS it?" Emma asked, after they had exited the taxi in the Marais. "You look like someone just walked over your grave."

That was precisely the feeling that gripped Lilith. It had started as they passed through Immigration at Charles de Gaulle, had increased during the taxi ride to the Périphérique, the city's ring road, thence through the Porte de la Chappelle, into the heart of Paris.

The feeling escalated as soon as the taxi dropped them off and they stood on the sidewalk three blocks from rue des Archives. And yet even this far away, her nostrils flared.

"What is that?" She turned from Emma, wheeling in a complete circle. "Do you smell smoke?"

"A building has had a fire," Beleth said gruffly. "And believe me, I'm familiar with every form of smoke there is."

"Jesus God!" Lilith cried. "Hugh!"

She began to run, but Emma grabbed her arm, held her back. "Listen, listen," she or Beleth said—in her anxiety Lilith could not tell which— "even if it is Highstreet's flat, *especially* if it is, we have to be careful. Obarton would be smart to post a stakeout just in case you came back." She stared hard into Lilith's face as Lilith tried to free herself. "Isn't that what you would do if you were him?"

The wild look in Lilith's eyes slowly subsided. "But Emma, if it is, if that's what happened, then I'm to blame. I put him squarely in harm's way."

"Hugh's an adult, a very smart one, according to you," Emma said levelly, and now Lilith knew it was her speaking. "He went into this venture with his eyes open. He knew the consequences."

"And you think that absolves me?"

"I think," Emma said, in Beleth's deep timbre, "we would do well to stop speculating and find out what's what."

They headed off toward the block of rue des Archives where Highstreet lived. At first, Lilith took the lead as she knew where the building was, but soon enough the Power suggested it take over. "I can see things you cannot."

"But if people are watching they'll see Emma."

Emma smiled with Beleth's dark eyes. "Recall the bridge in Istanbul," was all it needed to say.

And, though reluctantly, Lilith gave Beleth Highstreet's address and flat number, understanding it was the prudent way to proceed.

She hung back while Beleth, looking out through Emma's eyes, turned the corner and scanned the block. "The fire was in his building, in his flat," the Power reported.

Tears glittered in Lilith's eyes. Ashamed of her display of emotion, she wiped them angrily away. Crossing the street, she entered a tobacconist's shop, bought the day's newspaper. Back out on the street she riffled through it. A small mention of the fire, a good sign, since if Hugh had been home, a larger news story would surely have reported his injury or death.

Feeling a bit better, she tossed the paper, went back to her position behind Emma. "Anyone watching?"

"One man," Emma said with Beleth's voice.

"Show me."

"Behind the wheel of the green Fiat. I think it would be better if I took care—"

"No," Lilith said sharply. "I want to save you for later, if things go pear-shaped."

"I do not understand."

"Fucked up, how's that," she said in Emma's ear, "better?"

"No." The demon under Emma's skin gripped her arm so hard she bared her teeth. "You will stay here, where you will be safe."

No sign of Emma at all; this frightened her, but she tamped it down, nodded. What else was she to do?

Brushing past her, Emma strode down the block at precisely the same pace as all the other pedestrians. Nothing about her set her apart, except, that is, if you were looking for her. And even if that were the case, Beleth made sure you'd miss her.

Hidden, Lilith watched, heart in her throat. The man in the green Fiat was on surveillance; she was certain of it. She recognized him as one of the goons who had wrapped the bodies of the three former Circle Council members and taken them out to the waiting trucks downstairs.

Obarton would have been incensed that she broke protocol, cut off communication with him. Of course she had taken this into account when Hugh had played her the incriminating video of Obarton and his underage boy toys Hugh's wonderful gadget she had planted on Obarton had recorded. That would keep him safe, she'd thought; once Hugh showed it to him Obarton wouldn't dare make a move again him. But she was wrong. Between bouts of formulating the plan with Emma and Beleth, she had finally worked out the flaw in her thinking: Killing Hugh would trigger the release of the video. Whereas if Obarton abducted him, kept him isolated, well, then Hugh couldn't call his lawyer; Obarton would be safe.

And yet he wasn't safe, not at all. As soon as they were finished here, they would take care of that.

The man sat behind the wheel of the old, battered Fiat, windows down, smoking idly, as if waiting for his wife or mistress to put on the last of her makeup in their flat. Emma walked up beside the passenger's door, lifted the lock button, and slid into the seat in one smooth motion.

As the man turned in her direction, his eyes opened wide. Instead of reaching for his handgun, he jabbed the glowing tip of his cigarette butt toward her left eye.

Beleth evaded the shaky attack, brought the man's head down until his forehead met Emma's raised knee with a satisfying crack. His body lost its tension, the muscles slackening, and Beleth throttled him, squeezing tighter and tighter, cutting off all oxygen. And, then, because it was really pissed off, because it had not tasted the thrill of killing in some time, the Power struck a blow so forceful it jammed the man's nose up into his brain.

He was dead before his head hit the steering wheel. Beleth guided it away from the horn in the center, treating his head gently now that he was dead and its spasm of rage expended. Beleth breathed slowly and deeply, willing the mind to calm the host body. For a time, then, it sat quite still in the passenger's seat, inhaling the aftermath of the fire.

"Why did you kill him?" Lilith said as she leaned in the open window.

"He was a threat." Its voice had taken on a new thick and throaty tone.

"We could have squeezed him for information. Maybe he knew where Obarton is keeping Hugh."

"We'll find him through—what do you call it?"

"The GPS."

"Right." Beleth inhaled deeply.

"Well, that's blood under the bridge now." Lilith watched Beleth in Emma's eyes. "Turned on by death, are you?"

"Always." Emma licked her lips. "Should I feel ashamed?" A rhetorical question. "I don't feel shame."

"But your host does." Lilith took Emma's hand, looked into her lover's dark eyes. "Let her speak, Beleth, if only for a little while."

"For you, Lilith, anything." Again the curious thick and throaty tone.

And then Emma's eyes lightened, along with her expression.

"Look what he's made you do," Lilith said softly. "Are you—?"

"Let's have no more talk of that." Emma smiled. "Now for God's sake let me get out of the car, so we can get out of here."

Emma exited the Fiat, but not before taking the man's mobile and rolling up the windows.

"I have no intention of leaving just yet," Lilith said. "He looks like he's asleep. Or drunk. Besides, check out the sidewalk side windows. The sunlight is turning them opaque. I figure we have about fifteen minutes. Plenty of time for what we planned."

Emma followed Lilith into Highstreet's building. Lilith knew the codes to get them in. Upstairs, the front door was cordoned off with police tape. Apparently, an investigation as to the cause of the fire was ongoing, but Lilith was familiar enough with the Paris police to know that they'd get around to it when they got around to it, never mind the grumblings of the neighbors, who were complaining of the stink and calling for smoke and fire remediation. Besides, she was ready to bet that the infamous French government red tape was already mummifying everyone involved.

Unpeeling one end of the tape, she used her key to enter the apartment. The door, which had been split in half by the firemen, had been crudely hammered back together, using raw wood crosspieces.

The place stank of smoke, but she was grateful that the firemen had smashed all the windows in an attempt to air out the flat after they had extinguished the fire. As expected, the rooms were a mess—what was left of them. What furniture remained identifiable was ruined and still sopping wet; it wouldn't be long before mold set in.

"What if it's not here?" Emma asked. "What if it was destroyed in the fire?"

"Have faith," Lilith replied.

"Faith!" Beleth's dark voice. "Another God-word!"

The kitchen was a complete disaster area; it was clear the fire had started there. In the bedroom, the door side of the bed was a staved-in mess, but the far side was only streaked with ash, the rucked coverlet patterned as if with graffiti. The dresser had collapsed on one side and, like a horse, kneeling, bowed its head. She opened the closet door, stepped inside. Hugh's neatly folded clothes were intact but were of course unwearable, covered with snowy ash, stinking of smoke. Pushing aside the array of suits, she exposed the back right corner. Reaching up, she removed a plaster-covered wooden peg. Digging her forefinger into the opening, she pulled down, revealing a recess in which resided a USB thumb drive.

"Gotcha!" she said.

# 37

**THERE WAS NOTHING MORE TO SAY, WAS THERE? OBARTON**
escorted Cardinal Duchamp out of the Reliquary, back into the late afternoon, the granite angels weeping rainwater, the gutters along the pathways
gurgling. The sky was low and still ominous, though the clouds were driving swiftly eastward. When he looked at the cardinal's back, he did not
even feel anger. He had passed beyond that stage, into the familiar territory most men dared not even dream of. But Obarton was not most men;
he had gotten ahead in the world and, most importantly, had stayed there
by ruthlessly manufacturing his own reality. Duchamp was no longer a
part of his reality. He had dismissed him as a cardinal, as a man, the moment Duchamp had denounced him. Now the cardinal was but a shadow
as he stepped into the car and the driver rolled away, down the winding
paths toward the entrance far below.

Obarton watched the car out of sight, then lifted his arm, signaling his
own vehicle. He climbed in. There was no reason for him to speak to the
driver; he already knew the destination.

Once outside Père Lachaise, Obarton again caught sight of the car
taking the cardinal back to Charles de Gaulle Airport as his driver followed at a discreet distance. He sat back, crossed one leg over the other,
called up the app one of the tech people had installed on his mobile, and
tracked Lilith's presence in Paris. Hugh Highstreet might be enisled, but
his cadre of people were still working like diligent mice, only now under
Obarton's relentless whip. None of them had Highstreet's brilliance, true
enough, but that only meant Obarton had to find someone of equal genius
to replace him. In fact, he was determined to hire someone far cleverer
than Highstreet, one who was in thrall to him, not Lilith Swan.

He paid scant attention to the streets as they passed by, so immersed was he in his vicarious pursuit of Lilith's whereabouts. She was in the Marais. According to the app, on the very street where Highstreet used to live. He closed his eyes for a moment, nostrils dilated as if he could smell the wood char, savoring in his imagination the look on Lilith's face, the heaviness in her heart, as she came upon the ruin of Highstreet's fire-ravaged flat.

Idly, he texted Denis to ensure Lilith was, in fact, there. After some time, he received the expected reply. Then, because they had reached the Périphérique, joining the endless traffic that circled the city, he put away his phone and concentrated on the moment to come.

Sunlight began to peek through the clouds in the west, as the sinking sun lowered itself into its coffin for another night. The light was such that he could see his face in ghostly reflection in the window, superimposed over the factories, warehouses, and company headquarters that dominated the outskirts of Paris. At length, the car carrying Duchamp exited, following the signs for the airport, and his own car exited as well. On either side of the highway rose more of the industry of France, faceless, full of massed signage, looking more or less indistinguishable from the industrial areas of any other country in the EU.

Approximately halfway to the airport, Duchamp's car pulled off the highway and into a roadside gas station. It stopped alongside a petrol pump; the driver emerged, dipped a credit card, began to fill the tank. Then he ambled into the station itself, perhaps to relieve himself or to buy cigarettes; it really didn't matter. Obarton's driver pulled his car onto the leading edge of the petrol station.

Obarton took out his mobile once again, counted to ten, then pressed a six-digit string of numbers into the virtual keypad. There was an instant's silence in his head, as everything save the car carrying Duchamp ceased to exist. Then with a hellacious *whoomp!* it and the pump itself exploded into a massive fireball plumed by thick acidic black smoke.

"Back to the Reliquary," Obarton said to his driver, and the car pulled out into traffic, which was just beginning to come to a virtual standstill. Car horns blared angrily, fearfully; sirens began to wail; people jumped out of their cars, screaming and gesticulating wildly in the wake of the disaster.

Obarton's car drove on. He seemed to feel the intense heat of the conflagration at his back, but that might only have been an illusory part of his immense satisfaction. Cardinal Felix Duchamp was gone, gone, gone, to meet his Maker or, more likely, into the arms of some demon caretaking the lowest pits of Hell. Either way, it was of no concern to Obarton.

He began to think of his favorite scene from *Witness for the Prosecution*, when Sir Wilfrid says—and so pleased was he with the afternoon's success that he recited the line of dialogue out loud in Charles Laughton's plummy tones—"'The wheels of justice grind slowly, but they grind finely.'"

He was chuckling, still in full Laughton mode, when the focus of his vision changed. Upon the window he saw not only the reflection of his own face but also, just behind him, the horrid horned, grinning countenance of the Fallen Seraph he had glimpsed at the Vatican.

**THEY ESCAPED** the police presence by about a minute and a half, rounding the corner at the far end of the block even while hearing the familiar high-low, high-low bleat of sirens. The sun was obscured by clouds stretching upward from the west, where it was already dark and raining. A wind had arisen. It skittered along the street, as if hurrying them along.

The rain came soon thereafter, and they descended into the Métro at Arts et métiers, where Lilith threw her phone into a trash bin, keeping the phone that Emma had lifted from the dead man in the Fiat. They changed at République, rode two stops, emerging at Saint-Ambroise.

Under low, ugly skies that intermittently spit at them, they headed down rain-slick sidewalks toward a side street off boulevard Voltaire not far from the Saint-Ambroise church that gave the quartier its name. The buildings were gray and faceless. People hurried by, hunch shouldered, under deployed umbrellas.

Halfway down the street, they entered a patisserie on their left. The plate-glass window was filled with luscious-looking napoleons, fruit tarts, and Saint-Honoré's. The floor was much-scuffed tiny tiles, the ceiling pressed tin. The smell of caramelized sugar and melted butter permeated the air. Two middle-aged women, one with a child in tow, were being served by a pair of young women, while a third manned the cash register.

Lilith went up to the cashier. "Monsieur Boyer. Please tell him Mademoiselle Swan is here to pick up her strawberry tarts."

The woman went into the back, returning almost immediately, followed by a stolid middle-aged man with unruly hair and small, unblinking eyes. He wore a full apron over his trousers. The sleeves of his shirt were rolled up past the elbows.

"Mademoiselle, your order was for eight tarts," he said. His face revealed nothing.

"Pardon me, monsieur, I ordered a full dozen."

The muscles of his face seemed to relax. "So you did." He nodded. "This way, if you please."

They stepped behind the counter, followed him down a corridor dim with pastry flour dust. Past the kitchens, they made a sharp left. The end of this elbow revealed a door, which Boyer unlocked, gesturing them to pass through.

They found themselves in a laboratory, filled with all manner of computers and related electronic equipment. Staff members went about their work without even glancing up at the newcomers. Emma could feel Beleth's bewilderment, felt almost sorry for the Power.

Lilith handed over the dead man's mobile. "I want to know who he called last and most and where those people are."

Without a word M. Boyer set to work. He did not ask who Emma was; he scarcely glanced at her. She didn't matter to him. Only the job of work Lilith had handed him mattered.

He plugged the mobile into one of his computers and began. After several minutes, he said, without looking up, "You must be hungry. Ask Agnes to feed you."

"I've got more important fish to fry," Lilith replied.

At which Boyer at last looked up. As he caught sight of the thumb drive Lilith held up, his mouth twitched in what Emma could only surmise was a smile. He pointed his thumb at a laptop across the lab, then went back to work.

Lilith crossed the lab, Emma following a step behind. She plugged the thumb drive into a USB port on the side of the laptop, then opened a secure VPN connection to the Internet. Now whatever she did from this computer could not be traced. Her fingers flew over the keyboard and, moments later, the first of Highstreet's several layers of firewalls popped up, preventing her from gaining access to the Knights' server. Minimizing that window, she navigated to the icon of the thumb drive, which showed up on the screen as Drive N, and opened it. There were four folders: Huey, Dewey, Louie, and Uncle Scrooge.

Lilith let go of a grim laugh. "Oh, Hugh," she murmured to herself. She hovered the mouse over the Hughie, clicked to open it, returned to the server screen in time to watch the first layer of firewall dissolve. You could almost see it happening brick by brick.

Sensing Emma hovering over her shoulder, she said, "I assume you know the codes to copy the material to the Gnostic Observatine servers."

"I don't," Emma said. "But we have a satellite server I can get into."

"Do it."

Lilith moved aside, giving Emma access to the keyboard. When the first tier of folders had been copied, Lilith opened Dewie. The second firewall, more difficult to penetrate than the first, was breached, revealing more sensitive data, which Emma duly copied. The same procedure was repeated, dropping the third and even more difficult firewall to breach. Not for Louie, however. Now all of the Knights' secrets were revealed. Soon enough they were copied, too. Then and only then did Lilith activate the files in the fourth folder. Like the original Uncle Scrooge, this neat program undid all the temporary damage its nephews had wreaked, sealed up the firewalls one by one, at the same time removing all traces of the intrusion.

"There you go," Lilith said, removing the thumb drive from its slot.

Emma, who had given Beleth a silent request to butt out, bent over Lilith, kissed her on the nape of her neck. Sparks flew for both of them, but perhaps more for Lilith than her lover. The siege Emma was fighting, which up until now she had successfully kept from both Lilith and Beleth, had entered a new stage, one more savage, more furious, than anything that had come before. It was as if Lucifer's words, having been given life by being read, had called up hitherto-unexpected reinforcements. More violent troops, more complex siege engines, were massing around her defenses. Emma's resources were being taxed to the limit. And then a new and more terrifying siege was wheeled into place. The words of Lucifer—Arabic, Hebrew, Phoenician, Tamazight—began a siren song, a cord of twining melodies so beautiful, so magnificent, sultry, eloquent, compelling, they sparked, dazzled, exploded soft as fragrant flowers in the space behind her eyes. She felt drawn to them, magnetized, falling into a potent trance-like state from which she knew she would never return—never want to return.

The word-music was a warm tide lifting her into its embrace, rising up. A moment more and it would engulf her entirely. She would be beneath it, within it, swirling, ever swirling, to the celestial word-music. Sweat broke out on her hairline, her upper lip, in her armpit. Droplets of it slithered down her backbone, and she uttered a tiny moan as she swayed on her feet.

Lilith, whose senses were already highly calibrated to Emma's ever-cycling personalities, leapt out of the chair and held on to her to keep her from falling.

"Emma," she said, "Emma, are you all right?" And then, because Emma didn't or couldn't answer her, her tone changed. "Beleth, what the hell is going on?"

" 'Hell' is right." The voice, deep and perplexed, emanated from between Emma's half-parted lips as if she were a ventriloquist's dummy. "Something has hold of her."

Lilith flashed it a glowering look. "I thought *you* had hold of her."

"I do, but—"

"Then find out what's gone wrong. Maybe you've begun to poison her. Maybe you're killing her."

"Impossible, I—"

"Nothing seems impossible these days," she hissed at him with bare teeth. "You're a Power." She was trembling with rage and fear. "Find what's gone wrong, fix it, or by all that's holy I will find Leviathan and tell him how you've strayed from the Fallen straight and narrow."

"Get away from me," Beleth snapped. "Put her down. Go do something else. See how your friend over there is making out."

"I'm not leaving her side until I know she's okay."

"There is nothing you can do," the Power said. "I do not understand you."

"I'm the luckiest woman on earth," she said bitterly. "No more talk." She gestured with her head. "Get on with it."

Emma lay insensate in Lilith's arms, but disconcertingly her eyes remained open. Black as pitch, unfocused, they stared at nothing.

At length, beneath the soft hum of the electronic equipment Lilith heard a sound. So softly at first that she was not sure that it wasn't inside her own head. Then it repeated, and repeated again, in a kind of rhythm like that of the hooves of a horse at full gallop.

"What's happening?" she whispered, as if to herself. "God in Heaven, keep Emma safe." Which was a foolish thing to say. Emma wasn't safe, and hadn't been since Lilith met her. She was at the mercy of occult forces so powerful Lilith could not have imagined them even a week ago. She recalled how Obarton had frightened her with the hologram of the Fallen Archangel, how Hugh had revealed the trick when she had returned to his lab. So skeptical, both of them. And where was that skepticism now? Crushed beneath the pounding hooves of the invisible oncoming steed.

As the sound of the thrumming rose she began to feel ill, sick to her stomach. Her head hurt in a way it never had before. She could no longer feel her feet; they were as inanimate, as dead, as blocks of ice. And now she began to fear not only for Emma but for herself as well.

"Beleth," she whispered in a dry husk of a whisper. "Beleth."

But there was no response. She took a quick glance over her shoulder. There was M. Boyer with his back to them, shoulders hunched, in the middle of following the electronic signals from the dead man's mobile back to their source.

Then Emma gave a galvanic start. She commenced to convulse as if a high current were being applied to her. The lids over her black eyes slid down, then immediately popped back again. Nothing in the blackness. Nothing at all.

Lilith felt the sting of hot tears forming, over-flooding her eyes, running down her cheeks, leaving tracks like war paint. And, as her heart constricted, she thought, Love is a weapon as well as a solace.

Now Emma was convulsing so hard and so rapidly Lilith was obliged to hold on to her all the tighter in order not to lose her. But I am going to lose her, she thought. And then, What hasn't she told me? Is this the end-game of her resistance against Beleth?

She bent over, put her lips against Emma's ear. "Emma, I'm here. I want to help you." She kissed the tip of the ear, then the lobe, like she did when they were making love. Emma was cold, so cold Lilith gasped. "Oh, Emma, please tell me. How can I help you?"

And then, most horrifyingly of all, Emma's mouth hinged open in a way that made her seem both more and less than human. Her tongue, black as her eyes, fluttered like a banner on the battlefield, and words deep, harsh, ragged were forced through her voice box with what seemed a strangled effort:

"The . . . end . . . is . . . near—"

In one final convulsion her head swiveled on a neck corded with immense tension, and she vomited up a gluey substance, thick and black as tar.

# 38

BRAVO FELL THROUGH A THICK VELVET NIGHT, TURNING, turning. Small fish came to investigate. When a larger shadow approached, they turned tail as one and vanished. Ayla, who had scrambled after Bravo, reached him as he sank. Grabbing fistfuls of shirt at his shoulders, kicking out and up, she arrested his downward trajectory.

Above them, the speedboat's running lights stabbed down through the water. Diadems, glimmering like stars, floated below them. An octopus, curious but shy, stared up at them before whooshing away in a cloud of ink.

Ayla, kicking hard, her legs working in apposition, drove them upward. They broke the surface, Bravo gasping for air and for the surcease of pain. She maneuvered them over to the rowboat, where she could lift him far enough out of the water to see the swollen flesh on his cheek. The bruise was just starting to darken, like a port wine stain.

"My God, we have to get you into the boat and lying down."

"No," Bravo said.

"No? What no? We're treading water here and freezing."

"If we waste time getting me into the boat we could lose them."

"Them? The people who grabbed you and beat you up?" Her eyes sparked in the starlight. "I don't give a fig about them."

"Well, you'd better," Bravo told her. "Ismail has the rood."

"So what? It's not the real, one. This one's made of bronze."

"The bronze is camouflage, just a covering," Bravo said. "Underneath, it's made of solid gold."

"I don't care—"

"Ayla, we need the rood. Along with the apple it's part of the Unholy Trinity."

"But you saw for yourself they repelled each other."

"Yes, and you wondered if perhaps we had the wrong apple. But it was because of the bronze covering on the rood." He winced.

"Bravo, I can't help you while you're still in the water. At least, on board I can make you warm. Here, you have no chance."

He seemed to lose focus then, his gaze drifting far away toward something she could not see.

"What? What is it?"

But he didn't answer. It was unclear whether he even heard her, for in his mind rose the apple tree under which he and Conrad had spoken, not only as grandfather and grandson, he realized now, but as progenitor and heir. He could hear the leaves rustling in the wind, the thrush calling from one of the topmost branches. Warm sunlight spilled in golden droplets through the labyrinth of leaves. The fruit, red and ripe, swayed, gave off its intoxicating perfume. And as he watched, Conrad rose from his wheelchair and, no longer disabled, plucked an apple from a branch overhead. He held it in the palm of his hand, a prize as well as an offering, but Bravo did not take it. Then Bravo knew that it wasn't yet time.

*Now I will tell you a secret,* Conrad said from across all those years and yet as close as if he had flown through the glittering night to land on Bravo's shoulder. *I did not fall—at least in the manner I told everyone.* His laugh was as soft as velvet. *Me fall off a ladder? Please!* He shook his head. *No. I lost the use of my lower limbs in my final encounter with Verrine.*

And the here-and-now Bravo thought, Verrine. I have encountered that name in the *Nihilus Inusitatus.*

*Yes, you have,* Conrad said in his mind. *Verrine is the Commander of the Four Thrones. Be very careful when you meet this terrible Fallen Angel. Do you understand me?*

As an answer, Bravo reached out for the apple sitting in the palm of Conrad's hand. It seemed to be waiting for him, and him alone.

*Now you are ready.*

As he picked it up it turned from red to gold.

"Bravo?"

Ayla's voice broke through his vision. Was it a vision, or . . . ?

"On the contrary," he said with a peculiar clarity she had never heard in him before, "right here, right now, is my only chance." He held out his free hand. "Give me the golden apple."

A frown pulled her eyebrows together as she dug it out of its hiding place against her skin and placed it on his palm. "What are you going to do with it?"

Closing his fingers around the orb, Bravo placed it against his bruised abdomen. A lightning flash, electric blue. A certain pain came to him, as if from a very great distance. A pain altogether different from any he had ever experienced before.

"What is it?" Ayla said, clearly alarmed.

"Nothing. I didn't know what to expect." Steeling himself, he pushed the apple harder against his flesh.

"My God," she said again, staring. "I feel like I'm in a dream."

"Perhaps you are," Bravo replied. "Perhaps we all are. Or maybe you're just feeling the chill. You've been in the water a long time."

Then he gave a little cry and doubled over.

"Bravo!" Ayla clutched at him, pulling his head out of the water. "What's happening? It's the apple."

"Yes," he managed to get out. Water cascaded over his face as she pulled him up. "The apple."

"What is it doing to you?"

"It's . . . I don't know."

"How can you not know?"

"It's opening a doorway." Bravo shuddered, and Ayla wrapped him as tightly as she could with her free arm. "I know where we have to go."

"We have to get out of the water. We've got to get you lying down. I'll row you to shore. I'll get a doctor."

"The pain is receding. My strength is returning. I don't need a doctor." As if to contradict his words, he convulsed, and Ayla cried out, holding him even closer. His heart seemed to beat as fast as a bird's. "The Four Thrones." His voice was thick, strange, as if emanating from a part of him that had been inaccessible to him up until now.

"What are the Four Thrones?"

"Not what, who." Bravo shuddered again. "Murmur, Raum, Phenex, Verrine. The leaders of the Fallen."

"Not Lucifer?"

"They are Lucifer's outriders, his generals. You know how some humans chain and starve attack dogs? This is what Lucifer has done to the Four. They are the epitome of evil, trained and bound to Lucifer. They are ravenous in their thirst for power. It is impossible to convey in language how dangerous they are."

"The golden apple of the sun has shown you all that?"

"That and more," he said.

His voice held a timbre that frightened her. "Bravo, where have you gone?"

"To the threshold of the doorway. But not through it. Not yet, anyway." His eyes, which had been slipping away, caught the moonlight, stars reflected in them. "Ayla, if we don't stop them, the Four Thrones will come through from the Hollow Lands to our world. They will wreak havoc and destruction. They will pave the way for the Second Coming, as Yeats predicted. 'The darkness drops again but now I know / That twenty centuries of stony sleep / Were vexed to nightmare by a rocking cradle, / And what rough beast, its hour come round at last, / Slouches towards Bethlehem to be born?'

"It's Lucifer, Ayla. Lucifer is on our doorstep."

"We're only two people, Bravo. What can we do?"

"We're Shaws," he said. "The battle for mankind's soul is what we were destined for."

Now it was her turn to shudder. "Where must we go?"

"First, we need to retrieve the rood."

"And how on earth are we going to do that?"

"Swim, Ayla," he said, pushing away from the rowboat. "Swim."

THE SPEEDBOAT was tied up to the stern of the Syrian mother ship, a hundred-foot vessel gotten up as a tramp steamer in order to fool the police and navy boats of various nations patrolling the Mediterranean. Lights streamed off the steamer; the pumps worked overtime clearing the bilges of seawater. Maybe the Syrians' ship was as old as it looked. At the moment, the speedboat was deserted, its cockpit and running lights off. The mother ship was weighing anchor, the rusty chain protesting vigorously as it was winched off the seabed.

"This way," Bravo said as they rounded the promontory that had hidden the ship from their view.

His strokes were long and powerful, and Ayla with all her expertise had no little difficulty in keeping pace. They hauled themselves over the rail of the speedboat moments before the anchor, bearded with brown kelp, rose in a thundering cascade from the sea. Presently, it was secured, and the steamer, engines rumbling, got under way.

"Thank you," Bravo whispered as he lay back against a bench.

Ayla was still in a state of comparative shock. He drew her to him. They huddled beneath the rail, backs against the curving hull, sharing what warmth remained in them. It wasn't enough. They kept shivering.

"We need to get out of these wet clothes," he said pragmatically. "The wind will dry our bare skin."

Without another word being spoken they both peeled off their sopping clothes, laid them out on the deck before returning to their spot. They spoke in low tones even though their voices even at normal volume would have been drowned out by the diesel engines.

Ayla rested her head against his shoulder, slowly relaxing her mind, which had been spinning insanely like an out-of-control top ever since he had pushed her overboard to keep her safe. "Bravo, tell me, have you ever been in love?"

"Once. At least I think I was. Now I can no longer remember her."

"I was never. Not even close." She shifted farther into him as the warmth started to build. "There was someone in London. A smart guy. It didn't take long for him to disappoint me, though. Is it the same with all of you?"

"I'm the last person to ask about things like that."

"No. You're far too busy saving mankind to think about such mundane things."

She sounded hurt, angry even, and this bewildered him. "I'm a Shaw. There's a burden—"

"Yes, yes. I'm fed up with hearing about the Shaw legacy," she snapped.

"If you don't feel it, Ayla, then it doesn't exist for you."

"That's not what I want to hear." Her face screwed up and she put her hands over it. "Don't you understand?"

He put his arm around her. He could not understand what was happening.

But then his mind—his *self*—had been pulled away from her. "Tell me," he said softly.

"Oh, I don't know." She shook her head. "I don't think I was cut out for this—for being a hero. My mother dragged me into this. Because of you."

"Because she had to."

"Have it your way," she said shortly. "In either case, I had made a life for myself in London. I was happy."

"No you weren't. You were made a scapegoat and fired from your position. And then there was the guy who disappointed you." He put his knuckle under her chin, lifted her head up. "He wasn't smart enough to make you happy."

She gave him a weary smile, like a lightbulb about to go out. "Well, you're right about that. But the last thing I wanted was to come back to Istanbul and get involved in my mother's . . ."

"Your mother's what?"

"My mother's other life," she said. "The one my father knew nothing about."

"She was protecting him."

"She was lying to him, withholding an entire part of herself."

"Did you tell your father about your other life?"

"I didn't want any part of it."

"That's not what I'm asking."

She turned her head away, said nothing for the longest time. The grinding of the ship's engines was all there was in the pallid moonlight.

"I loved my father. I wasn't of his blood, but I could not have loved him more if I had been."

"And he you. Omar Tusik was a great friend and a remarkable man."

"I miss him."

"More than your mother?"

"In a different way. You know, fathers . . ."

But Bravo didn't know. His own father had remained a mystery up until his untimely death. He was practical, highly intelligent, and cold as ice. Had he even loved his own son? Maybe. But he also begrudged him having Conrad's specialness, which by a fluke of genetics had passed him by.

"I'll understand—certainly I will—if you want out. Just because Conrad was your father . . ." His voice dropped off. He stared at the white water churning in the ship's wide wake. "Look, go home. Maybe I was wrong. Maybe you did make a home for yourself in London. So go back there. It's all right."

But there was something in his voice, some metallic edge. He was not capable of talking down to women, but he could cut them down to size as well as men. Ayla felt this happening to her now, felt the metaphoric ground slipping away under her feet. Leaving her where, exactly? Was that what she really wanted, to go back to London, resume looking for a job, even though she knew she had been blackballed from every law firm in Britain? What was waiting there for her? Contentment? Peace? Not hardly. And then she heard him say:

"The war is hidden now, but it's just around the corner. The enemy's advance guard is already here. Do you want to wait until the fire comes, until people are dying in the streets? It takes a certain kind of courage to stand up now, the kind that's not so very different from faith. I, as a Shaw, took a vow, just as Conrad did, just as my father did. It's as binding as the vows of priesthood, of taking the veil, pledging yourself to God.

"There is a choice to be made here, Ayla. It's yours and yours alone to make. But either way, I beg you not to take it lightly."

There were shouts from on deck, high above and in front of them, but no one was looking in their direction. It was a call to prayer. Everyone on board was on their prayer rugs, facing Mecca. It was a different world up there, one they could never really know.

She touched the apple tentatively, as if it might burn her fingertips. "Does this mean that you've become immortal?"

"I hope not. Who wants to be immortal? Fra Leoni constantly struggled with the changes he saw around him. It's a hard lot not being a part of an age. Like being an orphan."

"No direction home."

"Exactly." His watery smile was almost wistful. "We used to have a routine, he and I: when he got too depressed, I'd call him Fra Diavolo. It always made him laugh."

"He was your mentor. You must miss him terribly."

"Coming upon his decapitated head was a dreadful moment. Our enemies—"

"Yes. Our enemies knew how to deal with him."

He heard the emphasis, knew what it meant, looked straight into her eyes. "Which is why we must be careful when we approach Emma. The Fallen inside her will know how to deal with us, as well."

"How d'you know we'll be able to find her?"

"I think," Bravo said, his expression grim again, "that she'll be able to find us."

# 39

AFTERWARD, WHEN TANIS DID NOT IMMEDIATELY RETURN TO
her post, Yeats, seeing the look she gave his friend, stepped away toward
the aft rail, watched the last of Diantha dissolve in the dancing sparks of
sunlight glittering on the water. He missed Ireland, missed his bride-to-be,
but he would never have traded this adventure for anything in the world.
In a moment, he drew out his pad, began again to write with the same
fervor that had come to him in the presence of the underground Sphinx
in Lalibela.

"I am so sorry," Tanis said. She stood close to Conrad, and yet very
much apart from him. It was a curious thing that Conrad, even in his state
of grief, did not fail to mark. "I wish I'd known her."

"Thank you," he murmured. It was so hard. Throwing her ashes overboard, as was required, was the most difficult thing he had ever had to
do.

"She must have been a remarkable woman."

"She was . . . most remarkable."

But this was all small talk, condolence talk. Useless or necessary? It was
difficult to tell. In the end, it meant very little. Unlike what Tanis said next:

" 'I am carried away, the time of my nonexistence has come, my spirit
has disappeared, like the day, from whence I am silent, since which I became mute.' "

Conrad turned to her. "That is a quote from a royal Phoenician tomb."

"In Arvad."

He started. She had used the original Phoenician name for the small
island off Syria that was now known as Arwad. "Yes. Have you been there,
Tanis?"

"Alas no. But my family is originally from Arvad."

"You're Phoenician?"

She smiled. "My family name is Ahirom. We knew the Safitas very well."

EVENTUALLY, TANIS returned to her post. The sun was slipping through the traceries of western clouds. Gulls were calling, ibises were stalking the reeds on the western bank. The boat, sails huffing and puffing intermittently in the heavy air, kept plowing northward toward Cairo.

Yeats said to Conrad, "You'll marry that one, mark my words."

Conrad laughed softly. "I'm not the marrying kind." Nevertheless, his gaze alit for just a moment on their captain, and he thought, Perhaps he's right. A fellow Phoenician. My mother would like that.

"The artifact frightens me." Yeats's voice was soft but urgent. "Look what it did to Diantha." He moved them farther from the crew. "Perhaps we should throw it overboard. Let the tide of the Red Sea take it, and be done with its dreadful power."

Conrad, standing at the railing, hands clasped, the last remnants of his mother's ashes powdering his fingers, considered this for a long time. Presently, he took the artifact out. His hands moved over the piece in ways Yeats could neither follow nor understand, but which resulted in the rood and the apple separating.

He looked up at his friend. "We will travel to Cairo. There I will have a metalsmith of my acquaintance coat the rood in bronze. That metal has unusual properties in the world of my mother and Gideon. So long as it is intact, it will keep the rood's power at bay. That way we may conserve it without fear."

"And the apple?"

"Must be hidden, and hidden well away from the rood."

The worried look did not leave Yeats's face. Sunlight flashed across the lenses of his spectacles, briefly concealed his eyes. "And in the future should the bronze crack or be pried open?"

"Has your Farsight told you something I should know?"

The great poet removed his spectacles, pressed his thumbs into his eyes. "I have seen murder, my friend." His myopic gaze fixed on Conrad. "The death of your grandson, killed before his time."

Conrad looked stricken. "How do I prevent that future?"

Yeats shook his head. "I am sorry, but there are limits." With his ever-meticulous attention to detail, he hooked the ends of the spectacles' wire temples around the tops of his ears, made all the necessary adjustments.

"What I do know, what I have seen, is that if there is an answer, it must come from within, not"—he swept his arm wide—"out here."

THEY TRAVELED to Cairo by train, arriving in the middle of the night. Lights glimmered, reflected off the station's high soot-patterned walls. Shouts and murmurs went on all around them; it might have been mid-day instead of midnight. It was here trackside that W. B. Yeats said his good-bye.

"But we're not through yet," Conrad said, taken aback. "We have more questions that require answering."

"The only question I require an answer to is how fast I can return to my beloved Ireland." He smiled as he patted his friend's arm, aware of Tanis hanging back, watching them out of the corner of her eye. "She has been patient, perhaps overly patient. The truth is I have been selfish. This journey . . . well, it has certainly been extraordinary. Its echoes will doubtless reverberate in my mind and in my writing for decades to come. For this and for your extraordinary friendship I will forever be grateful."

He extended his hand, shook Conrad's; then the two men embraced. After a time, Yeats picked up his much-battered suitcases. "Be well, my friend. May God go with you always."

"And you, as well." Conrad watched the great poet pick his way along the platform, through merchants and Berbers.

It wasn't until he disappeared through the grand archway into the hall proper that Tanis approached Conrad. "He is a good man."

"Yes, he is," Conrad replied. A deep melancholy swept through him, and his shoulders hunched, as if from a stiff wind. "An extraordinary one."

"Interesting. He used that word also."

"You were listening?"

"Not intentionally." She presented him with a sly smile. "I have excellent hearing."

"You wanted to talk with me?"

"Actually, I wanted to inform you."

They began to step away from the train, following the path Yeats had taken toward the grand hall that gave out on to the streets of the city. Behind them, the locomotive sighed like a rejected lover.

"What might that be?" He was only half-listening. He was exhausted from the impossibly long journey. His mother's death as well as his father's betrayal weighed heavily on him. Though his parents put him in boarding school early, because it was the custom among their class, Diantha came to Cambridge to see him, spending as much time with him as she could between her trips abroad with Gideon. After graduating from college at the tender age of eighteen, he more or less followed in their footsteps. No time for women friends, for falling in love, for getting married. Those bonds were for other people, not him. He almost wept in remorse and fury. Who am I? he thought. More to the point, *what* am I?

They passed under the grand arch. The hall echoed with weary footfalls, like the slow progress of ghosts across a gray landscape. Fewer and fewer people seemed to be about now that the last train of the day had pulled in. An old man with a hump on his back swept the floor with desultory strokes, tiredly pushing dirt from one place to another. But the kids were still about, begging, scamming, on the lookout to pick the pocket of anyone too naïve or inattentive to pay attention. None of them approached Conrad and Tanis, however. They had a sixth sense about these things.

"Here's what I wanted to say: the past is immutable; the present is chaos; the future is like water running through your hand."

"Why are you telling me this? Is it supposed to make me feel better?"

"Even those gifted with Farsight cannot be certain what they see will actually occur, or occur in the way they have seen it."

"How d'you know this?"

"Because," she said, "the very nature of chaos makes a mockery of Farsight."

They had come to the line of grimy doorways that opened out on to the street. The hot air of the desert brought sweat to their brows and grit to their eyes.

"You understand," she said, pulling wisps of her hair back from her face, "I'm speaking about your grandson."

He turned to her. "I'm starving. Do you want to get something to eat?"

---

**THEY FOUND** a small joint off El-Zaher. It was one of Tanis's favorites, one reason being it was open all night. It was small, not much more than a hole in the wall, but it was cozy and welcoming at this time of the morning; that was all that mattered. The food wasn't bad, either, but perhaps that was only because he hadn't eaten all day. One old man with skin like a tobacco leaf and a skull as polished as a cue ball sat in a corner drinking tea out of a glass and reading the local paper. After their food had been served, the cook appeared, bringing a plate of sweetmeats to the old man's table. The old man folded away the paper as the cook sat down opposite him. They began to talk about the war just ended. This part of the world was scarcely touched, but there was the British presence, of course.

"How long have you been with us?" Conrad asked.

"You don't know?"

"If I did, I've forgotten."

She cocked her head. "I don't think you have. I don't think you forget anything." She produced a small smile so intimate he was sure she had never given it to anyone else. "You have an eidetic memory."

"True."

"Then why did you ask the question?"

"Answer, please," he persisted.

"Five years."

"Always in Cairo?"

"No. I was brought in from Safita."

"Where you were born."

"That's right. Syria."

"And how was the transfer effected?"

"Mr. Shaw—your father—recruited me."

This gave Conrad some pause. In the corner, the cook had told a dirty joke. Both he and the old man were suddenly full of mirth. He looked away from them, reengaged Tanis's eyes. "Did you ever meet Gideon?"

"No. I was greeted here by Mrs. Safita."

"My mother."

She nodded. "That's right."

Two transit workers entered the place, slouched at a table near the front. They were smoking like chimneys. The cook rose and went over to them, had a brief conversation, then returned to the kitchen. The scent of mixed spices filled the small room.

"I had no idea you knew her. I would have included you—"

She waved away his words. "I had a job to do."

"What did you think of her, my mother?"

"I'm hardly the one to ask."

"Still. I'm asking you."

"Mmm." She leaned forward, elbows on the table, chin supported by her cupped hands. "I didn't like her at once. At the time, I couldn't say why. Perhaps it was the way she looked at me."

"How did she look at you? As if she had known you all her life?"

A smile like a scimitar curved Tanis's lips. "As if she had raised me herself."

"She must have liked you a great deal."

"I came to like her immensely. So much so I confided in her. And then, well, she took great pains to keep me away from her husband."

"I'm not surprised."

"Mr. Shaw is like that, is he?"

Outside, the streets were abruptly devoid of people, as if life, like water, had swirled down a drain.

"I'm Mr. Shaw now," Conrad said. "My father died in Lalibela shortly before my mother passed."

"Oh!" One hand flew to her mouth. "I didn't know. I'm so sorry." And then, after a beat: "Why didn't you bring both of them to the boat?"

"He was better left where he died."

"I see." Though he knew she didn't, not by a nautical mile.

There was a small silence as the cook came bustling out of the kitchen to deliver the order of the transit workers. He wiped his hands on his apron as he passed them. He smelled of Za'atar and hot oil.

"On the boat you said your family knew my mother's."

"That's right. They were business partners, I believe. That is the story I was told, anyway."

"What happened?"

She shrugged. "Their interests diverged. I imagine that is why most partnerships dissolve."

"Your family didn't want any part of the Gnostic Observatines."

"They've been Muslim for centuries."

"Always religion," Conrad muttered.

She leaned in closer. "What was that?"

He sighed. "Sometimes I think the world would be so much better if religion did not exist."

"Human beings are aware of their mortality. How then could they face the chaos of life and the terrible reality of death—or tragedy—without a belief in a higher power? Having said that, for people like me, religion is mutable. I could not join the Gnostic Observatines if I was still a Muslim, could I? But what is it I really believe? I believe that deep down, at bedrock, beliefs are what you make them. God is God. Holy is Holy. If, in your heart, there is Light, then all the rest are simply trappings."

It was an excellent point, one that Conrad could only admire deeply. He wanted to tell her, to discuss the matter further, but at the moment he was bone-tired.

"Have you a place to sleep tonight?" Tanis asked abruptly. It was not difficult to read his body language.

In truth, he hadn't thought about it, too many other matters cramming his mind, too much grief. "Cairo is not unknown to me. I expect I'll find a hotel room."

"At this time of night?" She shook her head. "Best to come home with me."

"Have you a spare bedroom?"

Again that intimate smile meant only for him.

CONRAD AWOKE alone in bed. Sunlight streamed through lace curtains. A lacquered screen, featuring cranes flying amid clouds and below them a lone fisherman in a straw hat, was propped against one wall in lieu of a painting or photos. A small but exquisitely carved gilded Buddha meditated atop a Japanned dresser. Behind it, he could just make out a framed photo of a couple—no doubt Tanis's parents—a little girl between them. Apart from the family photo, the decorations were strange for a Muslim, though, now he thought about it, not so strange, considering her beliefs.

Her scent was still on the pillow, a heady combination of rose attar and sandalwood. He sat up, blinking, turned his head toward the window. The city sprawled away from him toward the desert, the Great Pyramids perfect monuments to a long-dead culture. He thought of the Sphinx, and shuddered. The moment he rose, he smelled coffee already brewed. Outside the window, the morning's bedlam was well under way. After hasty ablutions, he climbed into his clothes.

He found Tanis sitting at the kitchen table, her gaze fixed on the rood and the apple. His heart turned over. Had she touched them, tried to fit them together? Did she have any idea . . . ?

"So that's why you wanted me to come home with you."

"One of the reasons, yes."

He should have been angry; he found it curious that he wasn't. But then he found her forthright answer refreshing. There was no embarrassment, no self-consciousness, in her whatsoever. Crossing to the stove, he poured himself a glass of coffee, brought it back to the table, and sat down at a ninety-degree angle to her. As he sipped the strong, bitter brew, he watched her, studied her hands, which were sun browned, long fingered like a pianist. They lay on the table, in an indeterminate attitude, somewhere between advancing toward the relics and retreating to her lap.

"Do you know what these are?" she asked. Conrad set down his glass. "Two of the three manifestations of the Unholy Trinity." He placed his hands on the rood and the apple.

"Careful," she said.

"I know," he replied. "Now." And could not keep the darker notes of dismay and regret out of his voice.

"They disrupt life, these things." She was looking at them, not him. Then her gaze lifted, her eyes light and dancing upon him. "They open a doorway."

"I've witnessed that." Conrad involuntarily took his arms off the table, reminded once again of how the power of these artifacts invaded his mother, caused her to entreat the Sphinx to end her life before . . . what?

"But even with the power that took your mother they are not complete, and that presents a very serious problem."

"What d'you mean?"

"I cannot tell you," she said.

Now, at last, anger rose within him. "Why the hell not?"

Tanis regarded him, unperturbed by his outburst. "Because words are useless when it comes to such matters. You must see for yourself."

More or less what he had told Yeats to induce him to come with him to the Levant.

"You know where the third piece is."

"Indeed I do."

"Then take me there."

Tanis rose, and Conrad with her. "It will not be as easy as that. The way is dark and dangerous."

"Then," he said, "we must fly like the wind."

# 40

THEY WERE HEADING DUE EAST. IF THEY KEPT TO THIS COURSE,
Bravo knew, they would wind up in Syria. That made sense. But on the
other hand, this band of extremists had wandered very far afield. It was
more than a thousand nautical miles to home. Why would they do that
unless they were desperate for money, guns, war materiel? He could not
think of another reason.

Clouds coming in from the south had obscured the moon. The stars
were no more. Apart from the steamer's lights, the night was black as pitch.

"They've been waiting," he said softly to Ayla. They were no longer
naked; their clothes were as dry as they were ever going to get out here.
"My guess is there's an armament shipment they're going after. They were
lying low off Malta. That's why they were so alarmed when they saw us."

A subtle high whining in the pitch of the roaring engines alerted them.
Rushing to the bow of the speedboat, they peered out as best they could
past the wake and the blackened bulk of the steamer.

"There's another ship out there," Ayla said.

"And we're turning toward it," Bravo added. "At full speed."

Now they could discern activity on the rear deck high above them. A
complement of men were arming themselves.

"They're going to man the speedboat for a run at the target," Ayla said.

But Bravo shook his head. "If that were the case they'd have slowed
for the transfer. No, they're making a run at the arms shipment with all
guns blazing. Most likely because that ship is armed to the teeth."

"A pitched battle then. That fits your theory that they're desperate."

"Right. A pitched battle is just what we need."

"What?"

Bravo grinned. "Cover for our boarding the steamer. In the chaos of battle it'll be easier to get the rood from Ismail."

"If he has it on him."

"He'll have it on him, all right."

"And finding him?"

Bravo's grin widened. "I'm counting on you for that."

"Me? Won't the battle give you sufficient distraction?"

"Distraction is one thing, diversion quite another." He grabbed the rope attaching the speedboat to the steamer. It was cold and wet, leaving traces of slimy seaweed beneath his fingers. He'd have to remember that—seaweed was slippery. "Divide and conquer, Ayla. We need to cull Ismail from the rest of his crew. You're our best chance to do that."

They could make out the other ship as it plowed through the water. It was heading east by northeast. The steamer's rear deck was deserted now; the militants crowded forward to engage the enemy.

Bravo waited for the first volley before launching himself onto the thick hawser. He turned his head, saw Ayla hesitating. "C'mon now! It's now or never. Go, go, go!"

He resumed his crawl over the hawser as soon as he was certain she was behind him. Using hands, knees, and ankles, he made his slow, deliberate way forward and up the steeply slanted rope. The idea was not to hurry, to concentrate on the next foot forward, but it was difficult to keep to the pace he had set for them, what with the shouts, imprecations, and the hail of gunfire erupting from both ships, lighting up the way ahead like fiery streamers.

Below them, the churning of the water, the knowledge that should either of them slip off they would be sucked into the undertow caused by the steamer's massive screws. He had wisely not mentioned this possibility to Ayla; she already had enough to occupy her mind. He had, however, warned her of the slime on the hawser, and she was lagging behind even his deliberate pace. Making sure each handhold was secure enough to hold her weight.

As a consequence, Bravo made it onto the stern of the steamer while she was still shy a third of the distance. He had turned back to reach out for her as soon as she came into range when he heard a shout. Whirling back, he saw one of the Syrian extremists leveling an AK-47 at him. Immediately he raised his hands high, came walking at a normal pace toward the man.

The man shouted at him, but Bravo cupped one hand behind his ear in the universal sign that he hadn't heard. The staccato gunfire and the roar of the diesels helped him sell it. At the same time, as the Syrian automatically shifted his gaze to the gesture, he picked up his pace considerably.

Now he shouted at the Syrian. It was gibberish, but that was the point. The man squinted, shook his head, and again Bravo picked up his pace. The Syrian recognized what was happening too late. By the time he squeezed the AK-47's trigger, Bravo was already inside his perimeter of defense. Grabbing hold of the barrel with one hand, shoving it aside, he slammed the heel of his hand into the Syrian's nose with such force he shattered the cartilage. A great gout of blood fountained, then began a rhythmic spurting.

The Syrian howled in shock and pain, his grip on the AK-47 loosened enough for Bravo to rip it out of his hands. The butt of the Syrian's own weapon rendered him unconscious. Crouching down, Bravo went through his pockets, salvaged a knife with a six-inch serrated blade in a stained and well-worn leather scabbard, and a two-way radio.

He switched on the radio, tapped out *I am here* in Morse code, repeating it twice more before shutting off the radio and throwing it overboard. Returning to the stern rail, he helped Ayla aboard.

"Keep your feet at shoulder width, knees slightly bent to counteract the pitch," he instructed before recalling she was a diver and would know how to keep her sea legs in all kinds of weather. "Stay ready," he said over the constant noise before retreating into the shadows.

The steamer, having come alongside the arms freighter, had slowed to neutral and was now wallowing in the waves and troughs.

It wasn't long before Ismail appeared. He saw his man sprawled on the deck, then looked up to see Ayla, her face appearing and disappearing in the swinging, shifting ship's lights. His eyes narrowed.

"Who are you? Where did you come from?" But he didn't seem in any mood to find out. He lifted a Makarov pistol. As he did so, Bravo threw the knife. The shifting of the deck worked against him. The knife entered Ismail's right shoulder, causing him to lower the pistol, but it did not bring him down as Bravo had planned.

Instead, he twisted to face Bravo as he pulled the knife out of his muscle. Bravo didn't wait to see what he'd do next; he rushed Ismail and bulled into him with his shoulder. They both went down; the Makarov went skidding;

Ismail smashed his fist into the side of Bravo's neck. Digging his thumb into the knife wound, Bravo fought to gain control, but Ismail, imbued with the peculiar fire of the fanatic, drove an elbow into his windpipe.

Bravo coughed heavily, gagging, and Ismail took the initiative, burying his fist into the place he had kicked Bravo. Bravo cried out, still trying to catch his breath, his strength drained by the pain and the fury of Ismail's counterattack. Straddling Bravo, Ismail fought to gain a grip on Bravo's head, to sink his thumbs into Bravo's eye sockets.

There was a moment when the two men were locked in stasis, grappled, arms twined, muscles bulging, teeth bared like animals in a death spiral. And then, so slowly it was only discernable to the two combatants, Ismail found an edge. His thumbs moved ever closer to Bravo's eyes. They were almost upon them now, Bravo's head locked in a fierce vise-like grip. Bravo could feel the other's rough, calloused skin against his eyelids; then a terrible pressure commenced against his eyeballs, compressing them.

An explosion. Ismail's head fractured, spraying Bravo's face with blood, bits of brain and skull like hot sleet. Ismail's torso wobbled, the pressure came off Bravo's eyes, and with a violent twist, Bravo tossed the Syrian's corpse aside.

He looked up to see Ayla standing over him, legs spread, two hands on the Makarov. Then she grinned. "You see," she said, "feet at shoulder width."

**AS HE** had predicted, the rood was secreted inside Ismail's clothes, nestled against his skin. The gold gleamed against the darkness of his skin. There were still streaks of darker metal on it; Ismail hadn't had time to completely free the rood from its bronze overlay. They could still see part of the crack that had led him to discover the gold.

The two of them crouched down on either side of the body as Bravo cradled the golden rood.

"Are you all right?" she asked.

"I am now," he answered, and gave her a grin to reassure her. There was no point in clueing her in to how much pain he was in, But, knowing her, she'd find out for herself sooner rather than later. His head pounded and his ribs felt like they were broken. Every inhalation was agony.

She was about to ask another question of him when the firefight rushed back in on them. They had both been so concentrated on their own private battle they had blocked out the larger war being fought between the crews of the two ships. Now the incessant barrage of gunfire was all that could be heard.

Ayla, leaning over the corpse, said in his ear, "Okay, now what? How do we get out of here?"

"We don't." Bravo said. "We'll let the crew of the other ship do it for us."

Ayla looked intrigued. "How d'you propose we do that?"

Above and ahead of them loomed the ship's superstructure—the crew's quarters, wardroom, kitchen, and, above, the pilot's wheelhouse—intermittently illuminated by livid tracer fire. The smells of cordite and blood, bittersweet, filled the air.

He reloaded the Makarov from Ismail's ammo belt, handed it back to Ayla. "Where did you learn to shoot like that?"

"My father taught me. You know what a crack shot he was."

Bravo did. Once, when he and Omar Tusik went hunting in the Turkish mountains, a Eurasian lynx, all tufted ears and carnivorous eyes, leapt from an overhanging tree branch. It would have landed on Bravo, would have sunk its teeth into the back of his neck, had not Omar shot it dead in midair.

"I'm going forward." He pointed. "You take the high ground. The wheelhouse." He looked at her levelly as she rifled through the Syrian's pockets, found cigarettes and a cheap plastic lighter. "I'll tell you this once, Ayla. The more of these Syrian extremists we kill the better our chance of booking passage on the arms ship. Are you listening to me?"

She looked up at him. "Absorbed every word."

He nodded. "So . . . shoot first and often."

She nodded grimly. "I understand."

"I hope you do. Your mother will leap out of her grave and kill me if I let anything untoward happen to you."

AYLA WAS in the kind of shock one feels at a loved one's death—the autonomous nervous system, in full play, had taken charge of a body whose mind had gone numb. These dire, life-and-death circumstances were off the charts. Hell, they were part of another chart altogether. On the other hand, she thought, as she climbed the steep metal gangway to the helm's crow's nest, they had hurled her backward to the time her mother had taken her to Tannourine, to the red tent of shadows, introduced her to the infernal presence that would allow her to access her powers and mark her forever. She had to get used to the fact that her life was here, now. She was a Shaw, as fully committed to the extraordinary destiny of its lineage as Bravo was. And this recognition, which she felt flowing from her mind to every cell of her body, worked like a trigger. She had never before understood who she was, where she came from, what her lineage was, what responsibilities and powers that carried. All her adult life, until the moment she met Bravo last year in Istanbul, she had fought against her mother, fought against what had happened in Tannourine when she was a child, aligning herself with her father, who was as normal as she wished to be.

As she opened the door to the wheelhouse, she felt her father's—both her fathers', actually—strength, intelligence, and nerve flow through her, unfreezing her mind. She no longer fought the unknown inside her but relaxed into its flow. She felt her mind moving forward in time, in the smallest increments, but dictating her actions and reactions as, she guessed, Conrad had been taught by his mother, Diantha.

With one father on each shoulder, she shot to death three of the four armed Syrians manning the wheelhouse, protecting the pilot. They had been fixated on the firefight raging below them, could not imagine that they had been boarded from the stern by another enemy.

The fourth guard swung his pistol and fired off-balance. Ayla leapt at him. The bullet grazed her cheek. She felt its passage as one might a lightning bolt, the proximity to such raw power electrifying, as terrifying as the events in the red tent of shadows when she was just a girl, when, in mortal fear, she had set fire to it.

And this she did again, engaging with the fourth guard, shooting him in the abdomen while the pilot scrabbled for the pistol he never thought he'd need. He shot without aiming, putting two more bullets into his guard, bleeding out, whom Ayla was using as a shield. She shot the pilot between the eyes, and then started work on the dried-out, oil-streaked wooden deck boards.

NO ONE had been assigned rear guard duty, no one was looking behind them, occupied as they were with exchanging fire with the crew aboard the arms ship. Bravo came at them enfilade—that is, from the side. He had counted twenty or so armed Syrians. Six went down in his first volley, before he switched positions. As the men were blown backward by the fusillade, some of their compatriots rose out of their positions hunkered down behind winches and crate, and were taken out by fire from the other ship.

Ten down, Bravo thought as he fired again. Three more. That left seven. He was unconcerned by what would be a small complement belowdecks in the engine room. That would be the arms crew's problem.

His own problem stemmed from the three Syrians who were now coming after him, while their brethren kept up their fusillade across the short span of water between the two ships. But already the nature of the firefight had changed; the arms crew had realized the attacking fire had been more than cut in half and were reacting to it. Emboldened, they took less protected but more advantageous positions, concentrated their fire at the remaining Syrians. Then grappling hooks flew through the air, drawing the two ships close enough for members of the arms crew to leap aboard the steamer.

It was at this moment that flames burst through the shattering windows of the wheelhouse. The three Syrians, stunned, were easy to pick off. Bravo advanced along the length of the ship. He shot the last remaining Syrian on deck as the first contingent from the arms ship approached from the opposite end. They were wary, their killing blood on the surface, ready to shoot anyone in their way, including Bravo. Then they saw the men he had shot, and allowed him to direct three of them belowdecks to mop up whoever was left aboard.

Moments later, Ayla joined him, face and clothes smudged, but unhurt.

"Good job," Bravo said. Then he turned her to get a better look at her cheek. "That was close. Are you all right?"

"Better than you, I expect." She gave him a crooked smile, and he laughed.

**"QUITE FORTUITOUS,"** Captain Kreutzer said, eyeing them in his quarters aboard the arms freighter. "We owe you a debt of thanks. How about a hot meal, a shower, and a new set of clothes." He tilted his head toward Ayla. "That is, if you don't mind some oversized men's clothes, Fräulein."

"Not at all," Ayla said with no little relief. "Thank you very much, Captain."

He nodded to her in a formal manner. Everything about Kreutzer was formal, from his well-combed hair, to his scent of expensive cologne, to his well-cut trousers and pea coat. He wore, of all things, made-to-order John Lobb loafers with deck-gripping soles, which must have set him back $1,200, if Bravo was any judge.

"Pardon me for saying this," Bravo said as a mate set steaming mugs of coffee before them, "but you look more suited to be captaining a mega-yacht than a freighter."

Kreutzer laughed. He had a marked widow's peak and large, square hands. A semi-circular scar stood on the point of his right cheek. He flipped open a silver hip flask, poured generous slugs of dark rum into their mugs. "Drink up, *meine Freunde.*" He lifted his mug and they clinked them together. "To money," he said jovially. "The root of all evil. And pleasure!"

He studied them, his deep-brown eyes twinkling. "You make quite a pair, I must say. And that fire you set, Fräulein. Quite ingenious." He spoke with a peculiar accent, part German, part British. He lifted his mug to her in a salute that held no measure of irony. He was clearly impressed with them.

Two crew members, one of them the cook, served them a delicious-smelling Moroccan meal: pigeon *bastilla,* lamb, prune, and green olive tagine, rounds of freshly baked unleavened bread. They fell to, the captain seeming as famished as they found themselves.

Afterward, over more coffee, Kreutzer addressed their curiosity. "I used to captain a mega-yacht, just as you surmised, Herr Shaw. But I grew tired of taking orders from the rich and famous. 'Vain and stupid' is more like it." He chuckled, a warm, throaty sound that put them completely at ease.

He spread his hands. The nails were manicured, shining with clear lacquer. Clearly, this tanker did not lack for amenities. "I make no excuses for what I do now. It pays far more than anything else I could do on the high seas. I work less and make more."

"And the stress levels?" Ayla said.

"I have a hearty constitution," Kreutzer replied. "Lucky for me. Otherwise, I'd be popping stomach tablets like candy."

Ayla pushed her chair back from the table. Through one of the portholes, she could see the Syrian steamer on fire, the ship diminishing rapidly as they pulled farther and farther away. "Now about that shower, Captain."

"Certainly. I'll have my steward show you the way. New clothes are already set out on a berth in a spare cabin, now that our complement has been somewhat . . . reduced."

"You feel no remorse, Captain?"

"These men are all mercenaries, Fräulein. They knew the risks going in. They don't expect to be mourned."

"That doesn't mean you can't."

"Fräulein, you'll pardon me for being blunt, but I have no time for such luxuries."

"We fully understand, Captain," Bravo interjected.

"It might interest the Fräulein to know that ironically my six men died for nothing. We off-loaded our cargo ten days ago in Tunis. We're running light now." His heavy shoulders lifted, fell. "*Die Idioten* got their intelligence mixed up."

"One more thing," Bravo said.

Kreutzer lifted an eyebrow. "Anything, if it's in my power."

"I believe it is. You're heading east?"

"That's right."

"So are we."

"You're welcome to take passage, both of you. Though some of my men will grumble about a having a female—"

"I can take care of myself," Ayla said, her back up.

Kreutzer's smile was soothing, not in the least condescending. He'd seen what she was capable of. "I don't doubt that for a moment, Fräulein. I assure you that everything is in hand." He turned to Bravo. "And where might you be headed, Herr Shaw?"

"Arwad."

The captain's thick eyebrows rose. "The island where those Syrian extremists who attacked us are from, so I'm given to understand."

Bravo nodded. "That's right."

"Is that wise?"

"It may not be wise," Bravo said. "But it's necessary."

# 41

PARIS: PRESENT DAY

*THE . . . END . . . IS . . . NEAR. . . .*

Emma heard these words in her mind, each one like a thunderclap, but she was unaware that her lips moved, her voice box vocalizing. She lay splayed, like Christ on the cross, bleeding from a thousand and one wounds. Drowned in the words of Lucifer, privy to the dreadful autobiography of his creation, "the birth of the Lord of Night," in Satan's own words, the raising of Beelzebub by a creature unknown to neither man nor angel, if he was to be believed. But why should I believe anything Lucifer says? the part of Emma's mind still nominally under her control thought. He who worships at the filthy altar of lies, deception, and slander. And yet the words were there, all around her, dragging her under, where they swirled thickest, a blizzard of were-history.

*The . . . end . . . is . . . near. . . .*

And Lucifer was not alone in his creation. Twins were born to the thing with neither face nor name. The words of Lucifer, filled with fire and smoke, told of the twins only in the vaguest terms, given short shrift, one embittered, spiteful sentence.

Emma was flattened, shredded, ripped asunder. And yet the core of her abided. She had clutched the lifeline Conrad had extended to all his progeny, held it in her heart, kept it safe and secure against all assaults. And this vigilance now stood her in good stead. The lifeline bore the Shaw-Safita-Ahirom's imprimatur, the combined wisdom of Conrad, Diantha, and Tanis, twined like strands of DNA that rose through the core of her, a part that the Power Beleth could neither alter nor touch.

But something more powerful than Beleth had used the doorway opened by the words of Lucifer that had invaded Emma's mind at that first and only reading. And because, like her brother, she had an eidetic memory, those words could not be forgotten but repeated themselves endlessly, pinging off the folds of her brain.

In this extraordinary state, she was separated from Beleth for the first time since it Transpositioned into her body from Maura Kite. And for the first time, she could hear the whispered voice of Conrad.

*Djat had'ar,* he whispered in her mind's ear.

"*Djat had'ar,*" she said. He is present.

A jolt went through her. A dark presence, colossal, many winged, face shrouded, halted on the threshold of the doorway the blizzard of Lucifer's words had opened. It looked like the sum of all shadows, and her soul quailed before it. She could feel its rage like the heart of the sun. A rage beyond the scope of mere human senses. *This . . . is . . . the . . . end . . . of all things.*

*Et ignis ibi est!* he whispered in her mind's ear.

"*Et ignis ibi est!*" she cried out with all her might. Let there be fire!

Blue flames erupted, coursed through her, enveloped her, slammed the door on the many-winged presence, locked, bolted, and sealed the door shut.

**"SHE'S DYING!"** Lilith screamed. "She's dying, Beleth, you lying piece of shit! Do something!"

"I have tried," Beleth said. "I am locked out. . . . There is nothing . . ." A gasp. "He comes! He is coming!"

"Who?" Lilith cried. "Who's coming?"

"The King of the Four Thrones." Beleth's voice quivered. "The Beast. The Reaver. Verrine."

Lilith trembled at his words, at the thought of confronting evil. Nevertheless, she held Emma all the tighter, kissed her temples, her forehead, the trembling lips. She ignored the black tar-like substance Emma had vomited up, just as she ignored M. Boyer, who had at last abandoned his work at the sound of her scream, and who, along with his assistants, crowded around her. Dimly, she was aware of someone summoning an ambulance, and she shouted, "No! No ambulance!" without quite knowing why, and yet with such utter conviction that the call was canceled. Instead, someone contacted Building Services to clean up the strange black vomit.

"What's happened?" M. Boyer asked without any apparent affect.

"She's fine. Petit mal," Lilith said, vamping, making it up as she went along. "Missed her meds time, but all will be well now."

M. Boyer nodded, lost interest, striding purposefully back to his work. The others followed.

"Beleth!" she called. "Beleth!" But there came no reply.

And then the foreign words erupted from between Emma's lips:

*"Djat had'ar."*

Emma arched up, almost coming out of Lilith's embrace. The cords of her neck stood out, a vein in her forehead pulsed, and for a moment Lilith, terrified, was certain the end had, indeed, come. But then came a loosening of Emma's rock-hard muscles, and a sense came to Lilith as of a stream of clear cool running deep beneath the surface.

*"Et ignis ibi est!"* Emma cried.

And blue flame engulfed them both. M. Boyer and his staff turned to gape in a welter of shouts of surprise and shock. No one moved. No one felt the least bit of heat. The blue flame now seemed to implode, to shoot inward, if that was even possible. Some, at least, suspecting they had taken leave of their senses, became dizzied. Others looked away, frightened of their own shock.

The smokeless blue flame vanished, perhaps to the same nether regions from which it had come. Lilith was unharmed, and as for Emma, she was stirring in the warm cradle of Lilith's arms, her face normal at last.

"Emma," Lilith whispered. "Emma, I'm here. I love you."

Emma opened her eyes. They were as clear as the morning sea. As they regarded Lilith, a smile curled her lips.

"Lilith." Her voice was cracked and desert dry.

"I'm here. I never let you go."

"I know. I felt . . . I knew."

Their lips touched, opened. Heat rising off their bodies. M. Boyer, hunched over his task, had his back to them. The staff was slow in recovering their equilibrium, speculating among themselves in hushed voices. They were all scientists of one sort or another. Their expertise was in electronic instruments, the laws of physics, and suchlike. What they had just witnessed went beyond their comprehension—so much so that some of them refused to believe what they had seen and heard, putting it down to mass hallucination. Several of them went to check the ventilation system on the off chance fumes from elsewhere in the building were affecting them.

At length, Lilith broke away. "You scared the hell out of me. What happened to you?"

"Where's Beleth?"

"You tell me."

"I don't feel it. I don't . . ." Maybe it was caught in the doorway when the blue fire slammed it shut, Emma thought, shuddering, closing her eyes for just a moment. When she opened them she saw the expression on her lover's face. "Don't worry," she whispered. "I'm a Shaw." So much of her history she didn't know. Bravo had never told her and she had never asked.

"That's not an answer. Emma, please tell me. It's not fair to keep me in the dark."

She was right, Emma thought. "I read something I shouldn't have. Bravo warned me not to, but my curiosity got the better of me. Anyway, the words kind of took me over, drowned me, opened a door to . . ."

"A door to . . . what?"

"I don't know. Some place of eerie darkness, of pure evil, some place I had no business being. That door should never have been opened. And it's because of me, because I couldn't keep my curiosity in check."

"You couldn't help yourself?"

"That sounds so weak."

"You're human, Emma. Weak threads exist in all our weaving." The cleaning crew showed up then, and she slipped her hand into Emma's. "Let's get you to a chair."

"I'm fine. I'm—"

Lilith steadied Emma as her knees gave way slightly. Out of the corner of her eye she saw M. Boyer on his way over. He very studiously side-stepped the mess on the floor, indicated to the crew to hurry up. He had a printout clutched in one hand. Lilith got Emma to a task chair as he came up beside her.

"How is she?" he asked.

"She's fine," Lilith said. "With a little bit of water . . ." She looked expectantly at M. Boyer. Then when he made no move: "Oh, for God's sake!" She fetched a paper cup of water from the cooler by the wall. No one in the lab would touch tap water, out of paranoia or elite-think she could never tell. Possibly it was the same thing.

"Look what I have." He fluttered the printout in front of Lilith's face after she had handed Emma the water.

"I can't make out a thing," she said. "It's Mandarin to me."

M. Boyer gave a rare laugh. "Oh, well, yes. But what's of import to you is that I finished my search. I know where the man you're looking for is right at this moment."

"And where would that be?" Emma said, having been refreshed by the cold water.

"Ah, well, that's the fascinating part." M. Boyer looked at her for the first time. "He's right in the middle of Père Lachaise Cemetery."

# 42

OBARTON ARRIVED BACK AT THE KNIGHTS' PÈRE LACHAISE Reliquary after spending a restless night tossing and turning in his bed. He dreamed he was Julius Caesar, alone in the Forum of Rome. He was searching for something, but all he saw were the blind eyes of the marble statues arrayed around him. He had awoken, amid twisted bedsheets, a question on his lips that he could not recall.

Now, showered, shaved, and impeccably dressed in a brown linen three-piece suit, he stood for a moment before the Memorial to the Dead, smoking a cigarette. The day was clear, filled with bright sunshine beamed down from a nearly cloudless sky. He hardly ever smoked, except when he was highly agitated. That image or vision of the horned head—better call it a hallucination. Well, whatever it was had unnerved him. He'd seen it twice now, the first time when he was with the cardinal at the Vatican, the second following the explosion that had ended Duchamp's life. Why always with Duchamp? And why . . . ? He was not a person prone to nerves—or hallucinations, come to think of it. But, look here, the sky was blue, the grass green. Birds sang as they always did, swooping from tree branch to tree branch. All things bright and beautiful; all things in their accustomed place. He took one more draw on his cigarette, decided he didn't need the nicotine, and exhaled all the smoke in a single puff.

By the time he reached the subterranean precincts of the Reliquary, he had put the incident entirely out of his mind and was feeling uncommonly cheerful. Cardinal Felix Duchamp, that vexing thorn in his side, was no more than a carbon cinder. Mission accomplished.

He noticed the prisoner's mobile on a side table as he took himself to the room where Hugh Highstreet was under lock, key, and guard. There had been no point in taking it with him, and he liked that it was in plain sight for all to see.

Being in the presence of this particular prisoner gave a jolt to his endorphin levels, just like, it was said, a good, long run. Obarton wouldn't know about that. Even as a young man he eschewed all sport, save, of course, fencing, which was a physical endeavor appropriate for a gentleman. Already at the age of twelve he was too large for epée, so he took his instructor's advice and opted for the sabre. Not as popular as epée, of course, but, in Obarton's estimation anyway, quite a bit more enjoyable. That the matches stopped short of being fun said far more about Obarton than it did about the sport itself.

Before he had the guard unlock the room, he gave a food order to Naylor, the only one who knew his tastes enough to be trusted. So full of good feeling was he that he included his prisoner in the order. Why not give the poor devil one good meal? he thought with what he considered was a gentleman's magnanimity but was in actuality condescension.

Highstreet was not in good shape. He'd never been an athlete. Accordingly, his incarceration, not to mention what Obarton euphemistically thought of as interrogations, had drained him of what little physical vitality he had once possessed. Sitting in the middle of the bare room on a straight-backed metal chair, to which he was bound by wrists and ankles, he was whey-faced, spotted and daubed with crusted-over blood, heavily bruised and wounded all over his body and limbs. A comfortable club chair, upholstered in waxed leather, had been placed opposite him, a reminder of what he did not—and could not—have. In one corner was a stainless-steel lav.

"Hullo there, Hugh," Obarton said heartily. "How are we today?" He sat on the club chair, wriggling his jelly buttocks into the buttery leather to make himself more comfortable. "Feeling at home yet?"

Obarton did not, of course, expect an answer to these unreasonable questions, and Highstreet, his eyes half-shut, the surrounding flesh the color of raw meat, no longer rose to the bait. All flippant response had been beaten out of him days ago.

Obarton leaned forward, his nostrils dilating as he sniffed. "You smell that, Hugh? It's the odor of decaying flesh, of insects tunneling through desiccated flesh and brittle bone." He smiled benignly, a favored uncle at

Christmastime. "It's the smell of death, Hugh. That's what it is. Why, you might as well be dead yourself, seeing where I have put you."

Highstreet stared at him as best he could through his slitted eyes. His lips looked flayed; in one corner of his mouth an ugly sore had begun to suppurate a greasy yellow liquid.

"Oh, Hugh." Obarton sat back, laced his fingers across his belly, as if they were in a London gentleman's club instead of in the underbelly of the most famous Parisian cemetery. "I warned you. Now you know what it feels like to back the wrong horse. Tell me, how did that happen, hmm?" He shrugged. "I mean to say, Lilith couldn't have seduced you—not you. You might as well be a eunuch, for all the interest you have in sex. And how did *that* happen, I wonder?" He shuddered. "What a diabolical aberration. Poor thing."

He cocked his head. There was pitcher of water on the floor, along with a glass. Dust motes danced on the surface of the water, moved along by who knew what form of insects. Obarton made no move to offer Highstreet any. "A tart and a eunuch walk into a bar, bound together by God alone knows what unholy means." He laughed shortly. It was very much like Charles Laughton's bray. "What's the punch line, Hugh? I mean to say, the relationship is something out of the *Arabian Nights,* isn't it? Extraordinary, really."

There was only the whir of air in the ductwork, circulating through the grill high up on one wall. A bare bulb in a metal cage was screwed into the ceiling, its cruel light centered on Highstreet. Obarton could count precisely how many prisoners had been incarcerated here over his lifetime in the Knights. To his knowledge, Highstreet was the first who was not a Gnostic Observatine.

"You know, Hugh, this room is like the Roach Motel: guests check in, but they never check out." His laugh was discordant; there was no humor in it.

He sighed, as if his favorite pupil had disappointed him. "Well, Hugh, despite it all, today's your lucky day. I've ordered food for the both of us. A four-course meal, the works." He leaned forward so abruptly that Highstreet flinched. "Now, now, old son, I'm not going to lay a hand on you. No, today we shall share a meal together, as equals, as friends." He bared his teeth. "A last meal, as such."

Suddenly the sound of raised, querulous voices pierced the door. A gunshot.

Then someone gave out with an unearthly scream.

"YOU'LL THINK I'm crazy."

"And that would be bad, why?" Emma said.

Lilith laughed, but it was an uneasy laugh, for all that. The two women, for the moment sans Emma's otherworldly companion, were in a taxi heading toward the 20th arrondissement, one of Paris's outermost northern districts. Morning had turned into late afternoon, sunlight burnishing the tops of the buildings, gilding the trees lining the wide boulevards. Occasionally the aroma of freshly baked bread for the evening meal came to them, reminding them cruelly of how long it had been since they had last eaten.

"So tell me," Emma said.

"We tell each other everything, right?"

"You told me you had been in the Knights' Reliquary with Obarton and how to get in there, so yes, I would say we tell each other everything."

"So here's the thing." Lilith paused, her unease manifestly present now. "When you were—I don't know what to call it—under the influence . . ."

"That's as good a description as any," Emma acknowledged.

"There were—" Lilith broke off.

"Oh, for God's sake, say it already."

Lilith licked her lips. "Lean forward."

"What?"

"Just do as I ask. Emma. Please."

As Emma leaned forward, Lilith palpated her back in the area between her shoulder blades.

"What are you doing?"

"Looking for them. The bumps."

All at once, Emma seemed alarmed. "What bumps?"

"There were three sets of them—right here, and here. I felt them as I held you."

"Three sets, you say."

"That's right."

Emma saw again the great shadow with the hidden face. It had three pairs of wings. Her face drained of all color.

"What is it?" Lilith asked. "What did I feel?"

"Wings."

"What?"

"The stubs of three pairs of wings." Emma was shaking, and she sought to calm herself through words. "You said that Beleth told you that Verrine, the King of the Four Thrones, was coming."

"Yes, but that's all. I don't know a thing about the Fallen Four Thrones beyond that they exist, and that Beleth thinks they may be coming— that's the kind of esoteric knowledge you Gnostic Observatines special- ize in."

Emma had kept searching for Beleth, shining a revolving beacon into the darkness inside her, ever since she had revived. No sign of it as yet. "The Fallen are ordered in ranks of power," she began. "Three Spheres, the First being the most powerful. Within the First Sphere are three categories: Seraphim, Cherubim, and Thrones. Leviathan, who we both have met, is a Seraph of the First Sphere, Lucifer's right-hand angel. But the Thrones have a specific place in the hierarchy of the First Sphere. Like Beleth, they are warriors. But unlike Beleth, they are the generals of the Fallen Legion. They are pure evil, hungry for power, and therefore incal- culably dangerous. Murmur, Raum, Phenex, Verrine, these are the Four Thrones."

"And Verrine was the shadow you saw in the open doorway?"

"The Four Thrones have three sets of wings, Lilith. Yes, I'm sure."

"And the bumps I felt."

"He was meant to use me—use my body—to return to our world in the form . . . well, like Leviathan."

"God in Heaven, you would have been gone! And what of Beleth?"

"Excellent question," Emma said. Already in the 20th, they were climb- ing now, heading for the lower reaches of Père Lachaise. "My sense is he's in hiding. Verrine's appearance frightened him beyond measure. I sense that if the Throne King had been successful, not only would I have ceased to exist, but Beleth would have, as well."

"So, basically, Beleth is a coward."

"Well, he's Second Sphere, so there's that, but, yes, I'm afraid he is a bit of a coward."

"Huh. It would be amusing if the situation wasn't so dire."

The cab pulled over, came to a stop outside the gates to the cemetery.

Lilith paid the driver and they got out, stood amid kiosks hawking maps and postcards of the most famous gravestones and crypts. A gaggle of German tourists on one side, neat, martial ranks of Japanese tourists on the other.

"Well, dammit, we need Beleth now," Lilith muttered as they strode through the gates and into Père Lachaise proper. "The creature is like the police. In your hair all the time, but where are they when you need them?"

Emma smiled grimly. She was dealing with so many things her head was spinning: the inexorable march of Lucifer's Testament, the unspeakable horror of the open doorway into another realm, and Beleth. Stupid bloody Beleth, where are you! she cried silently.

Not even an echo answered her back. Wherever the Power was, it was securely hidden against the might of Verrine.

*The door is closed,* she whispered in her mind. *You're safe now.*

*But for how long?* The reply came from nowhere and everywhere at once.

*Ah, you're still alive and well.*

*Of course I'm alive. As for well . . .* She could feel Beleth shudder inside her.

*It's illuminating to know that you fear some things.*

*Of course. Leviathan, for instance. But the Fallen Seraph is nothing compared to Verrine.*

*The Reaver, yes, I know.*

*When it comes to the Four Thrones you know nothing—nothing at all.* She felt the Power shudder again. *Shall I tell you a story illustrating what I mean?*

*By all means, but why don't we take this vocal so Lilith can hear the story, too.*

Emma's eyes grew dark as she drew Lilith off the cobbled path they were following up the hill. They stood by a cold slab of marble engraved with cherubs fluttering their small wings. How wrong the traditional depiction of Cherubim were, Emma thought. Or was it Beleth? The two were intermingling now, but unlike before the experience was more of a merging, rather than a hostile takeover.

Lilith stared into her lover's altered eyes. "Beleth."

"I have returned." A beat, a hesitation. "But then I never left."

"Oh yes, you did. You vacated the premises."

"That, as you know, I cannot do. Not without killing Emma."

Lilith noted his use of Emma's name, rather than the usual "my host."

Something significant had occurred. The landscape was now altered. Was the change temporary, she wondered, or permanent? In any event, she had to make the most of this opportunity while it presented itself.

"But you hid from Verrine."

"When I tell you about the Throne King perhaps you will understand more clearly the imminent peril you are in."

"We're wasting time," Lilith said. "Every minute we delay could be Hugh's last."

"Let's walk then," Beleth and Emma said together. "You said the Memorial to the Dead is some way up the hill."

Lilith nodded; there was nothing more to argue. Besides, if she was honest with herself she could not deny her curiosity about this so-called monstrosity they might at any moment be up against.

Beleth told them the story of Leviathan and Shemhazai, the Grigori, a member of the Fallen who metamorphosed into human form in order to maniacally fornicate with female humans, an action that was forbidden to all angels, Fallen or not. This was ensured by the simple fact that they had no genitals. Leviathan annihilated the Grigori once and for all.

"But it was Verrine who got the idea in its head to kill all the offspring of Grigori-human couplings. One by one, whether they be teenagers, toddlers, or babes still suckling at their mothers' breasts, Verrine hunted them down and broke them in two. The Thrones King's hands were soaked in blood, a state in which Verrine reveled."

"But how did Verrine move from one realm to another?" Lilith asked. "The doorways were sealed by God himself."

Emma wondered how it could be that Verrine had missed Gideon Shaw, her great-grandfather. For an instant, she was taken by a powerful presentiment of a future she wanted no part of, but which she knew she must learn to navigate, or be taken under by an altogether different force than the words of Lucifer.

Simultaneously, Beleth was speaking: "That is an excellent question. There have been, so I am given to understand, momentary breaches in the membrane between realms, all caused from this side. But how Verrine could spend an extended period of time in your world is a mystery."

"Perhaps it has to do with The Testament of Lucifer," Emma said.

"You witnessed what almost happened to me. Lilith felt the stubs of the triple wings sprouting between my shoulder blades."

"And those words you spoke," Lilith said.

"What words?"

"You mean you don't remember?"

"With what was going on inside me I'm surprised I remember who I am."

Lilith put her arms around Emma, held her close. "Here's what you said," she whispered in her ear. "'*Djat had'ar.*'"

Emma stiffened. "That's Tamazight. It means 'He is here.'"

Lilith held Emma at arm's length. "Who is here? Who were you talking about?"

"Conrad," Emma said. "My grandfather."

"I don't understand." Lilith's eyes narrowed. "Is your grandfather still alive?"

"No. He died years ago."

"Then how—?"

"Enough!" Beleth roared, turning heads, causing tourists to shrink back at the sound. But since nothing more of the sort issued from the beautiful woman, they directed their mobile phone cameras in another direction. "I will hear no more of this."

Lilith leaned in. "You know what, Beleth? Fuck you and the whiff of sulfur you rode in on."

Emma blinked. "I do not understand what you mean."

Lilith snorted. "What you don't know about human beings . . ." She made a curt gesture. "Come on, Beleth. We're wasting time."

She led the way up the winding path toward the memorial beneath which the Knights' Reliquary lay. They were almost in sight of it when Emma said, "How do you propose to get inside?"

Without answering, Lilith grabbed her, drew her off the path, into the shadows of a stand of pencil pines. "See that dark-haired man striding up the path ahead of us? That's Naylor," she whispered. The man who had leered at her at the entrance to the town house. The one who had supervised the cleanup crew getting rid of the bodies of the Circle Council members she had killed. "Obarton's most trusted guard dog." She moved them ahead, up the path, following in Naylor's footsteps. "He's our way in."

**IAIN NAYLOR** was concentrating on keeping a grip on the food while turning the key in the lock in the nether reaches of the Memorial to the Dead's macabre interior. Consequently, he did not hear the footsteps behind him until it was too late. With the door already open, he whirled, saw two women. In the gloom, their faces were shadowed, their identities unknown, but he did admire the curves of their bodies.

One of them said, *"Djat had'ar,"* words he did not understand, and immediately thereafter, *"Et ignis ibi est!,"* Latin he did understand: Let there be light! What light? he wondered.

And then it began.

Someone was screaming. He was screaming. He could not stop.

**CHAOS.**

It wasn't the gunshot that so unnerved Obarton, though that was reason enough for alarm. It was the eerie screaming, drawn-out, terrified.

Chaos.

Obarton had once been witness to someone being eaten alive by a pack of wild dogs. The victim had made just such a dreadful keening as he lost part after part of himself.

Chaos.

It was Obarton himself who had loosed the dogs.

Now he drew the snub-nosed revolver from its gleaming leather holster at the small of his back. No more gunshots—just the one. But that scream kept on and on, until he could bear it no longer. Unlocking the door, he yanked it open, only to be greeted by a scene out of a painting by Jackson Pollock. Blood splashed the walls in long, arcing swaths and wild asymmetrical spatters. His men—the ones left standing—were backed up against the walls, their bodies coated with blood, their eyes fairly bugging out of their heads. But the unearthly keening was coming from Naylor. He was writhing in the cold fire of blue flame. His face was a distorted mask, hideously blackened lips pulled back from bared teeth, his limbs already foreshortened; the unearthly fire had eaten away his hands and feet. He swayed back and forth like an abandoned marionette.

And through this chaos, this carnage, stalked Lilith Swan, his bitch-nemesis. How did she know where he was? Then he saw Highstreet's mobile, which had never been turned off. Damn. But how had she gotten in? Then he saw her reach out, push Naylor over. Of course. Naylor had a key. Damn-damn-damn.

"Hugh," Lilith said, not giving a second glance to the pistol pointed at her, "where is he?"

"Beyond your grasp, I'm afraid," Obarton replied with a false bravado. "Or he will be seconds from now." He thought he had pulled the trigger, but the edge of a hand came down on his wrist with such force that the bones shattered on impact. He moaned, dropped the pistol, cradled his hand in the crook of his other arm. Pain knifed through him like a chef's blade through muscle, and he moaned again. All the blood drained from his face. His eyes rolled in their sockets. And then he caught sight of his attacker, and abject terror gripped him.

He recognized Emma Shaw's face immediately, but what were those black talons grown out of her fingertips? He had no more time for speculation. He screamed as one of the talons punctured his flesh just beneath the breastbone, pinning him to the open door.

Lilith brushed by them, entered the cell, began to untie Highstreet, to minister to him as a mother would to her wounded child. Then she returned to where Emma Shaw had impaled Obarton, said, "I will kill him now, Emma."

"Wait," Emma said, in a strange, deep-throated rumble that sent a shiver down Obarton's spine.

"Look! Look what he's done to Hugh! He deserves—"

"I know what he deserves," Emma said. She eyed Lilith for a moment. "Go back to Hugh. Make sure he's okay. I need to spend some time with Obarton alone. Then he'll get what he deserves." When Lilith still hesitated, she added, "I promise."

When they were alone with the dead and the dying, Emma said, "We have breached your firewalls, Obarton. Every secret the Knights have or ever had is now in the possession of the Gnostic Observatines."

"You're a liar. It's impossible." He sputtered. "We would have known; I would have been told."

"And yet you weren't, and none of your IT people are any the wiser." She leaned in, pressed her talon deeper into the core of him, so that he shouted, whimpered. Tears overflowed his eyes, shuddered down his fat jowls. "Here's a little taste of what we've taken from the guts of your servers."

"They're Lilith's servers, too." Then, and only then, did it hit him how utterly and irrevocably the landscape had been altered. He felt like a child all alone in the night.

Emma waved a printout from the lab before his eyes, saw his gaze riveted by the information liberated from the deepest levels of the Knights' servers. He gave a little yelp.

"Now that we have cleared up who's telling the truth, Obarton, I have only one question you need to answer."

"Why would I?" he said, transferring his gaze to her face. "You're going to kill me anyway."

"Me? I'm not going to kill you, Obarton. Just extract information."

"You have everything. You just showed me—"

Emma shook her head. "I want more, Obarton. I want the location of the Knights' Reliquary."

**"HUGH, HUGH."**

Highstreet, safe in her arms, was weeping openly. All the pain was tolerable now, as the misery leached out of him, replaced by relief and a sense of the most profound love he had ever felt. He was so deeply grateful to Lilith for coming after him, for finding him, for delivering him from his own private hell on earth.

"I'm here now," Lilith said. "Obarton and his kind are over and done with. You can return to your life without fear."

"I don't . . ." Highstreet began to weep all over again. He was not ashamed, not with Lilith, who knew him like no other human being, who accepted him unconditionally.

"Take your time, Hugh." Lilith was using the water in the jug next to him, cleaning his wounds as best she could with the sleeve of her shirt. "No need to hurry."

"I don't want to go back to my life."

Lilith paused in her ministrations. "No? What do you want, Hugh?"

"I have no idea. Except . . ."

"Except what?"

"I want to be wherever you are."

Lilith burst out laughing, kissed him on the forehead. "But that's a given."

---

**"WHAT ARE** you talking about?" Obarton winced in pain. "You're standing in the Reliquary."

"Oh no, I don't think so." Emma leaned in farther. "There are no reliquaries in this underground bunker, only instruments of incarceration, interrogation, and torture."

"You're wrong. You—"

"Please don't insult my intelligence. You would never have taken Lilith to the real Reliquary. Would you?"

When Obarton refused to answer, she pushed the talon all the way in. Tears of agony appeared, and Obarton quivered. He looked like a waif with nowhere to run. "Would you?" she repeated.

His head dropped. "Please. Please don't let her near me."

"Would you, Obarton?" Emma pressed.

"N . . . no, I wouldn't." He gasped. "I never would have revealed the real Reliquary's location to that bitch."

"But you'll tell me."

"What? N . . . no. Why would I?"

"Because I'm the only one who can keep you from Lilith. I'm the only one who can keep you alive."

"Is . . . is that a promise?" His eyes, redrimmed in pain, searched hers for an answer.

"Yes." She cocked her head. "And unlike yours, Obarton, my word is a sacred oath."

He hesitated, licked his dry lips.

"Time is running out," Emma told him. "From the moment I withdraw this talon it will take you . . ." She shrugged. "Actually, I don't know how long it will take you to bleed out. But I do know that Lilith will get to you before that happens."

"How do you know—?"

"Because you're a coward, Obarton. There is no sacrifice in you. It's every man for himself."

He licked his lips again. His breath was hot and rapid against her cheek. "Al . . . all right." And then he told her, gave her the map coordinates to the Knights' most sacred of sacreds, the place that held all the secrets not enumerated on their servers—their Reliquary.

"You'll keep your promise," he said then. "You'll keep Lilith away from me."

"As I said."

"You won't let her kill me."

"No one is going to kill you, Obarton," Emma said softly. And when the tension had been replaced by profound relief, she added: "Death is too good for you."

Immediately his face paled again. "What do you mean?"

And then he screamed. One of the talons on her other hand pierced the fabric of his trousers, carved a bloody semi-circle, separating him from his genitals.

She grinned at him with grim satisfaction. "This is your life now, Obarton. Get used to it."

# PART FOUR

## THE HOLLOW LANDS

# 43

BRAVO'S AND AYLA'S FIRST SIGHT OF THE ISLAND OF ARWAD was of the high stone walls and fearsome fortifications that had successfully repelled wave after wave of would-be invaders. Within, among the ruins, Captain Kreutzer told them, was a sleepy fishing village and not much else. The war in Syria, though only miles away on the mainland, had not touched the island. In all, Arwad seemed a homely place, a rocky, barren isle with little to recommend it, save as a fortified outpost during times of war, but, ironically, not now.

The Phoenicians inhabited it first, eventually declaring it an independent island-state, one of the first known examples of a republic. These people at first called themselves Canaanites, meaning "merchants." They are recorded in the Bible, in both Genesis and Ezekiel, as skilled oarsmen and guardsmen. The Greeks renamed them Phoenicians, after the prized cloth of purple they made and exported.

The morning Bravo and Ayla were dropped off via launch, having said their farewells to Captain Kreutzer, was like any other in recent memory. Above them, gulls wheeled and cried beneath the blazing sun as the launch motored through the gap in the arms of the breakwater toward the sweeping harbor. Sails were strung from old spars, bleaching, caught now and again by gusts of wind coming off the water. Fishing boats were tied up, men working on repairs, or chatting after a long night's fishing. Above them loomed the great fortified walls from ancient times, throwing knife-like shadows onto the new but shabby apartment buildings shoved up against the rough shingle beyond the boat basin.

*The inhabitants are mostly Sunni Muslims, just like the extremists who captured you, so have a care,* Kreutzer had told them. *But here and there the ancient traditions of the Phoenecians remain, remembered and practiced by the remnants of the most influential families.*

The sea air had done wonders for Bravo's healing. His body bore only vague shadows of what had once turned much of his flesh black and blue, and only a touch of swelling, here and there, served as reminders of his physical trials at the hands of his sister and then the Syrians. As for Ayla's cheek, the wound was a brown slash, small, almost insignificant, giving her only a twinge now and again.

Their appearance on the beach provoked a predictable response. All heads turned in their direction, but keen eyes had spotted the freighter that had brought them to the shores of Arwad, and it seemed as if the ship was known on the island, for no gaze that landed on them was in the least bit hostile. Nor was it particularly friendly. A mild wave of curiosity fluttered through the bystanders before they returned to their work or their conversations. Only one woman was moved enough to head toward them, picking her way carefully over the broken-up shell shingle. She was barefoot, holding the hem of her robe up to her shins. She passed through the surf as if it were her home, belonging fully to neither the land nor the sea.

She was neither young nor old. Her hair was long, cascading thickly over one shoulder. She was handsome and strong, with good bones beneath her sun-burnished skin. As she approached, she watched them with an enigmatic expression, neither her wide-apart eyes nor her full lips giving away her thoughts.

After they exchanged the usual Muslim greetings, she said, "Good morning. My name is Kamar." She spoke to them in an Arabic dialect Bravo knew well. Her eyes were the color of sand. They were watchful, canny, but not hostile. "You have come a long distance to Arwad. Perhaps you would be good enough to tell me why."

"I am Bravo and this is Ayla." Bravo smiled. "And, yes, we have come a long way, and are hungry and weary. I wonder if you could direct us to—"

"But of course," Kamar said. Her returning smile was wary, circumspect. But Muslim tradition required that she accommodate the strangers no matter their objective. "You shall be guests in my home. You will eat and drink your fill, and afterward you may rest comfortably in the shade of my palm trees." She gestured. "Come now. Come with me. The heat of the day is just beginning."

———————

"NOW," KAMAR began. But before she could continue, a little girl came running into the dining area where they were sitting among the remnants of a veritable feast of small plates their hostess had whipped up while they were washing the days of grime off them. They shared the tiny bathroom. Kamar's house was old, low ceilinged, dark, and smoky, the rooms small but spotlessly clean and tidy. The sharp scents of spices mixed with the mellower aromas of caramelized sugar and ground pistachios. It was a homey place, a house you would always want to come back to.

The little girl—Kamar's eight-year-old daughter—looked at the visitors with the straightforward curiosity of a child as she climbed up into her mother's lap. Kamar wrapped her arms around her daughter, rocking her gently as she kissed the top of her head. The little girl seemed to be in seventh heaven.

"My name is Haya Ahirom," she said. "Who are you?"

"We are wanderers," Bravo said without missing a beat. But his heart rate went through the roof. Tanis Ahirom was his grandmother, Conrad's first beloved. Ahirom was not an uncommon Phoenician name, but Tanis and her family came from this island. "We search for the meaning of history."

"History?" Haya cocked her head.

"Your island, your home, has a great, long history." Bravo grinned at her. "Once upon a time, Arwad was a very important place."

"Is it now?" Haya asked.

"Well, I suppose it could be." Bravo shrugged. "No one knows."

"Is that why you have come?" Kamar asked with suspicious eyes. "You are not Muslim, but you wish to take that which was our ancestors', yes?"

"No," Bravo said firmly. "We're not tomb raiders; we collect nothing but knowledge." Not quite true, but there were moments in life when telling the truth was substantially more dangerous than telling a white lie. He leaned forward, looking at Haya, rather than her mother, feeling this was very important now. He was traversing a razor's edge. What he said next was of paramount importance. If he turned this woman against him, he could forget about finding what he was looking for.

"Haya," he said, "I have a surprise for you."

The girl's eyes lit up. "A surprise?"

"No gifts," Kamar said sternly.

"But what is it?" Haya's voice was high, plaintive. "What is the surprise?"

Outside the windows, mended sails billowed in the wind. Gulls called plaintively. Rough voices on the beach, raucous laughter, soon fading.

"My grandmother's name was the same as yours."

The girl's eyes opened wide. "Haya?"

"Not the beautiful name your mother gave you," Bravo said. "Your equally beautiful family name: Ahirom."

"Really?" It was Kamar who responded, her voice tight. Bravo wondered whether she was going to go for a weapon hidden somewhere about the room. "I very much doubt that."

"Her name was Tanis. Tanis Ahirom."

Kamar sat very still. In fact, she seemed scarcely to breathe. "Describe her, please."

There were no pictures of Tanis, but Conrad had described her to a young Bravo, his eyes closed against the sun, but seeming to gather strength from the light and the heat. Such was the loving detail of his grandfather's description that Bravo felt that he had actually met her. He closed his eyes, and spoke as Conrad had spoken to him so many years ago.

After he had finished, there followed the deep silence one experiences in a library or on a battlefield when the fighting is over, relief replacing fear. Not even Haya moved a muscle, attuned as she was to her mother's moods.

"Tanis Ahirom," Kamar said slowly and deliberately, "was my mother's eldest aunt."

Reaching around her child, she poured them more tea, then filled her own cup. "Please." She gestured, lifting her glass in the manner of a formal toast. "Let us drink."

And with that the bond between them was complete. Bravo was part of the family.

"NOW," KAMAR said, after she had cleared away the dishes and had sent Haya off to school, "tell me about your traveling companion."

"I think it's best if she tells you herself," Bravo said.

"As you wish." Kamar sat with her hands in her lap, an expectant look on her face. Her fingers were long and slender, as Conrad had said Tanis's had been. "So, Ayla . . ." Her hands lifted, wove complex patterns in the air as an inducement for her guest to speak, before falling back into her lap.

"My father was Conrad Shaw, Bravo's grandfather," Ayla began, but was forestalled by Kamar's knit brows.

"But how is that possible?"

"Conrad was an older man when he met my mother," Ayla continued, regaining the strength of conviction. "I never knew about Tanis; I don't think he told my mother about her."

"Well, why would he? I'm sure he loved your mother," Kamar said wisely. She looked from Ayla to Bravo and back again. "So you are Bravo's aunt, yes?"

She nodded. "Strange as it seems."

Kamar chuckled. "Well, in this family, my dear, nothing is ever strange." Her hands fluttered again, as if she were a conductor leading her orchestra in a prelude. "Tell me, Ayla, what is your mother's full name?"

"My mother passed last year."

"Ah, pity." She had a way of making you sure that she was sincere. Her eyebrows lifted, another inducement.

"Her name was Dilara Tusik."

"Her married name, yes?"

"That's right. But how—?"

Kamar shrugged. "Some things one simply knows. So." She slapped her thighs in emphasis. "The name she was born with. Out with it, my darling!"

"Balbi. The name she was born with was Dilara Balbi."

Kamar jumped up, crying, "Astarte and Baal!" invoking the names of the two principal gods of the Phoenicians. "I knew it! There was something in your bearing, something behind your eyes, and I knew. I knew!"

She appeared beside herself with delight. "I've waited so long for this moment." She was pacing back and forth, her expressive hands moving in a blur. "I had given up hope, you see. I had begun to lose faith. And then, lo and behold, an Ahirom and a Balbi are washed up onto the shore of my home. Not on any other place on the island, mind you. But here. Here where I am!"

"Kamar, what do you mean you were waiting for us?" Bravo asked.

Their hostess raised a finger, a mischievous smile on her face. She left them alone for some minutes, disappearing behind a beaded curtain into one of the bedrooms. Ayla glanced at Bravo, but he just shook his head. Neither of them knew what Kamar had in mind.

She returned holding a box of tulipwood, banded in bronze. She carried it with the reverence reserved for something beyond price. Setting it down between them, she produced three small keys. It took all three of them, used in turn, to unlock the box. She lifted the lid, brought out a golden apple. Reaching into the oilskin sea pouch gifted to him by Captain Kreutzer, Bravo showed her his golden apple. The two were twins.

"My God," Ayla exclaimed, "what does this mean?"

Kamar looked at them in turn. "In the beginning, there were three golden apples. One each was gifted to the three families that ruled Phoenicia—the Ahiroms, the Balbis, and the Safitas."

"My mother never told me—she never mentioned a golden apple."

Kamar's face darkened like the sky at the coming of night. "Yes, well, that is because the golden apple was stolen from the Balbis."

"Who would do that?" Ayla asked.

Kamar hesitated. "After what happened . . . happened, the offending family name was stricken from all written records. It was as if it had never existed." She shook her head. "But, of course, it did. One of them stole the apple and left this island, never to be found, though they were pursued by members of all three families, who banded together for this one purpose. It is said they searched for a hundred and one years, a mystical number for us, as well as other ancient peoples of the East."

Bravo stirred. "What was the name of the family?"

"The family name is unimportant," Kamar said. "These are most precious heirlooms. We are guardians. The apples have been handed down from generation to generation."

"For what purpose?" Ayla said.

Kamar eyed her judiciously. "Let me answer your question with another. How did your mother pass?"

When Ayla remained silent, her gaze upon the floor at her feet, Bravo said, "She was beheaded."

Kamar's eyes grew fire bright. "Ah."

"By one of the Fallen in human form."

She nodded. "But of course. She was one of the immortals." Leaning forward, she placed a hand on Ayla's knee. Her touch was light as a finch alighting there. "I'm sorry. Truly sorry."

And Ayla, nodding, meeting her fierce gaze, knew she was, though Kamar and Dilara had never met.

After a short reverential silence, Kamar started up again, like a train that had switched from the local to the express track. "So. The person who stole the apple from the Balbis used it in a manner in which it was never to be used."

"Who was it?" Bravo and Ayla asked together.

"Her name," Kamar said, "was Chynna Sikar."

CHYNNA SIKAR. The name reverberated through the folds of Bravo's brain like a bullet ricocheting from wall to wall. Chynna Shaw, Bravo's great-great-grandmother, was the one member of the family no one—absolutely no one—spoke of. Even Conrad. No one purported to know where she came from or anything about her origins. Kamar had just provided him the last link.

On one visit to the great library in Alexandria in Egypt, Bravo had come across a reference to her. His father had developed the habit of taking his young son, a voracious reader and astonishing polymath, with him to the library. What Dexter studied there was a complete mystery to young Bravo until one morning, when his father was called away by the librarian, he wandered over to the table at which Dexter had been sitting. A large tome, thick as his torso, was open. It was very old, its pages fragile with extreme age. He saw the names of the four most prominent families on the Phoenician island Arvad, as Arwad was called in ancient times: Safita, Ahirom, Balbi, and Sikar, of which this was an exhaustive history. What caught his eye, specifically, was that the word "Sikar" was partially rubbed out, a heavy line drawn through it. The one short paragraph someone had tried to destroy concerned a particular Sikar. There was a notebook and pencil just to the right of the book. On it, Dexter was attempting to reconstruct the paragraph in its entirety. The subject was Chynna Sikar—specifically that she had stolen something Bravo could not read, something clearly very valuable—from the Balbi family.

According to the author or authors of the book, it was an impossible feat—impossible, that is, for a human being. Even an invading army would not have found its hiding place, so the tome claimed. How then had Chynna Sikar done it? By occult means. She had help, this theory posited, dark help, conjured from the netherworld—the place between the Underworld and here where humans dwell.

"It was said that Chynna Sikar was a sorceress of exceptional powers," Kamar said, as if reading his mind.

"Which was how she managed to steal the Balbis' golden apple," Bravo said.

Kamar pointed. "Is that it? The Balbis' long-lost apple?"

"No. This one belonged to my grandfather Conrad. It's the one belonging to the Safitas. But I believe he was searching for the stolen one. He wanted to right a wrong."

Kamar stared at him, wordless.

Bravo waited a beat. "My great-great-grandmother's given name was Chynna."

Kamar was thunderstruck. "Are you saying—"

Bravo nodded. "After Chynna Sikar fled Arvad with the golden apple, she changed her name to Shaw."

"I don't—"

"It makes sense. No one in my family would speak her name; no one knew where she came from." He told her what he had seen on his visit to the Alexandria library that fateful morning. "My father was very interested in her. Now I know why."

His fingers skimmed the silken contours of both apples. "The rumors were correct. Chynna was a sorceress. Her powers were so great that it was believed she was somehow able to summon one of the Fallen to help her steal this apple. It was supposed that she was in thrall to the Fallen, that while in its power she was impregnated, and later, after it had abandoned her, she gave birth to Gideon, my great-grandfather."

"A Nephilim!" Kamar gasped the words out, one hand to her throat, as if terrified to speak the name. "And you two are its descendants."

Bravo nodded. "But now the narrative has been turned on its head. It seems far more likely that the Fallen was under Chynna's spell, that she lured it with the promise of the golden apple, mated with it of her own volition, and, afterward, when she was done with it, banished it back into the netherworld from which she had summoned it with some dreadful spell using the apple she had stolen."

Kamar frowned. "The Fallen are said to have long memories, that they never forgive. Which Fallen did Chynna mate with?"

"That I don't know."

Their hostess considered for a moment. "Listen to me, Bravo, I know

the Fallen are here. I know what they want. They are far more powerful than even you realize. I would advise you to use every trick at your
command to find out the identity of the one Chynna used for her own
purposes and then discarded."

Once more Bravo dipped his hand into the sea pouch. This time he
brought out the gold rood. Kamar gasped audibly as he set it down beside
the two apples.

"Is that . . ." Kamar almost choked on her emotions. "Is that the real
thing?"

"It is," Bravo said.

She looked up at him. "May I?"

He nodded. "Of course."

Slowly, her hand reached out, her long, slender fingers wrapping themselves around the crucifix with infinite care. When she lifted it up to hold
before her face, she was weeping. "How was it kept out of sight for so
long?"

"There is something in the composition of bronze that defeats some of
the Fallen's powers. Conrad had the rood clothed in bronze armor, protecting it from both identification and use."

"Bless him! Then there is a chance against the fall of eternal night," she
whispered.

# 44

**"LOOK AT THEM!" LILITH REACHED OUT TO TOUCH THE RAZOR-**sharp tips of the ebon talons, then drew her hand back. "What the hell?"

"'What the hell' is right." Emma looked into her eyes. Sunlight spun off the glossy surfaces of the newly grown talons. It was time to tell her the truth, the whole truth, and nothing but the truth.

Salt air ruffled her hair, still thick enough to hide the stubs of horns sprouting up just above her hairline. Beyond the hull of the boat they had boarded at the southwestern cape of Cyprus rose Arwad's ancient walls. The eighty-seven-nautical-mile journey was almost done. The boat swung around to starboard, skirting the scimitar-shaped southern shore, on the way toward the long breakwater toward the mouth of the harbor.

"It's The Testament of Lucifer," she began. "I told you I read it when I shouldn't have. What I didn't tell you is that, like Bravo, I am blessed with an eidetic memory. In this case, however, it's a curse. I can't forget what I've read; the Testament has a life of its own. The words, sentences, paragraphs, magical in their nature, are working on me. They're changing me." She pushed her hair off her forehead, revealing the beginnings of the horns.

Lilith grasped her. "Oh, Emma, no." Her trembling fingers traced the circumference of the stubs that were threatening to break through her skin. "Oh, my God."

"I've fought against it, Lilith. You don't know how hard I've fought, but the opening of the portal, even for that short a time, strengthened the dark sorcery of the Testament. Conrad's blue flame served as only a temporary respite."

The look of horror on Lilith's face made her appear gaunt, ashen. "What's going to happen to you?"

"I'll change. I won't be Emma anymore."

"And Beleth?"

"He knows. Beleth will die."

"That's why he's in hiding."

Emma nodded.

"Coward!" Lilith shouted into Emma's face. "Get out here! Save her, you fucking baby!"

Emma's eyes darkened, the sigil returning to her pupils. "I cannot." Beleth's deep voice rumbled out of Emma's mouth. "I am only Second Sphere. I lack—"

"Think, Beleth!" Lilith shouted. "You're from that realm. There must be a way."

"Leviathan said I am a tactician, not a strategist, and he is right. My mind was not bred to see the big picture. I win battles, not wars."

"You have shit for brains, you useless *thing*."

"Epithets will not win the day," Beleth said evenly.

"Perhaps not," Lilith spit, "but they make me feel a whole lot better."

"What may make you feel better," the Fallen Power said, "is that Emma's fate is not set in stone."

"You mean *your* fate isn't set in stone."

"No one wants to die, Lilith. Not even me, I find, now that I've met the two of you. Now that I understand . . . things I've never been privy to before."

"But back to Emma."

"Yes, back to Emma. She can still be saved. But there is a deadline fast approaching, after which the transformation process will have gone too far. If that happens, no one, nothing, will be able to stop it. I will die and she will become—well, she will become . . . something else, some dark angel enslaved by the words of Lucifer himself. A creature that, frankly speaking, none of us have ever before seen or read about. A creature wholly of Lucifer's making. Not one iota of God will dwell in her heart or in her soul. She will be nothing . . . and everything."

Lilith drew back, as if from a dreadful shadow, an enemy as yet unseen or fully formed. She stared into Emma's face, blank but for those ferocious black eyes holding at their center the sigil of the Unholy Trinity.

"Emma." Gathering her courage to her like armor, she grasped her lover's shoulders. "Emma!"

But there was no answer. Only Beleth's sorrowful stare.

"How long?" Lilith whispered. "How many days do we have?"

"I am not good with temporal matters, even when in this corpus," Beleth said. "But I would say some way must be found to arrest the transformation, to reverse it before moonrise."

Alarmed, Lilith said, somewhat breathlessly, "Moonrise when?"

"Tonight."

Lilith gave a little cry of dismay. Despair gripped her.

Moments later, the boat glided alongside the dock, lines were tossed, the boat tied up. They had arrived at Arwad.

**"THIS WAY!"** Kamar, crooking a forefinger, hurried them along the shingle. "We must hurry! My husband is due back at any moment, and if he sees us he will try to stop us."

"Does he not know who and what you are?" Ayla said.

"He knows nothing. He can know nothing." Kamar's voice was husky, breathy with the pace she had set. Out in the blazing sunlight they could discern the lines at the corners of her mouth, along the meridians of her forehead. There were mini-starbursts at the outer corners of her upswept eyes. "It is afternoon. At any moment, his ship will appear between the arms of the breakwaters."

"Why did you marry someone like that?" Bravo asked.

"My husband is powerful. No one dares bother me or interfere with what I must do in his absence. No one dares even gossip about me." She grimaced. "It was a marriage of convenience, I admit that freely and without shame. And look what I got in compensation. I love my little girl with all my heart."

"But it must be a strain when he's home," Ayla said, "keeping your secret life from him."

"Everything is a strain when Ismail is home," she said, and so concentrated on guiding them was she that she failed to see the meaningful glance exchanged between them.

"Is Ismail the captain of a fishing fleet?" Bravo asked, after a moment's silence.

"Would that he were." Kamar shook her head. "Ah, no. My husband is a certain kind of Sunni Muslim. From an early age, his mind was steeped in hate. He interprets the Qur'an in a different way than I do, in a strict way I do not approve of." She shrugged. "But this is his way and there's no talking him out of it."

Bravo and Ayla exchanged another glance. Now they were sure that the Ismail they had encountered was Kamar's husband. It was difficult to say how either of them felt; the situation was too complex, their time not enough of their own to ruminate about what they had done. Besides, there seemed no love between the two, at least on Kamar's part.

Still, Ayla felt it incumbent on her to ask, "What would you do if Ismail failed to return now or in the future?"

Kamar paused for a moment, turned to them. "I have been on my own most of my life, my darling. I would do what I always do: put one foot in front of the other." She shrugged. "Ismail's protection will survive him. I would be his widow. Untouchable, unassailable." She shrugged. "In any event, he's served his purpose."

She regarded them with her sharp, quick eyes. "He's dead, isn't he?"

Bravo saw no point in lying to her. Besides, she had given them enough information to gauge her reaction. "His ship was set on fire," he said. "It sank with all hands on board."

"Ah, well. That was the life he chose." She did not look sad, did not seem in any way moved. "He was the kind of Muslim I could not abide. Haya has nothing to fear from him now; she can go to school without him punishing her."

She paused. "Did you see him?"

But Bravo knew she already knew the answer. "He was just as you described him. It was impossible to reason with him."

A slow smile that was perhaps half sneer crossed her face quickly. "He met his fate," she said. "What happened was supposed to happen." She gave the ghost of a nod. "Haya thanks you, both of you."

They had mounted the seawall via a flight of stone steps, crumbling with age and the ceaseless pounding of the sea, and had now crossed over onto the other side. Traversing a steep decline, they found themselves beyond the precincts of the village. Only a scattering of scarecrow houses were to be seen on the hillside beyond. Now they approached the black mouth of a sea cave. Its sandy floor seemed to be the only thing not moving, for the upper reaches were infested with bats. The acrid stink of their guano was so pungent it stung the eyes, made the backs of their throats sore with each inhalation.

Inside the mouth, she paused, facing them again. Beyond, the long afternoon was on its last legs. There was almost no wind. The water seemed deeply asleep. The heat was almost unbearable. Far out, the coastline of Syria was a fuzzed-out line, wavering in the heat. Every once in a while a war jet could be seen. But its sound never reached them. Arwad was in its own time and place, separate from everywhere else.

"Listen to me now," Kamar said. "You must find the third apple. Without all three the sacred instrument is not complete. It will not work—worse, it will work in unintended ways. Chynna found that out. Others too, I have no doubt." The skin of the apple she handed Bravo was like molten gold in the shadow and the light. "The addition of the gold rood gives you three out of the four sections of the instrument. You must assemble it. The instrument is the only thing with sorcery powerful enough to arrest the coming invasion. Without it, the Four Thrones will destroy you—do to you whatever they choose—and then the path to their incursion into our world will be open. We will be defenseless."

"Even you, Kamar?" Ayla asked. She had become very fond of the woman.

"The fact that I am an immortal like your mother will make me one of their very first targets."

"We will stop them," Ayla said. "That's a promise."

"Look at this one, Bravo. What she lacks in experience she makes up for in bravado."

Ayla gave a nervous laugh. "I'm still scared as hell."

Kamar replied with a warm smile, "That fear will keep you alive, my darling. Cherish it; keep it close. It will protect you."

Ayla took a step toward their host. "I must ask you—"

"About your powers." Kamar laughed softly, the bats picking up the vibrations, fluttering and squeaking as if speaking to her. "Don't look so surprised, my darling. One sorceress recognizes another, just as sorcery knows sorcery." She took Ayla's hands in her. She held them loosely, and yet had Ayla wanted to withdraw them she knew she would not be able to. Once, she had swum with dolphins, had felt the gentle tingling of their sonar as they scanned her, getting to know the contours of her body and then the person within. This was now precisely the same sensation passing from Kamar to her. She relaxed completely. Her eyelids grew heavy, and they slid down. She was now inside herself. Kamar was with her. Information passed from mentor to acolyte at such a furious pace Ayla at first became disoriented. Then she relaxed into the flow and, like a diver, allowed it to take her where it would, into a deeper and darker part of an unfathomable ocean.

Songs came to her from out of the indigo, incantations in Tamazight, in Assyrian, in all the mother languages of the human race. One after the other, they rose and fell like a tide, buoying her up, carrying her along, penetrating through the pores of her skin, circulating through her blood, rushing pell-mell through the millions of corridors of her brain. And then in an instant she went from being conducted along to conducting the inflow herself, guiding this incantation here, that one there, housing them as she saw fit, until they inhabited every room of the memory-mansion she built for them. Then she had to build another one, and another, so on and so forth, until the torrent abruptly ceased, having expended itself on her own private shore.

BRAVO WATCHED the transfer with a combination of awe and delight. At last Ayla was finding the destiny her mother had seen for her but could never tell her about for fear of changing the future revealed to her by her Farsight. For, as he had discovered, the future was mutable, Farsight a double-edged sword that, used improperly, could actuate a future the exact opposite of what had been seen. The law of unintended consequences was as true for those in the occult world as it was for everyone else.

At length, it was finished. Kamar's hands slid slowly from beneath Ayla's, and the connection was disengaged. Ayla slumped back against the wall of the cave, but when Bravo moved to help her Kamar held him back with a hand on his forearm and a shake of her head.

"Leave her be now. She needs time to digest, to come to terms with the vast amount of knowledge that is now at her fingertips." She led Bravo a little away, farther into the realm of the bats, who fluttered and dipped in the space between them, as if wanting to taste, with their echolocation, their visitors. Bravo did not mind; he liked bats, found them fascinating and misunderstood.

"Now," Kamar said softly, "I must tell you something difficult to relate."

Bravo regarded her with an unwavering gaze. There was no sense of foreboding, only a curious numbness at the heart of him that told him he was ready for anything.

"I knew your father," Kamar began. "Dexter came here to Arwad, came to see me in particular."

"What did he want?"

"Information. That's what Dexter always wanted. But then you know that."

Bravo said nothing. When it came to his father he was not agnostic. Dexter's antipathy to his own father—to the Shaw line, in fact—was something Bravo could neither forget nor forgive.

"What you don't know," Kamar continued, "was that he was obsessed with Chynna Shaw. He suspected that Shaw was a family name she gave herself, that she was born a Sikar. He journeyed here for confirmation."

"And, of course, you gave it to him."

"Was I supposed to lie?"

"No, but I—"

"You what?"

Bravo wet his lips with the tip of his tongue. The bats were getting thicker around him, as if he was a treat they had never tasted before. "My father and I did not get along. He was jealous of Conrad because Conrad had all the power and he had none."

"That's true enough. But he had another reason."

Bravo's heart felt like a bass drum beating against his ribs. "What other reason?"

"Every action has an opposite and equal reaction. This is a human scientific fact. But it is truer than humans can understand. Your father was angry at Conrad for what he had done. The rash actions of your grandfather had pushed further open the portals that had been unsealed by the Phoenician alchemists when they conjured the occult gold required by Solomon's foolish son."

She gave Bravo a level look. "He forbade you to spend time with your grandfather for fear that he would infect you with his rashness." She gave him a sad smile. "But it happened in spite of him. Your grandfather never died, at least not in the way we know death. He abides. You know this, Bravo. If I'm any judge of matters you have proof."

"Many times over."

"And now you and he are united. When I saw the gold crucifix I knew. No power on earth or in any realm, for that matter, can pull you two asunder."

"And my father?"

"Dexter is, alas, dead. He died in the explosion that wrecked his home. He cannot be brought back in any form. So." She lifted a finger. "You must learn to keep your head, while others all around you are losing theirs." She gave a short laugh. "Now you must accomplish what your grandfather could not. He was able to retrieve the golden apple that was the Safitas', but he could not find the stolen one."

"But he didn't have yours, either."

"He would have if he had found the third—I made him that promise." She nodded into the inky depths of the cave. "I sent him in there, just as I'm sending you now. My mistake was in not giving him the apple. Even if he found the missing one he could not have put the instrument together. I'm not making that mistake twice. You have everything you need for when you find the third golden apple."

"You put great faith in me."

"As Conrad did." She smiled. "Now you must have faith in yourself."

Ayla was coming around. Her eyes focused on them, her breathing normalized, and she pushed herself away from the wall, picked her way over the piles of bat guano to where they stood. She smiled at Bravo to tell him she was all right.

Including both of them, Kamar gestured. "The farthest reaches of this cave lead to the netherworld—the barrier between our world and the Underworld, where God imprisoned the Fallen. It is called the Hollow Lands, and it is there the portal between the realms lies. It is where Conrad believed Chynna hid the last golden apple.

"It is there where all the peril lies in wait for you."

# 45

THERE WAS A TIME WHEN LEVIATHAN STOOD AT THE LEFT hand of God. It is common knowledge who stands at his right hand. But Leviathan was not made for servitude, and even before the rebellion the Seraph chafed under the heavy fist of the so-called Almighty. That they rebelled, that they failed in their rebellion and were cast down, was proof that God was fallible. Or so Lucifer never tired of repeating. But Leviathan was not so certain. It came into the Seraph's mind that the rebellion, the Fall that mimicked the fall of Adam at the hands of Eve and the serpent, was also part of God's plan.

For what? The humans, in their dreadful naiveté, preached that these events occurred to teach them lessons on the nature of good and evil. But Leviathan knew that for a lie. In the first place, God was bored by peace. He relished war. In the second place, God was made more powerful by perpetrating vengeance, either directly or by proxy. "Proxy" meaning "Lucifer." For it was Leviathan's belief that even here in the Hollow Lands they were all God's pawns. In the third place, Eve was not to blame, nor was the serpent who, in any event, did not exist. It was God himself who gifted his creation with an insatiable lust for knowledge—the more forbidden the better. He had created, in effect, a social experiment, set his oh-so-clever inventions to working, and drew pleasure from watching them maim, rape, and kill one another. Who was the real sinner? Leviathan never tired of silently asking, mainly because he knew the answer.

And there was one other thing that vexed the Seraph mightily. Why were there only male-minds among the angels? Where were the female-minds? To be sure, there were female saints and oh-so-many female sinners. But as for angels, not a one. Why? the Seraph kept asking. Why?

It could not be an oversight. It was deliberate. Again, why? And the only answer the Seraph could come up with was this: a female-mind would be too powerful, too clever, for even God to keep under his fist for long. And to seal the deal he caused male humans to keep their females under lock-and-key, real or otherwise.

It was this injustice—God's violation of the natural order he himself created—Leviathan some time ago set out to rectify. And who better for a candidate than a direct descendant of a Nephilim? And not just a Nephilim, but a Shaw—or should we say a Sikar?—as well.

Emma Shaw.

He thought he had been prepared to see her at the rendezvous at the waterfall, but he hadn't. Her physical appearance nearly singed his eyes, if such a thing could happen to him. Her beauty was magnificent and forbidden. Too, there was the intense jealousy that raged through him, knowing that Beleth was inside her, part of her. He wanted to exorcise Beleth at once, subject the Power to a long and lingering death. But, of course, that was impossible. To do so would consign Emma to immediate death. And so, showing enormous patience, he gave space for his rage to subside, and when it did no such thing he was obliged to grasp it by the neck, shove it down, down, down into a musty recess of what passed for his soul.

He. Of course Leviathan thought of himself as he. More than a male-mind. Much more. But that memory was for another day.

Now as he strode through the never-ending night of the Hollow Lands, Leviathan kept Emma Shaw in the forefront of his thoughts, as he had so many times before. But this time was different. She was near— the Seraph knew it. She was entering the Hollow Lands, the Seraph's territory, for Leviathan had made this place that stretched all the way around the globe his beachhead, his outpost once the venal Phoenician alchemists had summoned from the Underworld the help they required to forge the tainted gold. That act had unsealed the portal between realms, allowed Leviathan, manifesting his power, to slip through to this netherworld, this Limbo. The waiting room to Hell.

Now the Seraph's long-gestating plan was coming to fruition. No one could stop it. Leviathan would be joined by a female-mind angel, and together they would defeat first Lucifer, then God himself. They would fulfill the dream of all the Fallen: they would rule the day as well as the night, together, side by side, as it was always meant to be.

**"YOU'RE GOING** to kill someone with those." Lilith smirked. But there was a sharp edge of terror in her voice that Emma could not fail to pick up on.

Taking her hands out of her jacket's deep pockets, she held aloft the black talons. There was a thin thread of dried blood on one of them. For a moment, it turned white in the glaring Mediterranean sun. Due to Beleth, no immigration official, no fellow passengers on their flight to Cypress, made mention or even saw the wickedly sharp implements. The hydrofoil they had hired to speed them to Arwad was private. The crew kept their distance, following the orders of their captain, who had been overpaid handsomely.

They arrived on the island late in the day. The heat was ferocious. Gulls screamed, wheeling incessantly over the fishing boats. The mineral odor of the shallows, redolent of kelp, barnacles, and dried fish guts, was overpowering. Emma was sweating profusely, but she couldn't risk taking the jacket off.

"Obarton's coordinates were specific down to the minute," Emma said, not wanting to talk about her transformation, even as a joke. She knew that was Lilith's way of dealing with fear, and was glad of it. But she had moved beyond that; part of her was already preparing for the inevitable—a fate, she was certain, far worse than death.

Having picked their way along the docks, they headed west, over the shorter arm of the seawalls, its crumbling steps washed with wavelets, slimy with poison-green seaweed. In the west, the sun, bloated into an oval, seemed to heave a sigh—of fatigue or relief—as it sank toward the horizon.

"It's underground; we know that much," Lilith said, and then pointing ahead, "There! The cave!"

**"IT'S AN** odd fact," Beleth said through Emma's mouth, "caves give me the shivers."

Lilith laughed shortly. "You're kidding, right?"

"I don't know how to kid," the Power said. "I never had much of a sense of humor. That was left for the First Spheres like Leviathan."

"As far as I could tell that horror has no sense of humor at all."

"You haven't been around Leviathan long enough."

"Look at you," Lilith said. "Speaking in contractions now. Maybe being in such close proximity to us has done you some good, after all."

Beleth, as was its wont when mocked, fell into a sullen silence. Both women, exchanging a glance, took advantage of its tactical withdrawal to launch themselves through the cave mouth, hitting the downward slope with long strides.

The bats kept their distance. Perhaps they too understood the dreadful transformation going on inside Emma, and wanted no part of it. Perhaps their echolocation fastened on Emma's talons, recognizing a predator of immense size.

Occasionally a shaft of amber sunlight shone directly down from a hole in the rock, through which, it would appear, the bats flew in search of nocturnal food. But these soon disappeared with the steep downward pitch of the cave.

"This cave is going downward too quickly," Lilith said. "It's no normal sea cave."

"No, it isn't." Beleth had returned. "It's anything but."

"Then what is it?"

"A passageway," the Power said.

"To what?" Lilith asked.

"If I tell you—"

"You're going to bargain? Now?"

"If I tell you," Beleth went on, unperturbed by Lilith's outburst, "will you teach me strategy?"

Lilith was brought up short. Emma stopped as well, turned back to her.

"You're serious," Lilith said.

"Never more so," Beleth answered her.

"Learning strategy could take weeks, if not months."

"Not for me," Beleth said with such conviction that they had no choice but to believe.

"Emma, what d'you say?"

"I say, what do we have to lose?"

Lilith grunted, then nodded. "You have a deal."

Relief flooded Emma's face. "This passageway leads to the netherworld. The Hollow Lands. It's a place without time or geography as humans know it. It's the place colonized by Leviathan when the portal between worlds was unsealed, the inner keep of his castle."

Beleth looked at Lilith with its dark eyes. "We must proceed with caution."

"Time is running out," Lilith reminded him.

"No one knows that better than we do." It was the first time Beleth had referred to itself and its host as a shared entity. Lilith marked the moment well. "But we do not want to go blundering into the danger without—"

"A strategy," Lilith said, her eyes alight. "Now I understand."

It was Emma who smiled at her—her beloved Emma. "Time to strategize," she said. "And I think Beleth's tactical skills will serve us in good stead."

Lilith nodded. "First lesson, Beleth. Battles are not won by strategy alone."

THE LION'S head stared straight ahead, its stony eyes focused on a future when it would become a war mount. The horse's torso, wicked spikes extending from the fetlocks and cannons of its four legs, already seemed flecked with the sweat of battle, a trick of the Hollow Lands' eerie light. Its serpent's tail, scaled and mailed, curled behind it.

Leviathan approached the Orus, placed a hideously malformed hand on its diamond-shaped chest, lifted it immediately, traced the triangle-circle-square engraved there with the tip of one of his ebon talons. The sigil turned briefly red, as if it were made of fire, then just as quickly subsided into what might have been ink.

At once, the chest of the Orus opened and out they slid, slimy as babes from a mother's spread thighs: Murmur, the mesmerist; Raum, the master of lies; Phenex, the Scryer; and, lastly, Verrine, the Reaver, King of the Four Thrones.

Three sets of leathery wings each, eyes that winked and moved about as if of their own volition. Broad of shoulder, massive of chest, strong as a dozen Oruses, these elite Fallen were made for war. They thirsted for battle as others thirsted for air or water.

They were the perfect killing machines, these four Thrones. The personification of Death, they were as hideous and malformed as the nightmares of a psychotic mind. That was Leviathan's opinion anyway, the only opinion that mattered. He smiled at them, but that smile was tissue thin. How he despised them.

# 46

"CONRAD COULDN'T FIND IT; KAMAR DOESN'T KNOW WHAT happened to it," Ayla said. "What makes you think you'll be able to find the stolen apple?"

"Kamar said Conrad knew Chynna hid it somewhere in the Hollow Lands," Bravo replied.

"Yes, but was Conrad right?"

Bravo was silent as they picked their way down to the lowest reaches of the sea cave. He inhaled deeply. There should have been moisture by now, perhaps even seepage here and there, for they were now far below the surface of the Mediterranean, but the rock walls were perfectly dry. No trace of salt or accumulated minerals was apparent, either.

He had much to mull over, such as what lay ahead and how he was going to find what amounted to a needle in a haystack. As they forged ahead, their way dimly lit by a phosphorescent vein running more or less horizontally through the rock, he was trying to put himself in the mind-set of his great-great-grandmother. He assumed Kamar had told the truth about Chynna stealing the apple that had been in the Balbis' safekeeping. After all, the theft fit in with Chynna running away from Arwad so precipitously, changing her name, mating with the Grigori—the Fallen Angel. She was a sorceress of extraordinary powers—Conrad had told him that much about her. Perhaps she knew that the golden apple would protect her from the Grigori. That hypothesis certainly fit the scenario he had pieced together. But given all that, why would Chynna stash the apple down here? Perhaps she had done it just before she had petitioned the convent to take her in as a novitiate. But, according to Conrad, she was already with the Grigori's child—the Nephilim Gideon, Conrad's father.

Bravo stopped abruptly. They had come to the end of the cave—if cave it actually was, rather than an access tunnel to the netherworld, as Kamar claimed. An unholy glow emanated from just around the last and sharpest turning.

"Are you ready?" Bravo said. And without waiting for an answer: "Here we go."

WITH A bloodcurdling shriek, Emma went down on her knees, doubled over. Moments before, Beleth had let out a groan that spoke both of pain and of recognition.

At once, Lilith knelt beside Emma. She grasped her shoulders, which shook along with the rest of her body, as if she were in the grip of a ferocious ague. But it wasn't an ague she was in the grip of, or any other earthly disease. She was in the grip of something else altogether.

For the past forty minutes, Emma and Lilith had been tutoring Beleth in the art of strategy. As it happened, both women had read Sun Tzu's *The Art of War* and all of Prince Machiavelli's works. Lilith had knowledge of much more, and they had spent the time fruitfully. Beleth hadn't been exaggerating; he was a quick learner, extrapolating one stratagem into others, some of which neither woman had considered.

Now, though, the crisis had arrived, somehow ahead of schedule. Had the moon risen already? Lilith wondered as she pulled Emma's damp hair back from her forehead. Impossible. The sun had not yet set when they entered the cave and encountered the bats. So many hours could not have passed.

She began to stroke Emma's back, and immediately let out a yelp of alarm. A set of wings were growing from between her lover's shoulder blades. Though they were only one pair, unlike the last time, these stumps were far thicker, sturdier, presaging wings of colossal span.

"Emma! Oh, Emma!" she cried. "Talk to me."

Instead, Emma raised her head. Lilith's heart gave a painful lurch in her chest. Emma's eyes were no longer human. They were as two faceted rubies set into her sockets. Neither iris nor pupil could be discerned. And then with a new wave of horror that made her retch, Lilith saw that each facet was, in fact, a complete eye.

"Beleth!" Lilith cried. "Stop this! You must stop it!"

Emma's mouth opened and Beleth's growl rose up. "Pull us to our feet."

Lilith did as she was told. "We must get to the guardroom as quickly as possible."

"The guardroom?" Lilith said stupidly.

"Yes, yes." There was a knife-edge of panic to Beleth's voice that caused Lilith to quake. "I'll guide you. It isn't far, but we have very little time."

But it was far—at least it seemed that way to Lilith, who was subject to Beleth's spit orders interspersed with Emma's piteous screams, as if she was being torn apart.

"She is," Beleth said, "literally," when she voiced her fear.

Through chambers big and small, down twisting corridors they stumbled. With each step Emma grew heavier, because either Lilith's strength was seeping out of her or whatever Emma was becoming weighed far more than she did. Lilith shuddered at the thought, kept on putting one foot in front of the other, staggering, pushing off her heels to keep their forward momentum. Once, she almost fell in her exhaustion, but she knew that if she did she might never get up again. So she gritted her teeth and kept on going. Sweat ran down her face, into her eyes, stinging, distorting her vision.

At last, they came upon an immense chamber. It appeared totally devoid of life, but at the same time Lilith could swear she heard a rustling coming from every side, as if they were passing through a field of long grass. As they moved, she heard an accompanying sound, somewhere beyond the rustling—the gurgle of a brook or stream. Then she spotted it, far off to her right, a dark crevice, as if the rock floor had cracked open. Beyond, she could dimly make out any number of doorways leading off in different directions.

"To the left now," Beleth said. His voice had turned slurred and halting. "Left!"

She found the opening in the wall, passed through it, found herself in a smallish chamber with a low ceiling. Unlike all the other chambers she had seen, this one was filled with thick iron racks bolted to the walls. The racks contained what looked like weapons, though she couldn't be sure; most of them were unfamiliar to her. There were also great iron rings hammered into the stone at two -and three-foot intervals, massive chains of iron and bronze and some black metal she could not identify. In all, it looked like a prison cell, or perhaps, now that she had a better look around, a torture chamber.

"The chains," Beleth said with some difficulty.

Lilith brought them close. "Which ones?"

"Bronze." Beleth gasped, as if in terrible pain. And then as almost a sigh, "Bronze, bronze, bronze."

Setting Emma gently down against the wall, Lilith took up the one set of bronze chains. They were very heavy.

"Now what?"

"Wrap them around us."

"What?"

"Tightly," Beleth said. "So we cannot slip the bonds."

"Are you crazy? This is your solution?"

"It's the only solution," Beleth said. "Listen to me. Soon the beast will be here in full force. If we cannot be saved before then the thing that is coming must be imprisoned."

"With these?"

"Yes. The bronze will bind it. The bronze will neutralize its power. The bronze will protect you."

"But it won't protect Emma, will it?"

"Nor me."

"Then I—"

"Do as I say!" Beleth's shout was so loud, so full of rage, that Lilith jumped. "It's a strategic move."

As if in a dream from which she could not awake, Lilith set about doing as it said. She wound the chain around and around her beloved's body, drew it tight as she could. At Beleth's terse direction she passed one end through the closest iron ring. And all the while, those ghastly compound eyes watched her with singular concentration, as if marking her out for a vengeful death. At one end of the chain was a large bronze padlock and key of the same metal. With shaking hands, Lilith passed the u-shaped locking bar through two links of the chain, snapped it to.

"There. It's done."

"Now go," Beleth said. "Find a way to save us."

"But I don't know—"

"Go! Just go!"

At last Beleth's meaning penetrated her numb mind. It wanted her gone before the transformation had gone far enough that she would no longer recognize Emma. Blindly, she instinctively grabbed the first weapon she recognized—a war hammer with a steel haft and a solid bronze head. Stumbling out of the cell, tears streaming down her face, her heart breaking, she began her search for the impossible.

"**WE'VE BEEN** here before," Bravo said.

"Under Malta." Ayla nodded. "The place with the underground river."

"Where I found the apple Conrad hid." They were moving forward, through the vast, eerily lit space larger than the interior of the largest cathedral.

"Surely this can't be the same place."

"Kamar said the Hollow Lands were without time or geography. Who knows where we are, really." He pointed the way forward. "The best way to find out is to look for the Sphinx."

"Do you think Chynna hid it in its mouth?"

"I have no idea, but the Sphinx is the best place to get our bearings."

"Considering its size, finding it shouldn't be difficult."

And yet it was. The netherworld was filled with numberless chambers, interconnected with corridors that twisted and turned in the most peculiar and dizzying ways. Sometimes they seemed to be heading deeper, until all at once they looked behind them to see that they had actually ascended. Other times, they seemed to be advancing along a wall, rather than the ground.

Guided by the whispered voice of his grandfather, Bravo never lost his way. Nevertheless, it was a very long way from here to there.

**THE SUN** was swimming in bloodred water. Kamar sat on the porch of her house, Haya on her lap, enclosed within her mother's embrace.

"Where are our guests?" Haya said in her high, piping voice.

"They have moved on." Kamar watched the sun continue to sink. "We were an oasis for them. An oasis in a very large desert."

"How large, Mama?"

"From here to the moon and back, little one."

Haya threw her head back against her mother's bosom to look at the sky. "That's a very long way," she said solemnly.

"Yes," Kamar replied, "it is."

For a time, nothing more was said. There was just the lapping of the wavelets, the creaking of the boats, the coarse laughter of the fishermen, the crackle of a fire out on the shingle. Cigarette smoke and broiling fish. Talk of the endless war on the mainland, boys who had died, men who had returned maimed, permanently scarred inside and out. Every once in a while a drone passed by overhead, streaking eastward toward the coast. Lightning flashes and then the dull booming, distorted by distance and the slow churn of the sea.

The fire and the laughter were evidence of a celebration. Kamar knew the fishermen were celebrating the death of her husband. Though they feared him, no one liked him. He and the fanatics he had recruited had brought the misery of death and plunder to Arwad, and for this he could not be forgiven. Now he and his followers were gone, drowned at sea. Cause for joyous festivities. Kamar did not begrudge them their relief; she was relieved herself. The reason for her marriage had passed. She was done with Ismail before he had left on his latest foray.

Haya stirred in her arms. "I liked them, Mama. They were like fish who came from the sea."

Kamar laughed. "Yes, they were, little one." But her laughter was short-lived. The sun was drowning. Soon enough the moon would rise.

# 47

THE HOLLOW LANDS: PRESENT DAY

"THANOS!"

"The fourth Sphinx! Bravo, could it be?"

The Sphinx loomed over them, black as a moonless night. Stars winked along its rippling obsidian flanks, its mouth open in a silent roar, but its great eyes were just stone, blind, aloof, and indifferent.

"It must be." Bravo, clambering onto the plinth and thence up to the Sphinx's colossal shoulder. "There it is, engraved behind its left ear. Ayla, we've found Thanos!"

"And the fourth artifact!" she said from down below.

Reaching over, Bravo inserted his hand into the Sphinx's mouth, felt around the entire cavity.

"No apple," he said. "Nothing but dust."

"If it's not there, where could it be?"

He descended the great beast, jumped off the plinth, stood beside Ayla. A worried expression on his face. "I don't know. This is wholly unexpected. Clearly, something's gone wrong."

At that moment, a figure appeared in the periphery of their vision. The odd, chthonic light threw quivering shadows across her face and body. Tense as they were, both Bravo and Ayla took a step toward her.

"Emma?" Ayla said.

Then Lilith stepped fully into the light, and Bravo let out a held breath.

"My name is Lilith. I've been with Emma for . . ." Her voice petered out and she bit her lower lip. "You're Bravo Shaw. I recognize you from—" She halted there, a flicker of a different kind of shadow crossing her face.

"You recognize me from where?" Bravo said, taking a second step toward her. And then he saw the war hammer she held at her side. Did she think she could hide it from him? "Where is my sister?"

"She's back there." Lilith appeared grateful not to answer the first question. "Behind me, where I came from. She's—"

Bravo's face darkened. "She's what?"

Lilith swallowed hard. "Dying." Tears glittered in the corners of her eyes. "Emma is dying. We need to—"

Bravo pointed to the war hammer. "Did you—?"

"No. Oh, God, no!" Lilith cried. "I love her."

It was at that moment they heard the heavy drumbeats of eight pairs of legs. They turned to stare at the chamber behind Thanos. Someone screamed as the Four Thrones moved swiftly from darkness into the light.

Murmur, Raum, Phenex, and Verrine. Each Throne sported three sets of wings—leathery batwings with small, claw-like hands at the apexes. Their skin was ebon, scaled in the manner of armored beasts. Their faces were angular, thrusting, demonic. Red-eyed and glowering. They advanced around the flanks of Thanos, strange, multi-bladed weapons in their taloned hands.

They moved terrifyingly fast for such huge creatures. Bravo wasted no time.

*"Djat had'ar!"* he cried. *"Et ignis ibi est!"*

The words were no sooner out of his mouth than a tongue of blue fire licked out from his extended fingertips toward Thanos, but before the flames could reach the Sphinx to animate it Verrine brought his war weapons down onto the carved basalt spine. Immediately cracks appeared, and with a great booming whoosh Thanos was reduced to rubble.

Stepping over the jagged chunks of rock, Verrine brought his Thrones to bear on Bravo and Ayla.

"Run!" he called to Lilith. "Run!"

But she did nothing of the kind, instead circling around the rear of the Thrones, the bronze war hammer swinging back and forth. The Thrones ignored her, keeping their attention fixed on Bravo.

Murmur broke away from the other three. Cocking his arm, he threw a mesh net over Ayla that adhered to the wall behind her, pinning her in place. Bravo, calling upon all his grandfather's power, sent a bolt of blue flame that sheared away one of Verrine's six wings. Still the Thrones came on, black of heart, murder in what remained of their twisted souls.

Verrine was about to leap at Bravo when Phenex—the Scryer—pulled back, hesitating. It knew something, or had seen something in a future that it did not like.

"What?" Verrine's voice put a shudder through the three humans. "What have you seen?"

Before Phenex could answer, the chamber was filled with a thunderous roar. The walls shook, the ground split asunder. The Four Thrones turned toward the rising detonations. And then, while their attention was elsewhere, Lilith swung the war hammer into the back of what she surmised to be Raum's right knee. Her instinct had been sure. The bronze head of the war hammer shattered the Throne's armor-like carapace, drove deeply into both nerve and bone. Raum let out a shriek. Phenex turned to come to its assistance when Phaedos, the Sphinx Bravo and Ayla had encountered in the Hollow Lands deep beneath Malta, made his appearance. Approaching with astonishing speed, his mouth open wide, enormous teeth glistening, he slammed Phenex aside with a hind leg, drove his teeth deep into Murmur's neck, and, with a shake of his colossal head, threw the Throne into the stone wall of the cavern. As Murmur slid to the ground, Phaedos stamped hard on its neck with his left forepaw. At the same time, his right forepaw ripped the metal netting aside. Coiling his tail around Ayla's waist with great tenderness, he drew her up, deposited her safe and sound upon his back.

Then he turned, stood side by side with Bravo, towering over him. Bravo inhaled the odor coming off him, like molten lava. Phaedos saw Lilith then, swinging the bronze war hammer with both hands. Again and again she struck the fallen Phenex, and a terrible sound emerged from the Sphinx's throat. It took Bravo's several moments to realize Phaedos was laughing, and he could not stop himself from laughing, too, even though they faced Verrine, the Throne King.

Phaedos batted away the first of the arrows Verrine sent his way, but the second buried itself in his left thigh. What the head was made of to penetrate the sorcerous basalt was beyond Bravo, but he sent a lashing of blue fire that enclosed the Throne's bow, disintegrating it. Unfazed, Verrine drew a double-bladed sword, red-and-orange fire flickering evilly along the honed edges of the blades.

Phaedos reared back, almost unseating Ayla, who grabbed onto his mane with both hands. Verrine raced at the Sphinx, evaded the swipe of his forepaw. Bravo encased the blades in blue fire, but he could not arrest its downswing. The blades slashed Phaedos's breast, the flames along their edges opening up both sides of the wounds, penetrating so deeply that the Sphinx staggered.

As Verrine stepped inside Phaedos's defenses Bravo sent a ball of blue fire into the Throne King's face. This slowed it long enough for Lilith, racing in, to deliver a blow with the war hammer. Something cracked, like a lightning bolt bisecting an ancient tree, and Verrine arched back. Phaedos drove his head forward, his gaping jaws clamped around the Throne King's throat. But there was armor there, protected with sorcerous battle incantations, and the Sphinx's teeth shattered. A dense liquid streamed from his mouth that Bravo could only assume was what passed for blood or the Sphinx's life-giving force. Verrine ripped at the hinges of Phaedos's jaw, and a horrendous noise issued from his mouth. Bravo slammed the blue flame again and again into Verrine's face, blinding him. Lilith swung the war hammer again, and Verrine's armor shattered along its spine.

And yet it still continued to punish Phaedos, inflicting agony beyond human comprehension. The Throne King, blind, its spine shattered, driven into a frenzy of rage, was intent on destroying Phaedos with a concentration bordering on madness.

That was when Ayla's lips began to move, as if of their own accord. Bravo could not hear what she was saying over the bellowing of the Sphinx approaching his death throes. But Bravo knew what she was doing. The air around Verrine darkened, seemed to congeal. Its actions slowed, the berserker energy seemed to be draining out of it and into the darkened air, which now began a slow, counter-clockwise rotation. It picked up speed, faster and faster until it was a blur.

"Now!" Ayla shouted over the turmoil. "Now!"

She didn't have to explain. Summoning the depths of his grandfather's will, he combined it with his own. With a detonation, silent but deafening for all that, he sent a blade of cold fire straight at Verrine. It pierced the Throne King's armor, penetrated its breast, then burst asunder inside it.

At once, all motion ceased. Verrine, still as a statue, stood burning from the inside out. It released its hold on Phaedos, the double-bladed sword dropped from its hand, and it burned on, with a fire that was without smoke, cold as a mountaintop, inimical, unquenchable.

———

**LILITH EXPLAINED** to them that they were running out of time if they wanted to save Emma. Nevertheless, Ayla did not want to leave Phaedos, or was it that Phaedos did not want her to leave? Perhaps it was both, Bravo thought, watching her small hand in his paw. The Sphinx was dying; that much was clear. That he had formed some kind of attachment to Ayla was just as clear—and infinitely sad.

As she leaned over to kiss his all-too-human face, he whispered something to her Bravo could not hear. But then Lilith was urging them to leave, desperate for their help. And as much as Bravo was grateful for Phaedos's sacrifice, his mind was preoccupied with the extreme peril his sister was in.

He knelt beside Ayla. "Thank you, Phaedos," he whispered. But the Sphinx only had eyes for Ayla. She was weeping openly now.

"I tried to save you," she said. "I tried."

"We all did," Bravo said, but the occult light was gone from Phaedos's eyes. He was dead.

Bravo pulled Ayla to her feet.

"Now we run!" Lilith called to them as she started off back the way she had come. "Run as fast as we can!"

# 48

## THE HOLLOW LANDS: 1919

"FINDING THE STOLEN GOLDEN APPLE IS OF PARAMOUNT importance to me," Conrad said.

"I hear a 'but' coming on," Tanis replied with a wry smile.

He nodded. "My friend Yeats's prediction that my grandson would be murdered—killed before his time."

"You know the future—well, there are many futures, all of them possible."

Conrad nodded. "So the Farsighters claim."

"You don't believe them?"

"Oh, I do," Conrad acknowledged. "But Yeats is something more than a Farsighter."

Tanis shook her head. "I don't understand."

"He's a Scryer."

She frowned. "What's the difference?"

"What he sees is truth. He sees the singular future that will be."

They were standing in a vast chamber of the Hollow Lands, where Tanis had led him. Far above them was the sleepy fishing village of Arwad. She had taken him here through waters filled with great peril from marauding pirates and the remnants of the war—soldiers half-mad with killing, grief, witnesses to the massive carnage wreaked by mustard gas attacks. Haggard men, hollow-eyed, shallow-breathing monsters, reavers whose minds had been perverted by death and more death. And now here they were, closer to the stolen apple than he had ever been, and all he could think about was his grandson, yet to be born.

"I want to protect him," Conrad said now. "I *need* to protect him."

Tanis cocked her head. "Why?"

Conrad looked at her in the most intense way. "He will be your grandson as well, Tanis."

There was silence between them, an odd, eerie presence that seemed almost alive. It hung in the air between them, now dark, now light, revolving, resolving itself. And then in the blink of an eye it was gone.

"I can help with this," Tanis said.

"In my heart I knew."

She gave him another wry smile, tinged this time with a peculiar sorrow. "There will be a heavy price to pay."

He did not hesitate. It was as if he already knew his grandson, could see him, speak into his ear, guide him toward the things he would never get to see or do. "I am prepared."

"I very much doubt that you are," Tanis said. "You must renounce your birthright. You can never be immortal."

Conrad seemed unfazed. "Immortality is overrated. Besides, what would I do without you?"

Tanis laughed. "Yes, yes, Conrad. I *do* love you as I have loved no other, as I *will* love no other."

"Let's get on with it, then."

She positioned them facing each other, put her hands on his shoulders. "Repeat what I say without hesitation."

He nodded. "I understand."

She spoke in Tamazight; he recognized the language immediately, but the words were wholly unfamiliar to him. They seemed ancient, even by Tamazight standards. The next thousand and one seconds were filled with this peculiar call and repeat. Soon enough he understood their circular nature, the composition of all spells and incantations. Tanis was weaving them both into the fabric of sorcery. He might have been frightened, but such was his faith in her, in her essential goodness, his surety that she was an emissary of the Light, that wherever she led him he would willingly follow.

And then it was done. He didn't feel any different, but he knew that he was. Something essential had been altered inside him, woven into his very nature. Was it protection, or something else altogether?

He was about to ask her, when she threw her head back and spoke a phrase that might have been Tamazight but wasn't. It was Phoenician, one of humankind's mother tongues.

A moment later shadows coalesced in front of them, towering, massive, looming like the tower of Babel.

Summoned by Tanis, Leviathan had come.

## 49

## The Hollow Lands: Present Day

**STOP, CONRAD SAID IN BRAVO'S EAR. *STOP!***

"I can't stop. If I don't do something Emma is going to die."

Lilith looked at him without breaking stride. "Who are you talking to?"

*Yes, she will die if you don't stop. Listen!*

Bravo heard nothing but the echoes of their feet slapping against the stone floor as they ran. "Stop," he said.

Lilith blanched. "There's no time—"

*Yes,* Conrad said. *Time is all you have now.*

When Bravo repeated this out loud, the two women paused, breathing heavily. For a moment, that was all Bravo heard. But as their heart rates slowed, there was silence. And then he heard it, the rustling as if a wind ruffling a field of long grass.

*Yeats was a Scryer. That was driven from my mind in later years. Part of the price I paid.*

Yeats. Conrad had given Bravo a book of W. B. Yeats's collected poems, much battered and worn—his own copy—and Bravo had read the contents many times. Not that he needed to. After the first read he'd committed them to memory. But reading them again and again gave him a kind of comfort he could not find elsewhere.

Now the rustling in this chamber called to mind the last verse of a poem, "The Song of Wandering Aengus," about a man who in his youth catches a silver trout with a fishing rod made of hazel—a magical wood. The fish becomes a beautiful woman who runs off. Throughout his life the man seeks her, without success:

*Though I am old with wandering*
*Through hollow lands and hilly lands,*
*I will find out where she has gone,*
*And kiss her lips and take her hands;*
*And walk among long dappled grass,*
*And pluck till time and times are done*
*The silver apples of the moon,*
*The golden apples of the sun.*

*The golden apple. In long dappled grass.* Bravo turned and turned again. The rustling of the long grass. The golden apple.

"It's here," he whispered.

"What's here?" Ayla said.

Lilith's hands, curled around the haft of the war hammer, grew restless. "Let's go, let's go!"

"We can't help Emma without the apple."

Lilith shook her head, appealing to Ayla. "What's he talking about?"

But Ayla was too busy looking with Bravo.

" 'I dropped the berry in a stream / And caught a little silver trout,' " Bravo said, quoting from the poem's first stanza. "A stream, Ayla. We're looking for a stream!"

"This way," Lilith said. "I heard it when I passed this way before."

The chamber was immense, but as they followed her the rustling as of long grass changed to a deeper pitch, became a soft liquid gurgle.

Bravo knelt on the bank of a sinuous stream, narrow but seeming quite deep. The water was entirely black, swift running. Here and there little silver highlights glimmered, reflections from the directionless light.

"We're looking for the glitter of gold," Ayla told Lilith as she knelt beside the stream.

Lilith stepped over to the stream, reluctantly looked into it. "I don't see anything," she said.

Bravo moved farther from where they knelt. Then of a sudden he saw something, a cluster, glimmering darkly. Like a bird of prey, he swooped down. His hand and arm pierced the icy water, drawing forth an object he held within the cup of his curled fingers.

"I have it!" he cried. "The apple."

Lilith frowned. "But it's silver."

Without a comment, Bravo slammed the apple as hard as he could against the stone wall.

"What are you doing?" Lilith said in horror. "Bravo—!"

Again and again he smashed apple against stone until a spiderweb of cracks appeared in the silver and one by one the pieces fell away.

"The golden apple!" Ayla breathed.

"Chynna protected it in the same way Conrad did with the rood—by coating it in another metal."

"What does all this have to do with saving Emma?" Lilith said with a hard edge to her voice.

"Everything." Bravo took out the two golden apples and the crucifix. At long last, the four elements of what Kamar had called the sacred instrument had come together.

"Now what?" Ayla said. "How do they fit together?"

It was then they heard the sound of buzzing flies, drawing closer. Lilith's head came up.

"God in Heaven," she whispered. "Leviathan!"

"Bravo!" Ayla said. "What do we do?"

"Run!" Lilith cried.

"No." Bravo forestalled them. Into his mind came another part of Yeats's poem:

> *I dropped the berry in a stream*
> *And caught a little silver trout.*
> *When I had laid it on the floor*
> *I went to blow the fire aflame,*
> *But something rustled on the floor . . .*

Bravo laid out the three apples and cross—a golden quadrangle—on the ground. Nothing.

The buzzing of the flies, a drone now, as if speaking with one fearful voice.

"Oh, hurry!" Lilith said. "Whatever you're going to do, for the love of God do it."

Bravo rearranged the order: the rood in the center, surrounded by a triangle of gold. At once, they slid toward the rood, melded themselves, melted into it until it itself began to alter its shape.

"Dear God," Ayla whispered. "What is happening?"

The melded golden artifacts began to rotate counter-clockwise, then stopped, reversed themselves, becoming what they were meant to be: a triangle within a circle within a square.

Bravo shook his head. "It's the Nihil, the sigil of the Unholy Trinity. Not what I expected."

*Take it,* Conrad said in his ear. *Use it!*

Bravo picked it up. His fingers tingled, then came a sharp pain like a jolt of electricity. He ignored it. "Let's go," he said to Lilith.

The horrific buzzing followed them, an army on the march, coming closer.

**"WHAT IS** that thing?" Lilith asked as she ran alongside Bravo.

"The instrument that will save my sister."

"How do you know that?"

"I don't."

Lilith, grabbing his arm, spun him to a halt, facing her. Ayla came up alongside, made to intervene, but Bravo signed to her to stand down.

"If you don't know . . ." Lilith was full of rage and fear in equal measure. "I won't let you use it on her."

Bravo kept Ayla close to him. With his arm around her he could feel the tremors of tension and anxiety rippling through her like a scythe through a wheat field. "Do you have a better idea, Lilith? You've told us that Emma is changing—changing into one of the Fallen. If the process has gone too far . . . Lilith, she's my sister. You must know that I don't want to lose her, either."

Lilith, staring at him with red-rimmed eyes, nodded. "I love her, Bravo. If this happens to her—"

"We'll see that it doesn't. I promise you."

"You can't promise that."

"You don't know him," Ayla said, breaking away from Bravo's grasp to take Lilith's hands in hers. "Now pick up that damn war hammer and let's go. That legion of flies sounds like it's getting awfully close."

**EMMA WAS** where Lilith had left her, bound to the iron ring by the bronze chains. But she was virtually unrecognizable. The wings, sprouting from between her shoulder blades, were almost fully formed, spreading outward, larger than the chamber. She stood amid rubble. Great gouges in the wall on either side of her spoke of the strength of her ebon talons. Her face had changed, as well, swelling in cheeks and forehead, mouth widened to accommodate rows of teeth. She stared balefully at them from out those dreadful ruby eyes within eyes.

"Good God!" Ayla said.

Lilith unwisely went toward her beloved, who lashed out to the extent of her bonds, teeth gnashing, causing her to rear back before retreating. "It's no use," she said. "Even if that instrument works you won't be able to get near her."

"I'll be able to," Bravo said. "I'm her brother."

Ayla stepped in front of him. "Have you forgotten that she almost killed you back on Malta? If not for Conrad's intervention . . ."

"It was Conrad? But how? He's long dead." Lilith said, but neither of them answered her.

Slowly, the expression on Ayla's face changed. "Oh," she said. "I see."

"What?" Lilith was frantic. "See what?"

Ayla crossed to where Lilith stood. "Just stay back," she said softly. "No matter what happens do not interfere."

"Why?" Lilith voice was jittery with her agitation. "What's going to happen?"

"Bravo is going to save her," Ayla said, "or die trying."

Holding the Nihil in front of him, Bravo advanced toward his sister— or what remained of her. He did not look to either side but stared directly into her eyes.

"Emma, be still," he said. "I'm coming for you."

The transforming creature in front of him rose up as if gathering itself for an attack. Its talons made new and deeper scrapes down the wall. Its wings fluttered, trying to gain freedom. Its teeth clashed together.

No matter to Bravo, this was still his sister, and Ayla was right—he was determined to save her or die trying. With that in mind, he rushed at her. The faster he could get near her, the better. Dodging those snapping jaws, he feinted right, darted left, slammed the instrument against her chest. At once, Emma began to convulse, and it was all he could do to keep the Nihil in continuous contact with her. He smelled a kind of burning, as of incense, of a mix of spices too rare and exotic to name. Something was melting, or rather folding in on itself. It seemed to him that a force beyond his reckoning was gathering all its strength and power into itself to repulse him. He was prepared. And then he wasn't.

Emma's head lunged forward, jaws gaping wide, and three sets of teeth buried themselves in the meat of his shoulder. He cried out, and Ayla had to tighten her grip on Lilith, who had taken up the war hammer.

"We have to help him!" she cried. "Look, she's killing him."

"What did I tell you?" Ayla said firmly. "If you move you'll divert his attention and doom us all."

At the same time, Bravo had turned his mind to shutting down his pain centers. One by one, he cut them off, until he felt nothing except the tingling in his hands, smelled nothing but the rise of rich spices curling up from the contact between the instrument and Emma's altered flesh. Then she began to thrash her head back and forth, trying to rip gobbets of muscle out of him, forcing him to return to shutting down deeper pain sensors. Writhing and bucking, she almost dislodged the Nihil. But he persevered, forgetting his pain centers, putting all his energy into one last push even while the agony of her bite threatened to make him lose consciousness.

At last, at the end of his rope, he called upon the cold blue fire, and at once it leapt from him, encasing her. And that was the end of it. He heard something utter a scream that almost shattered his eardrums, and then a release of tension, of animus, of the intent of evil. Then, in another voice altogether, a deeply felt sigh of relief. At first, he thought this was uttered by Emma, but it was a deeper voice, and he knew it to be the Fallen that had been inhabiting her corpus. The Nihil had released it.

His shoulder was bleeding, but Emma's mouth had withdrawn. He looked up to see the wings had vanished, as had the talons that had infested Emma's fingertips. Most joyous of all was Emma's face, which had been returned to her whole. Her eyes were clear and sparkling. Not a trace of the transformation remained, and he thanked God for that. He released her from the pressure of the Nihil instrument.

"Bravo," she whispered in a hoarse and husky voice. "Brother mine." And then she began to weep.

# 50

**"BROTHER, WHAT HAVE I DONE TO YOU? I'M SO, SO SORRY."**

Both the women rushed to Emma's side. Lilith unlocked the chains, pulled them off her, and Bravo collapsed into Emma's immediately outstretched arms. She held him close, rocking him as if he were a child. He was breathing hard; she could feel his heart pounding against hers.

Lilith kissed Emma's forehead and cheeks, while Ayla attended to Bravo's deep wound. Ayla bound his shoulder with a strip of cloth she ripped from her undershirt, laid both hands on top, and began one of the healing incantations Kamar had taught her.

"Beleth," Lilith whispered in Emma's ear.

Emma shook her head. "He's gone. Really gone this time."

"He must be relieved, the coward."

And then the buzzing was upon them. Lilith took up her war hammer, moved to block the doorway, but it was too late. The legion of flies entered the room just before the doorway was filled by the terrifying countenance of Leviathan. His skin was the color of fresh blood. His eyes flame ridden. A single horn protruded from the center of his sloped forehead. A serpent's tail, thick and powerful, flicked over his shoulder. His three sets of wings opened like black sails. Upon the bulging upper cartilage the flies rose and fell like a blackened tree limb, furred with toxic lichen.

Leviathan's saurian jaws hinged open, forked tongue vibrating as it took an in-depth sounding of the chamber.

"Emma," Leviathan intoned, like a godless prayer. The sound drove every ring, weapon, and chain to shuddering, a chain of inchoate noise that made their ears hurt. "Emma."

Emma had slid to the floor, her back propped against the wall, with Bravo in her lap. Lilith advanced upon the Seraph, lifting her war hammer on high to deliver a terrible blow.

"Fool!" Leviathan rumbled, and swatted her with such force that she struck the side wall and collapsed to the floor, insensate.

"You, woman," Leviathan flicked his talons, so they clicked together like stag beetles. "Get away from them." Ayla complied, backing up against the wall.

Leviathan grinned. "So here is the grandson. He kept you from Conversion. It seems that Conrad made quite an astute bargain."

"What are you talking about?" Emma said.

"Ah, yes, you were the protected one, Emma. You were never privy to your family's many secrets." He heaved a sigh, sending the legion of flies up toward the ceiling, before settling back down into his wings. "Your grandfather struck a bargain with me."

"Why on earth would he do that?"

"Well, he wasn't on earth, per se. But then neither are we." He swept an arm out, sending everything to rattling again. "His friend, the poet Yeats, prophesied that his grandson would be murdered before his time. Conrad did everything in his power to keep that from happening. In due course I was summoned by your grandmother, Tanis. Quite a power, in her time. But I digress. Tanis summoned me and a bargain was struck."

At Tanis's name, Bravo stirred, but Emma gentled him and he subsided.

"In exchange for keeping Bravo alive it was agreed that Conrad's son—what was that insect's name again?"

"Dexter," Emma provided. "Our father's name was Dexter."

"Right. Dexter. Well, Dexter, poor, poor insect, was born without the family's birthright—their powers."

"So you can't harm my brother."

"I don't want to harm your brother." Leviathan's laugh set their teeth on edge. "I want you."

Emma's eyes opened wide. Her heart began to pound in her throat. "Why? Of what possible use could I be to you?"

"You are correct, of course. It's not really you I want; it's your power. It's just that you have to come along for the ride. You see, you being of the female gender have a greater power than any male of the family. Once that power is combined with mine, Heaven, quite literally, is the limit. Together we will rule both Heaven and earth. A power never before seen, or even imagined."

"You're mad," Emma said.

"I do believe you are correct, Emma. But this is the nature of the beast, isn't it?" The Seraph grinned, a sight not fit for the human eye to absorb. "And, in any event, madness, like beauty, is in the eye of the beholder."

Out of the corner of her eyes, Emma saw Lilith, lying in a heap. Her heart constricted, but she fought against showing any emotion on her face, even now as Lilith opened her eyes, returning to consciousness. How badly was she hurt? Tucking her concern into the back of her mind, she resolved to keep Leviathan's full attention. "This Conversion you spoke of. How did you—?"

"Long and constant planning, Emma. Ages ago, I inserted rumors in the world concerning The Testament of Lucifer. In fact, there is no such thing. Perhaps as your keen mind comes to grips with reality that won't be much of a surprise to you. I laid a trap for you."

"I don't believe you. How would you know that Bravo would find it?"

"Clues," Leviathan said. "Clues, clues, clues. Bravo, like his grandfather, is oh so good at following them."

"And how did you know that I would be the one to read the Testament and not Bravo?"

"Curiosity killed the cat, that's a human saying, inane, but it applies here. In your case your curiosity began the Conversion. Your brother, being who he is, inherited his father's caution. You, however, inherited your grandfather's impulsiveness. I knew, given the opportunity, you would be the one to discover how to read it. And once you did, the trap was set. You were enmeshed in the words I had created." He shrugged. The flies, disturbed, buzzed angrily. "I admit that I have consistently underestimated Conrad. The bargain he made was, as I said, astute. Your brother is astonishingly resourceful. But, no matter, I myself will begin the Conversion and, as I am directing, nothing will stop it this time."

He beckoned with black talons. "Now come here so we may begin." When Emma showed no inclination to move, he swept his arm out, pointing it at Lilith, who stared at him with hatred through half-dazed eyes. "No? It seems that you are as stubborn as you are impetuous. But, really, all that is required is a bit of an incentive."

The hand extended toward Lilith curled into a fist, and Lilith cried out, her back arching as if the Seraph had delivered a blow to her spine.

He kept his gaze on Emma. "No? More?" He opened his fingers, closed them again. This time Lilith screamed, convulsing as if delivered an electric charge. "Emma. Really." And again, the gesture and the scream. "Do you want this to go on all night? I have infinite patience. Time means nothing to me."

"Stop," Emma said. She was defeated and she knew it. Gently, she laid her brother aside, rose and stepped toward Leviathan.

"Emma, no," Ayla said. "You can't do this!"

"What choice do I have?" Emma said in a strained voice. She kept coming. Lilith was stuck in her peripheral vision, like a mote in God's eye. She was watching Emma closing with the Seraph, and if there was an expression on her face Emma could not read it.

When she was an arm's length from Leviathan, she stopped. Her heart was pounding so hard she thought it might pop out of her chest. Her mouth was dry, and there was a sick feeling in the pit of her stomach. She could smell the Seraph, a mixture of shadow and light, sunlight and moonlight, sweet and metallic as blood, sour and earthy as a tree root.

Leviathan leaned forward, and Emma almost gagged on the stench. "Now that we have come this far I will tell you a secret. I would never kill you, either."

Emma looked at him. She was no longer afraid. She had passed beyond fear into a land wholly unknown to her. Curiosity killed the cat, she thought with a silent, bitter laugh. The Seraph has me pegged down to my toes. But had he?

"What's the big secret?"

"I mark the contempt in your voice."

"Mark it in your book of memories, The Testament of the Seraph Leviathan."

"Ha." But Leviathan gave her a peculiar look.

"We're all living that Testament, aren't we, Seraph."

"You will call me by my name."

"Seraph, Seraph, Seraph." Her eyes gleamed. "What? Will you kill me for my insolence? No. You said you wouldn't kill me."

"Of course I wouldn't," Leviathan said. "We are all family. You and Bravo and I."

"What?" Emma staggered, as if he had delivered a gut punch. "What the hell are you talking about?"

"Let's review your family history. Surely, you know that your great-great-grandmother, Chynna, took the name Shaw. Her real family name was Sikar."

Emma looked over her shoulder at Bravo for confirmation. He was fully conscious now, sitting up. His eyes were entirely clear, but they were filled with an emotion Emma had never seen before and could not identify. He seemed as changed as she had been, and she shuddered in the bare face of the unknown.

"The Seraph is correct," he said as he pulled himself up, stood shakily with his back against the wall. He was covered in blood, but it was dark, coagulated. Ayla's incantation had stopped the bleeding at least. His gaze flew past her, impaling Leviathan. "Go on. I want to hear this."

"I'm sure you do," Leviathan said mildly. "Because I'm about to tell you a secret that even your grandfather didn't know, though he spent fruitless years trying to find out. Well, it is this: Chynna mated with a member of the Fallen."

They all could hear Emma's indrawn breath. "Is this true, Bravo?"

He nodded. "A Grigori."

Emma stirred. "I thought all Grigori were destroyed," she said. "By you, Seraph."

"Ah, Beleth told you that, did he, that ignoramus." Leviathan gave a little laugh, imbued with something—something more vicious than contempt, repugnance, possibly—other than humor. "Well, that is to be expected. It's the lie I created and perpetrated." He gave that sound again, and it was as if he was pleased with himself. "Part of my legend, you might say."

Looking deep into Emma's eyes, he said, "But, you see, there was one Gregori left alive."

"You," Bravo said.

"Bravo!" Leviathan cried.

"You mated with Chynna."

"And, therefore, I am your great-great-grandfather."

They all seemed paralyzed with shock. Reaching out, Leviathan clamped his left hand on Emma's shoulder. "Welcome to the family, my dear."

He extended the talon on the forefinger of his right hand directly toward the center of Emma's left eye. It turned from black to bloodred, then to white.

"Ready or not," he whispered, "we begin."

Bravo pushed himself off the wall, murmured his two incantations, summoning Conrad. Blue fire leapt from the palms of his hands, crossing the distance between him and the Seraph, encasing him in a shroud of cold flames. Leviathan jerked in response. His white talon, his weapon for Conversion, turned bloodred. Fire broke out along the upper cartilage of his wings, instantly frying the flies slavishly clinging to them in hopes of feasting on dead flesh. That stench itself made everyone else in the chamber gag.

Hot fire met cold fire, pushing it back. Bravo, baffled, picked up the Nihil instrument.

"That's right." Leviathan curled his fingers, gesturing. "Bring it home."

*Don't!* Conrad whispered. *Don't give it to him!*

"The Nihil belongs to me, Bravo. It was stolen eons ago by the Phoenician alchemists, to cripple me. Broken into four sections, it was divided for safekeeping. Now, thanks to you, it has returned intact and potent as ever." He laughed, and they all winced. "I am a creature who thrives on fear and irony. It's ironic that the same instrument that saved Emma will now give me back the full measure of my power."

His fingertips clashed together as they beckoned. "Give it here, Bravo, there's a good little Shaw."

As if mesmerized, Bravo picked his way across the chamber, while Ayla and Lilith stared in outright horror. He was halfway to where the Seraph stood facing Emma when a shadow came rushing through the doorway, claws and clawed wings raking Leviathan's back.

"Beleth," Lilith breathed. "Emma, the Power has come back."

With a roar, Leviathan turned, slashed a talon across Beleth's neck. Black ichor oozed, then rushed from the wound. Still, Beleth would not give up. It bit down on the cartilage of one of the Seraph's wings, tore off a section with a vicious twist of its head.

With Leviathan's attention elsewhere, both Bravo and Emma were released from their thrall. Quickly Bravo transferred the blue fire to his sister, encasing her. He remembered what the Seraph said about Emma's latent power.

He told her what to say, and the instant she uttered the Latin for "Let there be fire!" fire erupted from her. Unlike Bravo's, it was a blue-green. The two met each other, twined, spiraling up and up to the ceiling, then spreading out in a mushroom shape, billowing closer and closer to Leviathan.

Beleth was bellowing. The Power was on its knees, trying to reach up to puncture the Seraph's armor-like skin, but it was too late. Leviathan sent a tongue of his pernicious flames down Beleth's throat, setting the Power on fire from within. Within moments, the fire had burned clear through Beleth, leaving it a hollow, ashy shell.

In almost the same moment, the combined cold fire of Bravo and Emma reached the Seraph. His shriek almost burst their eardrums. Whipping around, he tried to attack them, but he was already encased in the occult flames.

His eyes blazed; his lips drew back over fangs seeming to disintegrate behind the wall of blue-green fire. Leviathan screamed something at them they could not hear. Then he turned and ran. They pursued him, but by the time they reached the chamber of invisible rustling grass he was nowhere to be seen. At least a dozen corridors branched off from this space, making it impossible for them to follow. Nevertheless, they spent the next hour going from corridor to corridor.

"Quite possibly he's returned to the Underworld," Emma said when they made their way back to the massive chamber.

"That's what I'd do if I were him," Bravo replied.

"Thank God you're not."

"Thank God neither of us is."

**"OF COURSE** you can trust her," Emma said. "Lilith helped me kill Obarton."

Bravo stared at her in disbelief. "Obarton's dead?"

"That's right. And so are the Knights."

Bravo leaned back against the wall of the small chamber to which he and Emma had returned from their fruitless search. "How is that possible?"

"I invaded their servers, broke through every layer of firewall," Lilith said.

"We have all the Knights' secrets," Emma added. She had studiously avoided the cracked shell of what had once been Beleth. When it had appeared as if summoned out of her own head, she had been shocked at what it really looked like. For the life of her she could not put the voice, let alone the personality, to the monstrous being that had flung itself onto Leviathan's back. But how could she not look? How could she be horrified by its physicality? It had sacrificed itself to save her and Lilith. Was there any more human impulse than that? Who knew what lurked in the heart of darkness? "They've all been downloaded to our SSD drives."

Lilith looked from Emma to Bravo. "To be honest, we don't have *all* their secrets. Their Reliquary is here."

"Here? You mean down here in the Hollow Lands?"

"The coordinates Obarton gave us under duress led us here. Where we're standing is just a bit off."

Bravo frowned. "But the laws of our world don't apply to the Hollow Lands. His coordinates are useless here."

"He's right," Ayla said. "Obarton lied to you."

"No." Emma shook her head. "I'm convinced he was telling the truth."

"Then we need to go back up," Lilith said.

"The sea cave!" Emma cried. "The Reliquary must be somewhere along its length."

She was the last one out of the chamber. For a moment, she stood in the doorway; then she knelt down, drew one curved claw from the husk that had been Beleth. It had been the one sunk deepest in Leviathan's back, the only solid piece of the Power left. She hefted it in her palm, closed her fingers around it, then stepped out of the chamber. Lilith was watching her but said nothing as they joined the others on their journey up to the surface of the earth.

THEY FOUND it eventually, two-thirds of the way back up the sea cave toward the Arwad beach. It turned out that Obarton's coordinates were precise. Lilith, standing under one of the holes in the rock, had just enough signal in her mobile to guide them to the precise location.

"I don't know how I missed it on the way down," she said. "In my extreme agitation I must have misread the numbers."

"Lucky for us," Ayla told her, and Lilith smiled.

A section of the rock wall on their right had been jackhammered out, its replacement almost identical to the original. By borrowing Lilith's phone and using its built-in LED light at a raking angle, Bravo discovered the almost invisible seams that ran around the four sides of the panel.

Running his fingertips over the fake rock face, Bravo came across a machine-made indentation just below an outcropping, which, under the insistence of his forefinger, lifted up. They were looking at a small rectangular metal and plastic pad, on which were ten square buttons: 1–9 and 0.

"Let me," Lilith said. "There are certain master algorithms the Knights use. They translate into five numbered sequences."

The fourth one proved the charm. They heard a metallic click and Bravo pushed the door inward. The Reliquary was small, no larger than a walk-in closet. Not so surprising since it was the Gnostic Observatines who collected ancient artifacts, not the Knights. Apart from one painting, its walls were bare; no attempt had been made to soften the rough-hewn rock. An old-fashioned kerosene lamp stood in one corner. Bravo fetched it, lighting up the Reliquary. In the center of the space was a vitrine on a plinth, protecting, so the plaque read, the mummified heart of Saint Clement, shriveled, floating in a glass jar of what might be formaldehyde. Just in front was what looked to be the forefinger bones of the saint.

"That's it?" Lilith looked around, clearly disappointed. "This is what all the secrecy was about? A damn bone and a heart?"

No, she wasn't disappointed, Bravo saw now. She was angry.

"Well, that's it then," Ayla said. "Not every adventure ends in an important discovery."

"Fine," Lilith said. "I for one have had my fill of being underground. I don't know about anyone else, but I'm in need of some fresh air to breathe."

Lilith stormed out, Ayla right behind her. Emma was about to follow them when she turned back. Bravo had lifted the lantern to head height.

"What are you looking at?"

"This painting." Bravo moved closer to it, raising the lantern a bit higher the better to illuminate the painting. "Look, here." He pointed. "The paint is peeling off."

"It's no wonder," Emma said, "in all this damp."

Bravo peeled off a strip of paint.

Emma came to stand beside him. "It looks like there's another painting underneath."

Bravo was busy stripping off more paint. Emma was right. The years of damp had gotten between the layers so that the top layer, which was thick, almost like impasto, easily separated from what was underneath. "Not just another painting," he said. "It's the Last Supper."

"But that's impossible. Michelangelo's—"

"No. Look closely."

"The light is the same."

"Yes, but the figures are more primitively rendered. I'm betting this predates the one Michelangelo painted." He peered ever more closely. "In fact, it might even be the study from which he took his cues."

"Why is it here in the Knights' Reliquary?"

"Excellent question." Bravo handed Emma the lantern so he could take the painting off the wall. "We'll take it back to our lab where we can study it using the latest equipment. I want to verify its age, for one thing. For another, I want to find out why it was so important to the Knights of St. Clement."

"It may be nothing at all," Emma said with a wry smile. "Just a piece of decoration to keep St. Clement company through the ages."

Bravo returned her smile. "On the other hand, Ayla might have spoken too soon." He extinguished the lantern and they emerged into the sea cave where the others were waiting. "This adventure might have ended with an important discovery after all."

# EPILOGUE

**"IN THE END, BELETH WAS NO COWARD,"** **EMMA SAID, HER ARM** around Lilith's waist. The moon hung high in the sky, illuminating the water, the way ahead.

"Odd to say, but I miss him. I can't help thinking of Beleth as a *him*."

"I think he did, as well, in the end."

"We changed him, didn't we."

Emma nodded. "Perhaps we did." She opened her hand, revealing Beleth's claw.

"A souvenir?" Lilith asked in that bantering way of hers.

"If 'souvenir' means 'a remembrance,' then yes. But this is something far more to me." She was silent for a moment, then closed her fingers over it, feeling its smoothness, its weight. A part of him, still. A relic. "Maybe we were only facilitators. It seems to me that we triggered something deep inside him."

Lilith sighed, feeling her lover's warmth. Something she knew she never could get enough of now. "Perhaps you're right."

The four of them were on the hydrofoil Lilith and Emma had hired, racing back to Cyprus. Behind them, a hazy glow through the night in the backwash, lay the curved stone arms of Arwad. None of them were sorry to leave the island behind.

Emma was sitting between Lilith and a dozing Bravo. Ayla stood a little apart, staring off at a flock of cormorants, circling what must be some large sea creature, bloated with the gases only death builds up.

Lilith's face clouded over as she lowered her voice. "Do you think your brother will accept me?"

Emma smiled. "Once you know him better you'll never ask that question again."

"Well, I mean you three are family."

Emma took Lilith's hands in hers, twined their fingers. "You're my family, too, Lilith. Till death us do part."

Lilith's lips quivered. "My God, how I do love you."

Their kiss was long and intimate and tender.

FOR MUCH of the time as they had made their way up from the Hollow Lands the four of them had talked nonstop, catching one another up, laughing in relief. They could be forgiven if their laughter was more raucous and lasted longer than was necessary. They had escaped death with their selves intact. Bravo felt as if he had been through a meat grinder, wanted nothing more than to lie on a beach somewhere, drinking and eating and, most important, sleeping. He felt as if he could sleep for a month. For the moment, at least, the war to come was far from his mind. It had to be for him to regain his equilibrium and keep his sanity. In the back of his mind he knew that though they had won a great battle, they had gained only a brief respite. Even now, the enemy was regrouping, considering alternate strategies, planning the final strike that would send them headlong into the world of humans, and thence to Heaven's gates.

Now, however, as so often happens at the end of a long, exhausting journey, they were talked out. There was nothing important left to communicate. They had withdrawn into themselves, to lick their wounds and to heal. They slipped into a kind of daze; one another's silent presence was sufficient.

After a time, Emma disengaged herself from Lilith, who had fallen asleep. Bravo, his doze so light that he had awakened with the slightest movement, watched her speak to Ayla for several moments before moving on to the bow. He waited some time, then followed her.

Lilith, awakened by Bravo's absence, longed to be with Emma, but she understood the need of the siblings to be together after such a grueling time apart. She was glad of it, happy that they had such a close relationship. She wished she were close to her sister, but she preferred not to think about Molly. To clear her mind, she rose, went to stand beside Ayla, felt at once the other woman's prickliness, her sense of distrust.

"Where does your allegiance lie?" Ayla said without preamble.

It was rude, but Lilith couldn't blame her. She had been the enemy. Now she wasn't. But how could Ayla be sure? "I hacked into the Knights' database and sent a copy to the Gnostic Observatines."

Ayla appeared unmoved. "You should have cleaned them out while you were at it, wiped the damn database clean."

"And start a hot war between the Knights and the GOs with Bravo missing? Does that make sense to you?"

Ayla grunted, as much of an admission as Lilith was likely to get.

"Answer my question, please."

"My allegiance is to Emma," Lilith said. She meant it; it felt good to say to someone else what had been in her heart for some time. "Now and forever."

Ayla seemed to consider this as she watched the cormorants silently wheeling. At length, she looked away from them and sighed. "A love like that does not come along every day."

What an astonishing thing to say, Lilith thought. Not a twinge of jealousy or envy, just a statement of fact. She was so grateful she felt tears sting her eyes, before the wind carried them away. Everyone was vulnerable tonight. All at once, she felt a great love for this family. Not only for Emma but for Bravo and, yes, this thorny woman standing beside her, as well. And she was astonished anew at the realization that all of her tough stance, her iron will, her constant fighting and scheming to get ahead in a man's world, was in the service of finding a place for herself. Even as a child, she had been an outcast, an outsider. She had never really had a home and a family, a place where she fit in. She did now.

EMMA DID not turn when Bravo came up beside her. Her elbows were on the railing; the wind pulled her hair back from her face.

"About Lilith . . ." She turned to him. "She's very special."

"I believe you."

"I wouldn't have made it all the way to Arwad without her."

Bravo touched her shoulder. "Emma, you don't need my blessing."

"Need has nothing to do with it."

He nodded. "I know. I misspoke."

"But I do want you to like her."

Bravo's heart melted. Why, he wondered, did it take a near-death experience for him to realize how precious she was to him? "I don't even know her." He stroked her arm, lightly. "But once I do I have no doubt I will."

Her face clouded over. "How d'you know that?"

"You've always been a great judge of character."

That brought a smile to her face. "This is very important to me."

"Nothing could be more apparent, I assure you."

Her neck and cheeks began to color.

"So, Lilith aside, how are you doing?" he said softly. "Really."

She shrugged. "I wish I knew. This thing . . . Chynna mating with—"

"I meant you. Inside you. With all that's happened."

"I feel as if I've been hollowed out."

"Does that mean you miss Beleth?"

She gave him a sideways look. "It might sound strange, but I guess I do, in a way."

"It is strange."

"He changed."

"Emma, evil doesn't change. It's monolithic in its thinking."

"Then Beleth wasn't evil." She saw his expression. "You don't believe me."

"I want to, Emma, but it's not easy."

"You have to trust me."

"I do. You know I do." He shook his head. "What you've gone through—"

"We've both come back from . . ." She shuddered.

"The important thing is we stopped Leviathan from transforming you. Let's celebrate that victory."

She laughed bitterly. "You go ahead and celebrate. As for me . . . I so don't want to be who I am."

"Emma."

"I mean this family—our history." She shuddered. "Dad trained you from the time you were ten, Bravo. But I was left behind."

"Protected."

"Call it what you will. The fact remains I'm not built for this. I mean, I almost destroyed you."

"And were almost destroyed yourself." He gave her a bleak smile. "I don't think any human being is built for this, no matter the family history. But you're here now, with me."

"I survived."

"You did far more than that. You fought like a warrior." He took her hand. "Emma, believe it or not, what we've just gone through has made us stronger."

"Then why do I feel as weak and vulnerable as a day-old kitten?"

"Tell me, what are you doing now?"

Emma looked down at her hands, which seemed to be working independently of her mind. She had Beleth's claw in one hand. With the other she was scraping a small hole near the top with a small bronze-bladed knife she had picked up before they had left the interrogation chamber.

"Huh. I'm going to buy a thin gold chain when we get to Cyprus, hang this around my neck."

Bravo nodded. "That claw is proof, Emma, of who and what you are, no matter what you say to the contrary. You're exhausted; I get it. We all are. But tomorrow or the next day I promise you'll be able to appreciate the knowledge we've gained. That knowledge is what makes us stronger."

"Bravo, we're not even Shaws. Shaw is a name Chynna made up."

"So we're Safita, Ahirom."

"And Sikar."

He looked at her levelly. "You once asked me who we were. Now you know. But we also know that we're more than brother and sister. We're two parts of a whole. I will teach you everything I was taught." He smiled as he looked deep into her eyes, her soul. "Together, we'll explore the hidden places inside ourselves."

"What if we don't like what we find?"

"Either way, we'll both be stronger. Conrad somehow foresaw this outcome; Leviathan didn't. The bargain he made brought him pain, but it's given us our only chance to prevail in the war that's to come."

"The war?"

"What we've been part of is just the first battle." Bravo squeezed her hand. "The war itself is still ahead of us."

"Sweet Jesus," Emma breathed. "Let there be fire!" And opened her palm to the blue-green fire, cold as midnight in deepest winter.

THE MOON, bone white and beautiful, had risen, hanging like a paper lantern in the sky, so close that Haya could almost reach out and touch it.

"It's time," her mother said. "Are you ready?"

Haya nodded as her mother bundled her into a black cotton jacket, then slipped on a quilted coat, also dyed black. Hand in hand, mother and daughter stepped off the porch of their house, picked their way down to the shingle, where a small sailboat was waiting for them. Haya was lifted in; then her mother unwound the lines, pushed the boat out into the shallows, kept its momentum going until she was waist-deep before springing lithely aboard. She rowed a bit, then shipped the oars when deeper water opened up.

By the time they passed between the scimitar arms of the breakwater, the sail had gone up and had caught the offshore wind. She tacked starboard, coming around the outside of the southerly breakwater arm, until they were headed due west.

Moonlight fell upon the water like shards of ice. The stars sparked and twinkled. The water was pitch-black. Haya let her fingertips trail in the water. Her mother breathed deeply of the salt air and, for the first time in many years, felt the ecstatic brush of freedom against her cheek.

There were no boats about. She had placed them in an area free of both the fishing fleet and the shipping lanes. They were all alone in the night.

"Are you happy, my darling?" she said to Haya, though she could just as well have been talking to herself.

"Yes, Mama," her daughter answered. "Oh, very yes."

"Excited to meet your father?"

Haya screwed up her face. "I don't know my father."

"But, my darling, that's part of the excitement, isn't it?"

Haya, safe and secure in her mother's arms, allowed that it was.

The wind shifted and the sail needed tending to. The wind blew wide the open edges of Haya's jacket, lifted up her thin cotton shirt, exposing her belly to the moonlight. It was as smooth and unruffled as a porcelain vase. No navel indented its perfect velvet surface.

Her mother, finished with her brief tacking maneuver, raised her eyes to the moon, noting its position in the sky. A shiver of presentiment passed through her as the last barrier to her freedom was left behind.

"He's coming, my darling." She held out one arm, gripping her daughter tighter with the other. "Your father is here."

There, directly in front of them, loomed a darkness deeper than the night. Overhead, a flock of cormorants circled. As they closed with it, its six wings became apparent, then its massive upper body. For Haya's sake, the face was entirely angelic. No trace of the demonic was visible.

"Greetings, my husband." She put her hands on Haya's shoulders, presenting her. "Meet your daughter. Her name is Haya."

"How beautiful you are, Haya, just like your mother," Leviathan said. "And soon you will be strong like me." Then, he turned his gaze upon his beloved. "At last, Chynna. We are together again."

And with that, he scooped up the boat, gathering it and its passengers into his effulgent embrace.

# FURTHER READING

## HIERARCHY OF THE FALLEN

### LUCIFER

#### FIRST SPHERE

| *Seraphim* | *Cherubim* | *Thrones* |
|---|---|---|
| • Leviathan | • Azazel | • Focalor |
| • Belial | • Beelzebub | • Forneus |
| | • Berith | • Gressil |
| | • Lauviah | • Mammon |
| | • Marou | • Murmur |
| | • Salikotal | • Nelchael |
| | | • Phenex |
| | | • Purson |
| | | • Raum |
| | | • Sonneillon |
| | | • Sytri |
| | | • Verrine |

#### SECOND SPHERE

| *Dominions* | *Virtues* | *Powers* |
|---|---|---|
| • Balam | • Agares | • Amy |
| • Marchosias | • Ariel | • Beleth |
| • Nilaihah | • Barbatos | • Carnivean |
| • Oeillet | • Belial | • Carreau |

| _Dominions_ | _Virtues_ | _Powers_ |
| --- | --- | --- |
| • Paimon | • Lelaliah | • Crocell |
| • Rosier | • Purson | • Gaap |
| | • Sealiah | • Lehahiah |
| | • Senciner | • Uvall |
| | • Uzziel | |

THIRD SPHERE

| _Principalities_ | _Archangels_ | _Angels_ |
| --- | --- | --- |
| • Belphegor | • Adramelech | • Arakiba |
| • Imamiah | • Ananael | • Arakiel |
| • Ian | • Basasael | • Araxiel |
| • Nisroch | • Dagon | • Arioch |
| • Nithael | • Mephistopheles | • Armans |
| • Verrier | • Moloch | • Asael |
| | • Rimmon | • Asbeel |
| | • Rumjal | • Astoreth |
| | • Sarfael | • Caim |
| | • Thammuz | • Iuvart |
| | • Zagiel | |

[After the list compiled by the Order of Lux Lucis of Rose]

**William Butler Yeats** (1865–1939), one of the greatest poets of the English language, received the 1923 Nobel Prize for Literature. His work was greatly influenced by the rich mythology and turbulent politics of Ireland.

## The Song of Wandering Aengus
### (Based on an Irish folktale)
#### W. B. Yeats

*I went out to the hazel wood,*
*Because a fire was in my head,*
*And cut and peeled a hazel wand,*
*And hooked a berry to a thread;*
*And when white moths were on the wing,*
*And moth-like stars were flickering out,*
*I dropped the berry in a stream*
*And caught a little silver trout.*

*When I had laid it on the floor*
*I went to blow the fire a-flame,*
*But something rustled on the floor,*
*And someone called me by my name:*
*It had become a glimmering girl*
*With apple blossom in her hair*
*Who called me by my name and ran*
*And faded through the brightening air.*

*Though I am old with wandering*
*Through hollow lands and hilly lands,*
*I will find out where she has gone,*
*And kiss her lips and take her hands;*
*And walk among long dappled grass,*
*And pluck till time and times are done*
*The silver apples of the moon,*
*The golden apples of the sun.*